THE WAY WE GO

Olivia Norton

The Way We Go
Copyright © 2024 Olivia Norton
All Rights Reserved

Cover design by Fiona Norton

This book or parts thereof may not be reproduced in any form,
stored in a retrieval system, or transmitted in any form by any
means without prior written permission of the author.

This book is a work of fiction. All people, places, and events are
fictional or used in a fictional manner.

ISBN (ebook): 978-0-473-71031-6
ISBN (paperback): 978-0-473-71030-9

To those who defy what it means to be normal.

You are not alone.

One

My father is crying again, but he's been doing that a lot lately.

Only secretly, though, or so he thinks. He is a man set in his traditionalist ways, and "real men don't cry"—at least that's what his father taught him, and his father before that. It isn't something I agree with, but he needs to feel strong, to feel capable of holding our family together, so I go along with it.

I have never seen him outright cry. Even at Mom's funeral, as they lowered the casket, I remember looking up at his stone-cold expression. At the time I remember being angry at this, then envious at how he could remain so collected. I refused to look or speak to him for the rest of the day thinking he didn't really care. I also wished he was the one in the ground instead of Mom, but then I felt bad for thinking that and cried even more. It wasn't until later that night I awoke to his muffled cries coming from downstairs, so I crept down the staircase just enough to peer through the banister and see Dad cowering over the picture on the mantelpiece. It was the last picture taken of Mom and the one they used at the funeral. It shows her leaning down at an angle smiling towards the lens: her soft freckles showing, her long, light-blonde hair glowing gold from the sunlight coming through the silhouetted trees behind, her favorite peridot-green necklace dangling down in front of her turquoise cardigan matching the shade of her eyes. I took the photo myself, getting to use the last of the camera roll. Mom was the artsy type and preferred film cameras to digital, saying they had an authenticity to them. Given the amount of editing done nowadays I'd say she was beyond her years with photographic wisdom. Thankfully the film could be enlarged enough to hang on an eight-by-ten-inch frame and there was no debate that this was the picture to use at her funeral, to represent the natural, free spirit that was *her*.

This time, however, he is crying because he is about to lose the other woman in his life.

I close my bedroom door a little louder than normal which gives him the warning needed to collect himself. I pause, then slowly walk along to the staircase, making sure to step on every creek of the floorboards and thump the suitcase behind me. This causes Pippi to lift her head off the sofa and bark at my entrance. I reach the bottom of the stairs and turn to face Dad. He's already standing straight and firm. It's easy enough to tell he's been crying with his puffy, red eyes, but don't let it be known. I let him keep his dignity as he sees it.

I, on the other hand, have already turned into a blubbery mess.

"Dad," I snivel.

"Charlotte." He comes over, arm outstretched for a pat-hug. The pat-hug is usually as far as Dad goes in physical displays of affection when he's emotionally vulnerable. Again, that's his vice and I don't complain.

"I'm sorry," I sob. Pippi notices and licks my hand for reassurance. I stroke her thick fur. I will miss her, too.

"Now listen here, Charlotte Durane." Dad uses my full name and I know a fatherly pep talk is to follow. He is now in coach mode, his daughter another player for the Durane family team needing discerning advice, whether it be a quote from Sunday church or a debate on the best time to microwave sixty-second rice. "Sometimes you've got to venture out into the unknown as a leap of faith. Just like Moses did when he crossed the desert—"

"Yeah, yeah." I sniff a chuckle, which sounds more like a snort. "For we walk by faith, not by sight."

"I was going to say if you have second thoughts then come straight back home." He ruffles my hair. "Or just come back anyway. For a visit, to stay. Your ol' man will be here. Always."

I smile and get teary-eyed again. As hard as an old oak tree he is, with a trunk full of marshmallow. For the first time, I notice the lines in the corner of his eyes and the graying tint in his hair showing through the tawny brown. Age is creeping up on him and the mortality of life once again suddenly feels so real. I glance at the picture of Mom and wonder what she would have looked like now. Would she be graying too, or would her light hair turn into a whiter shade? Somehow I think she would have been one of those lucky few to age gracefully and look twenty years younger their age. Maybe one day I will show parts of her, but I've always followed my father's genetics with my darker eyes and hair. The few faint freckles I have on my cheeks, however, are from her, and while other people tend to cover theirs with makeup for a purer complexion, I proudly let mine show.

"Ten years." Dad must have followed my line of sight.

"Three months."

"And three weeks," he finishes before looking at the sonogram framed next to it, the one showing my brother who never got to be born. "Heaven is blessed to have them."

My eyebrows scrunch as they always do with such sentences. While my father is a bonafide Christian, just as his father before was etcetera, I follow the more liberal path of my generation, and all the bible camps and church picnics couldn't persuade me otherwise. My brother never got the chance to live. My mother is dead. And I don't care what or where Heaven is, they should be here too, seeing me venture off to college while joking about claiming my bedroom now that I've moved out. But instead there are two candles between their photos. I light one and then pass the lighter to Dad who lights the other. We light it on every occasion: Christmas, birthdays, anniversaries, graduations. I guess today counts, too.

"That reminds me." Dad takes his hand from his pocket and places something in my hand. I look at the delicate gold ring on my palm. "Your mother's. We couldn't afford a proper wedding ring at the time, but once I got that delivery job and a place to settle before you came along . . ."

My birth was five months eight days after their wedding date. I did the math; it turns out I was the product of my parents' not-so-Christian nightly encounters and the cause for a shotgun wedding, as demanded by my grandparents, as per suggestion of their church, as it was "the expected thing to do". When I brought it up one day years ago Dad's reply was, "We are all sinners, Charlotte. But under God's divine plan," and left it as that.

". . . I want you to have it now, to take a part of your mother wherever you go as you venture off into the adult world."

"Thanks, Dad." I slide it onto my finger and then outstretch my hand in front of me.

"And to show all 'em college boys you're taken, so they better not try anything."

I roll my eyes and smile. As protective as my father is, the eighteen-year-old part of me can't help but contemplate all the new people out there I will meet. It hasn't been easy growing up in this desolate small town, and the reason I chose a college four hours' drive away is for the fresh start, to play on the anonymity to be who I want to be.

However, unbeknownst to my father, as much as I love him, out of fear of repercussions from him I keep it a secret that my heart in fact already belongs to someone. Cole, my best (and only) friend in the world, the one person I can be my true self with—and, dare I say it, the person I have totally fallen for. I glance out the window to see him standing by my car, hands casually slung in his pockets, looking my way through his styled bangs and angled smile. I can't help but feel slightly giddy as I flash a quick smile back.

Under any normal circumstance I would like to think Dad would approve of him once he got to know him, which pains me that he never will.

Because Dad can't communicate with dead people.

Unlike me.

"I'm serious." He must have been looking at me and assumed I was caught up in boy fantasies (which wouldn't be wrong). "Don't go mixing with the wrong crowds, I raised you better than that. I hope."

"Yes, Dad."

"There are still good men out there, and you only need one Mr. Right, so don't go gettin' ya heart tangled up in anything in between. It won't be worth the pain."

Out of all my father's traditionalist ways, his devotion to my mother even after her death has been the most admirable, and he has yet to acknowledge the "til death do us part" of his vows. Maybe he just hasn't found anyone who can come close to filling my mother's shoes. Then again, maybe he's too scared to find someone who can. While he has Patricia, a dear family friend of ours, perhaps his wedding vows seem to clash with his faith of seeing his only love again someday, waiting for him at the pearly white gates in the clouds. As the years went by I had in part hoped for a mother figure around, someone to show me how tampons work or how to apply makeup properly. It was just embarrassing whenever Dad tried, and he was relieved when I said he didn't need to do any of that stuff (thanks to YouTube). But he did what he could. He always did what he could.

And now I'm abandoning him. I'm a terrible daughter.

"I'm sorry." Here come the waterworks again.

"Now, now, you have nothing to be sorry for."

"I should have enrolled at State."

Dad had hoped I'd pick State to be only an hour away and live at home to save money. Except the point of college for me is to get away from this town.

"You got better than State."

"What about the diner?"

"You sayin' I can't run my own business? Besides, I've got Pippi and there's still plenty of kick in that ol' retriever yet."

Pippi perks her head up at the sound of her name. I smile back, but it's a sad smile. She was a Christmas present ten years ago; the neighbor's dog had a litter of puppies so they gave us one in sympathy of what we'd been through, and we've loved her since. But even she looks old now. The sofa she's on has torn embroidery, the fabric faded. Come to look at it, the whole house looks worn. Why does everything suddenly seem so fragile?

"We'll both be fine. Please just worry about yourself."

"Okay."

There's a pause before Dad speaks again. "I know . . . school wasn't always easy for you."

The elephant has just been released into the room. Where would this elephant charge first, I wonder. The whispers about me across the classroom that were loud enough for me to hear? The rumors that I was schizophrenic? The endless lunch breaks spent in the library where even the school librarian pitied me enough to never tell me off for eating my sandwich in the corner? Or was he referring to the time I beat up the school janitor for trying to tear Cole into the afterlife (that part got skipped out in the misdemeanor report), or the fact that I had (again, with good intentions) ruined prom night by unleashing a vengeful ghost on the star quarterback (that part never made it to the misdemeanor report, either).

Dad doesn't know the full story, of course. It's better that way. I see him rubbing his chin, his gesture when uncomfortable truths about me resurface. He's been through a lot with me; raising a kid on your own must be difficult enough, let alone one that can communicate with ghosts and gets caught up in their post-death dramas. I can't imagine the stress I've caused him over the years, stress he's done well to manage.

Dad quickly tames the elephant. "But that's the past. You've got better times ahead, hmm? Now let's get your suitcase into your car."

One final goodbye hug to Dad later, I step into my Honda (my eighteenth birthday present—that, and Dad didn't want me relying on strangers or unreliable public transport for rides) and drive off.

Foxton is a small town (if a population of 7,000 is considered small) tucked into the rolling hillsides of farm country, nestled on the horizon of other such dotted farm towns across the South that eventually joins up with the rest of civilization. The surroundings are nice; woodland walks are plenty, and there is a popular country club nearby. But unless you are entering retirement then the only attraction of the place is the highway out. Doing just that, I pass by the high school I will never have to attend again. A smile grows on my face. For the first time I finally feel free.

∞∞∞∞

Compiling my grades (average) with my misdemeanors (many) and extracurriculars (few) I ended up applying to three universities, of which I got accepted to two of them. One was State (the backup), the other being Hillcrest: a small, largely unheard-of private university in North Carolina boasting a 9,000-student population. There isn't any particular reason for my choice; being four hours' drive away from home it's far away yet close enough to get back in one trip, and since I don't know anyone there it's the perfect place for a fresh start to have as normal life as I can. It also has a good health science department, which is what I decided to enroll in (again, for no particular reason except it's something I didn't *not* want to do). I'm not entrepreneurial, but I figure if I can see the dead, then maybe getting paid for my services for once as a grief counselor or nurse would be a good idea. Who knows, it will probably help *me*, if anything. And if that fails, then maybe I'll just be a crazy psychic lady with seven cats.

I slump down on the couch and place my feet up on an unopened box. It's the last box to unpack, but it can wait. I look around my new home. It's a small studio loft space, the type with the bed space above the kitchen and with nothing more than a small table and couch to form a lounge area by the front door. Its bare brick walls give a typical city apartment vibe, but with the right décor and homely touch I could make it work as something more homely.

It isn't much, but being within what I can afford and only a fifteen-minute walk to campus, it serves its purpose.

"Congratulations. You did it."

The words are beautiful, even more so from the person saying them. I turn to Cole and smile. As with being able to communicate with the dead, to me they're just like other people, minus the whole glowing aura thing. That would be the energy of what they are: their consciousness that remains after death. What their aura is like depends on the energy they give out. If they're angry their energy darkens, but if it's loving it brightens. It makes for easy analyzing of spirits, and I can see that Cole is currently content with his subtle light glow. It's his first appearance since leaving Foxton, and he looks deep in contemplation, something I usually see from him. The words are there but the feeling is more realization, like, "oh, I *did* turn the lights off after all" or "oh, it *is* already dark outside". Such expressions would make me question what he is thinking, but I let it go. He is probably just adjusting to things.

"This is it," I reassure myself. "Are you okay with the move? I know you're drawn to Foxton."

Cole strokes a loose lock of my hair. "I'm more drawn to you."

This makes me smile. A typical Cole response: humor with a dab of chivalry. The truth of the matter makes me more concerned, however. I first met Cole when I was seven and he hasn't left my side since. Even when I found out that fate orchestrated him to be the one driving the car that crashed killing not only him but my mother and unborn brother, I forgave him because I love him more. He's the only reason I made it this far, having saved my sanity dealing with spirits haunting me with their unfinished business, not to mention high school (I honestly don't know which one was worse).

With him around I feel that things can be okay.

"Which reminds me. Since my name is on the lease, I set the house rules."

Cole raises an eyebrow. "Go on."

"Well, I might be busy sometimes—"

"Uh-huh."

"So if I leave a plate or two out I'm not being lazy—"

"Okay."

"Or maybe I am. But I'm allowed to be—"

"Yes." He nods mockingly.

"I'll get around to it—"

"Sure."

I throw a cushion through him.

"And lastly, as you can see this is an open-plan studio." I subtly gulp. "So, naturally, the rule where my bedroom is forbidden territory without permission doesn't apply here."

This has his attention.

"Intriguing," he soon says, leaning in. "And the bathroom?"

"The bathroom is always forbidden," I quickly assert. "Always."

Cole smirks. "What, no shower show? I'm being conned out of my rent money I tell ya. Conned!"

"As for rent money, payment can be made in other ways," I suggest. "Like being my bodyguard on late night strolls in the park, or watching movie marathons with me."

I choose what I say carefully. There's only so much Cole can do, but I don't want that to hold significance. Since I opened up to Cole and kissed him a few months ago we have been in a good place. Caught up in our young love, we made the agreement to just live for the present, the notion of memories made together living on within us in this world and the next sounding romantic and beautiful. But for Cole especially, it's easier said than done. He still carries guilt. Guilt for being the one that crashed his car into my mother's, even though there were multiple factors at play that fateful night, and guilt for hurting me in the future when the inevitable happens.

It's on my mind too, I can't deny it. It wouldn't be a problem if Cole wasn't so, well, *dead*. As part of our agreement I have to acknowledge our different paths and allow life to take its course without making sacrifices for him, which is his way of saying there'll be a time when I'll have to let go of us.

But for now we find ourselves at the unknown boundaries of daring to be something more, a psychological game of chicken with one another, testing who will give up first.

Or give in.

Cole gives me a subtle look. He probably knows what I'm thinking; he knows me too well. I reassuringly place my hand on his. I don't feel him much but it's still there, his presence. I call it feather-touch; light and lingering on the fine hairs on my skin. Again, this doesn't bother me except in moments like this, moments when I want Cole to be *more*.

Cole notices the gold band between our hands. "You're wearing a ring."

"It's to keep the players away," I reply with a white lie, choosing not to mention it was my mother's. "So they know I'm taken."

Cole can't help but smile at this. I meet his eyes and the corners of his mouth curve slightly to reveal his dimples as his soft gaze lingers from my eyes to my lips. I shouldn't get too carried away; the fact still remains that I'm looking at a ghost. But my heart fights against logic with emotions that are both strong and shared between us, emotions that cannot be suppressed in moments like now as he leans in close to me.

"I want to do everything with you, Miss Durane," he says in a low, mischievous tone.

My heart knocks at my chest, demanding to know what the holdup is. I can feel something between us pulling us together, something raw. I begin to lean forward, an opening sign for more, but he suddenly pulls back, his usual demeanor returning. "But not tonight. You're tired. You need to sleep." He kisses me on my forehead, a consolation prize for what could have been, then stands and begins to walk away.

"Your rent just went up twenty dollars," I call out.

"Put it on my tab."

I can't help but chuckle as he disappears through the wall.

He is right; tomorrow I start university. Tomorrow I begin my newfound freedom.

I quickly wash up. As I snuggle into my new bed sheets in my new little home, I sleep happily, daring to believe that nothing can go wrong.

Two

My first day of university starts with a scream.

It wasn't the *first* thing to happen; that would be waking up to see Cole sitting at the end of my bed, looking at me with an almost-smile on his lips.

"Good morning, sleepy head," he says once he knows I'm fully out of slumber, the ghostly aura that is him light and glowy. "Just thought I'd pop by and make sure you don't sleep through your alarm."

I turn on my side to face Cole and smile, glad that he has taken to my new flat rules. "What's the rush?"

"Charlotte, of all the times in high school you turned up late to class, you can't be tardy on your first day of college, too."

I look at the clock hanging on the wall, ticking just after eight o'clock. "I have time."

Cole leans in closer, and I can see his eyes settling on my lips. "That's good," he says. "So do I."

That, I'm sure, would have been the moment to mark everything. To solidify our relationship, to confirm his feelings for me are as much as mine are for him.

Except that is the moment *she* appears, across my loft space, screaming at the top of her lungs. And it isn't the type of jovial scream you hear at a carnival either, unless it's the haunted house of horrors. And judging by the hues of grays that make up the glitching static that is her, she's doing well on the whole horror thing.

Cole and I look at each other as if to ask, "Do you see what I'm seeing?" before watching her disappear, her scream lingering into echoed silence, the image of her still blaring in my mind.

Whoever she is, she is absolutely traumatized.

Which, naturally, has me shaking.

"What," I eventually say, turning back to Cole, "was *that*?"

"I have no idea."

He's clearly as shocked as I am. He walks over to where she was, to my displeasure the intimate moment between us from before now long gone.

"What is it?" I ask.

"I'm not sure. Usually I can sense the spirits of other ghosts. Feel them coming or going, follow behind their trail. But it's like hers is barely there."

"What does that mean?"

Cole turns to face me. "I don't know, but since I only felt part of her I think she was . . . dying."

"What?" I ask. "You mean, she was in the process of dying? Like, *right now*?"

Cole shrugs. "Again, I don't know. And I don't think I'll get anywhere, but I'll try to find out." He looks at the clock and then says before vanishing, "You really don't want to be late on your first day."

I look at the clock ticking away slowly yet surely past the hour. I groan and throw my pillow over my head in protest. Not that I'm tired, no. The goosebumps still on my arms show I'm not going back to sleep anytime soon. I sigh, slumping out of bed. Is being normal too much to ask for? Can I not have this *one* day of normality?

Yes, I think to myself as I stomp my foot in protest. I refuse to give up so easily. Okay, so it wasn't the best of starts. But it is still early. The day has only just begun. So someone may or may not be dying in a not-so-pleasant way. Unfortunately that's just life. It's happening all around the world all the time. And as selfish as I feel for affirming it, today is a day for me. So I clip my hair back in a wispy bun, pucker up some cherry lip balm (my favorite), put on my best shirt and jeans, grab my satchel bag, and then head out the door with a spring in my step.

As it turns out, the first week of classes are more introductory than important, so when they finish early I take the free time to explore the campus more thoroughly. Hillcrest University is exactly what I hoped it to be: brick and stone buildings, some partially covered with ivy; oak trees lining the avenues, the large branches full of the last of summer greens; small circles of gathered friends sharing notes and food; and faces passing by me without a second glance, just another new freshman in the crowd of wide-eyed, overachieving and determined young adults. There are no whispers or rumors or judgements which admittedly excites me. I squint in the brightness of the sunny day, my hand lightly holding onto my satchel shoulder strap as I make my way across campus with a smile. The satchel-carrying, jeans-wearing, inconspicuously normal Charlotte Durane.

I also use this time to write up a to-do list. I like to-do lists. It sets out what I need to do and blocks off distractions. My stubbornness means I like finishing each task, even if it seems daunting or difficult. Today I am doing well to tick off my list. I haggle the price for the second-hand textbooks I need, I find all my classrooms—and turn up on time—and even make that awkward get-to-know-you small talk with a few class peers. I spend the early afternoon browsing through the stands and displays of various student support groups and clubs recruiting members, keeping flyers from the environmental conservation club and the university church group (although that one is more to appease Dad). I eat at the campus café, buy a university jacket, and even hang around to watch the student ninja warrior challenge.

I'm proud of my progress on my to-do list, and there is only one more thing in capital letters left to cross off: FINANCES.

Dad put what was left of Mom's life insurance into a savings account for me and it has collected a reasonable amount of interest over the years. In a way, Mom has saved me by allowing me the affordability to leave home and not have to worry about the immediate cost of doing so. Nonetheless, rent and tuition isn't cheap, and if I am to afford living on my own with three meals a day I need a means to support myself.

Which is why I find myself walking into a café with their WORK AVAILABLE sign in my hands.

"Hi there." I smile broadly at the man who looks managerial enough. "I couldn't help but notice you were looking for part-time help, and—"

"You have experience?" the man asks, not looking away from his clipboard.

I swallow. "Uh, yes, some. A diner during summer break."

"So you can waitress."

I don't know if that was a question or a statement, but I reply, "Yes."

For the first time he looks away from his clipboard and gives me a once-over. "How old are you?"

"Eighteen," I reply. "I just started university here—"

"The shifts are rostered. We work around your class times, but you should keep Sundays free. That's when we get busy, especially around exam time with students pulling all-nighters."

"That sounds great."

"Now I don't like any snowflakes who complain that the work is too hard or the pay is not enough . . ."

I expect him to continue talking but he's eyeing me. I hastily reply, "Not me, sir. I'm a hard-working, all-American capitalist Southern girl."

That makes him nod in approval. "Good."

He writes a few numbers on his clipboard and then calls out, "Kelly?" before turning back to me and saying, "Kelly will show you the ropes. You share tips equally with your coworkers at the end of every shift. Greediness won't go down well here so if you don't want a hard time with the others you'd best be honest about it."

"Yes, of course."

"Yes, boss?" A young woman, possibly my age yet easily

three inches shorter than me comes through the doorway. With a face of soft freckles and a thick bob of shoulder-length black hair in two braids with little ribbons on the ends, my first thought is that she could pass as a children's book character.

"Show . . .?"

"Charlotte—"

"Show Charlotte here the new employee application forms in my office and get her sized up for uniform." He turns to me. "Your first shift is Friday—it's a trial only. If you can make it through the evening without breaking anything or anyone, you'll work the weekend too and receive your shift roster for the following week."

A man straight to the point, down to business.

"Sure thing, boss." Kelly smiles broadly, her voice unusually chirpy.

"Yes, thank you."

He nods, then gets back to what I assume is stocktaking as I follow Kelly into the office.

"Motherfucker."

My eyes bulge as Kelly closes the door behind her. The busy chatter of patrons muffles out to newfound quiet between us.

"Sorry?"

"Not you." She swats her hand at me. "Mr. Dodgley." She notices my cluelessness. "Boss guy." She acts out in a chirpy voice again, "Yes, boss. Sure, boss. Anything you say, boss. Stare at my tits longer, boss." She pulls out some papers from the drawer and then in her normal voice again she says, "The average turnover here is ten weeks. He'll call you out for being late, calling in sick, weight gain—oh, and don't expect extra bathroom breaks when you're on your period." She places the papers in front of me. "Also, your uniform size will be 'out of stock'," she adds, doing quotation marks in the air with her fingers, "to get you to wear tighter shirts, so write down your measurements as at least one size larger."

"What about the male staff?" I ask.

"He doesn't hire guys. Sexist pig." She reaches into her bag from the lockers and pulls out a vape. She inhales into it deeply, and before exhaling she mutters, "Some people just shouldn't exist. His mother should have swallowed him instead."

I cough, but not because of her vape. Those were not words I expected to hear from cute little storybook Kelly.

"Thanks for the heads up," I say wearily.

"Why are you applying, anyway? Are you a student?"

"Yes, new to town. I don't know anyone here and I don't have much work experience, so this will have to do, at least until I get settled. Otherwise it's working fast food downtown."

"True." She takes another inhale of her vape. I taste apple in the air. "It's a tough job market. For anything decent, at least."

"How long have you been here?" I ask as I start filling out the forms.

"Eleven months," she replies, swatting away the vape smell with her arms. "Got promoted to assistant manager after five, only because I was the only one able to put up with him long enough. But I need the money, so what can I do?"

The boss—Mr. Dodgley, if I heard correctly—calls out Kelly's name.

"Coming, boss," she chimes with her well-rehearsed fake voice as she quickly puts her vape away. "Oh, and can you braid hair?"

"Uhm, I guess."

"Good. Get used to doing your hair that way. He thinks it looks more welcoming for customers."

He calls her name again.

"Coming!" she chimes louder before muttering, "Asshole."

Kelly closes the door behind her. I look at the papers in front of me, unable to hold back a small smirk as I sign on the dotted line. I will probably kick myself for it later, but this is the normal I wanted, right? "Shitty student job: check."

∞∞∞∞∞

It was dark before Cole showed up, interrupting my dinner of Mexican takeaways and a soda in my apartment.

"Sorry," he says as soon as he appears. "I didn't want to interrupt things for you. How was your first day as a college kid?"

"It was great," I chime as I bite into my taquitos.

"Oh? How so?"

"It was absolutely normal in every way. Got lost, found my way, made it to classes on time, looked into joining some clubs, socialized, all those new student things. And the best part of my day? No ghosts."

"I'm glad."

I throw two fries through him. "Minus you, Dumbo. How'd it go for you?"

"I didn't get anywhere," he says disappointedly. "Whoever she was, wherever she is, I hope she's at peace now."

I sigh, my appetite suddenly gone.

"Hey, don't go wasting any more fries. Eat up. You seem hungry."

"I am," I admit. With being so caught up with everything I only had a sandwich about six hours ago. It seems that takeaways would be a part of this new lifestyle of mine. I take a gulp of my soda before saying, "Oh, and I have a job—"

"A job? Already?"

"Yup. Just part-time waitressing at a café a few blocks away. It'll be . . . interesting. But I think my coworker and I will get along fine."

"That's good."

"Sure is."

"You're jumping right into this independent living role, aren't you?"

I take another mouthful of my taquito and mutter through a full mouth, "Eighteen years old. Who would've thought?"

"You're older than me now."

The words are quiet, and I wonder if they are meant to be heard. Cole looks contemplative; a slight slant of his eyebrows, his gaze lowered but far from focusing on anything. I hadn't thought of it that way. Not that it matters. Age is just a number, right? And if I was being *really* technical, he would be twenty-eight. That's, like, nearly *thirty*!

I shake my head at the thought.

"I'm not the little girl scared of the dark anymore," I say reassuringly.

"No, you're not." Cole turns and smiles at me. "You've grown into a strong young woman."

He instinctively reaches out to wipe the bit of sauce from my chin, but of course it's to no avail. I can tell it frustrates Cole even though he does a good job of hiding it. He wants to do things—not even big things, just small things like hold the door for me, or carry my heavy grocery bags, or wipe sauce off my chin, things a boyfriend (a decent one, anyway) would naturally do.

Only he can't.

I quickly grab a napkin from the takeaway bag and wipe my chin, then carrying on as if it is nothing I say, "A strong young woman who still eats like a neanderthal."

"As long as you enjoy every bite, Charlotte."

I swallow awkwardly. I try not to eat in front of Cole. Eating is one of the things Cole misses the most about living. He says that everyone alive is too busy being trendy with the latest fashions and flashiest gadgets, or keeping up with work or holidays or entertainment, but in death it's the basic things you miss, like the taste of chocolate on your tongue, or the feel of grass under your feet, or—as he so frequently comments on—the flow of nature happening all around that we're all too busy to notice.

"You know, if I eat one more bite I could burst." I stand, putting the rest of the taquitos in my empty fridge. "It'll have to be breakfast tomorrow."

"You should make time to go to a grocery store at some point," Cole mentions, eyeing the leftover fries and soda. "Get some real food into you."

"Yeah, I guess." I look at my stomach. I've been blessed

from my mother's genetics at having a slim frame, which means I never really put much thought into what I actually consume. Quick and easy is usually my go-to, whether cereal, fruit, toast, or takeaways. I take after my father in that retrospect; while we try here and there, especially with the vegetable garden we cultivate, unless we have guests both Dad and I aren't really into cooking beyond a pie or the odd catch caught from one of his fishing trips. But in caution of picking up some less favorable genetics from my father's side, I probably should start swapping out the taquitos for tofu.

My stomach growls, that bloated rumble. "Yeah, you're probably right. At this rate I'll develop a food baby by Christmas."

Cole is now in front of me, his hands on my hips, looking down. "One day you'll have a real baby in there."

I cringe. "I think I prefer the food baby."

It was meant to lighten the moment, but his eyes are still fixed on my torso. Cole would be a great father. He probably would be one now if he were alive, rocking his little human in a blanket, cooing it to sleep. I blink away the thought.

"You'll be a good mom," he says softly with a small nod, confirming his thoughts out loud.

"Right now I only care about being a good girlfriend."

Cole looks up and smiles at this. "Oh, you're good enough at that already."

He leans in and gently places his lips on mine and I feel the energy of him on me. I hope he feels it too, that yearning for more. Yearning to *be* more.

But then, as he has a habit of doing, he stops, abruptly drawing back, his demeanor returning to normal. And once again I feel a dwell of bubbling frustration.

I don't react, though. That just gets me more frustrated and Cole more reserved. Instead, I go back to clearing dinner away, my inaction perhaps leaving him addled for once, only I turn back to notice Cole has disappeared. I would be piqued, but he then reappears again and I know what he's going to say.

"There's a couple that need help crossing over."

Ghost whisperers, mediums, psychics, and clairvoyants are all commonly used names for people who have some sensual connection to the deceased. But for me they are almost as real as the living, with facial features and clothes 'n all. This supposedly makes me a 'Communicator', something so rare that less than a hundred of us are even known to exist in the world. And since I can communicate with them so well, this also means I am quite popular among the spirit folk—which, unfortunately, can intrude on my personal life.

So I scoff, but I can't say I'm surprised. Having a normal day was too good to be true.

"Should I tell them to come back another time?"

I look at the club flyers I left on the counter and quietly sigh. Full-time student, part-time waitress, full-time inter-realm ghost assistant service. I doubt I'll have time to add beach clean-up volunteer or bible studies member to my résumé.

"No, let them come." I put the club flyers in the trash before muttering under my breath, "It's not like anything else is going to happen tonight."

Three

Even though I feel uneasy about this new job, I make sure to arrive at work early to make a good impression.

"Hello," I say with a supporting smile. "I'm here for my first shift."

"Yes, yes. Follow me." Mr. Dodgley leads me into the office. Kelly is there too, folding uniforms away. "Bottom-left locker is yours. Extra bathroom breaks are on your time. Mints are in that drawer—do you smoke? Vape?"

"No."

"Huh, that makes a nice change." He shoots a glance at Kelly who manages to keep smiling as she closes up the uniform box. "We're out of size ten shirts, but you look like you'll fit size eight," he says as he hands me a t-shirt.

Kelly shoots me a look as she passes by, one that says, "I told you so".

"Great." I force a smile.

"Now remember: the customer is always right, keep smiling, and don't make a mess. If there's anything you don't know, ask Kelly. I'll be around here and there."

"Got it."

Mr. Dodgley holds the door open and nods at the customer walking in. "Time to shine, Miss Durane."

Waitressing really isn't as hard as it seems. Once you know where everything is it feels like clockwork. Smile, take orders, confirm orders, give orders, collect tips, and smile some more.

The shift goes by quickly enough, and Kelly shows me the ropes and the need-to-knows which keeps me busy. Mr. Dodgley seems impressed enough, judging by his one nod. Kelly assures me that him not hovering over my every move is a sign he approves.

We close early since it's a quiet day and nobody is really studying yet. Mr. Dodgley gives me my roster for the next week before leaving Kelly to lock up.

"So what are you studying?" she asks as I stack the chairs.

"Just a couple of generic health science and elective papers this semester. I'm still not sure what to major in."

"Oh, yeah? What classes do you take?"

"Criminology, Human Development, Introduction to Psychology—"

"Hey, I'm in that class, too!"

"Really? I didn't see you."

"Who goes to classes in the first week? It's all orientation and party, baby!"

And here I was thinking it's an unpopular class. I'm a geek, obviously.

"I'm studying part-time now that I've been clawed into this place." She turns on the faucet to fill up the mop bucket. "The pay is okay. Shift times are flexible with class times. It's alright *really*, I guess."

"*A* job is better than *no* job," I remark as I fling my French braids behind my shoulder. "Braids 'n all."

"Preach."

"So psych is your major?"

"Yep. I'm going to be a therapist. At least, that's my plan."

"Oh?"

"I feel like I'm good at reading people, ya know? Like, every customer that comes in, I can tell their mood, how to respond. The ones that are lonely and just want someone to talk to? I've got them, and they've got me a nice tip to match. The ones that want to be left alone will give you a bigger tip for letting them be, too. It's a good talent to have."

I grin as I pick up the broom. I like Kelly already. She's an open book who's not afraid to say it as she sees it. She's also been very helpful thus far. I would have to invite her to my place for takeaways or a movie sometime, or whatever it is friends do nowadays.

"What about you? Got any talents?"

I tilt my neck and half-shrug. Suddenly I remember why I don't do that social stuff. "None that I can think of."

"I believe everyone's got a talent, you've just gotta find it." Kelly stops to watch a group of guys walk past the front window. "There's the other type of talent, too. The yummy and scrummy kind."

I follow Kelly's gaze. They are big, in the gym workout kind of way. One of them notices us and smiles before rejoining whatever conversation they were having.

"I love when semester starts," Kelly sighs happily through the words. "Fresh talent in the mix." She leans against the counter, rummaging through her bag before taking out her vape. "I wouldn't mind showing that dark-haired one the back room."

I chuckle.

"So what's your game?"

"Game?"

"You know, choose your token."

I stare, confused. "Monopoly?"

Kelly coughs a laugh. "You're a special one, doll. I mean, what are you into? Your type. Your ideal guy." She inhales her vape before saying, "Or girl, I don't judge that way."

"Oh. Uh," I pause. I never really thought about it to be honest. There was Cole . . . and only Cole. "To be honest I'm not sure."

Kelly raises an eyebrow. "What? How can you not know? For me it's tall, dark and handsome. Literally."

I focus back to the broom I'm holding, realizing I've been sweeping the same spot over and over again. "I guess I just haven't really considered it."

"Come on, a girl like you, new to town? I know lots of people, I bet I can match even someone as unsure as you. Unless you've already got a special someone in your life?"

I hesitate, but this matchmaking of Kelly, while in good conscience, needs to be hampered sooner rather than later. "I have . . . someone," I say.

"Ooh. Name?"

"Cole."

"Ooh, *Cole*," she says eagerly. "What does this Cole look like?"

"He's . . . pale."

"Sell him up, why don't you?"

"I don't know what to say." Which is true. I haven't really talked about Cole to anyone else before, at least not in this way. "He's tall, about six feet. Athletic. He has sandy-blonde hair, light brown eyes, and a contagious smile. The cutest dimples, too. He's funny yet serious, mischievous yet caring, reserved yet intimate." I sigh. "I guess you could say he's hard to grasp."

Kelly giggles. "You're *so* into him."

"Yeah, I am," I admit.

"Is he a student here? I would have noticed someone like that on campus."

"No."

"He's not a lecturer, is he? Seriously, Charlotte, if he's a professor—"

"What? No, he's not from campus. I've known him for years."

"Ah." Kelly sighs in relief. "High school sweethearts."

"I guess so."

"You two live together?"

"Yes—no, not exactly. He . . . visits." I swallow, quickly regretting this.

"Well I hope to see this Cole soon."

"You won't." I chuckle beneath my breath. "I mean, he's not around much."

"Oh?"

I sigh. "It's complicated."

"They always are," Kelly says. "But if he's gonna be distant like that, you gotta get your game on and be ready to level up."

She places her vape back in her bag and then turns to me. "Hey, what are you doing after work?"

"Uhm, sleep, I guess." I choose not to say ghost counseling service.

"Sleep? On a Friday night? *The* Friday night of the start of semester? What are you, fifty?"

I shrug sheepishly. "I have work tomorrow."

"Tomorrow *afternoon*." She tuts, taking out her phone. "Here, add your number. After work, go home and get your game on. You're coming out with me."

I smile. This is what college is all about. "Okay."

∞∞∞∞

"Knock-knock."

"You don't need to knock, remember?" I say to Cole. He didn't knock, of course; saying those two words is his codeword for permission to enter my bedroom at home in respect of my privacy. "How was your day?"

"Same old, same old," he replies as he appears across the room. He rarely says much more on the topic and I gave up getting more details years ago, assuming it's some sort of ghost code. I often wonder what he gets up to; I can't imagine there's much you can do as a ghost, but then again, when you have all the world and all the time in the world I guess there's no stopping you. "How was your first shift?"

"Survivable," I reply, playing with makeup in the mirror. "Boss didn't micromanage me, which is apparently a good sign."

"That's good." Cole pauses, eyeing me up and down through the mirror. "And, uh, you look . . ."

I turn to face him, wondering what he's thinking. I'm not into the latest trends, preferring to keep my attire as blendable as possible. I thought I was keeping it casual: a ruffled shoulder-strap singlet, my favorite jeans, my hair—now even wavier than usual from the braids—is pinned back in a loose butterfly clip, and I'm considering wearing my heeled ankle-length boots. Topped with light eyeliner and mascara I'm not *that* bad. But Cole's hesitance to finish puts me on edge.

"What?"

"Sexy."

I blush. Not just a little; my cheeks are on fire. Cole has never called me *sexy* before.

Apparently I don't need confirmation either, because Cole is suddenly at my side, his fingers flowing down a lock of hair on the side of my face. "You look sexy," he reaffirms before his lips touch mine.

It's unexpected but I'm certainly not complaining. I only wish he isn't so fast to pull away, acting as if it's nothing. Because it's not nothing. It's something. To me, at least.

I want to protest, or at least pull him in for more, but there's a knock on my door.

"That'll be Kelly," I say as I walk to the door. "The coworker I mentioned. She's cool."

"Going out tonight?"

"Yeah. I am, actually." I can't help but giggle excitedly as I open the door.

"There she is!" Kelly beams as she pulls me in for a hug.

"Kelly! Welcome to my home away from home," I say, holding the door open.

"So cute!" She peers inside, totally unaware of Cole in front of her.

"I love the décor! Did you make these plant pots yourself?"

"Yeah, from clay and recycled glass. It's a pastime hobby of mine."

"Trendy *and* environmentally friendly. See, you do have talent, after all!"

"So much talent," Cole chimes in, giving me a peck on my cheek. I try not to blush again. If this is what dressing up does to him then I've got to do it more often.

Kelly talks into her phone, "Yeah, yeah, I found her, we'll be down in two." She turns to me. "You ready?"

"I am." I grab my bag, and giving Cole a subtle glance I ask, "Are you?"

"Girl, I was born ready," Kelly replies as she walks past me and back to the door while Cole points to himself and raises his eyebrows.

I nod discreetly and grin. "It'll be fun."

"Sure will," Kelly replies. "I've got my friend Juliet waiting for us in her car. You'll like her; she's like me but without the sass."

I can't help but laugh at Kelly's words.

"That's a pretty big laugh you got there, doll. Are you implying something?"

"Not at all," I chuckle as I look back at Cole and subtly hold my arm out to him. "Let's go have some fun."

Kelly was right; I do like Juliet. And like Kelly said, she's similar to her in her extroverted ways but more controlled in her choice of words and how she presents herself. I believe you can tell a lot about someone by their attire. Kelly would call this part of her "talent", but really it's just common sense. Kelly, for example, is in a short black sparkly cocktail dress that's tight to her frame with heels to match. Reinforced with thick eyeliner and mascara, she's clearly a girl on a party mission. Juliet has a gentler look: a jumpsuit with peach tones to match her pale strawberry-blonde hair, with a thick bracelet that looks like a souvenir from some foreign land in Africa or Asia. She's clearly looking to flirt, but also being pretty yet casual while doing it. I, on the other hand, am just looking to be social.

Kelly confirms my theory. "Now saying, 'I'm getting more liquor' is code for 'I'm liking this guy I'm with,' but remember, 'I'm getting another *shot* of liquor' is code for 'I want out from this guy,' and your girls will come save you. And as always, 'taking a tour of the place' is code for 'I'm with this guy for the night', and that means you're on your own." Kelly quickly applies more lipstick in the visor mirror before adding, "Not that Charlotte will care too much for that." She leans over from the passenger seat to Juliet who is driving and whispers as loudly as she speaks, "Charlotte's caught up in some unrequited romance."

"Oh?" Juliet and Cole say in unison, in that same inquisitive tone of expecting a further explanation.

"Tell me more," Juliet teases, her eyes fixed on the road.

"Yes, do tell more," Cole adds from the empty back seat next to me.

I avoid eye contact. "Just some guy I see sometimes," I reply.

"Yeah, but it's long-distance or something. And *complicated*," Kelly adds, doing air quotation marks.

"Oh," Juliet mutters. "They always are."

"That's what I said."

They high-five.

I look out of the window to avoid Cole's eyes that I know are on me as Juliet parks up on the roadside. The house hosting the party is clearly noticeable with the crowds and music. I always thought a fraternity house would be good for my self-esteem, but I have another tenant to consider, and while unexpected guests from the beyond would be problematic, having Cole surrounded by a bunch of peppy young women was my bigger concern.

"I think we need to talk," Cole says as I step out of the car.

"She wanted to set me up with guys," I mutter beneath my breath. "What was I supposed to say?"

"You're supposed to say yes and enjoy your life."

I look back and frown at Cole, something that loosens his own furrowed eyebrows in a vindication that pains me. Why would he say something like that, especially so bluntly? He should know how much I want him by now, expressed in the not-so-subtle ways I openly receive the few advances he gives. So why should I say yes to anyone else?

I don't reply to him however, because Kelly puts her arm around mine and starts walking.

"Now, Juliet is staying here the night, and I'm doing the midday shift tomorrow so I'm only having a few drinks. But you?" She places her finger on my chest, right on my breastbone. "Feel free to loosen up."

"Yay," I reply sarcastically. Not because Kelly seems to think I need loosening up or because I like getting on the booze (because I don't, not really). My response is towards the two ghosts standing by the door engaged in a heated argument with one another. Cole sees them too, but what can he do? They're obviously not here for me and clearly sorting out their own unfinished business with one another. So I simply avoid eye and body contact as I follow Kelly inside.

Once inside I don't need to find my own way in the crowd with Kelly the popular extrovert showing her new adopted introvert the way around. She takes me through the lounge, snaking between some people and saying hello to others, until she hugs someone she's obviously well-affiliated with.

"Kel-bel!"

"Hey, Lea!"

"Hey," Juliet waves with her free hand, the other on a six-pack of cider.

"So this the new recruit?" Lea eyes me up and down in some sort of girl initiation. Maybe she's checking if I'm a threat: am I pretty enough, or too pretty? Will I steal her boyfriend, or help proofread her essays?

"Nice shirt," she concludes.

I'm in, I guess.

"Lea worked at the café," Kelly informs.

"Yeah, for five whole weeks," Lea replies. "Hated that place. And the boss, what's his name?"

"Mr. Dodgley."

"Yeah, dodgy alright." She picks up her beer on top of the speaker and then eyes me again. "So we have this entrance fee for newbies, where you have to demonstrate a skill worthy of attending our parties." She takes a sip of her drink. "So what you got?"

"Oh, geez." Juliet sighs.

I double-take. "Sorry?"

"Charlotte's still discovering her inner purpose," Kelly says. "Be nice."

"Well she better discover it quickly. You know how it goes." She pauses the music and bellows, "New guest initiation!"

I blink. All eyes in the room are suddenly on me, my ear ringing slightly from the noise now strikingly quiet to what it was just a couple of seconds ago.

"I . . ."

"You have to earn your way in," Juliet mutters in my ear. "A talent, of sorts. I can't believe they're still doing this. Just juggle some fruit like I did."

"But I can't juggle," I mutter back, feeling uncomfortable with this sudden unwanted attention. Cole is next to me, his hand reassuringly on my shoulder.

"So what's your special talent, Charlotte?" Lea asks as Kelly elbows her.

I don't like this. But I'm not going to give Lea the satisfaction she seems to be after, either.

"Actually, there is one thing I can think of." I bite my lip, glancing at Cole who frowns back.

"Careful," he says on edge. "Don't do anything you'll regret."

"Yeah?" Lea asks.

"I can correctly guess how many fingers you show behind your back."

"Really?" Lea seems intrigued.

Cole rolls his eyes, but I'm sure I can see the little twitch in the corner of his mouth. We used to do this trick in the playground at elementary school. For a short time I became popular with my class peers, but whenever it came to inquisitive teachers Cole never played ball. I understand why now, but I really hope he throws me a line here. Or in this case, I really hope he stands behind Lea and relays how many fingers she shows.

He nods. I'm in.

"Yeah. Try me."

I grin smugly as I repeat what Cole says to Lea's amazement. Everyone else seems to be impressed, too.

Okay, so maybe this isn't a purposeful use of my gift. But hey, I have to have some fun sometimes, right? And I enjoy turning back around to see the look of dumbfoundment on Lea's face in the crowd of impressed onlookers who start chanting, "In! In! In!"

"Dang, doll," Kelly says. "You'll have to teach me that sometime."

"Well, looks like you're in." Lea turns the music back on and the party resumes. "That deserves a shot on the house. Name your poison." She reaches over to the table of tequila bottles and shot glasses before presenting two options. I point to the bottle in her left hand, not knowing the taste of either of them. Lea pours a few glasses and then hands them out. "Cheers."

Cole stands there, arms crossed but unable to hold down his smile. He's happy for me, I know he is. I only wish he would be happy for *us*, too.

I raise my shot glass, my eyes still on him. "Cheers."

The party hits off and I'm glad to say I'm enjoying myself. Lea introduces me to her boyfriend and a few others in my classes. It will be good to know some more faces on a more personal basis now.

But while this frat party is, as one of them puts it, "lit", my eyes still pan for Cole. He's currently trying to mediate whatever those two ghosts are arguing about, talking to one while the other waits on the stairs looking down at the ignorant partygoers below. Cole's always good like that, trying to understand where each side of a conflict is coming from. Except when it comes to us, then he's thick like a brick. I just want Cole to give in for a change, to let his barriers down and let us discover what we can be. Maybe I just want him to react.

And I know I've had a few drinks, but I can't help but want to find out.

So when I know I'm not the attention of anyone, I take a few steps up the stairs and then slide a look to the ghost next to me and smirk, "Hey."

Maybe it's his hunched forward stare or his thick bulky physique against my smaller frame, but he doesn't notice me.

I cough, then try again. "Hey."

He glances my way, annoyed at the distraction, until he realizes I'm looking straight at him.

"Woah." He flinches back. "Woah!" He waves his arm in my face. "You can see me!" Unconvinced, he hops side-to-side like a monkey. I don't know why *that's* his reaction, but it convinces him. "You *can* see me!"

I can't help but chuckle. Who says being a Communicator can't be fun?

"But . . . how?"

I remain silent and take a sip of whatever mix I have in my glass as a couple passes by me to seek somewhere more private before replying, "Just a talent of mine. What's your name?"

He tilts his head, his top lip curving upwards as he nods in approval at what I just said. "Brad."

I really shouldn't be encouraging him, but I flick my bangs back and shift my posture slightly. "How'd it happen?"

He knows what I mean. "Broken neck. Fall."

"Shit."

"At least it was quick."

I see Kelly waving me over from the lounge below. I nod, pulling my lips back. "Well, Brad, I'm going to dance," I say looking back at him. "Shame it will be alone."

"Alone? Well, do you want to dance with me?"

"Sure."

Brad seems to like this from the wide grin on his face. "Yeah!"

This frat house seems to be designed for parties. Each floor, divided by a small flight of stairs, seems to have something different going on. I know Brad is tailing me as I step down onto the dance floor. I mingle in through the crowds of bobbing people, seeing Kelly and Lea through the blue strobes.

"Where's Juliet?" I ask loudly.

I'm surprised Kelly can hear me. "She's made a friend. A *guy* friend." She winks and that's the end of it. Suddenly we're dancing away with our drinks in our hands. Kelly has a guy grinding up against her, one I'm sure she approves of since he's literally tall, dark and handsome, the way she said she likes them. I then realize I have someone grinding up against me, too. Not that anyone else notices.

Except Cole.

"What," Cole says, suddenly by my side, "are you doing?"

I act as naturally as possible as I say, "What? He asked, and I said yes. Isn't that what you told me to do? Say yes and enjoy life?"

Unimpressed, he seems to catch on. "Charlotte."

I tap Kelly's shoulder and point to my empty drink. She nods okay and I start making my way around the room to the kitchen-turned-bar on the lower floor.

"Did I mention you look really sexy?"

I thought those words were from Cole. I wish they were, but they came from Brad's mouth. Brad. Big, bulky Brad. He would probably be the center of attention right now if everyone else could see him. Everyone except me.

Nonetheless, I flash a smile. "No. But if you want to, you may."

He comes in close. I back up to the wall, my hand reaching the stair railing. His lips are only an inch from mine and with a smirk his hands snake up my chest. "You look really sexy."

That seems to do it for Cole because Brad is then shoved aside. Not far given his size, but enough to shove me along with him as I bump into someone.

"Hey!"

I twist and put my hands up with an apology before turning back to see Cole's hand on Brad's shoulders, clearly not fazed by their size difference. "You're getting really close to my girlfriend there, pal."

"Hey, man, I—wait, girlfriend?" Brad stops, eyeing me and Cole. "*Girlfriend*?"

"Wouldn't be the first time stepping on somebody else's woman, would it, Brad?" The other ghost is suddenly standing between us.

"Shut it, Ricky," Brad says, ignoring him. "What is this? Dating for the damned?" He shrugs Cole off him with a swipe and stands straight. "Wait, we can do that?"

Cole says no the same time I say yes. Then I say no.

"You can hear us?" Ricky interrupts, his eyes wide at me.

Cole says yes the same time I say no. Then I say yes.

"You can see us, too?"

"They're an item, apparently. However that works," Brad answers Ricky. "Hey, he's getting in on some action. Maybe we can, too?"

"Wait, *they're* an item?" Ricky points at us.

"How do we do that?" Brad speaks over Ricky. "Talk to chicks that are still alive?"

"So can others see us?" Ricky adds, glancing around.

"How's sex working out for you two?"

Ricky lights up. "We can have *sex* with them, too?"

I flush red, and I hope it's just the alcohol in my system. I slide a glance to Cole, waiting for him to answer that one, because that is one question I would like to know the answer to as well.

But he doesn't answer. Instead, he stands his ground, eyes and body deadpan.

"To be with Pam again . . ." Brad sighs, suddenly uninterested in me like he was a minute ago.

"Oh, so you want her even now, too? What's your deal, man? Go find your own woman!"

"My deal? *My* deal? You stole Pamela away from me!"

"You don't own women like that, man. Not cool."

"Don't you start that shit with me, you homewrecker!"

"Homewrecker? What about *life*wrecker? You ruined my life!"

"You ended mine!"

"You pushed me!"

"You dragged me with you!"

I'm not quite sure what their deal is, but judging by their wrestling and what is uttered through some very strong words,

Brad and Ricky were best buddies but secretly had it with the same woman named Pamela, and when Brad walked in on Ricky with Pamela, a scuffle quite like the one happening now ensued. Except it ended with a balcony, shattered glass, and two broken necks.

And even in death they're still fighting over her.

That Pamela must be some special woman.

The lights start flickering to their charged emotions, not that people notice or care with the other strobe lights flashing. I not-so-subtly step to the side as Brad jumps on Ricky, one pointless fist in the face after the other.

Now, while they lunge through other partygoers without their slightest inclination of knowing what is happening, for me that isn't the case. Because while they are energy compositions of consciousness (as far as we can figure out), I can still—as lightly as it may be—feel them.

Which is why, when I can't dodge Ricky fast enough as he drags Brad back through the wall, I am knocked into the stair railing. Except I realize, as I fall back, that there is no railing over the last two steps.

Then with a nasty thud everything goes black.

Four

When I open my eyes the first thing I see is Cole beating the other two away. It's a rare occasion to see Cole so riled up, his energy strong, radiating anger over the two feuding friends. And I have to say it's damn hot seeing him do so. I want to see more, but a small crowd gathers around me, asking what happened. Kelly is then at my side, carefully hauling me up, and I get a better view of Cole in action.

I tell Cole to stop, a warning before he actually manages to beat them into the afterlife.

"What was that, doll?" Kelly asks, taking my weight.

"Charlotte," Cole says, now crouched at my other side, trying to hold my balance as much as he physically can, which sadly isn't much. "You're bleeding."

"Really? I feel fine."

"Your head," Cole says, his eyes full of concern.

"My head?" I touch my head then look at my bloodied hand. "Oh dear."

"Geez, Charlotte, how much did you drink?" Kelly looks at me worriedly.

People quickly lose interest once alcohol is mentioned. They're probably thinking I'm just another stupid college freshman here to party hard. Not that a testosterone-fueled showdown went on with the unruly dead.

"I just fell over," I say, and that's enough. A trip of the toes, blamed on the booze.

"Charlotte, what the hell?" Juliet comes up to my side. "Here." She reaches over for some napkins.

"It looks bad," Cole says as Juliet places them on my head. "You need to get checked out at the hospital."

"I don't want to go to the hospital."

"I think you should," Juliet replies, replacing bloodied napkins with clean white ones.

"It doesn't hurt, though," I say.

"It could get infected," Juliet replies.

"That's just the alcohol talking," Cole adds. "It'll hit. Like a nasty hangover."

I wince at the pressure of Juliet's hand as my head starts to ache. "I think you're right."

"Uh, Charlotte," Cole says. "I'm dead, remember? People can't see me talking to you."

Oh, yeah.

Crap.

"Earth to Charlotte? I'm over here," Juliet says, waving her hand in front of me as a guy comes up to her side holding a drink and a can of Sprite in his hands. He's tall and well-groomed in a white polo shirt and blue knee-length shorts, the type of look that screams country club membership. He would look out of place at a party like this, but I somehow doubt that matters given his rich kid demeanor, cold and staunch, which is also how he's staring down at me right now.

"Maybe she has a concussion?" Kelly suggests.

"You're still sober, right? We have to get her to a hospital or something," Juliet says, looking at that guy again. He's probably the new guy friend Kelly mentioned before, annoyed that his plans for the night now risk being ruined as he tips the drinks out the window.

"Yeah," he says, giving me another look. He brushes his gingernut-colored bangs aside before saying, "Go grab some ice and more napkins. Keep an eye on her while I get my car. We'll take her to the university hospital. I know people there."

Spending Friday night in the emergency room was not what I had in mind. It's after midnight before anyone even checks on me, probably because I look like a stupid drunk college kid, and stupid drunk college kids aren't the priority of a city emergency room on a Friday night. Juliet happily keeps conversation while we wait, mostly with the guy who drove us here. Apparently his name is Rory and he's starting post-graduate studies in medical research. He seems to know the front desk staff since they're being friendlier to him than everyone else. He might not be such a fan of blood by the looks he gives me, but then again maybe it's just me sitting here in the state I am. I should stop feeling self-conscious and engage more, but I'm too busy trying to not react to Cole coddling me about self-care and, well, my head *does* hurt.

I tell them that they don't need to wait up, that I have money for a cab home, but Juliet doesn't seem to mind and Rory seems to have charmed the desk staff to getting me seen to shortly. Kelly was also fine waiting for me, although I assume that was more to do with the male nurse she was chatting up. He didn't seem to mind, either, because when he was paged to send me through, he gave me directions to go to the ward by myself while he carried on talking to Kelly. I follow his directions while Cole trails behind, going on about how I shouldn't drink because my safety is 24/7. Whatever. It's not like I drank a lot, and surely I should be allowed to party every now and then. Not that I am listening to what his lips are saying. I would rather pull him into me and show him my appreciation for his knight in shining ghostly armor duties, only my daydream gets interrupted when I hear my name being called.

I turn. "Yes?"

Two doctors stand across from me, one old and staunch, the other a young intern of sorts in his shadow.

"I'm Doctor Kahn, and this is Gareth Hamilton. He's a medical student and I will be assessing if that's alright with you?"

"Sure." I can't complain; it's a busy place and I should

probably be thankful that I'm getting seen to at all.

"Have a seat." The older doctor gestures to the chair across the cubicle space, separated only by a curtain from other patients in their own little cubicle area.

"Hello," the young doctor says as he pulls over a stall. I look up at him and smile sheepishly. He's clearly British, and looks like Harry Potter. An older, sexier Harry Potter, in a white lab coat instead of a black cloak, and with light, blue-rimmed rectangular glasses instead of the famous black circular ones. But no lightning scar.

"That's me. Hello," I reply, unintentionally mimicking his accent.

Yup, I am definitely drunk.

Or concussed.

Or both.

Thankfully he ignores my comment. "What brings you here on a fun Friday night?"

I lift the bloody tissue I'm holding. "I fell. Hit my head."

"Looks sore." He peers over to look at the bloodied patch on the side of my head as he puts on a pair of white gloves.

I shake my head. "It's nothing."

"Well, why don't you let us decide whether or not it's nothing, hmm? Follow this light with your eyes."

I comply, avoiding having to look at Cole's concerned dad stare on my left and Doctor Kahn's teacher stare on my right. I reassure them all that I'm fine by saying my date of birth, the name of the current president, and even the year the Declaration of Independence was signed.

"Impressive," the young doctor says. "No sign of a serious concussion, but I don't like the look of that gash." With a look and a nod from Doctor Kahn, he takes something from the adjacent drawer and I flinch slightly as the sting of the antiseptic hits me.

"A bit too much to drink tonight?" he asks quietly, his hand lightly dabbing an antiseptic wipe on the gash.

"How can you tell?"

"It's not the antiseptic I can smell."

I press my lips shut.

He smiles. A dimple forms on his cheek. It's cute. A single dimple. On his left side. What is it with me and dimples?

"Don't worry, we've all been there." His dabs turn into soft strokes and the pain becomes oddly pleasurable.

I look at his eyes. They're blue. Strong blue, with a green outer ring. His irises have lines of little zigzags coming out from his pupils. I wonder about all the things his eyes have seen. All the death. He must have seen a lot of that on the job, even only as a medical student. We probably have a lot in common.

His eyes meet mine. Crap, I've been staring.

"Yep, it'll need a couple of stitches," he says, throwing the swab away into the marked bin.

Doctor Kahn leans in and nods again. "Only three should do it."

"Will it show?"

"Not once your hair grows back. I'll just get the shaver."

"What?" I yelp.

"Joking." He has a goofy smile. And a dimple. Did I mention a sexy accent? "No shaver. We'll be right back with sutures."

"What are you so happy about?" Cole asks as the two doctors leave.

I roll my eyes. "Nothing you'd understand."

"Is this some woman thing?"

"Woman thing?"

"You know. Full moon. That time of the month."

I scowl at Cole. "Did you seriously just say that?"

"You're acting differently. I can't say I'm all that familiar with you in an intoxicated state."

I huff in disbelief. "I think it's a well-needed improvement, actually. Being more assertive. Open communication. Something you're not too familiar with."

"Charlotte." His voice gets serious, his aura darkens. He doesn't continue, however, because the doctors walk back in and the sexy British one sits down again.

"I'm going to do the stitches and Doctor Khan here is going to supervise me for training purposes if you're okay with that?"

I grin. "Sure thing, doc."

The young doctor manages a quick smile. "Okay, try to stay still, this will only take a few minutes."

He stitches me up, his face full of concentration, his touch gentle. I dare not talk, to distract him from his art, but I can't help but stare from the corner of my eyes. He notices this, a quick glance, an awkward tilt of our lips before we quickly look away. I wonder if this sexy Harry Potter has a Ginny Weasley by his side. I glance at his hands. No ring.

"And that should do it," he soon says. "Not a single tear. You're very brave."

Doctor Kahn leans in quickly. With a nod and scribble on his clipboard he then leaves to the next patient across the ward without another word.

I snicker. If Doctor Kahn manages a nod then it must be a good job indeed. "That's quite the magic power you've got there."

Sexy Harry Potter blinks. "Magic power?"

I lean forward slightly and say in the best Hagrid voice I can muster, "You're a doctor, Harry. "An' a thumpin' good'un I'd say."

He eyes me a stare that's probably looking for any missed signs of concussion and wondering if he should bring Doctor Kahn back. "My name is Gareth. See?" He points at his name badge.

"I take it back," Cole chuckles. "Intoxicated Charlotte makes for a laugh."

I feel my cheeks go hot with embarrassment. This Gareth Hamilton, as his badge says, probably thinks I'm not all there.

"I have a magical power of my own," I blurt out in ego-driven self-defense.

"Charlotte," Cole warns, suddenly all tense and serious again.

"Oh, really?"

"Yes," I reply. "I can correctly guess how many fingers you

show behind your back."

Sexy doctor Gareth Hamilton looks taken aback. "I—I'm sorry, what?"

"Go on, see for yourself." I say, giving Cole a chin flick. "Place your hands behind your back and I'll tell you how many fingers you have showing."

"Uhm, okay." Sexy doctor Gareth Hamilton complies. "How many fingers am I showing behind my back?"

"One. Five. Four. Eight. Four again." I smile, smug. "Told ya."

"Yes, two out of five is quite the record. If it got any higher MENSA would be knocking on the door to take you away."

Cole snorts.

"My psychic senses must be compromised while under the influence," I reply, shooting a glare at Cole.

Sexy doctor Gareth Hamilton laughs quietly, a short huff of air out his nose that is barely audible.

But I hear it, nonetheless.

Great. He thinks I'm crazy.

"Well, you're all stitched up and ready to go—straight to bed, I hope." He leans over slightly and adds, with that whimsical smile and sexy accent of his, "Doctor's orders."

I nod and stand to leave, eager to leave my shame behind.

"Miss Durane?" I turn back to see him half-smiling, a dimple protruding off the corner of his mouth. "Don't let the muggles get you down."

I'm swooning inside. And it's not the tequila.

I sign the insurance forms and hand them to the receptionist. Rory drops us off at our respective homes. I apologize for cutting their night short but they don't seem to mind; it seems that Juliet will have lunch with Rory tomorrow and Kelly got the phone number of the nurse she's determined to see again.

I wave bye as Rory drives off and then I enter my apartment. As soon as the door closes behind me Cole appears.

"As the doctor ordered, you need to get some sleep. Drink some water, too."

"Uh-huh." I grab a glass and flick the faucet on and off quickly. After a few gulps until Cole looks satisfied enough, I head upstairs, my mind on other plans.

He follows me, vanishing from behind me to in front of me to meet me at the edge of my bed while saying something about hangover cures when I walk straight up to him and kiss him.

At first he doesn't respond, but as I persist he releases a small, faint sound between his closed lips, his hands finding my waist. He pulls himself closer to me, now opening his mouth to my own, kissing me deeper as pleasurable sensations wave down my body. But then, as I expected he would, he pulls back with a look of disapproval with himself.

"I'm sorry," he says, guilt in his eyes. "I shouldn't—"

"Hey," I butt in, "You don't need to apologize. I'm not exactly pulling you off me here."

"You're drunk."

"Actually I'm pretty sober now," I try to say convincingly, although my lack of inhibitions and balance probably show otherwise. "And I know what I want. Okay, I'm sorry for leading Brad on. But at least he was interested in me."

"Sorry to break your heart but he's only interested in Pamela."

I roll my eyes. "I don't care about *Brad*, Cole. I care that he showed interest in me and wasn't going to flinch away after any and every display of affection like a timid little rabbit."

"Charlotte—"

"If you don't want me, just say it. Just try being open for once, Cole. Like we agreed."

Cole rakes his hand through his hair, a telltale sign he's stressed. He opens his mouth but quickly closes it again before looking back at me. Then, with a short sigh he speaks through tight lips. "It's not that I don't want what you want," he says slowly, tensely, his glow dimming. "It's just that it's never going to be enough. *I* am never going to be enough."

And with that, he's gone.

I sit there and pout, hoping he'll come back and give in to his urges, but Cole's words hit me with a reality check that brings on a wave of guilt. I soon feel embarrassed with myself and wash up with a sobering cold shower instead. Getting into bed, I reach over to open my bedside drawer and take out the framed photo of Cole, looking at the camera, a smile so pure after finishing a race. Okay, so I happened to visit Cole's romantic infatuation back from his time of living existence in an attempt to find out who he really was. And she might have given me this photo of Cole that I may be keeping in my drawer to ogle over when I miss him. But so what? It's the only photo of him I have, and this one right here would win over any other. Every time I look at it I wonder something different: what was he thinking at the time? Did he finish the run first? Was it a new record for him? How close was he to the runner next to him? Were his friends there, cheering him on? Did he actually know his photo was being taken?

I trail my finger down his face through the glass. I wish I could hold him, to rake *my* hand through *his* hair for a change, to feel his skin on mine, to smell him, feel him, even if he's sweaty in his track gear.

Just once.

I look back at the framed photo. Cole doesn't know I have this. I don't know why I don't just show him, but aside from having to explain how I got the photo, he'll probably just brush the image off with a simple explanation and then make a point about that part of him being gone. I prefer the mystery of not knowing, the fantasy of possibilities.

I sigh and put it back, my little secret kept hidden away.

I didn't see Cole the next day, nor the day after that. I probably deserved it though, after the way I acted. His words keep playing in my mind in class, at work, in bed as I try to sleep. Okay, so my idea of mixing Cole into my newfound social life didn't go as well as planned. Me and alcohol are never going to be a good mix either, I realize. But this sullen silent treatment isn't cool boyfriend material.

Especially when it happens again.

The screaming ghost, that is.

It is during class, just as the professor is changing the presentation slides from muscle development of infants to that of adolescents when she appears.

Only, it is a different woman.

I think.

It's hard to tell, what with the screaming and static. But she certainly makes herself known.

To me, anyway.

Cole too, because he's suddenly there, half-shielding me from her. His protection is appreciated if not pointless because she disappears after a few ear-piercing seconds, and so does Cole when he goes after her.

"Yes, abs have that effect on some people," the professor says, looking directly at me. There is a murmur of soft laughter from the class. It's a small class, no more than thirty of us, but I must have attracted attention, especially when I realize I'm up against my seat, panting and shaky. I giggle in embarrassment and settle back down in my seat. With the adrenaline rush still in me not even the growth rate of muscles will have me feeling dreary now.

I strain through the rest of class impatiently and am the first to leave when it finishes. Not because I'm nervous or scared, but between class and work I have a lunch date with Kelly which will hopefully take my mind off things, if only for the meantime.

"Hey," she chimes as she sees me approach. Kelly and I seem to be acquiring the habit of eating out when neither of us are working out of laziness to cook. Not that I'm complaining; it's another reason I believe we get on so well. "Juliet was meant to come too but she's caught up in a group assignment so it's just us. How was class?"

"Interesting." It's all I say as I take a seat and she doesn't ask more. "I'm starving."

"You like Korean, right? I love Korean food."

I pick up the menu. "You had me at the word 'food'."

We order and I start sipping my soda as Kelly talks about her vacation to Korea and Japan a few years back. Suddenly she asks, "Is that Rory?"

"Who?" I follow her line of sight out the large restaurant window.

"Rory, the guy from the party Juliet almost *got more liquor* with, remember? Kinda broody, father a commercial property investor, he drove us to the hospital in his *Audi*. Surely you weren't *that* drunk?"

I ignore Kelly, my focus on the guy walking next to him.

"Oh my gosh," I mutter, grabbing Kelly's arm. "It's him. The doctor from the other night."

"Sexy Harry Potter?"

I cringe and nod at the same time. I may have relayed my interaction with the doctor to Kelly at work a little bit too animatedly. She appreciated my literary references, at least.

"Get up, say hi."

My eyes bulge. "What? No way!"

"Fine, if you won't then I will."

"What?"

Before I can stop her, Kelly is skipping up to the entrance door they just walked through.

"Hey, Rory! And hi!" she beams at Gareth. I try to pull Kelly back but it's too late. "Ignore my friend here, she's naturally weird so this is normal for her. I'm Kelly." Kelly holds out her hand, her welcoming smile extending to Gareth.

Gareth shakes her hand but his eyes are on me.

Only me.

"I remember you," he says. "You fell. Bumped your head."

"And you stitched it up. Yay, all better now," I reply nervously as I pull on a loose lock of my hair.

"All thanks to you," Kelly continues the conversation. "And we are so grateful, by the way. You must have been so busy, and then having to squeeze Miss Two-Left-Feet over here into your rounds." Kelly tuts at me. "I always tell her to step carefully, especially in heels."

Gareth tries to hold back a smile. "I can't say I know of the struggles women today face. But I'm glad you're alright, Charlotte."

Charlotte.

He remembers my name.

"Come join us! We ordered plenty, too much for us. You like kimbap, right? We ordered bibimbap too if you don't. Here." Kelly doesn't wait for an answer, instead pulling out the two other chairs in offering. "I'll be right back, just *confirming our order.*"

She means adding to it, but I keep my mouth shut helplessly as she walks away, leaving me alone to face Gareth and Rory.

"You have a very . . . welcoming friend," Gareth speaks first, and it's only slightly better than the awkward silence.

"She's one of a kind," I say with a nervous laugh.

"So you like Korean food?" he asks.

"It's alright. I need a change from Mexican every night."

"You don't cook?"

"I can. I guess. When I have food."

Gareth tilts his head. "You don't have food?"

"I'm going through an eat out phase at the moment." I pick at my nails. Why am I feeling so awkward?

Gareth must sense something too because he changes the topic. "So I take it you know Rory?"

"We met. Briefly." I turn to Rory who's looking at us curiously. "Thanks for the hospital ride again."

"No problem."

"So you two are friends, huh?" Kelly asks Rory as she sits back down, her usual nosy self. Knowledge is power in her books.

"Rory is the reason I have a life outside of medical school with what little freedom I get. Since we both spend so much time at the hospital we sympathize with one another well."

"Oh? What do you do at the hospital, Rory?" I ask.

"Rory spends his time *downstairs*," Gareth interjects with a tone in his voice.

"Downstairs?"

"He means the morgue," Rory fills in. "It's where us students sometimes do medical research."

"You mean, like, cadavers?"

Rory nods.

"Gross!" Kelly exclaims.

There goes my fear of blood theory.

"So you're a student, I take it?" Gareth asks me.

"Freshman," I reply. "Studying health science. For now. I haven't decided on what to specialize in yet."

"Taking a sabbatical from MENSA?" he asks, holding back a grin.

I cringe inside but struggle to hide my smile. I can't figure out if he makes me nervous or embarrassed. "Something like that."

"I'm sure we could give you a tour of the hospital if you want to pursue health sciences," Rory interjects. "The world will always need people in the medical field."

"I doubt Charlotte wants to hang out in the hospital morgue," Gareth replies on my behalf. He says it in jest, but he's not wrong. While I have dealt with seeing the dead for as long as I can remember, I have only ever seen their spirit—that is, not their physical form left behind. Assumably this would make seeing their bodies less traumatic, given I know they are here, but it doesn't. Especially when they don't die under the, uhm, *cleanest* of circumstances.

"Sorry," I grimace. "I'm not really a fan of hospitals. Dead bodies would make me squeamish."

"Fair enough. Not many can deal with it," Rory replies. "Some say downstairs is haunted, anyway."

"Spooky," Kelly utters, half-listening while looking at her phone.

"Just nonsense from the admin girls," Gareth replies. "They probably believe in Santa Claus as well."

"You don't believe in ghosts?" I ask with only a slight crack in my voice.

"I'm a man of science. Of course not."

My heart sinks a little. I'm not quite sure why though, considering most people share the same views as Gareth. I guess I was just shooting for common ground. My mistake. Oh well.

He then turns to me, probably in expectation of an agreement. Fearing he may have just insulted me, his eyes widen slightly and he asks, "Why, do you?"

I can't bring myself to say no, as if it would jinx my abilities that are—for better or worse—an intrinsic part of me. I do, however, manage to remain the same as I say, "I guess I would need to see it to believe it."

"I believe in ghosts," Rory then says, leaning back. "As long as the admin girls do. I do them a favor like take a few pieces of paper downstairs for them, they do me a favor like let me use the good coffee machine or bump Charlotte here to the top of the emergency room waiting list."

Gareth and I chuckle.

"Cunning," Kelly remarks. "Well, I'm in no rush to find out."

"I heard kimchi makes you live longer," I add to the conversation, noting the small dish of the stuff on the table.

"So does not tripping over in heels," Gareth says to me. "Speaking of, do you mind?"

He points to my head before he leans in close and brushes back my hair. I can smell his aftershave now. It's a mix between pinewood and mint.

It's nice.

It's refreshing.

He smells so good.

"I don't know if you want to know this, but that's my first stitch job."

"No way!" I turn to reply to him, his face still close to mine. He's not wearing glasses today; I'm so close to him I can see the faint outline of contact lenses around the blue of his eyes.

"It's true. Typical understaffing and busy weekend nights. I knew I would have to do it soon, but I'm glad it was you."

Don't blush. Stop blushing.

"I was a little nervous but your cut is healing up well. Come by next week if the stitches don't fall out naturally."

I nod and then quickly look away, using the waitress serving up lunch as a distraction.

Kelly effortlessly picks up a piece of kimbap with her chopsticks before asking Gareth, "So, do you have a girlfriend?"

I gawp at Kelly. She really has a talent for being fearless.

It takes Gareth a moment to realize what Kelly is asking him. "Uh, not right now, no."

"What? A guy like you? You must be shy just like Charlotte here."

Gareth briefly glances my way before replying, "Something like that."

"Calm down, Kelly," Rory says. "He only just got off the plane."

It turns out that Gareth is American but has been in the country for only six weeks to embark on his medical residency. He moved back here from a fancy-sounding place called Buckinghamshire in England which is north of London, near Oxford. His parents are also American, but he's spent the majority of his life across the pond, hence his accent.

"I feel like a tourist in my own country," he concludes.

"That must be so weird. Isn't that weird, Charlotte?"

"Yes, Kelly," I reply.

Kelly has started doing a thing where she has to include me in every reply she gives. And while Gareth's life story all sounds rather exciting and impressive (he's helped his mother on Anglo-Saxon archaeological digs and thanks to his pilot father he knows quite a lot about planes), I'm still not able to fully distract myself from earlier. Because there's something about a screaming dying ghost popping up in front of you that does that, and I can't help but wonder where she is, and if she's okay. And on that note, I wonder where Cole is, and how he's feeling. I try to ignore these thoughts and pay attention to the living folk I'm sitting with and play the part. That includes ignoring the ghosts lingering nearby, especially the one staring me down, waiting for some eye contact for validation that I did in fact glance at her. When I ignore them long enough they leave me alone, including the one staring me down, discarding the rumors I'm someone special, someone who can help them.

"Enough about me," Gareth says, probably picking up on how far inside my mind I really am. "Tell us about yourself, Charlotte. Is that a slight Southern accent I notice?"

I proceed to tell him about my life, not that it's a very exciting talk. Foreigners seem to have this notion that the South is rodeo by day, steak barbeque in the evening, then barnyard line dancing into the night. Americans who aren't from the South tend to see it as some out of touch quasi-state ruled by rednecks and overrun with gun collectors and crazy men from Florida. It's not, though. It's just a place with people from many different cultures and backgrounds, different social and political beliefs, all just doing the best with what they have and what they've been taught. There are good people and there are not-so-good people, and when something bad happens, some of them help and some of them don't. It all blends into a very average upbringing environment. I mean, what can I say that compares to thousand-year-old skeletons and twin-engine planes?

Except for the obvious, of course. But I'm not going to mention that.

"It must be nice growing up in a small town where everyone knows one another," Gareth says to my surprise. "Because of my parents' jobs I moved around so many times I stopped counting."

I guess the grass always looks greener from the other side.

"Well, we have to get going," Rory suddenly says. "Gareth has to be back at the hospital soon and I have some family business to catch up on."

I get up to pay but Rory swipes the bill and then takes out his credit card without question.

"I insist," he says when I stand there awkwardly.

As chivalrous as that sounds, since we got them trapped here I figure paying for their food is the least I can do. "Let me at least contribute—"

"No need. It's my dad's card anyway."

He walks up to the counter before I can argue, but considering he has an Audi and a funded credit card I decide to let him be and pay.

"I think he's had a pretty sheltered upbringing so he can be a bit socially stiff at times. But he still insists on paying for outings or food. Must be a taught attribute from his family or something," Gareth remarks.

"No complaints from me," Kelly quips as she collects her belongings to leave.

When he returns we awkwardly say thanks and bye to one another. Gareth says he hopes to see us around sometime, and I'm sure that's the only reason why I can't help but smile sheepishly as they leave.

"What was that?" Kelly asks accusingly as she lightly whacks me with the back of her hand.

"What was what?"

"The opening was right there. And you skipped right over it."

"Opening?"

"He asked about your life story. *Life story*. He's interested in you! When he said he hopes to see you around sometime, you're supposed to give him your number!"

I shake my head, realizing where she is going with this. "He said that he hopes to see *us* around sometime, Kel. And I'm sure Gareth was just being nice. Besides, you heard him yourself: England is his home. Long-distance relationships never work out well."

"But that could be years away—"

"Or not."

"But Gareth is a *doctor*—"

"Medical student—"

"Whatever. That's a gold medal in guy material, doll. He's the stable bring-home-the-bacon kind. I mean, what does *Cole* do?"

I was going to say something smart like he's a teacher (what he wanted to be) or a private security guard (what he is. Sort of). But I can't bring myself to. Because the cold-hitting truth makes itself clear through the blockades in my mind: Cole will never be anything because he's dead.

That's when I start crying silent tears of hidden grief coming to light.

"Geez, doll. Don't get too pent up about it." Kelly passes me a tissue from her bag. "Some guys just take a while longer to figure themselves out."

She's trying to be supportive, but it only makes me cry more. I want to hold him in my arms and tell him I don't care that he's dead, that him not being here at all is worse than any obstacle of physicality.

"Sorry, Kelly." I start pacing to my car. "There's something I've got to do."

I drive straight back to my apartment, taking two steps at a time up to my loft room on the top floor and let the door slam behind me as I go inside.

"Cole?" I drop my bag on the table. It misses and falls to the ground, the contents spilling out but I don't care. "Cole!" I peer into the bathroom. Nothing. I pace up the steps to the bed. Nothing. I take a deep breath in and close my eyes. When I open my eyes next he'll be there, no matter how long it takes.

"Charlotte?"

I open my eyes and smile, a tear falling down my cheek. He asks me what's wrong but I don't give him the chance to finish because I place my lips on his. And this time I won't let him stop.

"Charlotte—"

"Shh," I press my finger on his lips in the small space he pulls between us. "It's okay."

"It's not okay, Charlotte. I'm—"

"I know what you are," I interrupt and look him sternly in the eyes. "I know there are obstacles and challenges, but I want you anyway. And *I* make that decision, Cole. Not you. *Me.*"

I kiss him again, and this time he lets me. His mouth moves deeper into mine, his energy more intense as he holds my waist and pulls himself closer to me. I sigh in pleasure feeling him close to me, not wanting to let go of him, to stop kissing him, to be anywhere else except with him. We find ourselves on my bed, feeling each other, exploring the sensations each touch and kiss gives. We eventually stop, the limit that Cole can—or is willing to—go, but that's okay. We lie there, talking about trivial things until slumber starts to take over.

"We can do this every night." I look back at Cole who is still shirtless. It turns out that clothing also isn't necessary for ghosts. I don't know why he's been hiding what lies under his shirt all this time, because I sure don't mind looking at his toned body. "I won't mind."

Cole holds back a smile, his shirt suddenly forming back on him, a trick of his consciousness. "Charlotte, I need you to know that . . . what I'm trying to make you understand . . . I won't always be around."

I feel a knife in my throat as I swallow. Cole being dead is only half the problem. Cole crossing over is the other half of the sad reality I refuse to face. I am reminded of this in the back of my mind now and then, and I know that one day I will have to face that reality. But I can't, not now. The selfish, stubborn part of me won't allow it.

"I know." It's all I can say, parceled up with another smile. "And we live for the present, day by day. As agreed, remember?"

Cole strokes my cheek. He then tries to move a lock of hair hanging from my face before quickly giving up. He nods then kisses me on my forehead, short but sweet, and I then snuggle under my bed sheets.

"Did you get anywhere with that screaming ghost, by the way?"

Cole's face hardens a little. "No. Gone without a trace. It's as if she's . . ."

"A ghost," I finish.

"Yeah. And it frustrates me."

"I'll check the internet for missing persons. Maybe that'll hint at something we don't yet know."

"That's a good idea. Tomorrow. But for now, rest up." Cole must have read my face. "Hey, we'll figure it out. Don't worry."

"Stay with me?"

Cole kisses my forehead once more and I close my eyes into slumber, awaiting pleasant dreams.

The dreams were terrible, actually. Nightmarish. Every night for the past few nights it's been the same. There was a shadow, static and dark, only when I look closer I realize it's Cole.

I'm glad to open my eyes and realize it is just that: a dream.

"Nightmare?" Cole is next to me.

"Cole!" I turn on the lamp, shocked yet relieved to see him as his normal self. "You're here."

"I was worried." He tries to stroke my hair. It feels damp. "Same one?"

I nod.

"Want to talk about it?"

I shake my head, wanting to cast it aside like the other recent nights. "What time is it?"

"Almost five-thirty."

"Dang." I sit up. "Well I don't want to go back to sleep."

"You know what will clear your mind? A good sunrise hike."

I moan and throw a pillow at him, only it goes straight through him and over the banister to the table below.

"Ow!"

I lower my eyebrows.

"I'm sensitive," he jokes, rubbing his chest.

"Why would I want to go hiking?"

"When was the last time you were out in the great outdoors? All you've done lately is work indoors, study indoors, and party indoors. Sounds pretty nightmarish to me."

He is right. I can't remember the last time I saw some greenery.

I groan. "Okay, okay. Where?"

"I know a place, about an hour from here."

"Oh?" I expect him to give a story about how he knows the place but he doesn't.

"I think you'll like it just as much as I did."

"It's a date." I smile. "Good morning, by the way." I kiss him on the cheek then slide out of bed before he has a chance to react. Not because I want it to be quick. I just don't want him to second guess the mention of a date. He doesn't seem to, though, instead choosing to watch me change into leggings and a light jacket before walking me to my car. Cole tells me the way, but I pause his navigation at the McDonald's drive-thru for a takeaway breakfast and coffee. I've never been one for coffee, but there's a first time for everything, and since I am about to go scaling the hillside the need for caffeine and a McMuffin calls.

After an hour or so we eventually come to the edge of a national park. It's by a lake that stretches out into the hillside, a quiet and forested area far from any main road. It takes nearly another hour to reach the viewpoint, and it's mostly steps to my disdain. I was even more annoyed to complete the climb only to see that there was a small car parking area just yards away from the viewpoint.

"That's cheating," Cole simply says as he tirelessly walks on ahead. He looks like a little kid at Christmas, excited and impatiently waiting for permission to start opening his presents.

"It's a good thing you don't need to breathe," I pant, lagging behind him. "Because the air feels pretty limited up here."

Cole looks back and chuckles. Of course there's not a single drop of sweat on his face, or puffy red on his cheeks. Just as usual, he's gorgeous.

"Almost there," he calls back. "It'll be worth it. Promise."

I push myself up the last flight of steps to meet Cole. "Told you," he whispers in my ear as I look to see the morning sunlight peak over the landscape stretching out around us, the lake below snaking around lush valleys of green and yellow-tinted foliage.

I close my eyes and inhale the crisp fresh breeze to open up my airway and refresh my body. The cool air slightly dries the surface of my lips, but I like the way it feels, emphasizing every detail of them. I bite my bottom lip, the sting oddly satisfying.

"It's beautiful, isn't it?" Cole says, looking out at the faint array of orange-stained clouds dotted across the sky.

"I guess it's worth it," I breathe. It is totally worth it, actually. And my body is now kicking up the endorphins in agreement. But I won't give him bragging rights. "Sit with me, Cole," I order, patting the ground next to me. I sit on a rock and close my eyes, getting lost in my thoughts to the sounds of nature. I don't know how much time passes; it could have been a minute or many more, until Cole gently says my name.

I open my eyes.

"Catching up on lost sleep?"

"No," I reply, my voice as calm as the surroundings. "Just thinking. About us."

"Oh?" Cole raises an eyebrow but his genuine smile is there, the one of mischievousness and humor. "You looked pleased."

"I am. Thanks for bringing me here, Cole."

"I remembered I have been here before," Cole starts, his voice drifting quiet.

Ghosts apparently have a different sense of time and space than the living; they go where their consciousness takes them, whether to a place or to a time as a return to memories, wanted or not. I can see in Cole's eyes he's sometime else, but unlike his usual past recollections, his light remains.

"I hiked around here sometimes, for track training. Nothing gets your fitness up like a fast-paced hike. It beat the treadmill, anyway." I expect him to say more, but he smiles softly, and as he returns to the present moment he concludes, "I enjoyed those days."

"What would you do? If you were alive for just one day?"

Cole raises his eyebrows at first, before narrowing them slightly and tilts his head before saying, "I used to think about that all the time. But then I accepted it's not a healthy thing to dwell on so I stopped."

"It's okay, you don't have to answer. I was just making small talk."

I expect that to be it, but he responds.

"I would ask you out." The words sing in my ears, a melody to my thumping heartbeat. "I would make a picnic—peanut butter and jelly sandwiches and fresh pineapple, then I would take you for a walk along the coast, the sun and salty air on our faces. I would expect some bikini action, of course." He winks at me. "And we'd watch an epic sunset with the greasiest diner takeaways we can find, and then build a campfire out of driftwood and make smores and drink beer, before sleeping under the stars wrapped up in blankets." Cole nods. "Yeah. That's what I'd do."

Two birds fly low, their cries lingering over the quiet until they settle in tree branches nearby. I let myself immerse in his words, the idea of it tantalizing. I thought the topic was over, something not to bring up again, but Cole continues, "And I would wrap my arms around you, feel you close to me. And when you turn to give me a look wondering what I'm staring at, that's when I would kiss you." He pauses. "And I wouldn't be able to stop."

I wouldn't want you to stop.

"Would you like that, Charlotte?"

"Yeah," I breathe above a whisper. "I would love that."

Cole smiles, a sad grin pushing through his mouth that's a flat line as he turns back to the sky. "If I were alive."

And just as my heart lifts it sinks. Cole is right; it isn't a healthy thing to dwell on. Because the more I want it to happen the more it hurts to know it won't.

I turn to take in the panoramic view, using the breeze to flush away the water in my eyes. Biting my lip slightly, I can't help but ask, "Are you scared? Of what comes after?"

Cole contemplates his answer. "No. Dying's the scary part. Crossing over is just . . . sad."

"What do you mean?"

"Whether it's Heaven or eternal nothingness or reincarnation in an endless cycle of lives that awaits me, it's just sad knowing that who I am, my life, my stories, my memories, will come to an end." He pauses. "I never got to properly experience my life as Cole. But I wanted to." His voice weakens to a croaky whisper. "I wanted to."

"I know you did." There's no stopping the tears now silently flowing down my cheeks. I pull up my knees and bury my face in them.

"Hey. If not this life then the next."

I look up and see Cole force a smile. It's all we can do for each other. Smile.

Returning to his usual self, Cole stands and stretches his arms out dramatically, a happy sigh released as he takes in the view again. "I don't know what's waiting on the other side, but it can't be better than this. Heaven is here. In this moment. With you."

He smiles, the energy of him radiating in a soft illuminating glow as he places his hand on my cheek and leans in to kiss me.

I could have died then and there. Maybe I did and he was trying to hint at something. Such moments feel so perfect, and while I want the seconds that pass to carry on forever, reality tends to get in the way.

Cole pulls back and then coughs subtly, nudging his head. "Human alert."

Following his gaze I see a small group of hikers approaching. Typical.

Cole must have read my mind because he chuckles. "It would look weird to them once they notice you."

I scowl. "I better start the hike back down. I have to work for a living now, after all."

"Hey," he says. "Remember this, Charlotte Durane. For me."

I kiss his hand cupped on my cheek. "Forever."

∞∞∞∞

"You look like you're in a good mood today," Kelly says as she sees me entering the café. "Don't tell me you had a reconciliation with this Cole guy?"

"Something like that." I smile. She's right; I am in a good mood after a refreshing—if not tiring—morning hike. I even completed my class readings early and helped an elderly couple who had been married for fifty-two years and who passed away within days of each other to cross over together. It's amazing what one can fit into a day.

Kelly smirks. "Uh-huh."

"Sorry about ditching you yesterday. That's not like me."

"Who am I to step in the way of love? Besides, I had plans with that hot nurse I met in the waiting room. Got him giving me a *tour of his place*, if ya know what I mean."

I choke up laughter as I throw on an apron. Kelly sighs as she picks up an empty coffee mug from the table. "Heads up. Dodge man is on the line today."

I groan quietly. I have been doing well on my work shifts so far, at least until Mr. Dodgley shows up. Then nothing I do is enough. But I've come to the conclusion that nothing will ever be enough, and acceptance comes from groveling in loyalty like Kelly has done so admirably. I was warned of this, I mentally remind myself, as I divide my hair with my hands and start tying them into two quick side-braids.

Apparently I am to only hand out one napkin per order, even if there are multiple people, because psychologically customers only use the napkins because they've been provided with one, and if given the choice they are likely not to take one unless they need one. Therefore, napkin usage isn't encouraged to save on costs and the environment (even though I think Mr. Dodgley cares about one more than the other, since I've seen the supply boxes and they are certainly not sustainably sourced and clearly bleached white). Kelly spuriously compliments him on his business smarts, but combined with his views of throwing away leftover food nearing expiry instead of giving it to staff or people in need because "it discourages selling and encourages scrounging", and only using half the recommended dishwasher soap because "the soap spreads enough", I just consider him stingy. Not that I say that out loud. Instead, I nod, smile, act interested and keep my shoulders back to avoid the "young generation hunchback".

When Mr. Dodgley eventually thinks I've had enough, he mercifully retreats into his office.

"Yeesh," I huff as I hear the door close behind him.

"It's all in the psychology," Kelly says in earshot. "Let them feel their power. Always make those above you feel superior. That's how they like it. But now he's gone, onto real business." Kelly throws a cloth down into the wash bucket. "You. And Gareth."

I groan. "What about us?"

Kelly flips a blender jug upright and pours a cup of ice into it. "It's a thing."

"What do you mean, 'a thing'?" I check the order she's making and then scoop up a cup of frozen berries from the freezer compartment.

"You and Gareth. It's there, I sense it."

"With your psychic abilities?"

"*Psych* abilities, not *psychic* abilities. Don't confuse me with my aunt."

I place a scoop of yogurt into the blender jug. "Your aunt?"

Kelly closes the lid, turns on the blender, and then waits ten seconds before turning it off and answering, "Yeah. She's really into that Feng Shui and crystal ball stuff. I'll introduce you to her sometime. But let's not get distracted here," she replies as she pours the smoothie into a glass. "He's British—"

"Technically American—"

"Well as long as he sounds like James Bond he's British in my books." She places a blueberry muffin in the microwave next to me and presses a button. "But my point is he's single, probably lonely, in a far-away land, looking for adventure and fun and probably romance. It's all there. The stage is set. Get in there, girl!" She nudges my shoulder except I don't know if it's in nudging support or if I'm blocking access to the microwave.

"I dunno, Kels. Gareth is twenty-three," I say, placing a napkin (only one) on the tray.

Kelly takes the muffin out of the microwave and places it on the tray next to the smoothie. "So?"

"So that's a big step from eighteen-year-old-freshman-and-waitress me. He has a degree already, is in medical school, and he's on the long yet promising path to becoming a surgeon. I don't even know what I'm doing with my life. I don't exactly have much to offer him."

"You're being too critical of yourself, doll. Nobody knows what they're doing, not really."

I shake my head dismissively as I place a straw in the smoothie. "It doesn't matter, anyway. I'm with Cole."

"Well, Juliet and I are keeping tight-lipped about this Cole guy so as far as Rory and Gareth know, you're single. We're all going to meet up at the mall for lunch at midday tomorrow. You should come if you don't have class. Bring Cole along and prove your point." She hands me the tray. "Or mine."

"Wait, what?"

"He's still in town, isn't he? Your grand reconciliation?" she says before turning to say goodbye to a customer leaving.

"Ah," I say in realization as I make my way to table five. "He left again."

"Hmph." Kelly picks up the rubbish left on table two. "Well, I want to meet him. See what he's got that Gareth doesn't."

The acceptance of who I am comes to mind. Or the ability to appear and disappear at will, but I don't say that.

I realize I haven't yet said anything to Kelly. I open my mouth to come up with a reply, something that doesn't arouse more suspicion. He's in the military? He's going overseas? He's a traveling wildlife photographer?

Only I don't reply, my focus suddenly on the ghost in front of me.

Because it happens again.

Seven

This one is louder, if that's even possible.

But Cole seems ready this time. He appears straight away, trying not to be taken aback by what's in front of us. I don't blame him if he feels as afraid as I do, but after a moment of hesitation he approaches her.

The tray I'm carrying falls onto the ground along with the blueberry muffin and smoothie. I don't hear the sound of shattering glass over her screaming, but I notice everyone stops what they are doing to look at me.

"Charlotte?" Cole turns at the sound and looks at me.

"Whoopsie-daisy!" Kelly chimes out loud. "Looks like we have a spill over here."

"Charlotte?" Cole asks louder.

I snap out of it, suddenly aware of the mess I've made. And Mr. Dodgley looking at me. I nod at Cole to follow her. He complies as they both disappear. I quickly yet carefully grab the wet floor sign and mop.

"We'll clean this up and get a replacement for you straight away," Kelly reassures the couple at table five with that hospitality service smile of hers as she picks up pieces of broken glass and china.

"Sorry." It's all I can think of to say as I help Kelly. At least that one napkin was put to good use.

Kelly gives me a reassuring smile and then carries on serving and pleasing customers while I clean up the rest of the mess I made. I get a grilling from Mr. Dodgley, but I manage to finish the rest of my work shift without incident which is just enough for him not to take the shattered glass and plate from my wages. Whether that would even be legal or not I don't ask; I'm just glad to keep my job.

"Geez, doll," Kelly says as we lock up. We were so busy the last couple of hours I haven't even had the chance to say thank you to her. "You looked like you were about to have a seizure or something. Are you sure you're okay? You need to get a second opinion on that head bump of yours?"

"I'm fine. Really. You shouldn't have put yourself on the line like that for me."

"Dodgeman needs me more than I need him. Besides, this friend's got your back."

I smile, feeling warm inside. I was never one to have true friendships; aside from Cole they were more or less just class peers or acquaintances. Kelly, however, even in all her frivolous and flamboyant nature, is definitely one for the books.

"Thanks," I say. "And tomorrow I'll be there."

∞∞∞∞∞∞

It isn't until after class the next day when Cole shows up. I was hoping he'd show up beforehand, but I know he doesn't want me distracted from lectures so I didn't get my hopes up.

"They're different. That's all I can tell," he says as we walk across campus to the student parking lot. I don't usually drive to class since I live walking distance away, but today I need to drive to get everything done, even though the only parking spaces left were so far away it probably would have taken just as long to walk from my apartment building.

I speak into my phone, a common tactic to avoid glances. "So three different women. All dying . . . or dead."

Cole stops and turns to me, his expression strained and sympathetic. "They're dead, Charlotte. That imprint is there.

Albeit in a weird way."

I sigh. "I thought so. Still, I hoped otherwise, especially since I found nothing on the missing persons website matching them."

We carry on walking as Cole continues, "I just don't know how to piece this together. They come to you, so they know who you are, what you do."

"Yeah, how do they do that, by the way?"

"Do what?"

"Sense me out."

Cole raises an eyebrow at me, as if to mock my cluelessness to the situation. "We just do. It's like . . . petrichor."

"Petrichor?"

"The feeling of rain in the air. You can sense it, even if you don't see it."

"I know what petrichor means. I just didn't think that's what I'd be compared to."

"Okay, how about . . . finding that parking space."

"What?"

"When you're in a crowded parking lot, but you want a space, and something makes you go where you decide to go, and voilà, a space is there." Cole suddenly looks pleased with himself. "Yeah. Seek and ye shall find."

"Again, not the comparison I expected, but I'll let it pass."

"My point is, it's a cry for help. And we just don't know how to help. We're helpless."

I grip my phone tight at that moment, suddenly feeling the heaviness of it. I pull it down from my ear and look at it. The pink glitter casing (not my first choice, but it was a gift from Dad's not-quite girlfriend Patricia who is lovely to me so I use it with gratitude) protecting my phone from damage and keeping important cards in. I pull the corner back, but hesitate and clip it back on again.

Cole realizes I've stopped walking. "You okay?"

"We'll figure it out." Cole's words, now my own. "*We'll figure it out.*"

My phone screen suddenly flashes. It's Kelly, her message an address to a Thai food bar.

"Almost forgot," I say as I approach my car. "Lunch date."

"Oh?"

I cringe at my choice of wording. "Yeah. Kelly and the others from that party."

"Really?"

"And that med student who stitched me up."

"That British guy?"

"Technically he's—" I shake my head. "Doesn't matter. He's a pal of the guy who drove me to the hospital."

"Really." It was more of an utterance than a question, and he doesn't ask further. And it's not like I have anything to hide, because I don't. I just don't want him to have any unnecessary ideas, especially now that we're in such an okay place.

I look around, making sure we're alone before standing on my tiptoes to place my lips on his.

If he was distracted before he certainly isn't now.

"What was that for?" he asks afterwards.

"Nothing," I reply. "Does there need to be a reason?"

"I guess not," he replies before looking around. "I guess there doesn't need to be a reason for this, either."

He then kisses me square on the mouth, his lips lingering on mine. When he eventually pulls away I tremble slightly, my body protesting the sudden halt to the pleasurable sensations within me.

"Don't be late for lunch." He winks, and then he's gone just as other students begin to disperse from campus to their cars.

With traffic and parking woes (maybe I need to practice that parking space sixth sense I apparently radiate) I walk through the doors fifteen minutes late.

"Took your time," Kelly seethes loudly. I know she doesn't mean it, though. "I saved you a seat." She nods at the space across from her. The seat next to Gareth.

"I know you missed me." I give her a quick hug before

nervously sitting down and saying hello to the others.

"How have you been?" Gareth asks, more perky than last time.

"Good, thanks," I reply as I pick up the menu. "And you? Not too many stupid drunks blocking up the emergency room, I hope."

He chuckles, that dimple on his left cheek making itself shown again. "Not any amusing ones."

I order a fried rice and a soda. Rory starts things off with a story of a body that an intern put in the morgue without turning the refrigeration unit on during the middle of summer. We all cringed, Juliet more so when she hit Rory for making her feel sick so close to eating, but it was a flirtatious hit. Soon we're laughing at Kelly's work stories and all the ways staff have quit on the job. We all get along amicably, as if we've been friends for a while now. Rory has loosened up a bit as well, and seems happier in this newfound friend group. I'm sure I could say the same about myself. It all feels great, like this is my new normal. Like I am normal. And I believe it too, for a while. And then the reminder comes, in the form of a thought of Cole, or the sight of a ghost walking by, or the voice of fear in my mind that this won't last. But I quelch such things, determined to play this out as best I can.

Once we finish lunch we stroll through the mall. There isn't anything in particular that we do; us girls browse the clothes shop and the guys walk slowly past the gaming store, but we're simply hanging out, enjoying each other's company.

I know Juliet has feelings for Rory, and it's clear Rory seems interested in her. They'd be good for each other. I've noticed the playful way she is with him and the way he does little things to protect her like making sure her shoelaces are properly tied and checking that there's no traffic coming when she crosses the road. Maybe if Kelly, Gareth and I back away a little they can grow closer and actually do something.

Then again, some things just need a little push in the right direction to get going.

Which is why I suggest, "Why don't we go check out that arcade?"

"Didn't know you were into that stuff, C?" Juliet comments.

"It'll be fun, trust me," I say, motioning them to follow me.

It doesn't take long for Rory and Juliet to pair up in a basketball throwing game, leaving Gareth and I to pester Kelly at Pacman.

"Oh my god go claw at each other will you!" She swats us away from the machine she's at, us taking the hint to try out the claw machine. We take it in turns, Gareth proud he manages to claw a plushie until I manage to get the golden treasure chest.

"Dang." He raises his hands. "I know when to fold."

I giggle, taking out the golden treasure chest from the prize door. "Beginner's luck, I'm sure."

"What is it?" Gareth asks, looking at his prize.

"It's Totoro," I reply. "You don't know Totoro?"

He looks at it again, pulling his head back and handing it to me. "You keep it. Plushies aren't my thing."

"Are you sure? I won't consider you any less of a man for having a cuddle toy in bed."

Gareth lets out a small chuckle before insisting it now belongs to me. "They're not what I want to cuddle in bed, Charlotte."

I try not to blush. Ugh, why do my cheeks ignore me? I laugh nervously as I take Totoro from him. "Don't worry, Totoro. There's room for you in my bed."

Gareth subtly clamps his mouth shut. I probably opened up an array of replies there, I realize, so I quickly change the topic.

"Well, better go and claim whatever it is I've won." We walk over and place the golden treasure chest on the counter in front of the store clerk. "I clawed the golden treasure chest, what did I win?"

"You win the fish game, you win a fish," he says with a thick accent, turning behind him and pointing to the shelves of giant fish plushies. "Toy fish," he then points to the aquarium tank, "or real fish."

"Real fish?" Gareth echoes.

I look at the options, my choice already made. I jump up and down like a little girl. "Real fish, real fish!"

Gareth chuckles as the store clerk says to wait by for a few minutes while he puts everything together. We decide to pull Kelly away from Pacman before she becomes too obsessed with the retro game.

"Ooh, I remember these," Kelly says, pointing to a machine covered in stickers. "I saw them in Japan. You go into the booth, make silly poses like this," Kelly pouts and does a V with her fingers, "then choose some effects and then the pictures come out. It's fun! Especially when there's a timer and you can't read the instructions because it's all in Japanese." She gestures inside. "Come on!"

Gareth reservedly goes into the booth first.

"Oh, it says maximum two people," Kelly says in a spin that lands her suddenly behind me.

"You said you don't know Japanese."

"I do now," Kelly utters as she shoves me into the booth to Gareth before closing the curtain.

I don't have time to apologize because Gareth has already placed the tokens in and the machine starts up. Just as Kelly said, there's a timer counting down from thirty and that's the only thing we understand between flashes of the camera in front of us between two mirrors. Pressing buttons in a random frenzy we apply various stickers and filters until the machine slides out polaroid-sized photos and shuts down.

"Look at you!" I laugh at the picture of Gareth with a dog face filter.

"I was going to say the same thing," he replies as he points at the photo of me as a cat.

I cough back laughter. "Fur isn't my fashion."

Gareth turns to me, flashing that side dimple of his. "Good. I prefer you without whiskers."

We both felt it. It was only an instant of something, an energy shared between us, through the way we looked at each other. It makes us stop in our tracks, wondering what just happened, and what should happen next.

I blink and quickly look away, ignoring the mild tingling in my stomach. "I like these ones." I hold up the collage of us doing various funny poses.

"Me, too." Gareth smiles, his eyes resting on one image in particular. "This one's my favorite."

I follow his gaze to the photo. It's the simplest of the lot, but the purest. The machine captured a snapshot as we looked at each other, laughing, lost and confused in the humor of it all. Added with a starry border filter that fitted surprisingly well I have to agree with him. "Mine, too."

"Come on, guys. I have to get to work soon," Kelly calls out to us from where Rory and Juliet are waiting.

"One set for you," I hand him the photos, "and one set for me."

He takes the photos. "Better get going."

"Yeah."

We pause, another moment of unknown between us before he clears his throat and we make our way over to the others. I pick up my goldfish, wrapped in a clear plastic bag and placed in a tank with a boxed filter attachment and a little aquarium plant to go with it. We all promise to do an afternoon like this again sometime before parting ways.

I stop by the grocery store on the way back, something I finally get around to doing, especially now since I have another mouth to feed.

I open my apartment door. "I'm home!" I call out for a laugh, but I always like it when Cole is there to respond. Like he is now.

"Is that food?"

"Yup. Real food," I reply as I place the grocery bag on the counter. "Or close enough to it." I quickly place the instant ramen into the cupboard out of his view. "And," I excitedly pace back to my front door and hold up the tank. "Our new roomie!"

Cole instantly laughs. "You bought a goldfish?"

"Sorta," I mutter, carefully placing it and the tank onto the table against the wall before filling a container of water in the sink. "It needs a name."

"Fish?"

"*Fish?*"

"It works."

"I was thinking maybe something a little more . . . unique." I lift the contents out of the tank and tip the container of water into it.

"Shark?"

I look back at the goldfish and laugh. "Shark? Really? It's a cool name, but it's the least intimidating goldfish I've ever seen. I mean, look at it. Its eyes look like they're about to pop out of its head. It's going around in circles, confused with itself."

"Shark is the confidence boost it needs."

I laugh again, refilling the container. "I like your reasoning." I fill up the rest of the tank with water and then place the plant in the tank. I then attach the filter and lift the plastic bag, admiring the new addition to my little household. "Okay. Shark it is."

"Hello, Shark."

I untie the plastic bag and carefully tip the goldfish into the tank. "There you go, little fella. Your new home."

I continue to unpack my groceries while I watch Cole take in his new friend, his aura bright and glowy. It's a good decision; back home Cole had Pippi and a couple of beehives for company whenever I was busy. I didn't think about how much lonelier Cole has been since following me here, especially with my busier schedule.

I blink away the guilt, not wanting to darken his mood.

"I'm glad you like it," I say, walking over with a small container of fish food. I sprinkle a few flakes on the tank filter. "You'll have to help feed him."

Cole glances at me, his light darkening, unsure.

"I believe in you," I quickly add, with a quick kiss on his cheek.

That seems to be the motivation he needs. Ghosts may just be energy, but everything is energy, and with enough emotion and concentration they can channel their energy enough to become more physical. This is only short lived; at most it's something dismissible like a light flickering or a wobbling picture frame. They may even be slightly visible for a second or two out of the corner of someone's eye, like a mirage or shimmer from their imagination. But anything beyond that is merely wishful thinking. Because they aren't physical entities, not anymore.

A flake of fish food, though?

He concentrates, eyebrows furrowed, channeling his energy on a single flake as he manages to lift it shakily. Once he manages to get it over the edge of the tank filter, in a sigh of exhausted relief from Cole it slides into the water.

"I knew you could do it," I whisper in his ear before kissing his cheek again.

He turns to me, making sure his lips meet mine, his light even brighter than before. I expect it to be short and casual, and wait for him to pull away. Except he doesn't. Not at first, anyway. He holds me there, his lips touching mine, wholesome and true. And when he does part his lips from mine, his words cement what I feel.

"You're the best thing that's ever happened to me."

I smile, my heart beating wildly. "That's good to know. I thought I'd be competing with Shark for that title."

Cole turns to Shark. "Sorry, buddy."

"We can continue this flattery upstairs," I suggest deviously.

Cole flashes a sly smile but it is met with hesitation, then I see his demeanor stiffen. "You have a test tomorrow to study for."

I groan. "How do you know that?"

"I saw your notes. Besides, I'm going to keep an avid watch tonight." He kisses me on the forehead. "Study hard. But sleep well."

I watch as he leaves the apartment. But even after he disappears, I smile as I wash up and settle into bed because everything feels good.

I then notice a message on my phone from Gareth:

Hey, how's the fish?

I pick up my phone and reply:

Shark is good. Happy in his new home :)

It doesn't take long for him to message back:

Shark?! HAHA XD
Lunch 2morro?

I pause, my mind drifting back to the arcade. I had a great time with Gareth, and there was something there, a tingling in a moment I can't quite explain. I'm surprised he's asking to meet for lunch again so soon. And directly, instead of as a group invite. Not that it matters, anyway.

Sorry, have a test :/

I bite on my fist, waiting for his reply. After one long minute it comes:

Good luck x

Good luck. With an 'x'. He replied with an 'x'.
I hover my thumb over the x, debating what to do with it. Every second he awaits a reply makes it worse. Panicking, I bite my lip and send the reply:

Thanks x

I hastily shut my phone off and throw it across my bed with my textbook. There's no way I'll be studying tonight. Suddenly the contentment I felt only a couple of short minutes ago seems so long gone.
What is going on? And why do I feel so . . . jittery?

I take a deep breath and sink under my duvet cover, wondering if I am already dreaming or if another nightmare is on the way.

Eight

Leaves begin to cover the sidewalks in hues of yellows and browns and the air is becoming colder every night. The resulting cooler mornings put most people in sweaters or a light jacket, but not Cole. He is still looking as handsome as ever in his white tee and jeans, oblivious to the elements. I'm glad he was athletic before he died. As vain as it sounds I enjoy basking at the way his toned muscles show through his shirt.

"You look like you've just seen a ghost," Cole remarks, noticing my staring.

I can't help but blush as I bite my lip to hold back a laugh. It has been two weeks since the last screaming ghost visit and we're no closer to figuring them out than before. I did spend some more time trying to research who the women are but to no avail, especially since it's hard to know what to search for when there's so little to go on. So we're not letting it hang over us, instead focusing on what matters most, like enjoying our time together. Nonetheless, Cole is sticking by my side. He says it's to protect me, but I assume it's at least partly out of desire more than necessity.

"Are you sure you want to come? I can imagine more interesting things to do."

"I'm a free spirit. Where you go, I go."

This makes me smile. His typical humor with the reassurance that I am not alone in the world.

Kelly pulls over in her car. "Hey," she waves out from her

rolled-down window. "Let's go shopping!"

I laugh as I hop into the passenger seat. Kelly has succeeded in dragging me out for girl time since Juliet is busy on a study trip for her class. To me, clothes shopping is something only usually done out of necessity, and a mani-pedi combo isn't something I can say I've done before.

Not any longer, though.

"I can't stop looking at them," I idly say, staring at my light green glittery nails.

"I can't believe you've never had a girl's time out before. You really must come from a farm town," Kelly replies.

I want to say that's the case, but I know it's simply because I never had any reason to pamper myself or had anyone to go with. I force a smile, refusing to let the past take over my present. "Well, I'll certainly make a habit of it from now on."

Cole whispers in my ear, "You look gorgeous either way."

I do all I can to not swoon over then and there. I'm loving this open, wholesome Cole. His light is slightly brighter, his smile slightly broader. And of course, it's mutual.

"Gotta get the attention somehow," Kelly says as she struts past the two guys on the sidewalk. She's now sporting a shoulder-length cut and styled waves, a look that she totally rocks as she slides them a glance with a thin smile. Both guys look back behind them as we pass.

I almost choke on my slushie. "They're checking out your ass!"

"Good. Let 'em look. I won't have this perky derrière forever."

I laugh.

"You're only young once, doll. Which is why you're going to be wearing out that skirt in that bag of yours."

I look at my bag of new clothes. I argued it's the wrong season for short skirts, but Kelly argued back that I'd look good and can support the seasonal look with a pair of tights and ankle boots, so I'm now carrying what is my new fashion style.

We turn the corner of the mall to a row of townhouses. We're stopping by Kelly's aunt's place to pick up one of her textbooks she left there.

"Now I have to warn you, my aunt is *quirky*, to say the least. But she makes great food, and she knows I'll always come back to her for it."

"Quirky? In her family? Who would've thought," Cole mutters quietly, not that Kelly can hear.

"Don't say I didn't warn you," Kelly adds as she opens the gate and goes up the stairs to the door. She enters without knocking, the door ajar. I put the rest of my slushie in the trash can before following behind her.

"Hey, Maria!" Kelly calls out.

"Kelly-bella!" The woman, maybe around fifty years old, in a long peacock-patterned skirt and an oak-brown wool poncho comes up to Kelly, arms spread wide for a hug.

"This is Charlotte, we're in the same class and work together."

Maria then comes up to me and without hesitation squeezes me into a warm embrace. "Bonjourno, Charlotte! I'm Maria."

"Pleased to meet you, Maria."

Maria tilts her head slightly, her angled grin growing, and asks in her faint Italian accent, in the excited way elders do, "And who's the handsome young man?"

Three emotions hit me in the moments following that question. First there is confusion as to who she could be talking about. There is nobody else here except Cole, especially when it comes to being handsome and young. Second is denial because while Cole is handsome and young, he is mine, as in for my eyes only. I follow her gaze to my side, right up at Cole, and then comes the third emotion: shock.

"I . . ." I don't know what to say. I glance at Cole but he is as speechless as me. "I don't know what you mean." My voice goes high, the hairs on the back of my neck tingle, and I do that nervous jittery smile I have a habit of doing when I'm anxious. I couldn't help but flash a glance at Cole again who also looked stunned. Cole is dead. Nobody else can see him—except for an unorthodox janitor-slash-priest-slash exorcist I came across half a year ago, but he's not the same vibe I get from Maria.

"That would be Charlotte's ghost of a boyfriend," Kelly casually replies. "The one who is never able to show himself." Before I have a heart attack she adds, "Don't act so surprised, doll. Maria says that to half the people who walk in here for one of her readings. Ooh, is that focaccia I smell?" Kelly follows the delicious smell of bread into the kitchen as I regain sensation in my limbs.

"He's stuck to your side like glue," Maria says in a hushed voice before winking.

I glance at Cole again. I (we) had tried out the psychics and self-proclaimed mediums over the years to see if they could see or at least sense Cole in the way I do, but aside from one having the "strong feeling of a young male presence" it was a waste of my money. I (we) had become so accustomed to assuming I was a once-in-a-lifetime phenomenon, neither of us seem to know how to react.

"You . . . you *see* him?" I ask, barely above a whisper.

Maria smiles. It's a warm and elated smile, and I know the feeling behind it. It's the feeling of validation.

At that moment Kelly walks back in, speaking over a mouthful of bread, "Maria, you're not scaring her away, are you?"

"Not at all," Maria replies back to Kelly. "Bring out the focaccia, please, dear."

As Kelly goes back into the kitchen Maria motions me over to the couch. "Come, sit, sit."

"Careful, Charlotte." Cole has his hand on my arm. It's not tight or tugging. It's a protective reassurance, and I love seeing him do all he can to protect me, to show his devotion and care for my wellbeing. I flash him a quick smile, a reassurance that I'm okay.

The house, from what I've seen so far, has a mystic theme to it. The pungent smell of incense, rows of stones on shelves, rock salt lamps, posters of star alignments, recycled artwork pieces on the wall. I see myself in Maria. I wonder if I'll turn out like her one day. It wouldn't be a bad result. She seems happy; wrinkles of many smiles frame her face, her deep brown eyes soft and clear. Which is enough for me to open up to her.

Kelly walks back in with the focaccia and puts it on the table in front of me. "Feel free to deny her spiel of reading your aura or whatever. Most of my friends do."

"It's fine, Kelly. Really," I reassure her. "I'm interested in this stuff, actually."

Kelly rolls her eyes. "Don't say I didn't warn you." She walks across to the recliner and puts her earphones on, plugging herself into her phone.

Maria claps her hands softly. "I knew something was coming. I felt it."

"Felt what?"

"Something like . . . *family*." She glances at Cole. "He is your family, yes?"

I smile, sliding a glance at Cole. "Something like that."

Cole squeezes my arm.

"He is special to you."

"Yes, he is."

Maria is interested in everything I have to say about Cole, which elates me for being able to talk about him to someone. I keep things basic, however, only letting her know how he's my protector from other spirits. I think my checkered lifestyle might be a bit much to take in, even for someone like Maria.

I was just telling her about his choice of name for my goldfish when she's taken aback. She asks in a subtle gasp, "You can *hear* him?"

My spirit drops at this. "You can't?"

Maria blinks twice before calling back to Kelly, "You have a special friend here, Kelly-bella."

Kelly must have heard. "I do pick 'em," she mutters idly before looking back at her phone.

"I only sense them, see their faint auras, Charlotte. What you can do . . ." She mutters something in Italian. "You have a divine gift."

I pull back. I've heard this all before and I don't care to hear it again. "Oh, uh, no. It's just something I can do."

Kelly must have noticed my hesitation. "I'm just going to pop to the bathroom. Then it's time to get going."

I nod okay to Kelly. When she's out of sight I lean in to say in a hushed voice, "I would prefer it if you didn't mention this to Kelly. It's just . . ." Kelly is my friend, and I feel bad about keeping this from her. But everything is great as it is right now. I am seen as normal in the eyes of the world around here. I'm the happiest I've been in so long. Why risk ruining that?

Maria puts her hand up. "I understand," she simply says. "Say no more."

"Thanks," I reply, my trust now in someone I've known for such little time yet it feels like I've known for years. Such a rare connection brings people together quickly, I conclude.

"I have one question, though," I suddenly decide to say. "Have you, uh, seen spirits that look, uh, different?"

"Different? In what way?"

"Sort of . . . static." I don't mention the screaming since she can't hear them. I don't want to scare her, either. "That sort of thing."

She shakes her head. "My dear, such spirits sound like there is an evil upon them." She walks over to her table of rocks and places a small purple rock attached to a string over my neck. "This has been blessed with cleansing energy. It could help keep you safe."

I look down at the rock, unconvinced of any such energies it has. Regardless, I say thanks. It's pretty and it's the thought that counts, after all.

Kelly walks back in, and with a takeaway offering of focaccia we say bye to Maria and make our way to work. We arrive just in time for Mr. Dodgley to freak out about the broken dishwasher, so we put in twice the effort to get things done at pace.

When we finally get a break I check my phone.

Dinner?

The message is from Gareth. We haven't seen each other since the arcade, but both of us were caught up with studies or work whenever the chance to socialize came up. I didn't mind, though. I've been busy, that's no lie. I think little of this offer as I quickly reply:

I finish work at 8..

He replies:

Perfect. I finish at 6 which usually means 8, fml..
Will meet you there?

I hesitate, my mind frantically wondering what to do.

Sounds great. Cya then~

It's just dinner. Dinner with a friend.
So why is my heart beating louder than usual?
"I've never seen you so into your phone before, doll. There better not be dick pics on the screen."
"It's Gareth," I reply with a friendly scorn at Kelly who simply shrugs. "We're just friends."
"And what does Gareth want?"
"I think I'm having dinner with him after work."
"Are you now?"
"Feel free to join us."
"Oh, geez, I would, doll. But you see, I've got this thing where I don't third-wheel dates. Besides, I'm closing up shop tonight."
"It's not a date."
"Sure, sure."
"Wait." I turn to Kelly. "You don't have anything to do with this, do you?"
"Who, me?" she asks too innocently. "Now why would you think that?"

"I told you I can't think about Gareth like that, because of—"

"Because of Cole, yeah, yeah," Kelly finishes for me. "But you know he's only holding back because he's not sure where he stands with you. I mean, you're not exactly advertising yourself with this Cole guy."

"Kelly," I warn.

"You don't hang out with him because you spend all your free time with us. You haven't yet introduced him to us, and we're your friends, right? Do we embarrass you or something?"

"What? No!"

"And you don't have a single photo of him in your apartment, or any memento of him. Even your phone background is of your dog—"

"I love my dog—"

"You're meant to love your boyfriend too, doll. Now with all of that I could turn a blind eye, but you don't even have his contact on your phone. That just can't be ignored."

I turn to Kelly, my mouth agape. "How . . . do you know that?"

"I guessed. Correctly at that, thanks for confirming. But it wasn't hard, considering other girlfriends are glued to their phones when they're not with their partners. But not you. You barely look at your phone unless I forward you a meme or your dad or Gareth messages. Who doesn't message their own boyfriend?"

Kelly is right—as usual—and I find myself stuck in a corner. I can't tell her, of course. Cole is a secret for a reason. And even if she did believe it, where would that put us? Would she consider me crazier than her aunt? Would she tell everyone? She is one to speak out loud without inhibitions. Not to mention the others. I finally have friends and a sense of belonging. I don't want to risk that. Not even for the truth.

I glance across the café to see Cole leaning on the window, glad he's out of earshot to what's being said. He's still, watching the world move without him, his mind no doubt deep with thoughts. Thoughts about us, probably. And the screaming ghosts. The whole other side of my life I can't—*won't*—let known.

Kelly sighs, her patience on getting an answer over with. "Upstairs needs closing off and cleaning up."

"Sure thing." I grab the mop and broom.

"Do you think I did the wrong thing, telling all that to Maria?" I ask as I finish sweeping. I'm making good use of the cleaning time upstairs alone by going over things with Cole.

Cole ponders this. I can tell he's caught up in one of his deep contemplative moods. "I don't know. But it's your choice to make."

"I think I trust her. I mean, I have no reason not to. Besides, she makes really good bread." I grab a cloth and wipe the table down. "And she gets it."

"She gets what?"

"Being different. She knows what it's like."

"I don't think she cares. About being different, I mean." Cole pauses as he watches a moth flutter at the window. He leans his face up to the glass, studying the motions of the moth. He places his finger on the glass before concentrating his finger slowly through it. As soon as he touches the moth it flies away. "I think it's a good thing you told her. She's clearly embraced who she is and is happy about it. I hope she can help you discover that for yourself." His attention goes to the window again as he softly says, "Still, Maria only sees me. You can communicate with me. And I thank God for it every day."

This makes me pause. I didn't take Cole for a religious person. I always assumed we were on the same wavelength when it came to religion and divine intervention and all that, which is a stand that usually favors logical reasoning. I am about to ask further when his eyebrows crease slightly. "That doctor guy is outside."

Crap.

"Ah, yeah." I gulp. "During my break Gareth asked if I was free for dinner."

"Oh?"

"I'm pretty sure it's casual. Rory might be there too, I didn't even ask." Except I somehow doubt it. "I said I have work, but he finishes late too, so then I said okay. But I don't have to. If it's awkward just say so and I'll cancel."

"You should go." His voice is flat, short of hesitation.

"I should?"

He nods. "Remember what we agreed on."

My shoulders slump, the chair I'm carrying suddenly feeling heavy. I don't need another reminder that life is for the living and I have to live my life with the living first and foremost. I am selfishly hoping he'd be angry, or at least a little bit reluctant. If he is then he's certainly good at hiding it.

"Okay, then."

He starts to come over. I can tell he wants to say something but then Kelly thumps up the stairs and chimes, "Charlotte! You have a visitor."

"Coming," I call out in reply. I look back to Cole who simply nods, then he's gone.

"Hey, Charlotte," Gareth says as I go down the stairs with the cleaning supplies.

"Hey." I smile.

"Someone owes me a couple of hours so I got off while I could. I thought we'd go for Chinese this time." He holds up a plastic bag. "You like noodles, right?"

I snicker. "We're becoming internationalized with our cuisine."

"There's a light display by the river. Want to check it out?"

"Sounds perfect," I reply. Casual, friendly, dinner outdoors on a mild early October night with a friend.

I turn to Kelly. "Upstairs is done."

"Go."

"Are you sure? I can finish up here—"

"Nobody's here. I'm going to clean the coffee machine and then spend the last two hours messaging Lea with a hot chocolate—without marshmallows of course, because we both know that Mr. Dodgley counts them."

I laugh. "I owe you one."

Gareth and I walk a few blocks to the river and find a bench to sit on as the lights flash changing colors and patterns.

"This is the way to eat dinner," I chime as I hold the pot of fried noodles in my hands. It's still warm and I notice there are even steamed dumplings mixed in. "How did you know I like steamed dumplings?"

"You're not the only one MENSA has an interest in."

I almost choke on my first bite.

Seemingly amused by this, Gareth says, "You really want to know?"

I nod.

"I had no idea what I was ordering. I just pointed helplessly and they pityingly put this together. The fact that they got it right has just bought them my customer loyalty."

I laugh.

"Oh, I almost forgot." He takes out the rest of the bag contents.

"My favorite beer! Wait, you know I'm underage, right?"

"The drinking age is eighteen where I'm from." He winks as he passes me a can. "Besides, it's just one. And age didn't stop you last time."

I blush at the memory. "Of all the patients you see you remember me?"

"We only remember the impressionable ones." He lifts his beer. "Cheers."

"Cheers."

We clink our cans, a quiet moment between sips. Talking to Gareth feels like the most natural thing. We talk about our shared political views and the progress of humanity before he talks about his summers spent helping his mother develop new exhibitions at some British museum.

"Wow, you sure know some niche subjects."

"It comes with being a nerd. Throughout high school—or do

you say secondary school?—I was a late bloomer and never got the attention of girls so I spent most of my time doing geeky stuff. It's why I got into medicine actually; I liked science and figured who doesn't love a doctor? So six years of university later here I am."

"You decided to become a doctor to impress girls?"

"Is it working?"

I almost cough out my beer.

"I guess not." He has a sheepish grin on his face. "But the feeling of helping those who need it, saving lives, seeing families leave the hospital intact is motivation enough to become a surgeon. Even through the amount of studying required, long hours and stretched resources."

"The most important jobs are usually the most thankless," I agree. "But surely there are lots of nurses and secretaries at the hospital who are down for going out with an up-and-coming surgeon?"

Gareth chuckles before shaking his head. "Been there, done that. Too messy."

"Oh?"

"My ex-girlfriend was in the same classes as me. I fell for her the first week I met her, then asked her out the second week. I was totally besotted by her. I was even thinking about engagement rings." He titters. "I really thought Ellie was the one."

"What happened?"

"She tried to blame it on the workload. She said with me doing medicine and her deciding to major in physio we spent too much time in our fields and not enough with each other." Gareth pauses to take a sip of his drink. "And I almost believed her. Until I caught her with one of the osteo majors."

"You walked in on her cheating on you?"

"I didn't need to walk in. I heard enough by the door."

"Shit."

"Osteopath majors are the worst. And they're so smug, acting like they're the center of the medical profession. Well, the only thing they ended up becoming the center of is the university's chlamydia outbreak. Guess I dodged a bullet there." He takes another few gulps of beer.

"Is that why you came here? To get away?"

"I was utterly heartbroken. And humiliated. I had wanted to visit home—the American one, that is—and with the transfer opportunity and nothing stopping me I thought why not? I renewed my American passport, packed two suitcases, and then took off." He finishes his drink before adding, "I still don't know if that makes me brave or a coward."

Gareth and I have more in common than I realized.

"Daring to find happiness isn't cowardly. It makes you brave," I finalize. "Especially when you're alone."

Gareth looks me in the eyes and smiles. "I think you're right."

It's there again. I feel it, that energy between us. Short and sudden, gone as soon as it comes.

I blink it away, a cough to clear my throat. "Girls are such bitches. And what sort of name is that, anyway? *Ellie*. Such a bitch name."

Gareth lets out a laugh. "A bit perceptive, don't you think?"

"You're still young. I'm sure someone like you will find someone better than *Ellie*." I gag dramatically at the name. "And you'll be happier than when you were with her."

"You think so, Charlotte?"

"I know so."

We share a smile before looking back to the river. Very few people are still out and the cool of the night is quickly settling on the tips of my ears and fingers.

"What about you? Did you ever sort out your guy drama?"

"Hmm?" I blink, confused.

He points at my head. "I was close to thinking maybe a guy did that to you until Rory verified that you fell."

"Oh, *that* guy drama." I chuckle nervously. "No, so you see— well, not see, but the thing is, there were these two guys fighting over a girl and, well, I don't know where this is going but I was tipsy and I fell."

Gareth raises an eyebrow and laughs. "Okay, I believe you." He leans back on the bench slightly, trying to keep a casual demeanor going when he asks, "So you don't have a boyfriend?"

I swallow, not knowing what to say. I am with Cole. Cole is my boyfriend. And, okay, so it's not the most conventional of relationships. But we manage. We're a team. Only, Cole's words replay in my head, the condition of us, that I have to put life with the living first. Even though I don't want to. Do I please Cole by hurting him? Or disappoint him by protecting him?

Gareth waits for an answer, and I suddenly realize it's not just about me and Cole. It's about Gareth, too. I would be deceiving him, not just about Cole whom I am having trouble conveying to Kelly as it is, but also about who I am. And after what he's been through, I can't do that to him.

"I . . . am single."

"Oh?"

"Yes," I say more assertively. "But I'm not ready to jump into anything right now." I look to the river. It seemed like a good answer when I said it, and I hope it works. This way Kelly lays off my back about Cole and dating while Gareth understands where I stand. And this way I don't technically break my promise with Cole, either.

"I understand," Gareth replies.

I smile. He already gets it. Now I just need to convince Kelly.

Gareth and I carry on talking about work and studies and crazy patient and customer stories into the night, and it's nearly midnight before he walks me home. With an uncertain hug we part ways until next time.

When he's gone I take a deep breath in before going inside.

"I'm back," I call out as I take my shoes and jacket off. I see Cole perk his head up from watching the fish tank. "How's Shark?"

"Well fed," Cole says proudly.

I walk over and give him a peck on his cheek. "That's great."

"How was dinner?"

"Good." I head towards the bathroom for a quick shower,

continuing to talk over the water. "Very casual. The food was good. Had a beer at the river. Colorful lights. Not much else to say."

"That's good. I'm glad you're having a good social life nowadays."

"Me, too. Any ghostly updates?"

"Not the ones you're hoping for. Brad and Ricky are finally making peace, though."

"That's good." I step out of the shower to change.

"They feel bad for what happened. I said you've since forgiven them."

"Water under the bridge." I step out of the bathroom, leaning on the doorframe. "What do you think?" I ask, twirling around in my new night dress. The lilac satin and black lace trim feels even better than it looks dangling above my knees on my waxed legs and painted nails. "Impulse buy. When you were by the florist convincing that ghost to stop trying to haunt his ex-wife—"

I don't get to finish that sentence because Cole is suddenly on me: his hands on my waist, his chest on my chest, and his lips on my lips. He pulls back to look me up and down again, his eyes wild, but he doesn't say anything before he kisses me again. A moan of pleasure escapes me as he kisses me down my exposed neck. His touch may be light, but I still feel him well enough, including *him* against my navel.

He pulls away suddenly, this realization sending him stumbling back in shock.

"I'm sorry," he panics, his light quickly dimming.

"What? No, Cole, it's okay—"

"It's just a reaction." He shakes his head, raking his fingers through his hair.

"Yeah, guys sometimes do have such reactions." I can't help but giggle as I say this. I at least hope it lightens the mood, but Cole is not swayed.

"Charlotte," he fists his hand over his mouth, backing up more. "It's not . . . *I'm* not . . . I can't . . ."

Oh.

"Cole—"

"No." His light darkens more. He hits his forehead in frustration with the palm of his hand. "I tried." He leans against the staircase, facing the ground, his voice strained yet trembling, "Tried to not let us get this far. I tried."

I can sense the pain it's causing him, which causes pain for me, too. I want to do something, say something to make it better. Except I can't. And I don't know what to do.

"This is why," he rakes his other hand through his hair, "this is a bad idea." He looks up at me, his eyes dark and guilty. "I'm sorry."

"Cole."

He's gone before I can reach him. And I know I'll be alone tonight.

Kelly and I finish work at eight o'clock precisely. It's a warm night, what will no doubt be one of the last for the next few months. I walk around the alleyway to my car and rummage in my bag for my car keys when I feel a hand on my shoulder.

"Geez!" I shout in startlement. "If you weren't already dead I would have killed you."

Cole grins, then kisses me on the head, the biggest act of affection he gives nowadays. We haven't revisited that night; it's as if it never happened. That doesn't mean it's gone from my mind though because I think about it. A lot. We've reached the limits of how far we can go, and once again we find ourselves in the unknown of what to do or where to go from here. So we fall back to our default of acting casual and ignoring the unspoken terrain as if everything's fine, even though it's not, and as much as it troubles me, as much as I try to think of a way to fix this, I know I can't.

But Cole is here, things are still okay between us, and for now that's what is most important.

"How was work?"

I open the door and sit in the driver's seat. "Boring and tedious as usual. You should be relieved you get to avoid having to be a wage slave for fifty years."

"Living is suffering," Cole reiterates, now sitting in the back seat. "But so is dying."

"Shit, when do we catch a break?"

"I'm on the assumption that the phrase 'rest in peace' has some truth to it. It's what I'm hoping for, anyway."

I glance back at him in the rearview mirror. What did he mean by that? Or, moreover, *when* did he mean?

"Why are you applying makeup?" Cole notices the mascara and lip balm I have in my hand.

"Juliet's place has a cool firepit in the backyard, and both her roommates will be away tonight so we're having an evening of candlelight supper, s'mores, and plenty of hot chocolate." I pucker my lips and apply lip balm. "So don't worry, no alcohol."

"Will that doctor guy be there?"

"I guess so." I know so, but I try to sound indifferent. Gareth and I have been hanging out more often between our busy schedules, mostly through our shared passion for Asian cuisine, but Cole has obviously picked up on it. And now this makeup seems like a stupid idea.

"He likes you, you know."

I cringe, putting the makeup back in my bag. "Well I told him I'm not looking for a relationship right now."

"Because of me," Cole says quietly, his eyebrows lowered.

"Because I decide so," I reply sternly. "Heads up."

The passenger door opens as Kelly gets in.

"That Dodgley!" She exasperates.

"Vent away," I say as I start my car.

"Nope, the shift is over. He doesn't get my free time." She opens the window and pulls out her vape from her bag. "And he wonders why I need this so much," she mutters as she inhales. "Got the marshmallows?"

"Yup. And biscuits and hot chocolate and potato chips and even popcorn if the weather doesn't hold."

"Got your toothbrush?"

"My toothbrush?" I breathe into my hand, trying to smell my breath.

I notice Kelly rolling her eyes. "For staying the night."

"We're staying the night?"

"Duh."

Crap. I didn't think that.

"Don't worry, just use Gareth's."

I shoot Kelly a disapproving stare. "You gotta stop pushing that, Kelly."

"It's not me you need to say that to, doll."

I look at Cole through the rearview mirror again, his expression unchanged. I sigh quietly. And they say that women are impossible to understand. Men are so confusing. I mean, here I am, giving them clear indications, yet they seem to want other intentions or take on different meanings in what I say.

After I turn onto the main road I glance another look through the rearview mirror, Cole's presence like a magnet to my eyes. His head is hanging low, his mind somewhere I wish I could enter. I wish he would share with me his thoughts, or at least express himself more. Cole isn't usually one to vent out his frustrations, rather keep them locked up, consuming him from the inside. I want to hold him, shake him like a kid shaking a rattle until he bursts out everything he's trying to hold in, just so he understands he doesn't have to suffer alone.

His face suddenly scrunches, and in that moment he looks up at me, our eyes meeting through the rearview mirror. He says my name, a caution of sorts. I don't need to respond, however. Because suddenly I see it, too.

I hit the brakes. Kelly yelps and grips onto the car door, her vape falling to her feet. The car gives out a small screech as it comes to a stop, my head lifting at the inertia to see another screaming woman standing just yards in front of my car, with the same all too familiar static about her.

Suddenly Cole stands in front of the car between us, and as she vanishes so does he.

"What?!" Kelly shouts, eyes darting around in alarm.

I try to speak without hyperventilating. "There . . . was an opossum."

"An opossum?" Kelly looks left and right. We're on a road of town houses, but only a few blocks from the CBD. "*Here*?"

I nod.

"Are you seriously saying you almost killed us over an opossum?!"

"It could have been a racoon. Or a big rat. Or a cat." I should have said cat first. Kelly likes cats. "Are you okay?"

"Fuck!"

"Kelly!"

"Yes, I'm okay!"

A car lightly toots its horn behind us. Kelly sighs heavily and I shakily carry on driving. "Sorry."

"It's a good thing you drive within the speed limit." She rubs her neck, turning to me. "Are *you* okay?"

I glance at the rearview mirror, but this time the reflection is only me. I notice the tears in my eyes, my mascara disturbed. "I'm fine," I say, trying not to smudge the mascara. "Sorry. Again."

"Someone better hug their cat extra tight tonight," Kelly mutters. "Or their big rat."

I huff a laugh. So does she.

The drive to Juliet's place was another fifteen minutes, but only as I turn into the driveway do my nerves start to settle. Cole hasn't returned, but I assume that is to do with my social plans more than with what happened. Another screaming ghost, the cause unknown. They have all been young, but this one seemed even younger, not much older than me. What happened to her? And why did her life have to end in such a way?

Those nerves start to come back, but I suppress them to the distraction of the night. At least we're not late since I don't see Rory's Audi parked up yet. I follow behind Kelly who makes her way inside. It's large and clearly recently renovated, the interior an unnatural stark contrast to the older exterior. We walk straight to the outside yard where Juliet is already sitting with Gareth, mid-conversation until Kelly jumps straight into dramatizing what happened.

"Are you okay?" Gareth asks in doctor mode. Or maybe it's concerned friend mode. Probably both. "Whiplash doesn't just come from an airbag.”

“We’re fine, really.” I force a smile and place the food supplies down in front of me. “Who’s hungry?”

The mention of food is all that’s needed to put the drive behind us. The night quickly takes off. With some lowkey music and snacks we enjoy ourselves, Juliet even more so when Rory finally turns up. As night time fully arrives we even get a view of some stars, which is rare for such an urban place. I feel a sudden yearn for my home at that thought. I used to see the stars almost every night, with Cole, on the front deck or lying on my old trampoline in the backyard. I didn’t realize how long it’s been since I haven’t seen the stars until now.

Gareth must have read my thoughts. “It’s been so long since I’ve seen the stars,” he says, following my gaze.

He sits down next to me, offering a stick with a roasted marshmallow on the end. I smile, pulling it off the stick and into my mouth with my teeth.

“Ah, the classic American tradition,” I chime as I chew into my marshmallow. Roasted along the edges and warm and gooey in the middle, just as they were intended to be.

“Okay, disclosure time: I haven’t done this before.”

I turn to him, shocked. “You haven’t roasted marshmallows before?”

“It’s not really a thing in England. Did I get it right?”

I nod, then swallow. “You, sir, are a natural.”

Gareth seems pleased at this. “I think I’ve found my purpose in life.”

“Not just a promising medical student or clairvoyant of my taste pallet.”

“Careful, Charlotte. You’ll make me blush.”

I giggle at his smile, that darn dimple of his noticeable from the light of the fire. His hair is slightly styled at the front, his short bangs settling to the side. I like that about guys: they can do so little with their appearance yet make such an impact. It makes me envious, especially when my wild and wavy hair has its own agenda.

Maybe I was staring because Gareth tilts his head slightly. "What are you thinking about?"

I inhale, sitting up straight. "Nothing. Just . . ." I look to the sky, the fire, my friends across the yard entangled with one another in a game of Twister. Here I am, eating roasted marshmallows in my new life with my new friends and a really nice guy by my side. The validation of my escape, my efforts to be what I want to be feels jubilant. "Life's just good in these moments."

Gareth smiles. "Yeah."

Cole's appearance startles me, but not for the obvious ghost reason. I quickly yet subtly lean back from Gareth, placing my arm out along the cushions lining the firepit seating. I cough nervously.

"You don't need to react," Cole reassures me. He can read a situation well, and knows when or when not to command my attention. "She's gone. The details can wait."

I turn to smile at the fire, but Cole knows it's directed at him.

"You want some more hot chocolate?" Gareth asks me. It's funny how he says the words. It just sounds so formal with him. So gentlemanly.

"I think, if I consume any more sugar, you'd have to diagnose me with diabetes."

He chuckles. "We'd have to compare our insurances to see who gets the best deal on insulin because I'd be going down with you." He looks at his empty cup in his hands before placing it on the ground.

I snicker. So much smiling, my cheeks start to hurt. Why am I smiling so much? I swipe a glance at Cole, surprised he's still here. He looks on intently, giving Gareth a look I can't figure out.

"He wants to kiss you, Charlotte."

I glance back at Cole, panic in my eyes. There is no anger from him, no disdain. Just words. Words without emotion.

Gareth follows my line of sight. "It's a nice fire."

"And you should let him."

"No," I breathe.

"No?" Gareth asks.

"I know," I reply to Gareth, forcing a smile.

I worry if he notices the falsehood in my eyes, but he continues talking, only I can't see or hear anything except Cole.

"As promised." The words are quiet, lingering in the air as he vanishes. I look at the fire once more, my mouth wanting to produce something, *anything*—an objection, a comeback, a scream of protest to the heavens.

But I have nothing.

I then see Gareth in my peripheral vision. Turning to face him, he looks at me in the eyes, his gentle blue irises are of curiosity and concern, that caring instinct of his wanting to assess, to help, to heal.

Which is why I then put my mouth on his.

I don't wait for a reaction; I place my hands on the sides of his head and hold us there. Instinctively I expect him to pull away, only he opens up to me, letting me in, him feeling me feeling him, knowing how to make each other better, healing the needs of our instincts, the wants of our desires.

Is this what I need? To fulfill the selfishness of my own hormones? Is this what I promised? What Cole is set on allowing to happen?

I can't explain the tingling feeling going down into my chest, then everywhere else. Unless . . . no. No, these are not *those* types of feelings, are they?

I pull away just as I hear Rory cheer.

"About time," Kelly says from across the lawn.

Juliet giggles loudly.

And Gareth, still taking in what just happened, looks rather flushed.

"Sorry," I whisper.

"No, don't be." He huffs, a quiver of laughter. He flicks his hand over his head and his hair effortlessly repositions itself from where my hand was. "I have to say that was . . . invigorating."

I lightly bite my lip. It still tingles, almost numb.

"Dude, don't analyze it," Rory hints as he walks up to us. "She's not a case study."

Gareth goes red. "Force of habit. Sorry."

"No, don't be." I smile again. That same smile, a mask of confusion and guilt.

I did what Cole wanted. Heck, I think I did what Gareth wanted, too. So why do I feel awful?

Because I liked it, that's why.

I swallow the sickly feeling in my throat. I wish I knew what to say or do, but it's like my brain has gone on vacation and I have nothing to go on. Except how I feel, which is a whole lot of things and makes me just as speechless.

We sit there looking at each other, not quite knowing what to do next. I fidget with the hem of my jacket before zipping it up tight.

"Are you cold?"

"No." Maybe? "Yes."

"It's late. We should head inside."

"Okay."

We pack up without any further talk on the matter and head inside for sleep. Since it's unspoken yet clear to everyone that Rory will be sleeping in Juliet's bedroom, Kelly takes the couch, leaving Gareth and myself on the pull-out sofa bed. I borrow a singlet and shorts off Juliet. Luckily she's roughly my size although I still head straight under the duvet, feeling exposed.

Gareth stands at the edge of the pull out, nothing but boxers and a tank top on, hesitant.

"I can crash on the floor," he starts.

"No."

I lift up the blanket for him. Okay, so Gareth wasn't the person I thought I'd be offering a place in bed by my side to, but Cole left me. He left me there, knowing what would happen, with no emotion or care. Besides, Gareth has medical school tomorrow, something that requires brain cells to perform at optimum function for. So no way he's going to sleep on the floor. And the gentleman in him won't let me take the floor, either. So here we are.

"You have work tomorrow. You're entitled to a restful sleep."

He nods and gets under the blanket, making sure to leave ample space between us. We idly play on our phones for a couple of minutes, nothing spoken until we all say goodnight to each other. Juliet and Rory head upstairs and Kelly turns off the lounge light leaving nothing but the streetlight outside coming through the gap between the curtains as a source of light. I can just about see Gareth turn on his side to face me, his arm muscles showing as he rests his head on his elbow.

"So I've got two tickets to this comedy show the theater students are putting on next week. I dunno, it's probably shit, but I was hoping, well," he fidgets with the edge of the blanket, "if you'd want to come with me? See what the local arts grant is funding. Who knows, we might even hear something funny."

I crack a laugh. "Sure."

Gareth hesitates before leaning in for a kiss. It's light and to the point, a simple goodnight message, but I'm not prepared for the magnetism his touch sends through me and I can't help but reach my hand for his cheek, the pull of attachment undeniable. He leans in closer, keeping his lips gently on mine as our bodies close in together. The same tingling as before comes back, a slower yet hotter veining through my body and it makes me grip my fingers into his skin as my arms and legs quiver from his touch.

"I better not hear any funny business from you two," Kelly warns from across the lounge, obviously hearing every movement made on the creaky pull-out sofa bed.

Gareth and I chuckle nervously as we pull ourselves apart, his outstretched arm keeping me within reach.

"Sleep well, Charlotte."

He kisses me once more on my cheek and I settle on my side next to him as we fall into slumber.

∞∞∞∞∞

When I wake up it is daylight outside, but I'm not all that surprised. I head straight to the bathroom, and luckily so because my face is a mess of yesterday's makeup and wild, unstyled hair. I tie my hair back in a loose bun, the most justifiable thing I can do with it right now, and then wash my face clean. I also use my finger and rub toothpaste on my teeth to get rid of the fluffy and gunky feeling on them before rinsing my mouth and then heading downstairs.

"Morning, sunshine." Kelly places scrambled eggs into a bowl. "Get it while it's hot."

"Coffee?" Juliet doesn't wait for an answer, probably assuming by my tired appearance I need one. I smile in thanks as she hands me a mug. I take a sip. I still don't like the taste, but the coffee bean aroma at work has grown on me so I assume the taste will also. But unlike at the café, I notice this is some instant stuff mixed in with milk. I can't make any promises this won't end up being discreetly poured down the sink.

"Where's Gareth?" I ask as I take a seat at the breakfast bar.

"Of course that's her first question." Juliet smirks.

"Just curious," I say with a mouthful of breakfast.

"He got called in early," Rory answers for me as he walks in from the bedroom. Juliet's bedroom. Kelly and I exchange looks. So do Rory and Juliet. "Scrambled eggs? Brill."

"Brill?"

"Gareth's vernacular must be rubbing off on me," Rory mentions before grabbing Kelly's breakfast.

"Hey!"

"Cheers, Kel." Rory smiles cheesily as he finds Juliet's hand with his. A gentle squeeze. A reassuring smile. A cement of what very likely happened between them during the night.

I take another bite of breakfast.

"Any plans for the day?" Juliet asks as she reaches for the orange juice. "Rory and I were thinking about catching a movie or something later on."

"Kelly and I have work later on," I say. "Same times. Three until closing."

"We can go at lunchtime, then?"

"Oh, Charlotte and I have a psych test coming up we need to study for. Don't we, Charlotte?"

"Yes." That wasn't a lie, regardless of the hinting in her voice. There's also the whole screaming ghost thing that I need to figure out, and where I stand with my ghost boyfriend and Gareth that I'll need to fit in today sometime, too. So while I want to crash out with a bag of popcorn and pointless entertainment, I have other priorities. Starting with Cole.

"I need to pop by home," I add. "To get my textbook. I have to feed Shark, too."

"That fish you won?"

"The one and only."

"Charlotte's all about animal welfare, as I experienced in her car last night," Kelly retorts. "Okay, we'll go to yours. We can work on our psych assignment there or walk to the campus library."

"Great," I affirm.

It didn't take us long to leave Juliet and Rory to themselves. When we get back to my apartment I offer Kelly the use of the bathroom shower first since I'll "use all the hot water", and she doesn't need telling twice.

As soon as I hear the shower running I turn to Cole. I've spent every waking moment of the day anticipating what to say, how to react, yet all I have is silence.

"Had a nice night?" he asks casually.

"A nice night?" I huff as I plonk on my bed with such force I almost bounce off it. "Seriously? Is that meant to be some sort of joke, Cole? Because I'm really not in the mood for laughing right now."

"It's not a joke, just a question."

"Cole, you told me to let another guy kiss me," I hiss in frustration. "I don't care how dead you are, that was unfair!"

"Gareth's a good guy—"

"He's a great guy. But that doesn't matter because I'm with you!"

"Did you like it?"

"What?"

"The kiss. Did you like it?"

I sigh, deflated. "Is that all you care about? Does it turn you on or something, your girlfriend with another guy? Does it not affect you even in the slightest that you so casually want me to get with someone else? I held him off, Cole. But you . . ." I refuse to cry. Not now. "When you told me to let him . . ."

"You didn't answer my question."

"Yes!" I snap and stand up angrily. "I liked it, okay? It was sweet and tasted of chocolate and marshmallow and my stomach fluttered like butterflies. I even went in for round two. Is that what you want to hear?"

Cole can see the shame in my confession. He waits for me to calm down, still void of emotion. "Open communication, remember?"

I roll my eyes in exasperation. "Only when it suits you."

"Charlotte?"

Shit.

I am so caught up that I didn't hear the shower turn off.

"It's Kelly," I mutter quietly before forcing a mood change. "Hey, Kelly. I'm upstairs."

"Who were you talking to?" she asks as she places her damp towel and overnight bag on the edge of the bed.

"No one," I reply assertively. "Just telling myself off for losing my textbook—oh, here it is." I pick it up from the bedside stand three feet in front of me. "Ready for study? My bet is we're going to be quizzed on the theology aspects the most, but—"

"Oh, no." Kelly takes out a pink makeup box from her overnight bag. "First we do girl therapy."

Ten

"I just don't know, doll," Kelly says next to me. We're sprawled out on my bed, staring at the ceiling so as to not let the hydrating facial masks slip off our faces. It would almost be relaxing if it weren't for the twenty questions in my right ear. "Gareth's such a sweetie, and I got the impression things with you and Cole had fizzled out based on what I saw last night. Do you have commitment issues or something? The psychology of love isn't until next week, but I can read up ahead on class notes if you want some insight."

"No, thank you." I try to hold back laughter; an emotion I didn't think I'd feel today. Trust Kelly to change that. "As I've said, things are just a bit complicated right now," I reiterate in the hope she will drop the subject altogether. I don't move but still give a side glance across the room. Cole is still here, listening on, which for the rarity of occasions annoys me.

"Nail file?"

"Top drawer." I put my hand out in front of me and spread out my fingers. The glittery green is still there, even though I chipped it in a couple of places at work. "I might try the purple next time. What do you reckon?"

Kelly is now sitting up, however, her attention elsewhere.

"You have a picture of Cole hiding in your drawer?" she asks, holding the frame in front of me.

Crap.

Now I'm sitting up. That was meant to be my little secret.

Cole has a look of stupefaction. "You have a picture of me hiding in your drawer?"

"Is that not allowed?" I ask both of them defensively.

"Where did you get my photo?" Cole is suddenly by Kelly to get a better look.

"Why is it hiding in your drawer?"

"Damn," Cole utters, intrigued at his own image.

"Well, I . . ."

"I remember this," Cole mutters. "I was—"

"Stop!" I snap, snatching the photo from Kelly's hands, not wanting to hear Cole's recollection.

"You're dating Gareth but you're keeping a picture of Cole hidden in your drawer?"

"Danielle took this . . ."

"I don't even think we're dating."

"Seriously, Charlotte?" both of them say in unison.

"What?!" I bellow defensively.

"Do you like Gareth?"

"You saw Danielle?"

". . . Maybe." I don't even know whom I'm replying to at this point.

They both exasperate.

"Well Gareth *maybe* likes you, too."

"When did you see Danielle?"

"And he's a good guy, Charlotte," Kelly continues, unaware of Cole next to her. "I'm sure you know his relationship history. He doesn't deserve to be played around like this."

"Why didn't you tell me?" Cole pushes, aware of Kelly next to him yet not seeming to care.

"Sorry." It's the only word I can get in.

"Yeah. I'm sorry for thinking you two are meant to be." Kelly stands and walks to the door. "I'm going to study at the library. I could do with the walk."

"How do you even know where she lives?"

"Just let me explain—"

"I don't think you can, Charlotte. You're hiding stuff. Stuff

I don't think I should know." She kneels down to put on her shoes. "Gareth's my friend, too. So you do you, but I don't vibe off white lies and deception."

With a sigh she stands to leave, a half-smile on her face fighting through her frustration when she looks back at me to say, "He's cute, by the way. Fucking adorable."

When the door closes behind her I turn to Cole.

"Answers," he orders, clearly not falling for my scowl.

I roll my eyes. "I may have done some research."

"Research?"

I flop onto my bed, hoping it will help shield me from the scolding I know I'm about to receive. "You're hard to find. No social media, no online presence. Nothing on Google. So I furthered my field."

He appears next to my bed, standing over me, arms crossed. "Like stalking my ex?"

"Are you really that surprised?" I ask angrily, facing him. "I had no idea who you really were. I needed closure of my own, Cole. Besides, I'm allowed a photo of you, aren't I?" I pick up the picture and with a tissue wipe the few specks of dust and symbolic disapproval of Kelly from it. I sigh, blinking away the tears forming in my eyes before muttering, "It's the only thing of you I have."

This mollifies Cole, his aura now dimmed. He slumps, not quite knowing what to do or say, but I don't blame him, I feel the same way. Then he's sitting next to me on my bed, putting his arm around me comfortingly. I curl my head into him. It's all we can do, but it's enough.

Cole eventually speaks, "Back in my day, the need to be photographed and uploaded with a hashtag wasn't as common as today. I never cared for social media. I was just a guy in some rural nothing town. I was easily forgettable."

"Okay, Gramps," I say, trying to lighten the mood. And his aura.

"So you met her? You spoke to Danielle?"

"Yeah. I pretended I knew you as a kid or something. Not

technically a lie.”

Cole looks at me, his voice soft and vulnerable. “And what did she say?”

“Who, Danielle?” I realize then that Cole may have never gotten his closure with her. I turn to face him, careful to speak softly. “She said you saved her, and that she escaped her past to live on for you.”

Cole listens on, his aura healing to its natural light, his mouth a soft smile.

“And honestly it made me love you all over again.”

Cole reaches his hand up and gently strokes my cheek, his feather-touch leaving a tingling sensation on my skin I feel down to my heart.

“If you want we can go to her. I can play ghost guru, give you two closure.”

Cole thinks for a long moment, his face solemn and contemplative, his mind briefly somewhere else. “No. Like everyone else, she found her peace and moved on.”

“I’m sorry.”

Cole shakes his head. “No. I’m sorry, Charlotte. I should have been more sensitive. I never really considered things like photos after all this time. Maybe it’s a guy thing, or maybe it’s a ghost thing. Maybe it’s just me.”

“It’s okay. Just let me have this one.” I hold the photo frame to my chest.

Cole kisses my cheek. “Of course.”

It’s surprising how different things were between us only a minute ago, yet now we meet in the middle like this. I guess it’s down to that open communication we agreed on.

“Bring your laptop over.”

I raise my head. “Why?”

“I’m not that ancient, Charlotte. We had smartphones, back in the day when I was less dead.”

I cringe at that last part. “I would have assumed so. Why? Do you know where yours is?”

“Nah. Destroyed in the car crash, no doubt. I wasn’t into

social media, but my best friend was."

Best friend? Cole has mentioned his best friend Heath on occasion as part of his opening up experience. It was mostly stories of how his family was more loving to him than his own family, which was sad to hear. It is only now that Cole brings up Heath's passion for social media. "You mean . . .?"

"He was such a paparazzi; no wonder he ended up as a private investigator. Instagram is still a thing, right? There has to be something."

This excites me. I rush for my laptop, letting it rest on my bed as I turn it on. A quick Facebook stalk later and we find a matching Heath Marsden.

Cole points at the screen. "That's him!"

I squeal in excitement as I scroll through Heath's public photos, back to over a decade ago. There aren't many, but lo and behold, a few profile pictures make Cole known. We look at each photograph and I let Cole narrate each one as he returns to the memories. Group selfies with his class peers, drinks at night by a fire, his model-like stare (unintentional, so he says, but sexy nonetheless). I coo over younger Cole, laugh at dorky Cole, and cringe at smug Cole. But I love all of them, combined to form a small lifeline of his life; snapshots of moments in time that were his.

The mouse hovers over a post, the last one we find of him.

I gasp, turning to Cole. "It's a video."

Would he sound different? Would he *be* different?

Cole gives me a reassuring look, his hand on mine as I click it. It takes four long seconds to upload. The quality isn't the best, although I guess it was good for a phone ten years ago. It's dark, but Cole is seen straight away, approaching the camera from the crowds of teenagers and young adults drinking and socializing.

"You look happy." That must be Heath talking, holding the camera and zooming on Cole's unavoidable smirk.

Cole nods his head slightly. "I've got reason to be." Then, realizing he's being filmed, chortles slightly as he jokingly pushes the camera away.

The footage ends. And then there's silence.

"At least he got my good side," Cole eventually utters.

I snicker. The typical Cole response, trying to lighten up the dark he's trying his best to fight. And it almost stops the tears in my eyes.

Almost.

He holds me as best he can, his arm a blanketing comfort as he kisses my face over and over again with each sob that escapes me.

It takes a few minutes for me to settle down, a damp tissue-riddled mess around me. Cole tries to change the subject a couple of times, and I only let him when he mentions the fourth screaming ghost.

"Whatever happened, she's gone."

I sigh. "There has to be something about them. What are we missing here, Cole?"

"I really don't know. Maybe they've been in a hospital?"

"I can ask Rory and Gareth if they've seen anything," I suggest, reaching over to the bedside stand for my phone. I notice the message on my screen from Gareth, asking if I want dinner with him tomorrow night. And just like that, reality hits again. Cole must have seen it too, because he stiffens, subtly sitting up straight. I place my phone back down. "Later."

"Charlotte." He rests his forehead on my shoulder, closing his eyes. "What am I going to do with you?"

"Lie here with me and forget the outside world exists?"

Cole strokes a lock of my hair with his hand. "As much as I want to, you can't ignore the world. You're alive, Charlotte. You'll have a career, get married, have babies, and stare out of windows all day long in a rocking chair when you're old and saggy."

I cringe at the thought.

Cole notices and chuckles. "And how lucky you will be."

I turn to face him, unable to hide the guilt I feel.

He speaks so I don't have to. "You should reply to that message. Gareth is a good guy."

"He's not you."

"He's alive," Cole adds, brutally to the point. "Be honest with yourself, Charlotte. That's all I ask."

I scowl. It hides the sorrow.

"Fine. I'll date Gareth. But if it doesn't go anywhere I'll break things off with him and you'll drop it."

"Okay."

"And you're still my number one."

"Always."

I pick up my phone but put it in my drawer. "Tomorrow," I say. "Today is still ours."

Cole can't resist a smile before moving in closer and we're back to lying down on my bed, our own comfortable cocoon I could happily lose myself in.

"You know you're lucky to keep your youthful looks," I idly comment.

"Didn't you hear Kelly? I'm cute."

I turn and lean in to kiss him. "Fucking adorable."

∞∞∞∞

The next day, Cole leaves me to catch up on some needed study and house cleaning. I'm on such a roll with getting tasks done that I pick up a pasta salad and orange juice from the store and then walk over to the hospital. I figure I'll drop Gareth off a surprise before work. I know I'm seeing him for dinner, but I want to see him to figure out if the other night was just some infatuation or if the feelings I felt are still the same. That, and I'm on an official snoop for anything screaming ghost.

I walk up to a receptionist at the information desk.

"Excuse me, could you please contact Gareth Hamilton to pop by quickly if he's not busy, I have his lunch."

"Sure thing, ma'am. I'll see if he's free."

While the receptionist does her thing I idly look around. I hate hospitals. Always did. Too much death; too many dead. In

∞ 111 ∞

the foyer alone I count four ghosts.

"You see us, don't you?" A little old lady comes up to me. Clearly I didn't look away fast enough.

"He'll be here in just a moment," the receptionist says. I nod in thanks.

"You need to pass on a message," the little old lady says, nudging my arm with her frail ghostly hand.

"Sorry, but I'm a bit busy right now," I mutter as I walk out of the way of patient traffic.

The little old lady ignores me. "It hasn't been long for me. But it's my husband, you see?"

I stop listening as Gareth enters the foyer. I hold up the paper bag and smile, but the warm greeting isn't returned. Gareth looks at me, his clenched jaw a giveaway of his mood. He opens his mouth just enough to ask, "Who's Cole?"

I blink twice. "Sorry?" I ask, my voice not hiding the surprise.

"Cole. Come on, who is he then?"

"How . . . how do you know about Cole?"

"Aside from you saying his name in your sleep, Kelly and Juliet were talking about how hung up you are on the guy."

Crap.

"I am so, so sorry," I say. And, although it's cliché, I don't know what else to say when he rolls his eyes and starts walking away except the words, "It's not what you think."

"It never is, is it?"

"It really isn't," I reply after him, ignoring the pandering of the little old lady by my side about her husband sitting in the other ward.

"You know, I thought you were different."

"You have no idea," I mutter under my breath.

"He needs to know I'm okay," the old woman trails behind me.

"Especially after I told you about Ellie. But it seems you women are all the same."

"If you could let him know—"

"Not now!" I hiss back at her.

"Are you even listening?" Gareth and the little old lady simultaneously ask, and I'm left turning my head between the two.

"Yes?"

Gareth rolls his eyes again. "I've got patients to see." He doesn't even look back when he says, "Don't bother about tonight. Or any other night."

I stand there awkwardly, his lunch still in hand, as the receptionist look on nosily. I frown at her and she quickly gets back to work. I then turn to the little old lady angrily, but there's only so long I can be annoyed at a little old lady, especially one who has just passed away. Besides, none of this is her fault.

I sigh. "Tell me which room."

Eleven

When I get to work I don't hide my frustrations from Kelly. There's a clear tension between us, but it's hard not to be frustrated with her right now. It makes the shift slower and quieter, to the point I almost wish Mr. Dodgley was around to direct some of the tension on himself.

I thankfully keep myself busy with cleaning up a birthday party mess upstairs, but once the place gets quieter and my mind gets louder, I know things need to come out between us.

I roll the mop bucket back into the cupboard and close the door. "So I went to see Gareth earlier today."

Kelly, counting the last coins in the cash register, doesn't look up. "Oh?"

"Apparently you were talking about me earlier today?"

This gets her attention.

"What?"

"Yeah. He said that you and Juliet were talking about me. Is this a common thing? Talking about me behind my back? I thought I left high school already."

"Okay, so I may have mentioned things to Juliet in the hospital waiting room while we were waiting for Rory to finish studying a brain in a jar or whatever, and maybe Gareth passed by unknowingly. But I was just saying how it seems like you need a little bit more time before you can commit again." She writes down some numbers on the clipboard before adding, "I guess Gareth didn't wait around for the last part."

I place a pile of napkins down frustratingly. "It's not your place to say this or that. Why can't you just butt out of my personal relationships?"

We both smile and say bye to a customer as he leaves, and the café is now empty except for us, our fake service smiles gone as fast as they came.

"This isn't on me, Charlotte. You're the one being deceitful," Kelly mutters angrily before closing the cash register harder than needed. "You know, I may seem a little eccentric, I get that. But as a friend I have your back. And things would be a lot easier if you could just be a bit more honest and trusting."

I stop sorting napkins, suddenly full of remorse. Kelly is right. Trust is essential for any relationship to work, and I haven't placed any trust in her. I'm used to being so sheltered, scared of vulnerability from a lifetime of being judged and rejected and betrayed that I've resigned away from trusting people.

But Kelly is her own person, and I shouldn't place her on the judgement of everyone else. I don't want who I am to ruin this friendship. But who I am needs to be known to make this friendship real. And to do so I need to take a leap of faith.

Which is why I then drag her into the office against her objections and as soon as the door closes behind her I take a deep breath and open up to her. I explain to her that I can see ghosts, and the reason why she'll never meet Cole is because Cole *is* a ghost. I watch her taking it all in, her lips pressing tight, her face unreadable. I believe I've blown it, that I'll be ostracized and ridiculed in the way she mocks her aunt, except it will be Juliet, Rory, Gareth, Lea, and the whole campus. I brace for the words, knowing I'll get over it eventually. Maybe after moving to another state again. And changing my name.

That is until Kelly replies in the most casual tone, "Well, why didn't you just say so?"

I blink. "Sorry?"

"Well, you feel better now, don't you? Now that you've let it all out."

I huff, speechless. I watch Kelly as she rummages in her bag for her vape. "You . . . believe me?"

"Well it all makes sense now. No photos, no phone contact, the boyfriend who's never there but actually is."

"Aren't you shocked? Freaked out? Want to call the psych ward on me?"

"Are you kidding? You've met my aunt; you aren't even on my top three list of people I'd recommend being institutionalized." She inhales her vape before adding with a wink, "Top five, maybe."

I sigh in relief, a sound which draws out into an exasperated laugh. "You have no idea," I manage to say, fighting back the tears in my eyes, "how much of a relief it is to hear that."

"Oh, doll, I didn't mean to beat the truth out of you. Here, take a napkin to dry your eyes—but only one, of course."

I chuckle and comply.

"No wonder my aunt won't stop raving about you. She's making lasagna this weekend by the way, if you're interested." Kelly inhales her vape. "And it's a good thing I know now. Because, well, the thing is, doll, you sometimes talk to yourself, and it's weirding the customers out."

"Shoot." I need to work on that.

"But I got your back now. See? We can have a codeword for when you go all ghost mode in public. Like . . . 'Hey, stop *ghosting* me'."

I raise an eyebrow at her.

"Or, 'you seem in good *spirits*'." Kelly snorts. "Or how about, 'that's the *spirit*, Charlotte!'"

"Are those the only options I have?"

"Eh, we'll work on it." She shrugs. "Oh! That number of fingers behind your back thing, that was him?"

I nod sheepishly.

"Of course." She clicks her fingers in an "ah-ha!" moment. "So he's met me?"

I nod.

"Geez, doll. A little heads up next time."

"Sorry," I say sheepishly.

"Is he . . . here?" she asks, eyeing the air around us cautiously.

"No, not right now."

"But he lives with you, in your apartment?"

"*Occupies* would be a better word for it."

"And he's been *occupying* your life since you were seven?"

"Uh-huh."

I may have skipped the part on why he's been at my side all these years; I'd rather that be on a need-to-know basis only.

"I guess *complicated* really is the word to use for you and Cole."

"Yep."

"So . . ." Kelly gives me a look before her eyes bulge. "No."

"What?"

"No!" she bellows.

"What?!"

"You know what!"

"What do I know?!"

"You can't commit with Gareth because you have feelings for a ghost, that's what!" she hisses.

"Well, when you put it that way . . . yes."

"Charlotte, you can't be with a *ghost*. People don't have relationships with ghosts, they just *can't*."

I feel sudden anger rising within me. But Kelly is right. We cannot be together. Not until I died, at least. Which would be unproductive to my existence and morbid to say the least.

Instead, I mutter, "So I've been told."

Kelly sighs. "I don't know, doll. This goes beyond even my talent."

"Psych101 not doing it?"

"I think you're beyond Ph.D. level."

We both snicker.

"How are things going with that nurse you were interested in, anyway?" I ask, wanting to shift from the topic of Cole.

"Oh, I'm ignoring him. I'm going on a date with a dating app match tonight."

"What? Why? What did he do?"

"Nothing. He's been very good, in fact. Paid for dinner *and* dessert."

"Then why are you ignoring him?"

"Don't worry, doll, it's just part of my game plan."

"Game plan?"

"Get him jealous, get him competitive. Fight for the prize."

"You're terrible."

"I prefer calculative, sly, devious. A good investor of sorts."

I chuckle. I don't approve, but that's just Kelly. She may be the most free-spirited person around, but her backstory is that along with the vaping, drinking and tattoos she showed me during one shift, her sexual activity (particularly aimed at ethnically diverse males) is a phase of rebellious freedom from her parents. Maybe she's in denial with herself; maybe she just wants to be sure the guy's a keeper to not be disappointed by her parents or with herself. But I don't push it. As long as she's happy and safe.

"Customer." Kelly jumps to her feet. "Better get back to it. You're okay?"

I nod. "Better than okay."

"Good. Because the bathrooms need cleaning."

I cringe, but I can't hide my laugh. The rest of the work shift breezes by with filling Kelly in on all sorts of details of the dead. She's particularly enthralled in the stories from high school, but I keep details short as the shift soon ends with the promise to fill her in more on future boring shifts.

By the time I get back to my apartment I'm barely able to contain my excitement to tell Cole what I've told Kelly.

"Cole?" I ask as I close the door behind me.

"How was work?" Cole asks, watching Shark eat its fish flake. He must be getting good at feeding Shark because I notice there are no more flakes on the tank filter. I walk up to the fish tank and quickly sprinkle some more out on the tank filter for later, then with a hug and a peck on Cole's cheek I take a deep breath, braced with excitement.

"I told her, Cole. I told Kelly about me. And you. And she accepts me!" I look to Cole for approval. "She accepts me."

Cole pulls away, unsure with this new information. "You told her? How did she take it?"

"She wasn't even that surprised. I think alongside her aunt it's just another weird person in her life." I laugh nervously. "She's keen to meet you, too."

Cole looks at me, perplexed. "Oh? And how will that happen?"

"I'll translate, I guess."

Cole snickers. "I don't know if we'll have much in common. It'll be a short conversation."

I elbow him, not that it has an effect. "Be nice."

He wraps his arm around me. "I'm always nice. Don't you trust me?"

"Of course I trust you," I say, smiling sweetly. "Especially since I get the final say."

"As long as it makes you happy."

"It does." I grin. "And now I can talk to her about me—the real me, and you, and us—"

"Wait, you told her about us being . . . together?"

"Well, not exactly."

"Good."

I recoil. "Good?"

"It's for the best. Besides, you're dating Gareth now."

The reminder pulls us both apart.

"About that," I start. "I don't think Gareth and I will be going out, after all."

"What? Why?" Cole asks. I can't tell if he's happy or disappointed.

"It doesn't matter why," I dismiss the topic. "It's over between us. In fact, I don't think he ever wants to see my face again."

Cole is skeptical, but he can tell I don't want to talk about it. "I'm sorry, Charlotte."

I shrug. "It's what happens. With me, that is. I mean, let's be real here. Dating is for normal people. I'm not normal."

"Charlotte—"

"It's fine. Really. At least I have you."

Cole glances down at the floor, his eyebrows creasing slightly. When he looks up at me his eyes soften, a tight smile making itself known. "Of course."

He leans in for a hug, one that feels almost forced. I almost pull back and ask him what's wrong, but I feel his energy soften in my embrace, a healing touch between us, and decide to leave it.

Things with Gareth may be over, but at least I now know it wouldn't have worked out. And that makes the sums in this guy equation easier to calculate.

I offer to snuggle down with a movie, but he tells me to utilize my time and study more instead. I groan but comply. He is like having another parent at times. Tough love, they call it. And according to my Psych101 textbook I've got seven pages to read about it.

Cole is right. Living is suffering.

∞∞∞∞

The following morning I find myself needing a coffee to get myself going. I admittedly got so into study it was after midnight before I realized what the time was and went to bed. So I take the plunge and stop by the campus café before class for a small latte. My morning classes drag on forever, almost making me excited for work later. I have back-to-back anatomy class with a reproductive anatomy test, followed by a lecture on lifespan development, all of which require me to actually pay attention which is hard to do when I can't stop thinking about things. There are the screaming ghosts, which I never got to ask Gareth about. I'll have to ask Rory (if he'll even speak to me after how things went down with Gareth), although with the number of possible hospitals in the state area the bodies could have ended up at, compiled with the number of bodies the hospitals must have to sort out on a regular basis, I'm not hopeful I will get very far.

There's also Kelly now knowing about me. This makes me smile, and I still stand by my judgment of telling her. I can't help but wonder, however, how this will work with the others around. Kelly was a big enough step, and I don't feel comfortable with anyone else knowing, at least for now.

College is so different to high school yet so similar at the same time. Even though we're supposed to be all mature and grown up now, I know friend circles may come and go, arguments may ensue and gossip still spreads. Such as with Gareth. Yeah, Gareth is on my mind, too. Mostly for the way he looked at me before he stormed off in the hospital, but also the way I felt curling up to sleep next to him, and the way it felt kissing him that night . . .

I force the thoughts away. That doesn't matter now. I don't know how dynamics will work between the friend group now that there's a rift between us. Rory is Gareth's numero uno; Kelly is mine. And poor Juliet is now caught in the middle. I guess nights by the firepit and lunches at the mall will become a thing of the past.

I sigh as I pack my notes up, class now over.

Luckily (or not) I see Rory soon after leaving the lecture hall. I run into him between classes from time to time since we both have classes within the same department building. This time, however, he acts as if he didn't see me.

"Rory," I call out as he passes.

"Oh, hey." The greeting is a typical guy response: short and unassertive.

He doesn't stop to talk, so pacing up to his side and going straight to the point I ask, "I was wondering if you have had any unusual bodies turn up at the hospital?"

This makes him stop.

"What?"

I certainly don't want this conversation to become any more awkward than it already is, so trying to not sound too weird I reply, "Just a case study project for criminology class. I figured any ongoing investigations with young women would be more interesting to follow."

"Criminology class?"

"My elective."

"Huh. Well, not that I know of. If there are any at the hospital then they'd be in the autopsy area under priority if it's an active police investigation. I don't usually go there; it's not exactly an open-door policy."

Rory gives me another look before saying he's late for class, even though we both know that the next classes don't start for another ten minutes. I wave bye and leave him to it. It's clear he's brushing me off politely, no doubt to pledge his loyalty to Gareth. Not that I blame him for doing so.

I sigh and glance at my watch. My stomach rumbles, not satisfied with just coffee. I grab a panini lunch from the campus café, choosing a lone bench across the pavilion to sit on for some peace and quiet.

"Any such luck?" Cole asks me, now sitting next to me.

I shake my head as I swallow the last of lunch down. "Rory's clueless. I doubt Gareth would know anyway. Back to square one in the mystery of the screaming ghosts. But we owe it to them to find out what exactly is going on."

"Maybe that's something you should go into? *Detective Durane* has got a good ring to it."

I snort at his words. Only, I have thought about it, more than once. I guess that's why I chose a criminology elective. Having access to case files would certainly make my job easier. I just don't see myself as having the stamina to start out as a police officer, doing years of highway patrols or having to taser rowdy protesters fighting for causes I'd probably be supportive of. Not to mention all the dead bodies I'd have to look at and coming across even more ghosts than I do already.

"I've got to get to work," I say, noticing the time. "Walk with me?"

Cole doesn't need asking twice. Or at all, I'm sure. We take the fifteen-minute walk side by side, just like any other couple on the street. We even talk about everyday things like the weather and study. I'm sad when I see the café approach into view, but at least I see Kelly smiling, and this makes me smile too, knowing the façade doesn't have to end just yet.

Kelly approaches me. "Judging by the look on your face I can only guess who you're with. I assume he's here?" She waves her hand as she looks around, then says loudly and slowly, "Hello, Cole."

I laugh. "He's dead, Kels, not deaf."

"Well I don't know," Kelly utters back.

Cole bites back a smirk. "Dead but cute."

I hold back a giggle.

"What?"

Cole teasingly kisses my neck. "You offered to translate."

"He said he appreciates you calling him cute. A really big boost to his ego, by the way."

This makes Kelly giggle.

"Tell her I also say thank you," Cole says in my ear.

"He also says thank you."

"What for?" Kelly asks.

"Yeah, what for?" I also ask.

"For being your friend. For accepting you." He wraps his arms around me when he says, "You're the happiest I've seen you in a long time."

"For being a good friend. For putting up with me," I say to Kelly sheepishly. "Ghosts 'n all."

Kelly smirks, a slanted grin of appreciation. The sentimental moment is cut short, however.

"Kelly!"

Kelly rolls her eyes and says a very bad word under her breath, one that makes both Cole and I raise our eyebrows.

"Dodgley's on a tirade today. You'd better get ready quickly. And up your hair in the snippiest darn braids you've ever done."

I chuckle as she leaves.

"You heard the woman," Cole quips. "I'll leave you to it, but I'll be close by."

With one more kiss on my cheek he leaves me to it, and with a big inhale and braiding of my hair I enter the café doors.

I don't think I've ever worked as much for my minimum wage pay as today. The café was continuously busy, the blender broke—twice—and one other waitress called in sick at the last minute. It was dark before Kelly and I could catch a break, but even then it was short-lived when a birthday gathering entered. I serve up the last of the carrot cake, my stomach making its own rumblings of protest for dinner when I start to clear the other tables. It's right when I pick up some candy wrappers from the floor that I glance up and my attention suddenly goes to the news report on the television screen, headlining how the bodies of four young women have been found in a nearby national park. But it's the next image on the screen, the one with pictures of the suspected identities of the four bodies, that makes me stop in my tracks.

Everything goes quiet bar a ringing in my ear and the beat of my heart.

I hear Mr. Dodgley's voice, but it's more of a murmur than the anger I'm sure it is.

Cole says something too, I feel his hand on mine, but I can't figure out what.

"Charlotte!"

I snap out of it.

"What are you doing? I don't pay you to watch television!"

"Sorry."

I shakily walk into the kitchen and place the candy wrappers in the trash. I tell Kelly I'm taking a bathroom break and don't wait for a reply. Out the backdoor in the dark alleyway I stagger forward, resting my hands on my knees for balance. It's noticeably colder and quieter here which allows me to think, even if there is an odor of trash in the air.

"It's good," Cole tries to reassure me. "We now have names. We are closer to knowing what happened to them."

"What?" I turn to Cole. "The police are investigating, Cole.

They were probably *murdered*!"

"It happens."

"Yeah, it happens. But I don't witness them happening!" My voice is faint, cracked, pushing through the tightness in my throat. "Whatever happened to them . . . there's likely a killer out there, Cole. There could be more!"

Cole grips my arms. "Calm down, Charlotte. It's going to be okay. I'm here with you, see?"

My eyes gloss over. "Okay."

"You need to get back inside, finish your shift."

He's right, but I don't move. I pull back my phone case, revealing the card holder. I slowly take out the lone business card, the one I wanted to forget.

Cole notices the name which makes his eyebrows furrow and face stiff. He then looks at me, his voice neutral when he asks, "Are you sure?"

I look at the card again, hesitating. I want to put it back and pretend I never saw it, but this is beyond me and Cole. Three lives have already been lost, lives I was too distracted to give enough attention to. What's more, other lives—innocent lives— could be at stake.

I dial the number displayed on the front. It rings twice before the call is received. There is silence on the other end, but I can hear the faint sound of his breath.

My lips tremble as I speak, saying the name I didn't want to have to say ever again.

"Beasey."

Twelve

It takes exactly forty-eight hours for Beasey to show up. I wish
he didn't have to show up at all, but here we are.

"Charlotte." He almost flashes a full smile as he walks up to
me, right on time. "So good to see you again." He looks to my
right, his eyebrows rising slightly but his smile holding. "And
Cole. Of course."

Like me, Beasey can communicate with the dead. He found
me earlier on in the year when I was in high school, trying to
stop him from exorcising Cole. He was the school janitor,
although that was more of a cover up because he's actually some
priest—slash—exorcist figure that sends ghosts packing to the
other side. It's part of a secretive Communicator club he's part
of, something he tried to get me to join. While it's something I
still idly consider, the reg flags attached to Beasey put me off.
I know little about Beasey and what he's really up to. In fact,
come to think of it, I don't even know his actual name. That's
how discrete he is. But he knows more than he lets on, which
means if anyone can help solve this mystery it's him.

"Beasey."

Cole doesn't say anything else, but I don't hold that
impoliteness against him considering their history. We both
know that when Beasey is around, bad things happen. Not in
the way of misfortune but of manipulation, in the way ideas are
planted in your mind and before you know it you've become it.
He did that to me and Cole back in high school, beguiling us to

think differently and doubt ourselves to get us to give in to what he wanted: Cole—like all ghosts—to cross over and me to follow him off the radar into his secret organization of Communicators. Kelly would have a field day trying to psychologically analyze him, using fancy words from her textbooks. But for me I'm just warily cautious. I don't like people I can't understand. It makes me vulnerable. And he preys on vulnerability.

Beasey turns back to me. "You've grown up since I last saw you. I take it you have been well?"

It hasn't really been that long, but I guess I've done a lot of growing up recently. And I feel my efforts show, at least with my newfound confidence and wardrobe. Beasey, on the other hand, looks exactly the same as before: his tinted dark gray hair, his staunch yet slightly butch figure, the slight stubble around his face, the strongly defined frown lines, even his worn buttoned shirt and carpenter pants that showcase a fifty-something year-old bloke that lives alone. I know he travels light, but I guess I was expecting some seasonal styles, at least.

"Yes. Did you find your way okay?" I don't ask how he's been or where he was; I doubt he would even tell me. And whatever he was doing I doubt I would approve of it, anyway.

"Aside from parking. Such is the case in cities, especially with my home on the road to find a space for. I take it you decided to try out city life, then? Not a bad choice, I guess."

I nod, keeping it simple. We're in the park opposite the hospital. I figured an open public area would be best since I'd rather not have him know where I live or study. Beasey is a man who likes power, and knowledge is power.

To slide over awkward greetings I gesture to an empty park bench. "We need to talk."

I don't know how Cole is responding to all this; I don't look. My eyes are only on Beasey, trying to read his every move, which is almost impossible considering he's a master of hiding intent. But I won't be fooled, not again.

"To what do I owe the pleasure?" he asks as we sit down.

I want to get this over with quickly, which makes me get

straight to the point.

"There's something going on."

"Yes, I can see it's almost a ghost convention amassing here. I'll have it gone by morning."

I cringe in disgust. Beasey's exorcism approach to those caught between worlds is not something I agree on morally, along with most other things about him.

"I'm not talking about them," I say, although now it has my attention that there really are a lot of ghosts hanging around. Maybe it's something about the manicured lawns and duck ponds that draws them, although it's probably just the hospital itself, anchoring them in their newfound limbo. "I'm talking about others."

"Others?"

"Ghosts are appearing. They're different." I swallow. "I think they've been murdered."

"How many?"

"Four of them. So far." I hand him a printout of the news report. "I saw the first one—Maya Tilly—a couple of months ago, followed by the second one—Monique Sharpe—about a week after, and the third one—Lucia Turnball—a few days after that. There wasn't anything for about three weeks until number four—Paula Voss—appeared. I had searched for missing persons online, but they were found across the state border and I didn't think to search that far out. We were just about to give up finding any information about them until the news . . . well, you can see for yourself."

"Oh. I see." He takes a moment to scan the article. "Fascinating. So they come straight to you?"

"Yes. Just before they cross over. It's all so quick I barely have time to comprehend them. Except they're screaming. Loudly. And they're . . . *glitchy*, I guess is the word."

This seems to garner a reaction in Beasey. It's quick, but the flustering twitch of his face gives it away, especially for someone usually so stoic in appearance.

"I see," he says in monotone. "Looks like I've got my work

cut out for me here." He adjusts himself on the bench. "It's a good thing the local hospital is looking for a janitor."

"That's oddly convenient."

"Nothing to do with convenience. Hospitals are always hiring janitors. It's the cleanup duty nobody wants to do." He gives me a wink. "But someone's gotta do it, right?"

I don't satisfy him with an answer.

"We need to get these glitchy ghosts to talk and tell us what happened to them, which means we'll need to be ready when they show." He stands up. "I'll start with getting settled here, then we'll work on training again."

"Wait, what? Settled?"

"Why, yes. I might be here for a while." He glances at all the ghosts again. "There's certainly enough reason for me to be."

I moan.

"Chin up. It'll be just like old times."

"I regret calling you already."

"To be honest I thought Cole would be the reason for your call."

"Why would you think that?"

"No reason."

He glances at Cole who still hasn't spoken a word since Beasey's arrival. Although if Cole's feeling any negative emotion he's not showing it. He's probably hiding some thoughts, though. Thoughts about wanting to punch Beasey in the face, no doubt. I wouldn't blame him; I kinda do, too. Nonetheless, I'm out of options here.

He folds the news report up, places it in his pocket. "I'll be seeing you again soon, Charlotte." He then eyes Cole. "You, too."

I don't move as I watch Beasey walk away. "Did I do the right thing?" I eventually ask.

"Yes." Cole is contemplative. "You're right. People are dying. This is beyond us."

A ghost must have noticed me talking to Cole, because a small crowd quickly forms around us. I usually would have upped and left by now, but I don't want Beasey to have his full satisfaction. So with a small sigh, I get ready to start this other job of mine.

∞∞∞∞∞

It takes a couple of hours before the remaining ghosts are satisfied enough to leave me be, and I make it to my afternoon class just in time. One of the staff at work has called in sick and asks me to fill in until Mr. Dodgley arrives, which I agree to for the money and merit points, so it's evening before I get home.

"I'm home," I say as I kick off my boots and start unbuttoning my jacket.

Cole appears, his face different from the usual welcoming. "There's a spirit I think you should see."

"Cole, I'm tired. I've done my ghostly duty for the day. Can't it wait?"

"I think you'll need to make an exception for this one."

I sigh, rebuttoning my jacket and sliding back into my boots as I let Cole lead me. After a few blocks, we pass through a recreation park and I am about to ask how much farther we have to go, but then we suddenly stop, and I see why.

Oh no.

Dealing with ghosts is something I've had to just learn to get used to, and that includes all their gone-too-soon stories and tales of woe. Most of what they say just illustrates how unfair life can be. Some just need to accept their age and the natural way of things.

But children? That never gets easier.

"Hey," I say gently, coaxing the little boy with a wave. "My name is Charlotte. What's yours?"

The little boy, no older than five years old, looks up to me, his eyes big in shock. "You . . . you can see me?" He looks to Cole for confirmation of this crazy lady.

"Yes, I can. What's your name?" I ask again.

"Timothy Secker. From Brighton Crescent."

"It's good to meet you, Timothy," I say, except it isn't.

Kids, with their ripe young souls, don't tend to hang around with unfinished business or the heavy weight of karma that comes with the freedom of choice until at least adolescence. So I know that whatever reason Timothy Secker from Brighton Crescent has for hanging around, chances are it requires a degree in child therapy to deal with.

But he doesn't have a child therapist. He only has me.

"Why are you here, Timothy? Do you like this place?" Cole asks.

Timothy nods. "Mommy and I come here a lot."

"And where is your mommy?" I ask.

He shrugs.

"Mommy told me to wait for her. She said she'll be here soon."

"Oh?" I glance at Cole, hand reaching in my pocket. "How long have you been waiting, Timothy?"

He just shrugs before holding the handles of the climbing apparatus.

"He won't have much comprehension of time," Cole mutters to my ear as I swipe open my phone.

"My friend Cole told me about you. We thought we could keep you company for a bit, until your mommy gets here. Is that okay?"

Again, he shrugs. I guess he wouldn't care to do much else. "I guess."

"I bet you won't be able to catch Cole, he's really fast."

This gets his attention. "Yes I can."

"Really?" Cole starts. "I'm pretty good on the monkey bars, you know."

Timothy reaches out to grab him, but Cole dodges. The next thing I see is Timothy trying to catch Cole who is already acting like a monkey climbing up the slide.

"Come on, Charlotte," Cole goads. "I want to see how fast you can climb these monkey bars."

The competition doesn't last long. I want to complain that I am at a disadvantage with all the body mass I carry, especially when I get stuck (much to Cole's amusement and lack of sympathy). But Timothy finds my struggles entertaining enough to accept my defeat with what little dignity I have left and so I leave them to it while I sit down on a nearby bench.

I like ghosts like Timothy Secker, stating their full name and location. It makes finding out about them a lot easier. Unfortunately, however, it's not always the news you want to hear.

Cole cries out in defeat as he is caught. He high-fives Timothy and says that he'll be right back as I signal to him to come over.

"His mom won't be coming anytime soon," I say, showing him my phone. "His father's out of the picture, too."

Cole's light dims. "Shit," he mutters, reading the screen. He scowls, half-punching the air before resuming his composure. "I'll let him know."

"Cole," I call out feebly. "He's just a kid."

"I know. But we can't just leave him. He has to know so he can cross over."

"How is knowing *that* going to help him to cross over?"

"What else do you suggest?"

I glance back at Timothy who is idly stepping along an old chalk hopscotch marking on the ground. He's had it tough, and he doesn't even remember it.

Not now.

Not tonight.

"He can stay with us."

"*What?*" Cole gapes at me like I've gone mad. "Charlotte, he's not a lost puppy."

"But he's a lost spirit," I argue before muttering, "and cute and innocent like a puppy."

Cole gives me an unconvinced look, his eyes jumping from me to Timothy and back again before raking his hand through his hair.

"Fine." He sighs. "He stays. But he'll have to be told soon enough."

"I know," I admit. "But we can't speed through this one."

"Yeah," Cole agrees. "Just don't get attached," he warns me before facing Timothy, his demeanor suddenly one-eighty. "Hey, kiddo," he says as we approach Timothy. "Charlotte just got off the phone. Your mom will be a while longer, but you can stay with us until she comes."

Timothy scowls. "Where is she?"

"She's busy. At work. With other adults. We know Sandra—your mom—and she said it's okay for you to hang with us for a while."

The use of his mom's name must have convinced him because he says okay and takes Cole's hand as we stroll back to my place. It's evident in the way he talks that he's clueless as to what's going on, and aside from the whole being dead thing he's just like any other kid his age, talking about his favorite dinosaur (the Spinosaurus) and wanting ice cream (chocolate chip, of course).

When we reach my apartment, Timothy quickly makes himself familiar with the new surroundings, his attention settling on Shark, following the fish around the tank in happy curiosity.

"His name is Shark," I say. "Do you want to watch some cartoons?" I turn on the television for the first time since I've moved in and scroll through my limited channel selection. I will have to set up a subscription later, but for now he's settling for whatever animation show that's currently playing on the screen. I turn to Cole and shrug. I mean, what does a child ghost do for fun?

"Life is still pretty abstract for kids his age," Cole whispers to me. "He probably hasn't acknowledged he's dead, or even understands what being dead really means."

My heart pangs in guilt for the little guy.

I watch him sitting a mere couple of feet from the television screen, just like any other kid would. It's not fair. He had his whole life ahead of him, and through one selfish action it was all taken from him.

"Hey," Cole reads my expression. "Nothing can be changed."

I subtly wipe my eye. "I know," I mutter as I look away, only my eyes then meet the print-out on the table of the now-found young women. "It just sucks."

"You care. That's also the difference between you and Beasey. Don't change."

I sigh with a sad smile. Cole has a point. I can't imagine how long poor little Timothy would be sitting at the playground, wandering all lost and confused and alone if Cole and I hadn't reached out to him. And caring may make my job so much harder, but it also makes it so much more worthwhile.

Cole notices me yawn. "You're tired."

"It's okay," I reply.

"No, it's not. You're holding up full-time study and a part-time job with irregular shift times, as well as trying to uphold a social life, fulfilling the desires of the dead, and now training with Beasey."

I shrug. "It's a good thing I didn't sign up for any extracurriculars. And I have a feeling my social life will be on the downturn now, anyway."

Cole looks at me sympathetically. "It's not fair on you. Surely it won't be that bad with Gareth?"

"I don't know. I mean, we're bound to see each other around here and there, especially through Kelly or Juliet with Rory. He should at least be mature enough to be amicable about it. Not that it matters, since it seems I'll be spending a lot more time with Beasey for the next while." I throw a cushion over my face as I hit the couch head-on.

Cole crouches down beside me. "His loss."

I lift my head and slowly pull the pillow down from my face. That lock of hair hangs over my face which makes Cole's mouth scrunch up slightly as he tries in vain to flick it aside. A directed blow from the corner of my mouth does the trick. He then grins as our eyes meet; my timid hazel eyes welcomed by his jovial bronze eyes. I wonder if he feels the same butterflies I do, but then he stands up, his casual demeanor back.

"Speak of the devil."

The door knocks.

"Who's that?" Timothy asks.

"Hey, Timothy, I bet I can beat you on the monkey bars this time," Cole teases him.

"Nuh-uh!" Timothy calls back, then he's gone.

I look back to Cole but he is also no longer there. I nervously turn off the television and then open the door, bracing for a breakup finale.

"Look, Gareth, it's been a long day—"

"I'm sorry."

The words are unexpected, the flowers even more.

"May I come in?"

I open the door wider. He comes inside, fidgeting with the rim of his glasses as he leans on the kitchen counter, a sign he is nervous.

"I feel like a stupid sod, just assuming the worst. Like you're no better than my ex." He taps his fingers on the counter, frustrated with himself.

I take my scented candle on the counter out of its glass holder and then place the flowers in it and turn on the faucet. It will have to do on the whole unexpected first time receiving flowers from a guy thing currently in progress. I smell them. Lilies. My favorite.

"I didn't even give you a chance to say anything about Cole."

I flinch, the makeshift vase now overflowing with water around the sink.

"I mean, how can I ever be a good surgeon when I'm like that? Just jumping to conclusions." He then mutters to himself, "Gareth, you prick."

"Uhm, say what about Cole, exactly?" I start wiping the watery mess I made around the sink, confused about this whole situation.

"That Cole was your first love. That you thought the world of him. And that he passed away."

My eyes bulge, my mouth unable to form words. Gareth notices my reaction because he fills in, "Kelly clued me in."

Oh, Kelly. What have you gone and done?

Gareth suddenly has his arms on my waist, gently turning me to face him. "Hey," he says softly. "You don't have to suffer in silence. I'm here for you if you want to open up."

"Open up?" I echo. The concept is still strange to me. I haven't been able to open up about Cole to anyone except Kelly and Beasey, except one of them was only recently and the other was only to stop Cole from being exorcised so that doesn't even count. I guess Patricia counts too, but she took a lot of convincing even with the help of her dead husband next to me. For everyone else it's been denial or discomfort, including my own father. Besides, Gareth doesn't believe in ghosts so what's the point?

"Yeah, you know, that thing people do to connect with each other." He smiles reassuringly. "Or, if you'd prefer, I can get you in to talk with someone at the hospital, if that's what you want—"

"No," I quickly say. "No, thank you." I internally cringe at all the therapy sessions I've been subjected to in my lifetime. "I'm okay. Really."

"Well, I promise I won't be such a pillock in the future—if you're still willing to put up with me, that is."

I blink. "You mean, like, you and me? As a couple?"

Gareth nods. "I missed you more than I thought I would. And when Kelly told me, I wanted to be here for you more than I realized." He takes a step back, leaning eye level to me. "But only if you want to. I can wait, or totally sod off if you prefer."

"No, I don't want you to *sod off*, Gareth."

"Phew," Gareth replies. He pulls me in and kisses my forehead.

I feel a wave of guilt sink over me. This isn't wrong, is it? I was just accepting how this is something I'm not capable of doing, accepting my fate. Gareth just apologized for something that he isn't technically wrong about, and I just accepted his apology for something that I technically did do.

And just like that, it begins again. The façade of normality.

"Oh yeah," Gareth notices the time on the wall. "Remember that stand-up comedy sketch show I mentioned? It's starting soon if you feel like going. I totally understand if you don't feel like it and just want to watch a movie or have a night alone, but it might take your mind off things? Whatya say, feel like laughing at some drama students?"

"Like a date?"

He smiles. "Our official first date."

I hesitate in panic, not able to hide away from an answer. Once again finding myself in a predicament, but once again with a prior agreement to uphold. It's just a date, right? Many people end things on the first date, the chemistry or commitment not there. I want Cole here for guidance, but I know from last time what he would say.

"Okay." I hesitantly smile. "Let's go."

I grab my jacket and keys, looking back at the empty apartment before closing the door behind me.

<h1 style="text-align:center">Thirteen</h1>

Of all the world cuisines I like, Italian has to be my favorite. Luckily for my waistline it's hard to find an authentic Italian place. That was the case until I met Kelly's aunt, at least.

"Thanks for the lunch, Maria," I say as I place my knife and fork down on the empty plate that had displayed the utmost delicious lasagna I have ever eaten.

"Anytime, dear."

The evening has been casual, void of any such ghostly conversation which is honestly a little disappointing compared to my expectations. I let Maria know that I told Kelly about Cole, but it was probably his absence that led to the lack of the topic. Even if I knew that this would have been the case, Cole has his hands full. That's what happens when you have a kid to look after, I suppose.

"Oh my god Aunty, that was the best." Kelly burps before covering her mouth. "I'm so glad you're Italian."

"One day you will cook this, too. The lineage must continue."

"I dunno, Aunty. Have you seen me try to cook for myself? Anything beyond toast or scrambled eggs needs a caution label."

"You young Americans, forgetting the important things like how to properly cook and clean. I was at the laundromat yesterday and these college boys didn't know how to use a washing machine. They had never washed their own clothes before. Sure, become a doctor or scientist, but wash your underwear? Separate whites from colors? Too difficult."

"On the note of cleaning, I insist." I stand.

"Yeah, Aunty, you've done enough." Kelly takes her plate. "Let us young Americans save face and clean the dishes."

"Are you sure? I don't have a dishwasher, you know."

"Even better," I reply. "No scary buttons to figure out."

"Besides, work has trained us well for this."

We laugh as Kelly and I head into the kitchen with the plates and glasses. Kelly and I haven't had a chance to talk since Gareth and I became an official couple, so as soon as we're alone in the kitchen she begins the talk I know she has been eager to have.

"So how was your first date last night?" she asks as she squirts dish liquid into the sink and holds her finger under the gush of water until it's warm.

"It was good." It was great, actually. The show itself was terrible, so bad in fact we only laughed at how cringeworthy it was. But that just made it all the funnier. Gareth apologized profusely for subjecting me to that, especially on a first date, but he made up for it with ice cream and walking me home.

"And how did Cole take it?"

"He . . ." I don't know what to say. I don't want to say anything. Since I went on that date with Gareth, Cole's been giving me the cold shoulder romantically. It's both frustrating yet sadly understandable.

I force myself to sound as casual as possible as I scrub a plate clean. "He's fine."

Kelly raises an eyebrow at me, unconvinced. "So you're just living with a ghost guy you undeniably have feelings for while he watches you date another guy you are undeniably developing feelings for and he's *fine*?"

I pass Kelly a wet plate. Since she knows this place more than me I've automatically become the washer and Kelly the wiper and stacker.

"Well, since he was the one who insisted I give Gareth a go he has to be."

"Oh?"

"We have different paths, to quote him."

"He's right, you know. As sad as it is."

"I guess."

"Doll." Kelly places her hand on my arm. "That plate's not getting any cleaner."

I hadn't noticed how hard I was scrubbing the plate in the sink. I sigh. "Sorry, Kel. I'm as confused as you are about everything."

"Well, I'm sure the Halloween party next Friday will take your mind off things."

"Halloween party?"

"Yeah. At Lea's. It's their traditional frat thing. I went there last year. Went to *get some liquor* with this really hot exchange student from Brazil, if you catch my drift. Good memories."

"I'm sure."

"What I mean is a lot of people come out and socialize. There'll be darts and billiards, drinks—oh, and every second guy dresses as Zoro, it's hilarious watching them try to pull off their best Banderas impersonation."

"I dunno, Kel. Dress-up isn't really my thing."

"Oh, come on, it'll be fun! Besides, Cole will fit right in."

I flick some soap suds at her. "Very funny," I scorn.

"Surely he'd like to see you get your house bunny on?"

"My what?"

"Yeah, you're probably more of a vengeful bride type. Just don't wrap yourself up in toilet paper and stick your arms out, whatever you do."

I hold back a laugh.

"I already made sure we're both off work, so there's no excuse. And if you can't find a costume I have plenty. Gareth is coming, too."

"He is?"

"Yup. So now you have to go. If you don't want any other girls clawing their way at him, that is."

It's as if Gareth knows we're talking about him because I feel my phone vibrate in my pocket.

I can't help but smile.

"What's that all about?" Kelly teases, peering over my shoulder to read my message.

"We're going to the movies. I think Rory and Juliet may also come."

"Ooh, double-dating. You're going up in the dating world, doll."

"Feel free to join us."

"Nah, the hot nurse guy has just upped his game. He's got us tickets to a musical tonight. *And* a hotel afterwards."

I grimace. "You know one day you're going to have to properly introduce him to us, and I hope he has a name by then."

Kelly chuckles. "He's got to be Mr. Darcy for that to happen."

I snicker. I'm sure this guy play is why she moved here. She's trying to find a balance between her reserved parents and her flamboyant aunt.

"Come on, let's finish up. Can't keep them waiting."

Kelly and I thank Maria once more before we go our separate ways. I meet the others outside the movie theater, Gareth already holding the tickets as I walk up to him.

"Hey." I smile.

He kisses me on the cheek before saying, "It's either this indie movie or one of those comic-to-screen movies, and I figure superheroes are well and truly overdone so we chose the indie option.

"Good choice," I affirm.

Juliet and Rory come over carrying popcorn and soda, and then we make our way inside. Apart from a small group of retired folks sitting near the front row we have the theater to ourselves. Rory and Juliet call shotgun for the back row while Gareth and I naturally decide to sit a couple of rows in front for some alone time together.

The indie movie is terribly boring, but I don't say so. Instead,

I keep my mind occupied with mental revision of classes before drifting into an anxious mind tangent of upcoming bill payments, the maximum work hours I need to commit to compared to what I can do, the upcoming anatomy test to prepare for, Cole, Timothy, general ghost assistance and no doubt fitting in time for whatever Beasey has in mind.

Just normal young adult things.

I flinch at the nudge from Gareth. "Huh?"

"I said, can you believe he just did that?"

I look at the screen. As far as I can tell he did just do that, whatever "that" was. And I should or shouldn't be surprised about it.

"Uh, I wasn't really paying attention."

Thankfully I'm not the only one feeling this way either, because I glance at Rory and Juliet who are busy interlocking tongues. I smirk slightly but quickly look away before the ghost loitering near them notices me looking. That's the last thing I need right now.

"Sorry," Gareth whispers to me. "I really don't seem to be good at picking these things."

"Don't worry," I whisper back. "We can always find ways to make it fun."

He forms a devious smile at this. "And what ways do you have in mind?"

"I can think of a couple of things."

Okay, only one. But I've been wanting an opportunity all evening, and Gareth seems to be thinking the same thing because he places his hand under my chin and moves forward to where my lips are. Suddenly we're all making out at the back of the movie theater like a group of bored horny teenagers.

I can't say how long we do it for; I'm not really keeping track of time here. I can't say I'm fully enjoying it either because I'm consumed by guilt. I feel like a terrible person for trying to please both Cole and Gareth, but I need to let this play, to see if Gareth and I can actually be a thing. If not, then I can end it and get back to normal with Cole with our agreement intact. But if there really is something with Gareth, then I'm not actually sure what to do. To be honest I'm hoping it won't get that far, although I fear it could.

I'm ready to let this play out longer to find out, only it's suddenly raining popcorn.

"Knock it off, young'ns!" Rory chides quietly, throwing another handful down over us. Gareth, in all his agility, catches one in his mouth and we all crack up in a quiet laughter.

We leave early, all agreeing that the movie isn't worth any more time wasted. We decide instead to go get ice cream and hang out at a playground like naughty teens with nothing better to do.

Just as we exit the movie theater to the parking lot I hear my name.

"Charlotte!"

I turn, stopping when I see Beasey and Cole.

Beasey *with* Cole.

Beasey smiles in greeting. It's weird when he does that; it looks so fake yet genuine at the same time. The perfect customer service smile.

"You didn't tell me you have a boyfriend." He glances at my arm wrapped around Gareth's and then to Cole, a subtle movement I know was intended for me to see. "Aren't you going to introduce me?"

Trying to hide my scowl I say to the others, "Guys, this is my, uh, uncle."

Rory and Juliet come up behind me and say hello in unison, but Gareth straightens up at this, his arm now stretched out solidly. "Gareth Hamilton. Pleased to meet you."

Beasey seems to take amusement at this. "Uncle Beasey." He gives Gareth's hand an affirmative shake. "Likewise. It's so good to see my niece out dating such a *lively* young man."

Cole staunch face becomes less expressionless with every word Beasey says.

Beasey's rubbing it in. And he knows it.

"Thanks." Gareth politely takes the compliment, ignorant to

its real purpose which is far from flattery.

"I hope you don't mind, but I've come to spend some time with my niece. I'm sure she told you that we have this evening reserved, didn't you, Charlotte?"

If looks could kill, Beasey would be dead by now.

"I totally forgot. Sorry," I say sheepishly to the others.

"It's okay. I'll, uh, leave you with your uncle, then." Gareth gives me a look, one looking for confirmation. I smile and nod subtly to assure him I'm fine. He then begins to lean in, but stops and settles for a quick platonic hug. "Catch you around."

"Yeah."

Gareth turns to leave. Juliet says bye and then follows, and Rory gives us one long look before doing the same. Poor Gareth. I'm sure he's now thinking up a viable excuse to duck out of being the unexpected third wheel to Rory and Juliet.

Once they're out of sight both Beasey and I change our demeanor.

"How did you know where I was?"

Beasey starts walking through the parking lot. "Uncle Beasey cares about his niece."

"Shut up. Are you keeping ghost tabs on me?"

"Just making sure you're safe."

"That's what Cole's for." I turn to Cole. "Did you know about this?"

He shakes his head, unconcerned with our dialogue.

"I have to say, Charlotte, I'm surprised. I didn't think polygamy was in you."

"I said shut it, Beasey."

Beasey laughs off our conversation while he unlocks the door to his motorhome.

"What are you doing here, anyway?" I discreetly ask Cole. "Has something happened? Is Timothy—"

"He's good," Cole interjects. "He's watching a magic show right now. I told him I had free tickets. He was so excited."

Hearing that eases my vexation a bit. Picturing Timothy happy and playful lightens my mood instantly. With that high-pitched childish giggle and innocent bright spark in his light brown eyes it's hard not to.

"I tried to give you a heads up about Beasey, but . . ."

Cole doesn't finish; he doesn't need to. He couldn't give me a heads up because I was distracted. Distracted with Gareth.

I look away, embarrassed and ashamed.

For once Beasey's voice is a nice distraction. "Well come on in, then."

Beasey lives on the road, a nomad fulfilling what he believes is his duty for God, only stopping where he believes he needs to be. His camper is not bad for a home on the road. Actually it's quite good. I can't say it's something I'd willingly live in, but he's done an alright job at making it work. There's just about enough interior space for one person to walk through between the counter and table to what I assume is a tiny bathroom compartment and a small bed space behind the curtain at the end. For three people, however—or even two and a ghost—it's not going to work.

"Beasey, there's no way I can do practice of any kind in here. Cole is half-in, half-out of the wall as it is."

"You need to practice in private, where else do you suggest?"

I sigh. I know where this is going. And I don't like it.

"My apartment is small, but there's enough room for three people to stand in, at least."

"If you think it'll help you practice, fine. Now that we have a place, we need a test subject."

"A test subject for what?"

"How has your exorcism practice been?"

Beasey may have taught me a thing or two back in high school during afterschool detention, most memorably how to exorcise spirits. And yeah, I understand his eventual reasoning that some spirits are bad and self-defense is important for a Communicator, but I still only had to do it once.

That also means I'm not keen on doing it again.

"No!" I protest Beasey's look at Cole. "Don't even think about it."

"You need to learn how to hold a spirit in place to catch these ghosts in passing."

"Not by risking Cole." I feel sick at the thought. "Whatever you have in mind, we are not doing it to Cole."

"I don't know why you're disapproving. After all, isn't this the reason why he's here? To help you? Well, this will help you."

I open my mouth to argue but Cole, for the first time, joins in the conversation. "I'll do it. I'll help you."

I shake my head. "You don't have to, Cole. We'll find another way."

"No, this is the best way and we all know it." Cole is leaning against the door, his arms crossed, looking as if he's only half-bothered by the whole thing. "It makes me useful, at least. As Beasey said, it's why I'm here."

I eye Cole as Beasey claps his hands. "Splendid. Now all we need is to arrange times that match our schedules. You're on rostered shifts at that café, I assume?"

I scowl at Beasey. "You're verging on creepy, Beasey. Even for you. But yes, I am. As well as classes, midterms, and with everything else I'm a little short on time." I sigh. "But I should be free for a couple of hours at some point. I'll text you."

"Fine. I would like to start now, but it took time to find you and I have my first shift shortly." He starts the engine. "Of course, as an uncle I have to see you home safely. So tell me: left or straight?"

When I reach my door Cole follows me inside. While I'm glad Timothy is enjoying himself, I'm a little disappointed he isn't here to greet me. It is no secret I have quickly become attached to the little guy. Cole also has, although he's probably more resilient to admitting it.

Now I'm left to face Cole and the growing awkward drift between us.

"Gareth likes you."

Straight to the point. Sometimes open communication *is* more difficult, I now see.

"Cole, do we have to do this now?" I start idly cleaning the kitchen counter to keep myself distracted from facing him.

"You like him, too."

"Oh, do I?"

"It's in your eyes."

"And whose fault is that?" I snap. "You kept saying I should go out with him, date him, kiss him. This is what happens when two people do that stuff!"

"I'm not blaming you, Charlotte."

"Well it seems that way." I throw the dish cloth into the sink and sigh. "I kept our promise, Cole. But that doesn't mean I agree with it."

"You're right," he eventually says.

"I am." I say it as a statement, but it is more of a question.

"It's deceitful," he replies. "You shouldn't have to."

"Right."

"So I'm ending things with us."

I blink once. Twice. Then again. "What did you just say?"

"You can't hold back on living for me, Charlotte. I'm just in the way, a distraction holding you back."

"Cole—"

"I'll still be around to protect you, don't worry."

I can't believe what I'm hearing.

"But—"

"I'll take Timothy with me."

"What?"

"He'll visit, of course. When the time suits you."

I lean onto the kitchen counter and exasperate. How did I get from making out in a movie theater to talking custody rights in one night?

"Gareth is a good guy," Cole reiterates, expression solid. "He's good for you. Be happy with him for me, at least."

I don't know where the emotion comes from. I scream, throwing the vase of flowers Gareth gave me across the room with force. It hits the wall, a splatter of water left trailing down to the floor of shattered glass and strewn stems of torn lily petals.

"It's not fair!" I crash to the floor, thumping my fist into the kitchen tiles with every hot stinging tear forming in my eyes. "It's not fair!"

He shakes his head. "It's how it needs to be. Different paths, remember?"

He puts on a small smile but his eyes look sad. I'm done caring, however. Right now I'm over everything.

"Fine! Leave, then! It's what you always do, anyway."

"Charlotte—"

"Go on! Leave!"

He leaves, and I'm left slouched over and alone, in the empty dark, with nothing but my own conflicting thoughts and feelings to pain me.

Fourteen

The woman at the campus café knows me by my first name now.

"The usual, Charlotte?" she asks as I reach the front of the line.

I smile and nod. While she knows my name, I can't begin to pronounce what's on her name badge. I feel bad, and should probably Google it sometime, but it's just never a big enough priority to remember doing. Maybe it doesn't even matter what her name is. Like me, she's only a waitress. We see so many faces, write so many names of coffee cups with a black marker pen, our names shouldn't matter. We're forgotten about as they leave and door closes behind them.

Under that theory I should have a strong resilience to being walked out on. I mean, Gareth already did it once. Who's to say he won't do it again? And then there's Cole . . . I haven't seen Cole since that night he left, which was five nights ago now. He's still around though, keeping any unwanted or demanding visitors at bay, because no ghost has visited me since. Not even Timothy, which annoys me, but it wouldn't be the only reason for my moodiness. Grueling shifts at work, midterms, and the constant anxiety of having the screaming spirit of someone being murdered pop up in front of me certainly doesn't help.

To which there has been little in the way of official updates, not even from Beasey. I mean, these things can take time, I know. The hearsay seems to be that these women went out for a hike and got lost, which is why there's pressure to update trail signs and increase information on packing for the occasion. This gives me hope that it's not as bad as it seems. Because surely if it was a homicide investigation then there'd be a manhunt in progress by now. I think. I'm no criminal investigator. But it's been confirmed that they didn't know each other, they died at different times . . . people get lost in forests all the time, get disorientated, injured or eaten by bears. Maybe there was just a very hungry bear?

I shake my head, scrapping another scenario my mind comes up with. It's an attempt at reassurance, but it's in vain. These aren't normal deaths. I know it, and the police probably know it, too.

Usually I relay such thoughts to Cole who knows what to say to reassure me, but I'm left to do that on my own now it seems. I've had some resulting restless nights, but during work shifts and mundane classes I have started to come to terms with things as they are. Well, not so much thinking as much as feeling. Because although I assumed the whole dating thing would fizzle out, that's not the case.

Because I like it. And I like him.

This only angers me more, however. It must be about being physical, right? But that would only make me a more selfish person. And that would only make Cole more right.

I don't want him to be right, though. I want him to be wrong, I want him to appear before me and apologize for being so wrong and beg to come back into my life. With Timothy.

Only I know he won't.

So even though it's a surprisingly warm day with barely a cloud in the sky, everything seems like a drag, and I just want to wallow in bed watching reality television shows on my phone all day until I fall asleep. But while I admit being dumped by a ghost certainly doesn't help the ego, I can at least see it as one less drama.

Because let's face it, guys are drama.

Still, a day like this is not meant to be spent inside, which is why when the waitress with the unpronounceable name passes me my coffee, something I have now surrendered an addiction to, I place some coins in the tips jar, and with a quick thanks I then make my way back outside.

Kelly is waiting for me to return, sitting back on her picnic blanket, attempting to study for the last of her midterms while watching Gareth and Rory play frisbee. I take a long sip of my coffee as I join her. Kelly thinks the coffee here on campus is terrible, but since I don't know any better I don't complain.

I find myself actually smiling briefly at Gareth and Rory playing frisbee. They're like excited dogs jumping up to catch it, only with their hands instead of their teeth. I imagine Gareth being an active father one day, playing frisbee or ball in the front yard all summer afternoon for some one-on-one parenting time. I wonder if he's ever been fishing. Do they fish in Buckinghamshire, England? If not, I would teach him.

I flinch at the thought.

"And?"

"And what?" I've only barely been following along to Kelly with nothing but the odd "yeah" or "yuh-huh" thrown in here and there.

"Did you continue the date *into the night*?"

"What? No."

I'm sure Kelly knows the answer to this. Juliet would surely have told her that my weird uncle turned up and ruined the prospects of the night. I thought this would be old gossip by now, but I guess I owe it to her, having been so elusive the past few days.

"Is that because you're still an innocent little birdie or are affections with a certain spirit holding you back?"

I don't quite know what to say. Aside from Beasey and Cole turning up to abruptly end what was a good date night in progress, I technically am still an "innocent little birdie" as Kelly so eloquently put it, and affections with a certain spirit are definitely also in the mix. Not that they should be. After all, Cole was the one who wanted me to date Gareth, and it was Cole's choice to leave.

"Charlotte," Kelly fills in the silence, unsatisfied with my lack of reply. "Do I need to remind you that you will carry on aging, living, and desire more and more to properly date, get married and have children one day?"

I turn away, the words unwanted. My thumb rubs my mother's ring on my finger.

Kelly sighs, probably at my visible anger. "I'm sorry to say it, but you need a *real* man. To help pay the bills."

"I know," I mutter.

"To make you chicken soup when you're sick."

"I know," I repeat.

"To carry your heavy grocery bags."

"I know," I say louder, emotion building up inside me.

"You know it's different when Gareth holds you—"

"I know!" I snap back, louder than necessary as all the thoughts and feelings I've tried to avoid come flooding back. "And Cole knows it too. Which is why he's decided to no longer occupy my apartment. Or my personal life."

Kelly's now a blur behind my wet eyes. She places a napkin in my hand and I gently dab at my face, careful not to smudge the mascara I spent so long trying to perfect.

"It hurts now but it's for the best, doll."

"It doesn't make it any easier, though," I mutter.

"What's wrong?" Gareth and Rory approach us, frisbee in hand.

"Nothing," I quickly reply, forcing a smile.

"Charlotte has just passed another milestone of the grieving process," Kelly says. "Denial."

I curse under my breath. Gareth, Juliet and Rory have all been subjected to the narrative from Kelly that I'm grieving over a high school sweetheart who perished in a car accident. I mean, it's not entirely wrong, but there's certainly a degree of deceit to it. At least it works as an explanation for everything.

Gareth sits down on the grass beside me and that's Kelly's cue to leave. "Come on, Rory. Let's go see how Juliet's test went."

She leaves, making Rory follow, and I don't stop them.

"That Kelly," I mutter once I know she's out of earshot. "She's really taking her psychology degree to heart."

"She's headstrong," Gareth says. "But she cares."

"I know." I'm starting to really hate those words.

"Do you want to talk?"

"There's nothing to say, to be honest."

Gareth looks at the ground. I hope I didn't offend him.

"Can we just . . . lie here?"

He smiles softly. "Sure."

He straightens out across the grass and I place my head on his torso. As I do so he wraps his arm around my back, my hand gently rubbing along his arm.

"This feels nice," I speak my thoughts.

"Yeah," Gareth says.

"Your skin is soft."

"Thanks," he replies.

"You have hair on your arms."

His head turns. "Is that a problem?"

"No," I reply. "I feel it, that's all. And your muscles." I slide my hand along the slight bumps of his biceps. "Your warmth. Your breath. And your pulse."

"You know, this is probably the most awkward way I've been turned on. Just saying."

I chuckle back laughter. "Being alive is sexy."

Gareth leans up on his elbow, his eyebrows now furrowed. "Are you sure you're okay?"

I look up and nod. "Can I feel your lips, too?"

He smirks. Then he obliges.

∞∞∞∞∞

Walking into my apartment room feels dark and cold compared to the afternoon outside I just came from. I could have spent hours laying there in Gareth's arms for all I cared. It was certainly a nice enough place to be. Kelly is right; as much as I hate to admit it, there's something about being in the arms of someone physical that's so much more than what Cole can provide. My chest pangs with guilt at this thought, but it doesn't last long because my phone buzzes again, a reminder that Beasey is on his way. I told Gareth that I'm meeting up with my uncle again. I don't like lying, but the sooner this whole ghost situation is sorted, the sooner I can get back to some normality. Emphasis on the *some*.

I am back home only a minute before I hear it.

"Knock knock!"

The words startle me. It's been a while since I've heard Cole's knocking call, his permission to enter my private space.

I open the door, my frustration instantly gone from seeing Timothy smiling in Cole's arms. He reaches out to me and I happily receive him into my own arms.

"Timothy!" I gleam as I hug him. "I've missed you."

"We went to the zoo!"

I gasp in excitement and carry him inside. "The zoo? Wow! Did you see lots of animals?"

"Yes! We saw lions and bears and the elephants were so huge!" He outstretches his arms at the word as if it would represent an accurate size measurement. Kids are adorable that way.

"I bet. And what was your favorite animal?"

"The penguins, because they move funny like this." Timothy squirms through my arms to waddle across my room.

I laugh. "Wow, I almost thought *you* were a penguin for a second there, Timothy."

"No!" he teases. "Penguins would probably eat Shark. I don't want to eat Shark."

"That's good to know."

He peers through the tank glass. "I can't wait to tell Mommy about the cheetahs. She likes them."

My chest suddenly pings in discomfort.

"Go play in your garden, Timothy," Cole says. "I'll catch up to you soon."

Timothy leaves without so much as a goodbye, but it's not his fault. As Cole said, time and place are abstract to him at his young age, but it's probably for the best with him.

All sound in the room has suddenly gone, and like a balloon the mood bursts with it.

Cole stands across from me, his expression untelling. Several seconds pass as we stare at each other. I don't know why his silence is irritating me right now; maybe he doesn't have anything to say, or maybe he's like me, unable to speak because of the intensity building inside my chest.

"How were your midterms?"

"Fine, I guess."

"I didn't mean to keep Timothy away, I just wanted to give you space to study."

"Uh-huh."

In one second Cole disappears and then reappears.

"Beasey's arriving," he announces in monotone.

"You don't have to do this, Cole."

"I do."

"Whatever, then."

More silence.

The door soon knocks and without another word I open it.

"Welcome to my humble abode, I guess."

Beasey makes his way inside and puts his backpack on the table. Unzipping it he says, "Straight to business, then. I can feel the tension is already set up. Good job."

"What are the candles for?" I ask, ignoring his observation.

"Guidelines," he replies as he lays out a circle of candles on my floor. "Think of it as training wheels. See the heat energy as a barrier to contain the spirit in." He gestures Cole to the candles. "If you don't mind."

Cole stands in the circle of candles.

"You might want to remove the batteries out of your smoke detector and open the window a little," Beasey suggests as he lights the candles with his lighter. "Did you practice the chant I sent you?"

"I think so," I reply as I place the smoke detector battery on the counter. The gibberish that makes no sense yet seems to be some ancient tongue us Communicators have the ability to harness power from. "Whether I've got all the intonations and inflections right will need to be verified. Wouldn't want to unintentionally set loose a demon or something."

"As if demons are real." Beasey tuts.

I roll my eyes.

"I'll help you get the pronunciation right. Like the candles it's more for training wheels, but that's nothing to go into now." He turns to me. "Are you ready?"

"I guess."

Beasey looks to Cole who nods back.

"Very well," Beasey says with a clap of his hands. "Trapping a ghost is easy. Keeping the ghost trapped is the challenge. Watch."

Beasey starts the chant as I watch Cole tense slightly.

"How do you feel?" I ask Cole.

"Heavy. Tight. Like something's binding me," he replies with a strained voice. It's easy to tell he's uncomfortable.

"We're anchoring him down to Earth, that's why. Restricting the passage to cross over, the freedom of movement spirit consciousness has." He turns back to Cole. "Now try to move."

It takes a few attempts, but it doesn't take long for him to step to the side and move again.

"That didn't seem too difficult," I note.

"That's because I stopped channeling the energy. Now you try."

Doing as he says, I follow his words, channeling the energy I feel, containing it within the heat of the candles like he advises. Cole smiles in encouragement, although the adversity is clear in his eyes.

"Try to move."

Cole tries to comply and I feel the energy shifting with him. I strain to control it.

"Hold the energy," he cautions me. "Channel louder, harder."

I do as I'm told, determined to get this right. The quicker I learn the less Cole suffers.

"And . . . release."

I let go and Cole immediately falls to the side, taking out a candlelight behind him.

"Pretty good for a first attempt. Now this is where the fun begins."

He re-lights the candle.

"I assume you've received adequate enough learning in the national education system to know that everything is composed of atoms, and atoms carry energy?"

"Yup. Everything is energy, yadda-yadda."

"So you can understand that emotions emit energy, right? If you are sad you emit lower energies. Dark emotions are heavier than light emotions, which is why you feel sullen and heavy when upset or stressed. Therefore, the more distressed a spirit is, the more energy it channels and the stronger the energy is. Sometimes so much so it can even be heavy enough to seem physical."

I think back to all the times ghosts have managed to flicker a lightbulb or slide a glass off a table, and how emotional they were at the time. I guess thoughts, vibrations and emotions really do hold power.

"What about positive energy?"

"Positive emotions carry lighter energy. Remember the saying being on cloud nine? Or feeling over the moon? High on life? It all adds up in the grand universal design of everything."

"So if a ghost has really positive energy . . . when they're happy and have energy of peace and love . . ."

"It's off to Heaven they go. The Kingdom of the Lord. In the highest attainable energy there is of light and love."

"Oh. Right." I try not to roll my eyes. This is beginning to sound like those Sunday bible sessions I was forced to go to as a child.

"Exorcisms are a push in the right direction for them, by stripping them of that dark energy."

"Lord savior Beasey."

Ignoring my comment, he continues, "We can only assume that those poor women found their peace from whatever deaths they suffered for them to move on. We're going to veer away from working with light energy, however. Because if you can control an emotional spirit, especially one in dark energy, you can control any spirit."

Before I can react, Beasey turns back to Cole and begins chanting again. Taken off guard, I can feel him quickly stiffen.

"Do you remember this, Cole? This feeling? Just like that night when Charlotte found who you really were—"

"Beasey." I tense up.

Cole doesn't speak, but his darkening aura does all the telling.

"When you looked her in the eye and told her that *you* are the reason her mother is dead, the reason her brother never got a chance at life—"

"Beasey." I can't help but feel my throat close up looking at Cole, my head now starting to ache in tension, and I don't know if it's me or Cole I'm feeling.

"Do you remember her collapsing to the ground, how distraught she was?"

"Enough," I warn.

"How heartbroken she was."

"Enough!"

"No!" Cole interjects. He's now almost black, consumed with dark energies of guilt and regret. "I deserve it. I deserve it all."

I want to comfort him, to heal him, but Beasey blocks me with his arm.

"Good. You *do* deserve it."

I punched Beasey in the face once. Sometimes I think I should do it again. Right now is such a time.

"Charlotte." Beasey signals for me to repeat him. I grudgingly do so, and feel the heaviness of Cole's energy while he's in this state. Beasey is right, I'll admit. Methods aside, he knows this stuff well.

"Leave, Cole. Leave this place."

My eyes widen at the shift of energy flow. It almost feels as if an invisible wave is pulling to where he moves.

Beasey turns to me, his voice low and lecturing. "Hold it. Speak louder, harder. Disregard his own emotions or they'll flow into your own."

I try to comply, only I feel for Cole which means I pick up on his pain all too easily, especially when it's about me.

The energy hold quickly breaks as Cole moves quite easily to the side and then vanishes. I slouch forward in sullen defeat.

"You need to have better control of your emotions, Charlotte. You're empathic, remember? Highly sensitive to energies, part of the package of being a Communicator."

"Yes, I remember." I rub my forehead, trying to clear away this oncoming tension headache. "Sorry for caring. Something you wouldn't understand."

"You think I'm apathetic for the fun of it?" Beasey scorns.

I look up at him. He looks different, almost like he's . . . offended.

"It's not about caring. It's about control. If you can't control your own emotions then you take on the emotions of others, wanted or not."

I take in his words, his reaction, and wonder if that's the secret to his façade, the Achillis heel to his rustic and unwelcoming persona. Is he this way by choice, or because he has no choice? A coping mechanism to all the emotions and energies he would have come across all these years. Furthermore, would that mean that I too will become like that? Is that what being a Communicator comes down to, for survival? I mean, I can't even refrain from emotions from one ghost, let alone all ghosts.

I hold my gaze on Beasey, longer than I normally would, as if I'm seeing him in some new light.

Maybe I am.

I slump over to my refrigerator and take out two beers, sliding one across the counter to Beasey. This is my emergency stash, but I guess now counts. Beasey cracks open the can without hesitation and we drink quietly, mulling over our emotions.

"Aren't you too young for beer?" he soon asks.

"You're the cool uncle. You won't tell."

This brings out an almost-smile in Beasey, one of the few rare genuine emotions I've seen from him.

Cole reappears, now a lighter shade to the distressing sight he was before. Not great, but at least he can interact efficiently enough.

"How are you feeling?" I ask.

"Been better."

"Good."

I don't know why I say that. It's no secret I'm stubborn and can hold a grudge, but it's not like I don't care about Cole, because I do, especially right now. As closed off as he normally is, he's now no longer around me, which makes it even harder to know what's going on in his mind. But if I could get in, if he did go against his reserved personality and open up, I'm sure it wouldn't be felicitous in there because it's clearly no walk in the park for him either, having to do what he's doing.

Suddenly I feel as terrible as he's showing.

Beasey doesn't seem to notice, however. "It'll pass. Like a short-lived hangover. So we need to try again while he's down."

"I think he's had enough for now."

"Do it, Charlotte." Cole dares me as he positions himself in the middle of the circle of candles, his lips slightly scrunched and eyes tense. "Like the other night. Let it out."

My stern attitude falters, showing the exposed cracks I'm trying to hide. He wants me to let it out? Fine.

I thump my can of beer down on the kitchen counter and stand. "Dammit, Cole, why did you have to go and get yourself killed?" I start, feeling emotion erupting from within me as I walk near him. "You had your whole life ahead of you. You could have gone to college, become a teacher. You should be a father by now, with your own boy." I chant louder between the words, holding my arms out to control Cole's heavy energy as he tries to pull away, his energy quickly blackening. I see him crushing under the heavy emotions stirred from the words

I throw at him and it takes everything within me to withdraw any speck of empathy when I say, "You could have loved, Cole. *Properly* loved."

Maybe I went too far. Maybe Beasey will make me stop. It's a good thing no one else can hear his struggle. The lights start flickering and half the candles have suddenly extinguished. The mood of this place has become too dark to handle, and I struggle to breathe.

"You choose your emotions, Charlotte," Beasey reminds me. "You feel nothing."

I feel nothing? I feel everything.

You choose your emotions.

That's how Beasey sees it, anyway. That's how he can do this Communicator stuff so well. Because he has no emotions. Or, at least, he's very good at choosing them. I get it now. I wonder if that's a secret to getting by in this life, as I look at Cole fighting to get away from the weight of his dark energy. Just choosing to be happy and then bam, happiness. That's why some of the biggest sufferers out there dealt with the worst hands in life can also be the happiest. Happiness is a choice, after all. Why ponder with all the middle ground?

Cole goes limp and I fear I've gone too far. He hangs there, trapped and shadowed, his eyes dark voids looking my way. Beasey gives me a look as close to surprise as he'll show. I begin to panic, fearing he's going to tell me I've hurt Cole—or worse—I've lost Cole somewhere to some hellish dimension.

"Good," Beasey simply says instead. "Again."

Fifteen

Toying with so much energy takes it out of you. Seriously, I feel like I've been drained by an energy vampire. Beasey goes over some meditative exercises with me to reconnect to Earth's energies, whatever that means. It helps, though.

When I come out of my trance I leave Beasey to finish his beer while I go upstairs to Cole lying on my bed, lethargic and dark. I know it's because of me I'm seeing him conflicted, or whatever that look he's giving right now is, and I don't like it.

"Charlotte." Cole starts to wiggle away.

"Shh," I whisper as I crouch down to his eye level. If there's one thing I've learned today, it's that the balance of energies goes both ways. Cole doesn't have to feel this way. He doesn't have to suffer. And it's only fair I make up for that.

I place my hand on his cheek as I look him in the eyes and then gently tousle his sandy-blonde hair. I wish it really was his hair and not just some energy imprint of it. I've always wanted to rake my fingers through it the way he does, but this will have to do. And it's not like he can object; he can barely move he's so sullen. But I prefer to assume he wouldn't even if he could, because somewhere hidden within him I know he wants me beside him as much as I want to be beside him.

"I'm still annoyed with you," I warn, feeling his anxiety. "But I care about you more. So let me help make you better again. Starting with saying I'm sorry I said those things."

Cole raises his hand. "Don't apologize. You did it. You

trapped me in place. And if you can do it to a ghost as emotional as I was then trapping any other ghost will be a walk in the park."

"I don't care about any other ghosts. Not really. Ghosts are just invisible people, and like people they all have their own misfortune or problems. They aren't my problems, though. I only care about you."

His aura is slowly brightening again. I take his hand, caressing it on my own.

"You're with Gareth now," Cole warns, slowly pulling back.

"Yes," I agree before gently kissing his hand anyway. "But you will always be in my heart, Cole. Always."

Our moment ends with the knocking at my door.

"Shit, is that the time already?" I check the wall clock and pace downstairs, throwing the candles into Beasey's backpack and yanking the missing persons print-outs off the wall and into a drawer.

"Hi!" I pant as I swing the door open, although I try to make it sound more like an enthusiastic breath.

"Hey!" Kelly beams before noticing Beasey behind me.

"This is my uncle," I fill in.

"Pleasure to meet you." Beasey pulls a smile.

"He was just leaving." I turn to him. "Weren't you?"

I pray Beasey takes the hint. Even if he wanted more training time there's nothing more to give tonight, neither from me nor Cole who's only just summoned enough energy to appear nearby.

Beasey thankfully nods. "An evening well spent. Message me so we can do it again sometime soon."

"Will do." I force a smile as he pulls his backpack over his shoulder.

"Stay safe, Charlotte," he says as he leaves. "You never know what's going to pop out of the dark."

As soon as the door closes behind him Kelly says, "He's not really your uncle, is he?"

"Careful, Charlotte," Cole warns. His aura is nearly normal which is good to see, however if ghosts ever look tired then he looks like he could do with a long nap. We both could, actually.

I open my mouth to answer Kelly. I probably should lie, but I can't find enough effort to right now.

"How can you tell?"

"Please, the only thing you and that man share is the weird vibe," Kelly concludes.

I give her a look, one that Kelly immediately picks up on.

"Wait, he's . . . like you?" She huffs in surprise. "What, so there's, like, a club or something? Just how many people can see ghosts? Is this some new trend? It's the new cell network, isn't it? My cousin is always saying there's something up with the signal—"

"It's not what you think, Kel. There are only a few dozen of us in the world. I just happened to run into him in the school hallway one day, fist first. That's all."

Kelly raises an eyebrow. "This," she starts, "is definitely a story you will be telling me in detail sometime. But for now are you sure you're okay? You look half dead yourself."

I nod, reassuring the both of us.

"Good." She hands me a paper bag. "The others will be here shortly. Put this on."

I comply, although I wish I had not. I fiddle with the makeup Kelly slathers on me, trying to make it as subtle as possible without offending her. I keep the orange eye shadow and rosy blush, however, feeling it goes with all the red I'm wearing.

"You look fine," Kelly says, noticing me. "Doesn't she look fine, Cole?"

Both Cole and I look at her.

"What? You wouldn't have Halloween without the ghost." She leans in but whispers loudly, "And you keep looking at that corner over there."

I look at Cole, standing in the corner she points to. She's right. I don't know why he's still here since he was so adamant about leaving me, but I don't say anything. Instead, I want *him* to do the talking, to communicate something, *anything*, to me. But once again, he internally verbalizes everything and externally says nothing.

I pull myself away from my vanity mirror. I'm not that bad. I hope. At least I'm not when I stand next to Kelly, who's dressed up as a very naughty-looking maid. When it comes to having fun, Kelly goes the extra mile. She reassures me that she'll get more use out of it with one of her guys on the line and I can't help but let out a small laugh as I go to answer the door.

"We're here!" Juliet chimes. "Ooh, cute digs," she says as she squeezes through the doorway with her pixie wings.

"Charlotte!" Lea pulls me in for a hug, careful of the bottle of gin in her hand.

"Lea! Really? Underage drinking dressed as a police officer?"

"*Naughty* police officer, duh." Lea twerks her behind before setting the bottle down and pointing back to the door. "Needed one of these legal boys here to get me more alcohol. Gin's up!"

"Glasses are on the shelf above the kettle, snacks are on the table," I call back before turning to the door to greet Gareth with a laugh and a hug. "You're Harry Potter!"

"Dorky, isn't it?" He fiddles with his Hogwarts cloak.

"Definitely," I reply as I peck him on the cheek. "I love it."

"And you're . . . Little Red Riding Hood?"

"Apparently." I look down at my small tartan dress under my tight tartan corset and red cloak. "Although I don't think she wore such a small skirt with such long heels."

Gareth snickers. "Did I mention red is my new favorite color?"

I smirk in reply and pull him inside from the cool air outside.

"And you're . . . a ghost?" I say as Rory enters and closes the door behind him.

Cole takes particular notice to Rory, his eyebrow raised.

"Classic, right?" he says through the white bed sheet with three holes over his face.

"I can't say I see the resemblance," Cole says.

I bite down on my lip to hold my amusement in.

"What's so funny?" Rory asks, almost serious.

"Nothing," I quickly reply. Cole looks at me and tweaks a small corner smile, and for a moment things feel normal between us. I want to hold onto it, feeling how much I've missed it until now, but it's suddenly gone to the chatter of the others oblivious to us.

"It beats his original idea of being a tooth fairy," Juliet says, pouring herself a gin.

"Hey, who says I can't be a tooth fairy. It's the twenty-twenties, you know. Guys can wear a tutu if they want to."

"Oh, I'm sure you could pull off a tutu. I'm just not having my boyfriend upstage me as a fairy."

"Babe, no one can pull off Tinker Bell like you."

Juliet playfully hits him as he makes his way to the table.

I'm still looking at Cole, however, even as Gareth brushes my hair behind my ear and kisses me on the cheek softly before joining Rory. And then once again I find myself looking back at this new cold, distant Cole.

"So," Lea hushes as she passes me a glass of gin. "You and Gareth the medical student, huh?"

"It's early days," I say, trying not to glance at Cole. "We've just started dating."

"That's how it always starts," Juliet says in earshot. "Then before you know it you'll be exchanging wedding vows and holding your first child in your arms."

They giggle and start talking about their own guy stories. I slide a glance across to Cole, still unmoved, which I immediately regret. I foolishly expect him to pull a face or say another witty remark that only I could sneak a laugh at, but he doesn't. His gaze is on Gareth, and squinting a bit I think I can see tears in his eyes. My throat closes and I hope it's enough to remain composed.

"We're heading off shortly so don't get too comfortable," Lea announces. "I want first dibs on drinks since I'm playing host."

Kelly, in all her perceptiveness, asks out of ear shot from the others, "Will a certain ghost be joining us, too?"

I wait for a reply but instead Cole disappears.

"I don't think so, Kel."

I sigh, unable to do anything else, then join the others as Juliet and Lea decide they need final touch-ups of their makeup. I idly pack away the few candles I missed into a cupboard, all traces of what was going on before now long gone. Gareth is playing sober driver and we all squeeze into his car and head off to Lea's place. This time there is no need to prove ourselves; maybe it's the rum Rory was carrying or the tequila cradled in Kelly's arms, but we are greeted with a warm welcome from everyone and the night begins.

Given what happened last time I partied here, I have set my limit for only two drinks. It feels odd without Cole here by my side, but Gareth is a different kind of company. He confirms my thoughts when he slides his arm around mine, his cloak shielding me into his comforting embrace.

"Found anyone you know?"

I look around. People have really gone all out on costumes. Some faces I recognize from my classes, mostly pirates and cowgirls. But the others I can't. I also see Brad and Ricky again, surrounding a girl I can only imagine is Pamela. Pamela grinding up against some other guy.

I should leave it. I really should. Except they're clearly disheveled about the whole thing, their auras dull, and I know their mood will rub off on me one way or another.

I sigh. "Yeah. Do you mind if I go say hello quickly?"

"Go for it." Gareth joins Rory and Juliet as I snake my way past the Avengers and witches up to Ricky and Brad. I lead the way out the back door where it's suddenly cooler and quieter.

"I'm sorry," I say as I turn to them. "That's Pamela about to give Zoro a hand job behind the speakers, isn't it?"

"Yeah. Fucking sucks," Ricky replies.

Brad eyes me up and down. "Nice."

Ricky elbows him. I don't mind Ricky; he may be as thick as bricks, but his intentions are good, and if I were to guess whatever happened between the two I'd probably side with Team Ricky.

Ricky now looks broken when he speaks. "It's only been six

weeks. Who can lose not one but two lovers and be so okay so soon?"

"Maybe she's just trying to move on. Maybe she's suffering inside but just trying to cover the pain of losing you two."

Brad shrugs. "She has a point."

"I guess," Ricky mutters.

I attempt to reassure them with all my half-semester of Psych101 knowledge that grief makes people do weird things, and that I'm sure Pamela is secretly hurting. Except maybe Pamela doesn't care. Maybe she never really loved them, and it was all just a game for her. Either way, she's alive and they're dead. She's having fun and they're not. She's moving on and they're left behind, to watch on helplessly in torment.

"One path for her, one path for you," I conclude. I look down to the ground, suddenly feeling sick with myself.

"Where's your boyfriend?" Brad questions.

I open my mouth to say he's inside, but then halt, realizing he means Cole. "He's . . . moving on," I say. "And so should you two. You see the light, don't you? Pulling at you to cross into it?"

"I was wondering what that thing was," Brad mutters.

"Wait, we're supposed to go into that?" Ricky asks.

"Uh, yeah," I reply. I stop myself from saying "duh" even though I'm tempted to.

"And when we do we won't come back, right?" Brad asks.

I nod.

"Where does it lead to?" Ricky then asks.

Brad punches his arm. "Dude, don't you get it? That's *it*, man. The end game."

Ricky looks at me for clarification.

"Nobody knows for sure," I say. "Heaven. Reincarnation. Nothingness. The universe. But everyone will find out eventually. It's where we all go, sooner or later."

"I'm sorry, man," Brad says to Ricky, his tone now lower. "I would never have gotten with her if I knew you two were serious, if I knew we would . . . end up like this."

"Doesn't it suck?" Ricky snickers. "I mean, look at us. We

were tight, you and I. Ruined over some chick.”

“Her hand jobs sucked anyway.”

“Dude.” Ricky relaxes, his aura lifting the heaviness he carries.

“You’re still the coolest guy I know,” Brad says.

Ricky smiles at this. “You were pretty cool too, Brad.”

“Say, we went out together, reckon we should do so again?”

“Nah, man. Get your own light.”

“Dude, get a grip, it’s clearly *our* light.”

“That is *my* light! You’re always sponging off on what’s mine. What, can’t even go into your own light, now? Your light not good enough, you have to leech in through mine, too?”

“Seriously? You’re doing this now?”

“Yeah, everything’s *ours* when it suits you, Brad.”

I don’t know where their conversation goes, because their voices fade out with them until there’s a bright shimmer of light, one that I need to shield my eyes from with my arm, then they’re gone.

I crouch down against the wall feeling weak and pathetic. Am I like Pamela? Dragging Cole and Gareth along with me to my liking? Or am I not Pamela enough, failing to properly take part in the land of the living?

A shadow from the sensor light comes over me. I would say it’s a ghost, but a ghost wouldn’t cast a shadow, and a bed sheet barely passes as worthy of calling him a ghost, even on Halloween.

“Chilly out.”

“Hey, Rory.”

I don’t know how I feel when it is just Rory and me. He is Juliet’s boyfriend and Gareth’s best friend. We’re bound through third parties, but with his colder demeanor around me that is only emphasized when we’re alone, I honestly don’t believe he thinks that highly of me. I guess with Gareth or Juliet out of the equation we’re just two separate sums. So I don’t really know why his demeanor is warmer all of a sudden. He even slides down the wall next to me.

"Gareth's wondering where you got to."

"I just need a minute."

I hope he takes the hint, but he carries on talking.

"He likes you, you know. Gareth. And he's a cool guy. I don't want to see him get hurt, y'know?"

"I get it," I tell him. Except no matter what I do, feelings are going to get hurt. Including my own.

I think he begins to take the hint, because while he opens his mouth to continue, he pauses, before changing his tone. "By the way, are you still looking for a case study project?"

"Huh? Oh, yeah, I guess. Why?"

"Those missing women that were found in the national park—did you hear about that?"

I look at him, suddenly intrigued. "Yes."

"Well, I came across them on the system today."

I look up. "Really? You can do that?"

"Yeah. All the hospitals in the area are connected on the same database. It makes finding and claiming bodies easier."

"That's understandable. What did it say?"

Rory hesitates. "Are you sure you want to know this?"

"Yes," I reply instantly.

He hesitates again and I pray he doesn't chicken out before he says, "Suffocation."

"Suffocation?"

He nods. "All four of them. Apparently. There's no physical sign of pressure marks on the neck though, or a struggle. The windpipe wasn't damaged. Which can only really mean they were starved of oxygen. It's almost as if . . ."

"The life was drawn out of them," I finish.

"Yeah." He looks at me intensely. "Weird, huh?"

I shake my head. Then nod. "Thanks, Rory."

I stand to get back to the party.

"Hey." He quickly grabs my arm. "What I just said was a breach of protocol and patient confidentiality, not to mention an ongoing criminal investigation. I can get into a lot of trouble for that. Why them? Is this really just for a first-year case study project?"

"As I said, just finding an interesting ongoing case study for class. I won't tell anyone. I promise."

He scowls, unconvinced. But the others appear and he immediately drops my arm.

I feel myself going into serious mode. I should call Beasey. I should tell him straight away what Rory just told me.

"Shots!" Lea calls out as everyone cheers.

Tomorrow. I'll tell him tomorrow.

Because tonight is for me.

I stand up with Rory and we join the others. I skip past the shots though, and walk straight up to Gareth and greet him with a kiss on his cheek. He's surprised by this, but in a pleasant way. He pulls me close to him and that's where I stay for another hour or so before we make an early exit.

Gareth drops Kelly off first as she's spending the weekend with Maria and she doesn't want to keep her up, followed by dropping Rory and Juliet off at hers. We say bye and wish them a good night, fully aware that's what they'll be having.

With no traffic it only takes fifteen minutes to reach my apartment block. He pulls into an empty parking space and then turns the engine off. Our casual conversation suddenly turns off too, and I find myself feeling weird, my mind's thoughts from the long day all catching up to me in my newfound heavy sober state.

Which is why I surprise myself when I put my hand on his and say to him in all seriousness, "Stay with me the night."

This clearly has his attention, his face suddenly looking serious through the terrible circle glasses and permanent marker lightning bolt on his forehead.

For a moment I think he's coming up with some excuse not to, that work suddenly called him in or he has rekindled with his ex or something. Only he then twitches a little corner smile and replies, "Okay."

He gets out of the car first, meeting me by the passenger door as I get out. He flicks his keys and the car locks with a quick flash of light and sound. "But there's no way I'm letting you walk up all those stairs in those heels."

He lifts me up in his arms, ignoring my squeak of protest, and climbs up three flights of stairs to my loft apartment. He places me down gently so that I can fumble in my bag for my keys, and I then open the door just enough for me to peer through.

"Just want to make sure my, uh, uncle hasn't invited himself over."

"It's okay, Charlotte. I don't have to—"

"It's fine. Really." I glance around. No sign of any ghosts. It's a good thing Cole keeps his word. "Come in."

I hobble over to the couch to unfasten my heels. A sound emits from me when I see how red and swollen my feet already look.

"That's going to hurt tomorrow," Gareth comments.

"Then it's a good thing it's not tomorrow."

"Is it okay if I wash up? I don't want to sport the permanent marker lightning scar at work tomorrow, nor the smell of a night partying.

"Of course. Towels are in the cupboard here." I take one out. "There should be a pack of toothbrushes in the cupboard under the sink."

"Grand."

I start pacing nervously while Gareth is having a shower in my bathroom, now fully aware of what I initiated. But it's fine. It's what couples do. It's what Kelly has done plenty of times, it's what Rory and Juliet are probably doing right now. Even Cole's done it. Besides, it's not like I care about virginity, anyway. It's just sex. It's biology, what we're meant to do.

I play with my hair. Should I leave makeup on? What should I wear? Bra or no bra? I shake my head. Why would I wear a bra to bed?

"I, uh, don't have any other clothes with me." Gareth stands awkwardly at the bathroom door with nothing but his underwear on. Little is left to the imagination. Not that there should be. He's fine. No, not just fine; his tall frame, toned muscles and wet hair spiked to the side makes him more than fine in my books. All he needs is to hold a protein snack bar or a spinach smoothie for some brand promotion and his look would be complete.

"The good news is I smell of coconut and elderflower."

I can't help but giggle. Giggle and blush, both probably more than I should.

"I would offer you a shirt but I don't think any of them would fit you."

"Really? I thought the corset and tartan skirt would have worked better on me than you to be honest. But if you insist."

I look down at myself. I can't believe I'm still wearing this.

"Yeah, I would like to get out of this now. I turned the heater on; are you warm enough?"

Gareth strolls over to me, now more serious. "I'm fine. As long as you are."

I nod, feeling my cheeks flush. "I'll, just, wash up."

"Don't be too long."

I rush a shower, not bothering to wait for the water to heat up again. The cooler water is refreshing anyway, bringing me to my senses. Like what was I thinking, bringing Gareth back to mine for the night? And why am I so nervously excited about it?

When I step out in my purple and black lace sleepwear Gareth does a double take.

I like the way he looks at me. It makes me feel somewhere between cute and beautiful. I stand on my toes and do a little twirl.

"Wow," he breathes. I'm pretty sure he's the one blushing now, which makes me feel better about before. "Purple suits you."

I smile appreciatively as I walk up to him, our fingers interlocking in our hands. "You're cold."

"I'm fine."

"You have goosebumps. Now I'm feeling cold, too." I glance upstairs. "Come."

There's something about cuddling up to a guy—a physical one—that just can't be beaten. The way he holds you close to him, subconsciously caressing your arm. The natural smell of a man that comes through even after washing with coconut and elderflower shower gel. But most of all it's the feeling of protection. I breathe in the soft scent of him, feeling the warmth of his chest rising and lowering under my head. Gareth and I have been lying like this for a while now. It started out on each side of the bed, but once we established ourselves in this new environment it didn't take long to meet in the middle. With Gareth I feel safe and adored. I also feel normal, I realize, the other side of me forgotten when we're alone. I don't know how long this will be able to happen, though. Which is why, fighting the giddy feeling building up in my stomach, I turn to him and say, "I want to have sex with you."

Maybe he wasn't expecting that. Maybe he was, but was just surprised to hear it come out the way it did. He stops mid-sentence and turns to face me.

"Was my ranting about Halloween in the UK boring you that much?" he asks, both amused and surprised.

I shake my head. "No. And I won't ever get the image of seven-year-old you peeing your pants in front of the trick-or-treaters out of my mind," I reply. "But I mean it. I'm happy when I'm with you. I want to remember this."

Gareth keeps his smile, but his eyes turn more serious. "Are you sure? You still seem caught up on—"

"No." I don't want to hear his name. Not right now. "He's no longer here. Besides, it's what he would have wanted. I'm sure of it."

"Kelly would like to psychoanalyze you over this tomorrow, I'm sure."

"Probably," I chuckle. "What about you, though? You sounded pretty traumatized over what happened with your ex when you told me about her."

Gareth titters. "I was. Being cheated on and finding out like that changes a person. But I'm over Ellie," he says solidly. "Pretty sure I was over her the moment you walked into the ward that night."

Okay, now I'm really giddy. I brush my lips on his, testing the moment between us. It's both soft and welcoming, but Gareth gently pulls back.

"Charlotte." He puts his hands on my shoulders to make sure our eyes meet. "I'm not expecting anything, you know, *intimate* from you. I can wait."

"No," I say as I grab his arm. "I'm ready."

Before he has a chance to speak more I place my lips on his again. What starts as soft kisses become firm kisses, and before I even have the chance to pull back to breathe Gareth pulls me against him and we're lying face-to-face along the length of the bed. Feeling sudden discomfort, he wriggles and pulls Totoro out from the covers underneath him.

"No room for the both of us," he mutters and then flings the plushie to the floor.

We both laugh, our eyes give approval, and then as his lips touch mine again as his hands start moving impatiently up my arms. My body shudders as the tips of his fingers brush over my bare skin, gripping tighter as rushes of newfound sensations sweep over me. My breath catches as his fingers touch my chest, my body arching as pleasure shoots inside me down to my hips. A small sound from deep in his throat tells me he feels it too, and as he spins on top of me I know he wants more.

"Are you sure?" His breath is already short as he asks me.

I nod, my thoughts blind to my body yearning for more.

That's all the reassurance he needs. He pulls my sleepwear off over my head with a quick movement and flings it off the bed to fall on Totoro.

Being on such display in front of someone for the first time is daunting. My breath halts in my throat as Gareth's gaze moves down my body and then up again.

"Hello, gorgeous," he says in his thick British accent.

His mouth is then on mine again, then my neck, his chest rising and falling sharply with each short breath he takes as he kisses his way down my body. He places his hand between my legs which makes me tremble.

"I've never done this before," I suddenly realize out loud.

Gareth pauses to take this in. "You mean—"

I nod before he finishes. "Just so you know."

Most guys would probably snicker or maybe feel secretly disappointed they'd have to be slow and considerate. But not Gareth. He leans up and kisses me gently, and with a small stroke of my ear he says just louder than a whisper, "Thank you. For making this even more special."

That's all I need to hear. One hand pulls his underwear down, the other holds his cheek while I kiss him deeply. He accepts with a groan, filling my mouth with his. He places his hand on the bed by my shoulder, balancing his weight over me as he works his way down my body, one kiss at a time, and when he reaches my underwear he kisses me there too as he slides it off to join the pile on the floor.

"Do you have—"

"Drawer."

He's already there, leaning over to my drawer, feeling with his hand for the square wrapper. He pauses for a moment, the picture frame of Cole moved into view for both of us to see, but I refuse those thoughts right now.

He finds the condom.

"A free sample from orientation week," I whisper.

"Good. Always safe sex," he breathes with a wink. "Doctor's orders."

I smile and spin over onto him, feeling his hard up against my exposed navel. Our hands meet as he places the condom over where I'm touching, the excitement clearly emitting in his eyes as my fingers follow his.

"Charlotte!"

I spin in alarm to see Cole at the end of the bed.

Cole.

At the end of the bed.

With me.

Naked.

On Gareth.

Oh. My. God.

"What's wrong?" Gareth asks.

"It's your dad. He's in the hospital. Heart attack," Cole replies, eyes not leaving mine. And just as quickly as he appears, he disappears.

"Dad," I echo in panic.

"Dad?" Gareth asks. "Is that some kink?"

I quickly swing off him, grabbing a bra from my drawer. "My dad's in the hospital." I shakily try to slip the hooks of my bra on before not caring anymore and reach for my underwear instead.

"What? Your dad's in the hospital?"

"Yes." I run to the wardrobe and pull out a sweater and sweatpants.

"Is he okay?"

"I don't know, so I've got to go." I dash downstairs while pulling my arms through the sleeves of my sweater.

"What's wrong with him?" Gareth follows me.

"Heart attack."

"Wait, he just had one?"

"Yes."

What do I need to do? Assignments are in. I can email one professor in the morning about emailing me the upcoming lecture slides for her class. Kelly will cover for me at the café.

"How do you know he just had a heart attack?"

"I just do." I grab my bag and pace to the door. My car has just under half a tank of gas. I can fill up at the freeway stop. And fill up on coffee while I'm there, too.

Gareth thumps down the last of the stairs. "Look, Charlotte, if you don't want to go any further then just say so."

I slip my sneakers on my blistered feet that are already protesting in discomfort from the heels I wore to the party. Shark needs to be fed.

"Charlotte, can you just stop for a moment!"

I turn to face Gareth standing across my apartment. As much as I want to bask in awe at his naked body, his unimpressed expression feels like I won't be getting the chance to again.

"Shark."

"What?"

I scramble to get my spare apartment from the nearby shelf. "Can you please feed Shark for me?"

I throw him the key and even though my throw was uncoordinated he catches it in one swipe without even taking his eyes off me.

I can't believe I'm turning away from him.

"I'm sorry. I really am. It's not you. I'll message you later." I open the door and before closing it behind me I say once more, "Sorry."

Sixteen

"I really don't know what all the fuss is about," Dad says as I open the refrigerator for the chicken salad that the neighbors gifted. Thankfully it turned out to be angina and not a heart attack. Nonetheless, news spreads fast in this town (what's new?) and it doesn't always spread factually (again, what's new?), meaning we either have some very caring neighbors or some very nosy neighbors being misinformed that Dad had died. Either way, I'm keeping the salad.

"People care," Patricia replies, and she's right. She was there when Dad had his angina attack. She was there at his bedside. She was there for him when he needed someone. And I wasn't.

"There needs to be more people in the world like you, Patricia." I smile at the way she sits Dad down across the living room, her caring nature at full play. I flick the kettle on. "Coffee and apple pie coming up."

"Oh, I'd better be on my way."

"Nonsense. Sit," I demand as I serve up the leftover pie in the fridge. "You probably saved my father's life. You have indefinite access to the Durane household. Seasonal pie in the refrigerator is always guaranteed."

"She's right, you know." Dad says. "Can't thank you enough, Trish."

"Just happened to be in the right place at the right time," she replies. "All part of God's divine timing."

I subtly roll my eyes but smile, nonetheless. While I would

have much rather God not let my father get angina at all, especially *then* of all times, I welcome all the divine intervention there is. Including Cole.

Cole, who saw me naked on Gareth.

Cole, who hasn't shown up since.

"Isn't that right?"

I flinch. "What was that?"

"I said that while Patricia's place is getting renovated she could stay here. No nursing me, though. I'm not that useless. Yet."

"Of course," I agree. "We have a spare room that's never really been used. Stay as long as you like; the place could do with more people around. And Pippi agrees, don't you?"

Pippi perks up at her name and wags her tail.

"That settles it," Dad says as I pour hot water into three cups.

"Oh my, thank you indeed," Patricia replies.

"I'm the thankful one. It's reassuring to know Dad has someone around." I say as I place down a tray.

"Great!" Dad smiles and reaches for some apple pie.

"Oh, no. Not for you. Your cholesterol is too high, remember? Chicken salad for you."

I can't help but laugh at Dad's reaction as I hand him some chicken salad instead.

"Some recovery this will be," Dad mutters.

While Patricia starts talking about keto food alternatives, I nervously check my phone. Three missed calls from Beasey I can't be bothered responding to, but no messages. I haven't heard from Gareth since I rushed out of my apartment, leaving him standing there, naked and confused. I unlock my phone and the message bar appears from where I left it, an empty message space I can't find the words for. Do I lie? Lie about what? My dad did have a heart attack. And the small thing about how I suddenly knew just as I was about to have sex with him? Daughter's instinct? I got a message on my phone about it before but forgot about it? A ghost appeared and told me? None of those sound less obscene than the other.

I start texting:

Hey, fed Shark?

Too rude?

Hey, hav u fed Shark? I'm ok btw.

Too irrelevant?

Hey, hav u fed Shark? I'm ok btw. Dad too. Sorry about
last nite..

I sigh.

Hey, sorry about last night. Dad's out of hospital now.
Will make it up to you (somehow). Hope Shark is fed?

I press send and throw my phone aside. Communicating with
Gareth shouldn't be this difficult. Why hadn't I heard anything
from him?

"You okay, dear?" Patricia asks.

"Yes. Just making sure my goldfish is being fed."

I pretend to pay attention to their conversation but then make
my way to the kitchen and start portioning all the donated food
into containers for the distraction. While doing so, I notice my
old trampoline out the window. It's one of Cole's favorite spots.
Or at least it was. I wonder how often he comes back here. Am
I really his only anchor? Just me and Shark? He must be so
lonely. At least Timothy is keeping him busy. For now. But what
happens afterwards? What happens when I'm busy with Gareth,
or work, or classes? What happens after graduation when I have
a career, a fulltime job, a family?

These thoughts make themselves known again and I angrily
shake my head at them.

"Deep in thought?"

I didn't hear Patricia come in, but she's now at my side with an empty plate.

"No," I say.

"Your heart's not here."

I sigh. "I don't really know where my heart is right now. Somewhere caught between two guys, probably."

"One of those situations, is it?" She places her plate in the sink. "Do you know what you're going to do?"

I stare out to the trampoline again and rub my arms. "I have no idea".

"Your father would suggest more pie." Patricia chuckles. "But in this case I'd say that regardless of circumstances, if the first guy was truly meant to be then there wouldn't be a second guy in the picture."

Her words are both wise and painful. Except I don't think they apply to this situation, because if Cole were here in the flesh then there wouldn't be a problem and he'd be by my side.

"Oh, dear." Patricia passes me a tissue for my eyes. I must look like a lovesick fool in front of her. I randomly wonder if Pamela also had such a moment, too.

"Sorry," I mutter.

"You fight for those you love. And if they're really worth your heart, you live with the pain they inevitably cause. That's what unconditional love is all about."

"Being in pain?"

"Living with their flaws, not leaving because of their flaws." She starts to wash her plate in the sink. "You're still so young, however. I'd say ditch both of them and go wild for a while. Get all the lust out of your system. Discover what love and commitment is all about. Don't tell your father I said that, though. He might just have a heart attack for real."

I giggle, my eyes now dry again.

"Stay a while. Your father misses you. Pippi misses you, too."

I smile, but the more sense she speaks the more I feel the urge to do the opposite. As much as I want lazy days with pie and Pippi and Dad and Patricia, I miss hanging out with Kelly and

Gareth. I miss watching Rory and Juliet woo over each other. I miss Timothy and Shark. And I miss Cole.

"Actually, I probably should be getting back. I have work and don't want to fall behind on my classes." Not to mention a murder mystery to help solve, Communicator training, sharing custody of my foster ghost, and a lot of awkward explaining to do.

Dad comes into the kitchen, leaning uncomfortably on the counter. "So soon?"

"You should be in bed resting," I say disapprovingly.

"Resting's for the dead," Dad replies.

I can't help but scoff at his words. If only he knew.

"At least be here for Thanksgiving," Patricia suggests.

"Of course," I confirm. "Maybe I'll even bring a friend."

"A friend?"

"I do have them now, you know."

"That's not what I meant, bub."

"I know. I'll let you know." I take a dog treat out of the tin for Pippi and then give Dad a hug.

"You'll come back?" Dad asks again, anxious.

"Of course," I reply, neither of us wanting to let go. It troubles me how mortal my father really is. For someone in his early forties I didn't think I'd be having such thoughts so soon. Given I'd be able to see him after death should be reassuring, but it wouldn't be the same. Nothing would ever be the same.

"I miss you, you know."

"I miss you, too." I pull away. "Which is why you're going on a diet. Starting with no more beer. And that chicken salad better get eaten, too."

"Charlotte Durane, I thought I raised you better than that!" Dad looks at me as if I just renounced my faith or announced I'm pregnant, but I know he's half-joking. "You know pie is the staple food of this family. It's what keeps us going."

"I'm not sure it's the pie," I mutter.

Dad nods to the pumpkin on the counter, fresh from the market in a hessian bag. "It's pumpkin season, you know."

I sigh. I guess living is meant to be enjoyed. I reach into the cupboard and pull out the container of flour. "I suppose a pumpkin pie wouldn't cause too much harm."

∞∞∞∞∞

"He *what*?" Kelly feels around for her napkin to cover the mess on her chin, coughing out the last of the soda she choked on. It's a good thing we're sitting outside. It's mild with brown scattered leaves around the table we're sitting at, even though there's an uncomfortable cold breeze to signal winter is on its way. I thought Kelly should be the first person I see, if not for thanking her for covering for me at work so I have a job to go back to then for advice.

"He just walked—or ghosted, or whatever—in on you like that? Does he, like, not respect your privacy?"

"It was an emergency, and I'm glad that he did. I'm sure he wasn't expecting, you know, to walk in on *that*, though."

Kelly wipes her mouth, her breathing now recovered. "When I first met you I knew you would be good gossip potential, but *this*," she outstretches her hands, "is next level drama. I love it."

"I'm glad *you're* enjoying it," I mutter as I wipe her soda spray off my bag.

"And you haven't seen him since?"

"No." I feel my eyes hot with tears against the breeze on my cheeks. "I'm a terrible person."

"Doll," Kelly cuts in before I got too emotional. "You are doing exactly what you should be doing: learning independence, staying out late, being free, exploring your sexuality, all those natural young adult experiences." She casually slurps the last of her soda through her straw before saying, "He knows that's what you'll do. Live."

"Cole wanted to live, too."

"That doesn't mean *you* shouldn't," Kelly counters. I turn to Kelly. She shrugs at my expression. "I tell it as it is."

She is right, of course, as much as I don't want her to be, as much as it hurts. I have to carry on with my own life first and foremost. Not to mention I like Gareth, and Gareth likes me. Although I don't know where that could possibly go after the other night. What should I do?

Kelly must have sensed what I was thinking because she says, "You have to make the first move. Gareth doesn't know where he stands. I mean, a chick running away from him like that in such a vulnerable moment . . . you gotta make it up to him."

"How?" I ask. "He won't even reply to my texts."

"But he did feed your goldfish."

"Yeah. I would be shocked if he hadn't."

"So he has a spare key to your place?"

"Yes. Your point?"

"There you go. Have him return the key to you," Kelly says before smirking at me. "And finish what you two started."

Kelly's phone alarm buzzes to indicate she has to get going to work. We part ways, her reassurance that my shifts are covered, but only for the next two days because Mr. Dodgley is a "dipshit".

I debate whether to take her words seriously or not, but as much as I want to see Gareth right now, I need to see Cole.

When I finally reach my apartment and pull into my parking space I notice I already have someone waiting for me.

I sigh. Not the face I wanted to see.

"Of course you're here." I don't stop as I climb the stairs to my apartment room.

"I was concerned about you," Beasey replies behind me. "You didn't reply to my messages."

"Yeah, well, I've been a bit busy."

"So I've heard. How's your father?"

"Better, thanks for snooping."

"We've got work to do."

"I've had a long day, Beasey. And traffic was so bad coming back that it took an extra hour."

"This is important. I found out some stuff."

"Me too, actually."

"So we need to talk. Where's Cole?"

"Cole?"

"Yeah. The spirit that's been following you around for the past decade. You know him?"

I ignore his snark as I unlock my door. "The truth is, Beasey—"

I stop talking.

Cole is here.

Timothy also.

Timothy perks his head up, runs up to me and then hugs me hello. "You're back!"

"Hello, kiddo." I can't help but smile. "How have you been?"

"Good," Timothy replies to me. "Cole and I have played all day!"

Beasey can't hide his shock. "Good lord, you're adopting them now!"

I ignore him, my focus on Timothy. "Really? That sounds like fun."

"You're starting your own family of them," Beasey says at my side, still in disbelief.

"He wanted to be here," Cole says apologetically to me.

"Now I see why you have your own place," Beasey mutters.

"Where were you?" Timothy asks me.

"I was visiting my dad who was ill. He's better now, though. Next time you come to visit I'll watch cartoons with you, okay?"

"Okay."

"I see you really do have your hands full." Beasey makes his way back out the door and then points at me. "We'll be talking about this, too. Tomorrow."

"Noon."

"Deal."

When the door closes behind him Timothy grabs my attention again.

"Can I see my mommy now?"

"Timothy, your mommy's not well. She's at a place to get better."

"Like your dad?"

I grimace. "Not exactly."

"I couldn't see my daddy. Mommy said he was always busy."

Yeah, I bet. Busy with another family, not caring about the consequences of his adultery.

"Many adults are," I say instead.

"I want to see my mommy now."

"Timothy, the thing is, she can't . . . see you."

"What do you mean?"

Cole must have seen I'm struggling here, because he suddenly intervenes, "Let's go wait for her by the playground, yeah?" He turns to me, expressionless. "When do you want to see him next?"

I frown. Is this what we've succumbed to? The only communication being over visiting times?

With a sigh I reply, "I have some study to catch up on. Then Beasey, I guess. I want Timothy here when I get back."

"Sure thing."

Timothy leaves. Cole begins to follow.

"Cole," I say sternly.

He wavers, his back to me. Maybe I heard a sigh, but nonetheless he turns to face me.

"About the other night." I try not to let my voice crack. "I'm sorry."

Cole shakes his head and raises his hand. "No, I'm sorry. I didn't think. It won't happen again."

"No. I'm glad you told me straight away. I'm just sorry the timing was . . . unfortunate."

Cole titters at this. "Don't apologize for living your life. We've all got to move on sometime."

"What's that supposed to mean?" I cross my arms firmly. "Has Beasey been planting things in your mind again?"

"No."

"*You* left *me*, remember? So yeah, I am with Gareth, but it was you who seemed so quick to just give up and go!"

"You think this is easy for me?" he asks abruptly. His tone, though, isn't that of solemnity or self-pity. It's more hostile. "Playing parent, the snide comments from Beasey, having to always be on ghost guard duty while watching the one I'm in love with fall for another guy? I'm trying, Charlotte. But geez, cut me some slack."

My mouth is open, but I am utterly speechless.

Because Cole just said he's in love with me.

Not just love.

In love.

"You haven't said that before."

"What?"

"That you're in love with me."

"Of course I'm in love with you!" he blasts the words so casually, as if I'm stupid for not knowing it earlier. He grips the table edge firmly, tensing before going limp.

This should be the most exciting moment of my life, the declaration of love causing butterflies in my tummy and cartwheels in my heart. And don't get me wrong; the butterflies and cartwheels are there. Only I sense it coming, a heaviness in his eyes he isn't hiding as his aura begins to dim.

"Except now I'm tormented with wanting something I know I can't have," he continues. "And I knew it would come to this, and I tried to fight it. But the more in love with you I fall the more it hurts." I see the tears dwell in his eyes, his voice barely breaking through emotion bubbling up from his throat. "Which is why I have to let you go. Please let me let you go."

He's gone before I can speak, which is probably for the best, because when I break down in tears over a guy I'd rather be left alone.

Cole is in love with me.

Cole is *in love*. With *me*.

I mean, I guess I should have assumed that already. I knew he loved me, in the platonic sort of way, and I guess our relationship should have indicated that there was more to that. But being in love, to see him crack in emotion under those words he said so surely . . .

When I manage to regain my composure I pick up my phone. Still no messages from Gareth, but I've done all I can for now. It's as if the closer to him I get with ghosts in the picture, the more my new normal is threatened to the hidden part of me that gets exposed.

This isn't an equation that will work. And it's not just about me; Cole's thoughts and feelings matter, too. And Gareth's. Which is why the tears start flowing again as I break down to heaving sobs when the conclusion comes that I have to do exactly what Cole begged me to do.

I have to let him go.

Seventeen

I don't usually help the dead for compensation, but the odd favor here and there is justifiable in my opinion. Ross Kensington from ICU ward number four is more than fine with this, especially when I translate his final farewell to his wife as his body is carted away. And all Ross has to do in return is to find out and tell me the door codes used to enter the staff lounge the medical students are in.

I see Gareth with his peers through the glass panes. I feel like dashing back out in hope I don't get caught, but I'm not faking up my confidence by wearing my leather jacket and heeled ankle boots to chicken out now.

I swing open the door and need no introduction.

"Charlotte?" Gareth says straight away with wide eyes. "What are you doing here?"

I cross my arms, tapping my foot. Too much? Too late. "I need to talk to you."

"But how did you get in here?"

Someone next to him, presumably another medical student, waves hello awkwardly. Another one leaves the room, probably to get security.

Getting straight to the point while I can, I say, "Look, Gareth, there's not going to be an explanation as to why I ran off leaving you so . . . *exposed* like that when I did. I can only tell you it won't happen again."

"Now's not a good time to be—"

"Now's a great time," the guy next to him says with a big smirk on his face.

Another guy leans back on his chair and puts his feet on the couch in front of him. "Yeah. Do tell us more."

"Charlotte—"

"Just let me finish."

Gareth storms up to me and grabs me by the arm. For a moment I think he will be the one to usher me out, but he drags me to the adjoining locker room to the protests of his colleagues.

"Are you out of your mind?" He exasperates. "How did you get in?"

Ignoring his question I continue, "I mean it. I'm sorry. But this is the last time I am saying so. Because I'm not doing this anymore. I can't."

"What do you mean?"

"This," I say, flicking my hand between us. "Sneaking into the staff lounge just to see you because you're ignoring me with a man sulk."

"I wasn't ignoring you. I was giving you space. Giving *us* space."

"Space?"

"I don't know what you want, Charlotte. One minute you're interested, then the next you're not. And now I don't know what I want. And I don't think you know what you want, either."

"I want you." That isn't a lie, even though it hurts to say. But that pain is silenced by my newfound ego as I lean forward and hush softly, "*All* of you."

Guys are weak to the lure of a woman, at least that is what I'm banking on. I seem to be right, however, because his tough exterior melts away.

"Women," he mutters in one breath as his body is drawn to mine. "Can't live with 'em, can't live without 'em."

"We really do rule the world."

"You seem different."

"I guess some things came into perspective over the past couple of days."

"Is your dad . . ."

"He's fine. Really. Just some life perspectives. Starting with you. And me. I want us to start over."

It takes Gareth a long few seconds before saying, "I want that, too."

"Are you working tonight?"

"No. And with any luck holding, I should also have the next two days free."

"Good. Come to mine at six o'clock. I'm cooking."

"You're cooking?"

"Don't sound so surprised," I reply teasingly. "I hope you like pie, though."

"I like pie."

"Phew." I reposition the lapel of his coat. "My last class finishes at five. You have a key."

"I look forward to it."

He leans in for a kiss, caught out by the wolf whistling of his peers cramming their heads by the small window on the door.

"Maybe tonight," Gareth mutters.

I would nod to that, shy of any attention, wanted or not. Only that's not going to be me anymore.

"No," I say. "Maybe now."

I take hold of his neck and place my lips on his to the cheers of his fellow residents.

"All right, all right, bugger off, you lot," he says before nudging me out of their direct view and opening a locker next to him. I know it's his because photos of us from the arcade decorate the inside of the door.

"You keep those photos in your locker?"

"Is it cliché? I saw that in American movies and thought it's the norm." He looks at them and smiles. "I like it, regardless."

"I like it, too." I smile.

Gareth notices the clock. "I should probably get back to the ward. Doctor Kahn likes having an entourage of medical students following him around. I actually think he feels a bit glorified by it, but you'd never tell just by looking at him."

I nod. "I should go, too. I'm meeting my uncle at twelve."

I'm surprised by how naturally I refer to Beasey as my uncle, and it makes me shiver.

"He doesn't seem like the type of person who likes to be kept waiting."

"You're probably right. But I," I kiss him on his cheek, "expect to see you," again on the other cheek. "tonight."

I kiss him hard on the lips again before he answers. He gives in with a soppy "yuh-huh," so without another word I smirk and pace out of the building before security arrives, glancing back through the glass pane to see a flustered Gareth getting teased by his colleagues in what I'm sure is newfound popularity.

It's exactly noon when I knock on the door of Beasey's motorhome. It's hard to miss, sticking out like a sore thumb among the Mercedes and BMWs driven by the high-up staff this side of the hospital parking lot. At least I didn't have to walk far.

Beasey answers right on cue. He opens the door, cigarette in hand, but doesn't greet me. I was expecting a snide comment of sorts and am pleasantly surprised that for a few seconds he hasn't said one, until I realize he was just waiting for me to close the door behind me.

"Mommy and daddy had a fight?"

I give him a quizzical look.

"Where's Cole? Usually he sticks to you like glue."

"He's busy."

"Babysitting?"

"Probably."

Beasey takes a puff. "The kid needs to go."

"Go where?"

"You know where. This world isn't for the likes of him."

"Wow, could you sound any more fascist?"

"Charlotte!" He exasperates, stubbing out the last of his cigarette. "Whatever you think you are doing by helping that poor spirit, you're not."

"I'll deal with Timothy. When the time's right."

"And when will that be, hmm?"

"When he'll understand. He's just a kid."

"All the more reason to—"

"Drop it!"

Beasey grips onto the edge of his table and grumbles something, possibly in Italian. Or Latin. He then stands up and says, "Luckily for you we don't have time for that right now, because while you were playing happy ghost family I was doing some digging into those women."

"You're not the only one. I've done some digging myself. Get this: those screaming ghosts? They suffocated to death. Except there were no strangulation marks or signs of a struggle. It's like the air was sucked out of them or something. Maybe they were buried alive and then ran out of oxygen, but even those from the dead ringer days had broken fingernails from trying to break free from their caskets." I read the history books, unfortunately. Those poor souls. "Not these women, though. It's like they fell asleep and never woke up."

I expected Beasey to be surprised by this, or even impressed with my detective skills, but instead he sighs.

"Shit."

It's all he says, his tone only a fraction more emotional than usual. He stands and walks over to the partially open window and lights a new cigarette from his pocket. He inhales, eyes watching the traffic flow at a sluggish pace, his gray eyes untelling.

My face falls. "This isn't news to you, is it?"

He shakes his head, not looking back. "I was hoping this wouldn't be the case." He exhales before saying, "Do you remember that book I had?"

Of course I do. *Liber Manium*, or *The Book Of The Dead* in English. It was Beasey's bible, as he put it, containing all gathered information passed on from others like us over centuries and millennia, straight from the ancient civilizations of the earliest Sumerians right up to twenty-first century USA. There are only a few dozen copies in existence, only in the possession of those like us, upon pledging to the cause, the cause of the Communicators as they call themselves. I've been offered a hand of invitation from Beasey numerous times, however I'm not down for going off the radar to their headquarters somewhere in Italy to join some cult of the dead and practice exorcisms. I mean, I'm not that stupid.

Nope, I'd much rather do things my way, with Cole by my side.

Except he's not really by my side. Not anymore.

"Yeah, I remember. You ripped a load of pages out, wouldn't let me see them. Not until I join your cult, at least. You said it was *confidential*."

Beasey inhales his cigarette again, eyes still looking out the window. "I think it's time you saw those confidential pages."

"I dunno, man." I stand up cautiously. "I'm not signing any dotted lines. And I've done fair enough without your book."

Beasey doesn't seem to be listening, however. Instead, with his cigarette balanced between his lips he rummages in a compartment and takes a wooden board out before reaching up into the interior and pulling out the recognizable leather-bound black book. He flings it across the small space of his motorhome, gliding across the table to land so accurately in front of me.

I pick it up. It's clearly more tattered than before, the second half of the book held together by a quick tape job.

"I'm sure you're well aware by now we have the ability to exorcise ghosts to cross over."

"You think?"

"This isn't the time for joking, Charlotte. Read."

I open up to the first of the ripped pages. "Exorcising living vessels . . ." I give Beasey a look. "Living vessels?"

He ignores me, choosing instead to inhale another puff of his cigarette.

I continue reading. "Spirits encapsulated in living vessels, also known henceforth as active bodies, may also be exorcised given—" I pause. "Determining factors of age, health . . . case study one, Egypt, 1422 BC." I turn a few pages. "France,

1654, blah-blah . . . Denmark 1876, more blah-blah. Symptoms include . . .” I stop reading out loud. I don’t need to. Beasey knows what is written.

Static.

I put the book down.

“Wait, so what does this all have to do with those women?”

“Don’t you get what it’s saying? Exorcisms don’t just work for ghosts. They work for spirits. Dead *or* alive.”

“Woah.” I flinch back. “Let me get this straight. You’re telling me that those women were *exorcised to death*?”

Beasey nods. No words. Just a nod.

“We . . . we can do that?”

Another nod.

I huff. “Why . . . why would someone be given such power to end a life like that?”

“Murder is murder. It’s no different to stabbing or shooting someone. Anyone is capable of it, Charlotte.”

“Not like that,” I say. “Not like that.” The picture of what I’m hearing is building up in my mind. Those poor women, being sucked out of their own bodies, scared and confused.

“You’re missing the other punchline here, Charlotte: only Communicators are able to pull that off.”

I turn to him, even more shocked than I was before. “You mean . . . they were killed by . . .”

He nods again. Only this time he says, “One of us.”

I slump down, feeling numb. They say strangulation is an intimate form of murder as you are literally choking the life out of someone, at a close range, usually looking into their eyes as they die. To willingly take that life force and rip it out of someone . . . that’s a whole new level of psychosis.

“So basically there’s a crazy lunatic Communicator nearby who has figured all this out and is using it to *kill* people? Why? Why would someone do that?”

Beasey gives me a look, as if waiting for me to announce the punchline I can’t quite piece together. When I fail to come up with anything he sighs again before coming up to the table and flips the pages over before slowly pushing the book back to me, the bookmarked page clear and open for me to see.

I look at the words, faded and in old script yet clearly readable: 'BRINGING BACK THE DEAD'.

"What is this?" I ask, scouring over the pages, each one more manically than the one before. "Donor. Reverse exorcism. Spirit transfusion. Spirits can be transfused? Like blood?" I turn to Beasey. "Beasey, are you saying that the dead can come back to life?!"

"No," Beasey says quickly. "No they can't." He stubs out his cigarette in the ashtray next to me on the table, harder than necessary, before looking at me sternly in the eyes. "And I want you to remember that, Charlotte. The dead are dead. That's it."

I crease my eyebrows at his words. Of course that is the case. But then why is this even a topic of conversation?

"Well that's not what your book is saying, and it's proven itself worthy so far." I look at the pages again, wanting to absorb all of it in case Beasey changes his mind and takes the book away from me. "It's been tried. Look. The Ancient Egyptians . . . someone testing on a gladiator . . . oh, wow . . ." I scan the next few pages. "This account is dated only eight years ago!"

"But it didn't succeed." Beasey's voice is raised and sharp, a rarity that manages to take my attention from the pages in front of me. "Some people won't stop at anything to try, though."

I look back down at the page I'm reading. "I can see that."

"Keep reading."

I continue to scan over the pages again, annoyed that I don't have the time to absorb every word. This is huge. This is God-level huge.

Beasey fills in the gist of it, though. "To bring a ghost back from the dead you would need a bodily vessel. A body that's usable."

"Okay," I say slowly, not liking where this is going.

"Not many dead bodies fit that description, do they? If they did, they would be occupied by a spirit—*their* spirit—and they'd be alive. Unless, in theory, a healthy body has been provided. A body that was occupying a spirit just moments before."

I stop and look up at Beasey. He looks back at me, eyes solid, as I figure out the jigsaw puzzle in my mind, to put the final pieces together and say what the picture reveals.

I swallow. "The killer's practicing."

Beasey nods. Without saying anything further he lights another cigarette. The lack of ventilation in his motorhome is starting to fill my throat with second-hand tobacco smoke, but I say nothing. He looks like he needs it. Maybe I do, too.

"Shit." It's all I can mutter. "Maybe the killer's not really a killer and is just trying to help them?"

Beasey stares out the window as he takes in my suggestion. I notice how stiff he becomes, bar his cigarette bobbing slightly to his trembling fingers. "No." He shakes his head. "The screaming says it all. Those women had no other injuries. They were found in a forest. It wasn't voluntary. Especially the end result."

"But if it's so impossible then why does he keep trying?"

Beasey says nothing as he takes another puff. He looks agitated, stressed. No, he *is* agitated and stressed. I feel it emanating from him.

Beasey's cracking.

This isn't good.

"Because some people don't like to believe that." His voice is slightly hoarse, his eyes almost sympathetic.

"What do we do?" I feel almost too nervous to ask.

"We find out who the killer is."

"And how are we going to do that? The police have few leads as it is."

"The police can't talk to the dead."

"We can't either. They've crossed over, Beasey."

"We'll get the next one."

"Next one?"

"The killer won't stop trying. Not if they think there's a chance they'll succeed."

"But you just said that's impossible—"

"You need to leave." He strides across his motorhome, taking his book in the process. "My shift starts in fourteen minutes."

"Seriously?"

"Duty calls. Work duty, that is."

"So, what, that's it? Just wait around until the next poor innocent woman comes screaming out in front of us?"

"Yes. And we'll be ready. The spirit will probably be drawn to the closest Communicator. If that's you then you know what to do."

I huff, then start to leave.

"Charlotte," Beasey says as I step out of his motorhome. "Don't go tampering with forces that are beyond your understanding and control."

I want to say something back to him, something clever and cocky at the same time, but I have nothing. My mind is a chorus of a dozen thoughts at once, each one blaring over the other as I drive home.

Spirit transfusion.

The dead can come back to life.

Theoretically.

"Charlotte?" I barely notice Cole say my name. I don't even recall arriving at my apartment or passing by Timothy, yet I'm sitting on my couch. "Are you okay?"

I look at Cole. He has concern in his eyes. Concern and care, like he usually does. He's always so kind. He always puts others first, even at the cost of his own life. He deserves better, some justification for all he's gone through. If there is a chance . . . a small chance that he could . . . be *alive* again, I will find it.

I have to.

For him.

For us.

"Yes." I smile. "More than okay."

I don't know what to do.

That was the thought as I watched Cole and Timothy leave, the thought as I bailed on class, and the thought as I postponed dinner with Gareth, my mind unable to focus on other things. It was the thought as the time on my phone crossed over to the next day, and the thought throughout my classes in the morning. Even now as Cole sits across from me, that same thought rings in my mind, an alarm I can't seem to turn off.

Cole is a ghost. But what if Cole didn't have to be a ghost? However impossible that sounds. Okay, so a body would be needed. A healthy body. But does someone really have to die to make one available? Surely a body that's no longer in use could become viable under the right conditions, right? Rory probably has access to one or two every week. Not that I could just pick and choose a new Cole. But theoretically it could work. And Beasey knows how.

Maybe.

Only he's hiding things.

Possibly.

Am I hiding things too by not telling Cole?

Probably.

But I can't tell him, not yet. Not until I know for sure. It could make things worse for us otherwise. I can't get his hopes up. I can't get *our* hopes up.

Except there isn't any *our* or *us* anymore.

I sigh, frustrated with myself. As soon as I commit to one guy, life pulls me in the other direction.

"It's simple," Timothy says as if he can read my mind. We're sitting on my couch, Timothy intentionally placed between myself and Cole. We're supposed to be watching a cartoon, only he's seen this episode "five times already" so he's taken to playing twenty questions with us instead.

He turns to Cole. "Do you love Charlotte?"

"Yes."

He then turns to me. "Do you love Cole?"

"Yes, I do."

"Then why aren't you two married?"

The innocence in his question is uplifting, if not a heartbreaking reminder of the predicament I'm in.

"Because, Timothy," Cole says in that tone adults communicate to children with. "Look at my hand. Do you see how my hand is different to hers?"

"Cole," I whisper sternly.

Timothy looks from Cole's hand to mine, and then back to Cole's again before looking at his own. "Mine, too."

"Cole," I warn.

"Yes, yours too. We're different, you and I. Do you know why?"

"No."

"Cole," I hiss his name, but I give him a pleading look. "Don't."

He ignores me however, and while I want to stop him, I also know he's about to do what I've been too weak-hearted to do myself.

"Do you know what a ghost is, Timothy?"

"Yes. They're scary."

"What makes you think they're scary?"

"They stay in houses and scare people at night in their bed."

"Charlotte here can see ghosts."

Timothy looks up, surprised. "You can see ghosts?"

"Yes," I say. "And some ghosts are actually very nice. I'm

even friends with them."

"Ghosts are your friends?" Timothy asks. After I nod he looks to Cole for extra clarification.

"It's true," Cole says. "They're not scary. In fact, did you know that *I* am a ghost?"

Timothy's head jerks back at this. "*You're* a ghost?"

"I sure am."

Timothy then turns to me for extra clarification.

"He's a ghost," I say, forcing a smile. "Cole isn't scary, is he?"

Timothy hesitantly shakes his head.

"I'm a cool ghost, right? But that's why I can't marry Charlotte, even though I love her." Cole then jumps to his feet and makes a wooing sound. "Because I'm a ghost!"

This makes Timothy laugh, watching Cole do silly stints like fall through the chair only to reappear through the wall. And for a moment I warm up inside as I see myself in Timothy, the confused little child finding laughter again because of Cole's efforts.

Timothy claps at Cole as he reappears in front of us in a "ta-da" moment. I clap too, although I feel Cole tense up slightly by my side. We both see Timothy stare at his own hands, his light slowly dimming gray.

"Timothy?"

I think he knows. Deep down I think he's just figured it out. He looks at our hands and I see it in his eyes, putting the puzzle together. His mouth scrunches up, words forming in his mind, and he probably would have confirmed it himself if Cole had not gotten there first.

"Am I a ghost, too?"

"Yes. You're a ghost too, Timothy."

I don't know how Cole can remain so casual when he says it. It's the only thing keeping me poised.

"Why . . . why am *I* a ghost?"

"The thing is, Timothy, your mommy did something bad and, well, you died."

"Cole," I mutter harshly.

"No! She wouldn't do that! My mommy loves me!" He starts yelling, in the way children do when yearning for their mothers.

"I'm sure she does." I try to sound reassuring when I say the words. Except she doesn't, because loving mothers don't kill their own child in attempted murder-suicide. Not in my opinion, anyway.

"Sometimes adults don't always do the right thing, Timothy," Cole says. "My mommy was mean to me."

Timothy sniffs. "She was?"

"Yeah. Every day."

Cole rarely brings up his parents. His father was absent and his mother apparently cared for alcohol more than him. He doesn't even care for any reconciliation with them. If he asked me to I would, without hesitation, but he doesn't want that. I have come to accept that some families just don't work, which is more common than not. A happy family is a rarity, and looks can be deceiving. There are always skeletons in the closet, I guess. Always appearances being kept up. Until it ends up with cases like Timothy.

"But you're good, Timothy. That's the main thing. Because that means you can go into Heaven."

"Heaven?"

"Yes. Up in the stars."

"The stars?" Timothy shakes his head. "I don't like heights. I'll fall down."

Cole chuckles. "Don't worry. You can fly in heaven."

Timothy's eyes light up. "Fly?"

"Yup."

"What about mommy? I'm waiting for her. She said she'll be here soon."

"Your mommy will go later," I reassure him. "She's just a bit sick right now and needs to get better. Sick people can't fly."

"I want to see Mommy now."

"I'll take you there," Cole offers.

Timothy shakes his head. "No. I'll go."

He's gone without another word, leaving Cole and I to face each other alone.

"Are you going to go after him?" I ask.

"No," Cole eventually replies. "He'll probably just withdraw more if I don't give him space. Kids are like that."

Not just kids, Cole.

He points at the cupboard with the few candles in. "Are you ready?"

"Are you sure you want to do this again?"

"Yes. It's needed. Light 'em up."

I grudgingly comply. I can't even take in the added emotion from what just happened as well as everything else, so instead I focus on why he's here. There's a murderer out there, after all. A dangerous one.

"Remember what Beasey said," Cole says, business as usual. "Don't attach emotion to me."

"Fine. But I'm not tormenting you through the karma of your death. It's done. It's over with."

"Charlotte."

I fold my arms.

Cole sighs. Nothing is spoken, only the ticking of the wall clock prolonging the awkwardness between us.

"Fine," he eventually says. "Begin."

"But what stimulus do you have?"

"Don't worry about that." His aura is already dimming as he asks, eyes averted, "Ready?"

It turns out I don't have any other option because that's the moment it happens. A woman, a scream, only this one wasn't so much a panic scream as much as a loud whimper.

Cole and I glance at one another before I put my practice to the test, holding her spirit in place while I can. I then look to Cole for reassurance. I spent so much time preparing for this moment that I didn't plan for what to do after.

"What's going on?" she asks with a wail.

I start with the obvious. "What is your name?"

"Scarlet. Scarlet Barnes-Curtis."

Good. An uncommon name is easier to track down online.

"Where are you?" Cole demands to know, obviously more prepared for this than I am.

"I . . . I don't know," she stutters in panic. "Where am I?"

"We don't have time to explain," I reply, feeling my grip on her already weakening. "Think. Where were you? What did you see?"

"I don't know."

"Think!"

"A room . . . dark. Light. No, candles. Candlelight."

"Did you see anybody? Any pictures or faces or signs?"

"Yeah, he was there."

"Who is 'he'?"

"I'm not too sure. I just met him."

"Well then what did he look like?" I quickly ask.

"I don't know. It was dark."

"Anything! Hair color, size—"

"Tall. Quite young, maybe my age? Why can't I . . ." she looks down at herself. "What's wrong with me?"

"Anything else, Scarlet?" Cole presses.

Scarlet pauses to think, each second becoming more and more scarce. "He . . . he leaned over me. I couldn't understand him; he was talking gibberish, although he did say something about death throwing punches but he'll go for broke. I think he wasn't alone because he called for someone."

"She's slipping," I whisper to Cole.

"Who?" Cole asks.

Scarlet thinks as I strain to hold her. "Missy? Lissa? No. Melissa. Yeah, Melissa. Hey, did something happen to me? Am I . . . am I dead?"

I don't know what to say. But I realize I don't even have time to.

"I'm sorry," I reply. "I'm so, so sorry."

And with that she slips and is gone.

Cole goes after her, but I know there's nothing left to go after. This is confirmed when he reappears a few seconds later and we both collapse onto the couch together.

"It's something to work with," Cole eventually says, breaking the eerie quiet of the room and the chaos in my mind.

"Yeah," I agree.

"How are you?"

I shrug. "Just felt a life slip away in my grasp."

Cole turns to me. "Charlotte—"

"I'm in love with a dead guy but I like a living guy."

"Charlotte—"

"Timothy learned he's a ghost, killed by his own mother."

"Charlotte—"

"My father was in the hospital."

"Come—"

"I have to race against the clock to catch a serial killer between classes and work and dating."

"Let me—"

"And I could really do with a coffee right now."

"Hey—"

"Maybe an espresso."

"Charlotte stop—"

"And Gareth is coming for dinner soon—"

"Please—"

"I need to make a pie—"

"Stop!" It wasn't a shout but an order firm enough to take my attention as he places his hands on my own. "It's okay, Charlotte. It will be okay."

His energy is caring, reassuring, as are his eyes, just like the Cole I'm used to. But it's not enough to stop me from asking, "Will it?"

I don't know what to do.

"It's okay. I'm here. We'll figure this out together."

Bringing the dead back to life.

Cole raises his arm and places it behind me. It can't be hidden; we both know his arm was intending to hold me, something I want most in the world right now. That and Scarlet Barnes-Curtis to be back in her body, alive, where she should be.

"It's not okay," I whimper. "None of this is."

"She met the light," Cole utters softly. "She's okay. I felt it."

I hang my head low, holding hope to those words.

"I meant it, what I said before," I eventually have the nerve to say.

"The being in love with a dead guy thing?"

I nod.

"I know," he whispers back, although it was more of a sigh.

I turn to Cole, and even through the tears in my eyes I see the glistening in his own eyes. But he then straightens himself, professional demeanor back intact.

"One more try? Since you're the Communicator of choice for these women it's probably good to get the practice in."

"Uh, sure. If you're ready," I reply as if everything's normal again. "What was your stimulus, by the way? For going dark?"

Cole turns away. "That's not important."

I frown. "Open communication, remember?"

He frowns, but he eventually gives in. "I just thought about something I saw the other night."

I can guess which night.

I reach my hand out to him but he gets off the couch, the light of him becoming shadow as he backs away and begins to fade. "Don't."

"Cole—"

"I said *don't*. This has to stop. You need to accept that I'm dead, Charlotte. *Dead*."

"What if that could change?" I blurt out in a bout of emotion.

He freezes. "What?"

"What if that could change?" I ask again before biting my tongue. "Beasey said—" I shake my head, not quite sure what he said.

Cole takes two cautionary steps closer. "What did Beasey say?"

"I'm . . . not sure. But his book, the missing pages he ripped out, they're about bringing the dead back . . . back to life."

Cole is deadpan, taking in the words I say seriously and

thoughtfully. The wall clock echoes second after second until Cole brushes his hand through his hair. "I'll be back."

He's gone before I can get word in, but I have nothing to say over the alarm in my mind ringing louder than before.

What have I done, projecting false hope like that? And even if it's not false hope, if by any chance it could be something more, where do we stand now? What if Cole could come back? In whatever inconceivable way, what would happen then? What if I could save Timothy, too?

Bringing the dead back to life.

And what about Gareth? He's coming over for dinner soon. What was meant to be a grand reconciliation between us, a new beginning . . . how can I face Gareth right now? Am I just like his ex?

I pace to the bathroom and have a long hot shower, the need to let my emotions run adrift in the running water. Except when I step out I still don't know what to do. I start on dinner when two loud knocks at the door startle me out of my thoughts. I slip on a sweater and yoga pants, then running my towel through my damp hair I open the door to Beasey and Cole.

"We need to talk."

∞∞∞∞∞

I breathe into my hands, the signs of winter approaching no longer avoidable. I'm not outside because I want to be, but the people walking by in the local park helps to keep me calm. Because I'm more likely to remain composed with people around, and I don't know how composed I'll be after this.

"So start talking, Beasey," I demand, taking charge for once. "*All* of it, this time."

"Why are we out here? It's cold."

I fold my arms. I'm both angry and cold, but I want to show only one of those feelings. "I just feel like some fresh air, okay? Spill."

"You're getting ahead of yourself."

"Oh, am I?" I retort sarcastically.

"You should place a little more faith in me."

"And why would I do that? Since I first met you in the school hallway trying to exorcise Cole you've done nothing but lie to me."

"I really hope you're not still hung up on that. And I haven't lied to you, Charlotte. I work on a need to know basis."

I roll my eyes. "See? That sort of shit is exactly why you're a big walking red flag. I mean, I don't even know what your name is."

"It's Beasey."

"Your *full* name? And what sort of name is that, anyway?"

Cole backs away. "I'm going to check on Timothy. I think he's had enough time to process things."

He vanishes, but I don't stop him. It's probably for the best right now.

"Ah, yes. The adopted ghost child. Did you really think this would play out to happy endings, Charlotte?"

"This isn't about him," I rebuke. "You can't just leave me on the cliffhanger that the dead might be able to come back to life!"

"Cole is dead."

"No shit."

"That's how he'll remain."

The words sting in my chest, but I refuse to let it hurt. Not yet.

"Your book seems to say otherwise."

Beasey rubs his temples. "This is exactly what I thought would happen. Which is why I didn't let you see those pages in the first place."

He stops as someone strolls by slowly while staring down at their phone. I almost argue that she can't hear us but she glances our way, our sudden silence noticeable, before she paces onwards.

I turn back to Beasey who then continues, "Transplanted organs rarely ever get accepted by a body without a lot of drug intervention. Well the same concept can also be applied with spirits, except there's no such drug. One body, one spirit."

"But if we could for at least some time, just a short time—"

"At whose expense?" Beasey interrupts.

"Plenty of bodies in the world, Beasey."

"Charlotte."

"I can do it."

"Don't think that way."

"I'll find a way."

"It doesn't work like that."

"How do you know?" I demand to know. "You are always keeping things from me yet just expect me to blindly believe you?"

"Believe me on this."

"Why should I?" I retort.

"Because I'm trying to protect you."

"Protect me from what?"

"From the heartache I know you will endure!"

I flinch at his words. I've never heard Beasey speak like *that* before. Raising his voice was one thing, but the way he spoke, the emotion that escaped his crackled voice, the vulnerability in his eyes, his usual staunch composure fractured.

I open my mouth to amass some snappy reply, but I'm rendered speechless. I think back to what he just said to make him this way, the heartache he knows I will endure. What would Beasey know about heartache, and how could he know unless—

Oh my God.

Beasey knows.

Beasey knows the heartache I will endure.

Because like me, Beasey was in love.

With a ghost.

My anger mollifies. "What was her name?"

"Margaret," Beasey replies, knowing that I now know. "Margaret Dallas."

He closes his eyes, taking in the sound of the rustling leaves as I watch as the creases from his forehead relax and emotion form, as if—however rare the moment calls for—he's allowing some chaos in his own mind.

"I loved her. And when I lost her I lost part of myself."

He doesn't go into details, but it's enough, I realize, from the waves of empathy forming within me.

He opens his eyes, still looking ahead. "That case study eight years ago was *my* case study. I had help, too; multiple Communicators tried together. You can get a few minutes, or maybe half an hour if you're lucky. You keep thinking that next time will be longer, that you can break the God code. It almost becomes addictive. You start to think just one more body, just one more try."

I shouldn't pry, but I want to know. "So she left you to stop you from trying?"

"No, Charlotte. *I* had to make *her* go." He glances to the trees, wondering if he should say what he's about to. "She was okay with staying behind, and I was relieved at first. It didn't matter how she was because she was still Margaret. But the years went by and as much as I didn't want to see it, I did."

"See what?"

"Her depletion." He sighs softly. "Ghosts begin to lose themselves if they hang around for too long without unfinished business or trauma holding them here. Her memories meant less and started to fade. She was fighting the light for me, and once I realized that I knew she had to cross over."

I know where he is going with this, why he turns to give me a look. I shake my head. I don't know why; it won't change anything. I do it anyway though, and even whimper a quiet, "No."

"This is what I was protecting you from. This is why I warned you so many times, Charlotte, not to get attached to Cole."

"Charlotte," Cole hushes. How long has he been here for? "It's okay."

"No, it's not okay!" I almost weep, not even caring about the jogger who slows down to look at me. "It will never be okay!"

"Charlotte-bella!"

I turn to see Maria and Kelly approaching.

Crap.

"Maria, Kelly!" I force a smile. Glancing back at Beasey it's suddenly appearances as normal again. I wave a hello to them and once they reach us I say, "Beasey, you remember Kelly? This is her aunt Maria."

"He's Charlotte's *uncle*," Kelly quips slyly.

"A pleasure to meet you," Maria says to Beasey, offering a handshake.

I expect Beasey to flash his fake smile and say hello. Heck, even just say he has to go to work. But Beasey kissing Maria on the hand? Nope, wasn't expecting that. Nor was Kelly by the looks of it.

"Buonasera, Maria."

Maria places her free hand on her chest and grins cheerfully. "Il tuo Italiano è eccellente."

Kelly and I share a glance as her aunt and Beasey go over Italian small talk. At least, I assume it is just that. Maria seems very happy to be communicating in Italian again, while Beasey just seems somewhat . . . *happy.*

"Do I want to know what was going on here before we crossed paths? You look like you could do with a few shots of tequila."

Tequila shots would be a start to numb all I feel right now.

"I'm fine," I lie. "Just serious talk."

Kelly frowns but doesn't ask further. She may tell it how it is, but she is also figuring out when to leave it as it is.

"How are you?" I ask to change the topic.

"Good. Maria and I are making our way to the community orchestra performance down by the town hall. You're welcome to join us. Although," she glances back to Beasey and her aunt, "I think your *uncle* already is."

I look back to Beasey and Maria chatting away. I think I'll leave them to it, the serious conversation from before clearly over with. Cole must have left too, because he's not in sight.

"You go on ahead. I've got things to do."

"Things with Gareth?"

Crap, we're supposed to be having dinner soon. I put up a smile and excuse myself. At least this gets me away from watching Beasey impressing Maria. I excuse myself and head back, thinking over everything that was talked about while making dinner. Usually I would lie on the trampoline at home in such times, the calming sound of nature and the tranquilizing stars in the Milky Way to put my problems into perspective. Cole would also be there, a voice of reason and reassurance. But right now the muffled sound of the television from the apartment below and distant police sirens are all I have to hear, and social media pictures of now-dead Scarlet Barnes-Curtis once enjoying her life and the pie in the oven are all I have to stare at while I ponder things.

Then again, what is there to even ponder about? I had hope, and it's been quenched. Back to normal, then.

Life carries on.

For the living.

Three knocks on the door means it's action time.

I put Beasey's candles to another use and set up a candlelight dinner. It's not much, but it's a decent attempt at romance in my little loft apartment. And it works, because for a couple of hours I manage to forget about everything going on. Gareth does well to make me laugh, and if he doesn't like my cooking he doesn't show it because his plate is empty. He stocks up my emergency beer stash which is cool of him, although we go through half of it watching a movie on my couch together.

"You seem deep in thought," he says as the credits roll. "Too deep for *21 Jump Street*."

"I can't believe I've never seen this movie before."

"Just wait until you find out there's a *22 Jump Street*."

I laugh. "I'm fine, I just had a serious discussion with my uncle earlier, that's all. It's hanging over me a bit."

"Do you want to talk about it?"

"He's just trying to keep me in line, like the concerning

uncle he is. It's nothing, really. Thanks, though."

"He seems like a serious fella, your uncle. Was he in the military or something?"

"Something," I reply slyly.

He waits a short moment before nodding. "Well, I'll get going and let you sleep—"

"No," I reply all too quickly. "Please don't."

I don't even have to ask. He wraps his arms around mine and I sink into the warmth and comforting smell of him. I hold onto him tight, my rock, my life ring in the storm.

"Are you sure you're okay?"

I nod against his chest. "I'm just glad you're here."

He kisses my forehead. "I can sleep here if you want me to. I even have my own shower gel this time."

"Please."

"I'll sleep on the couch, though. I don't want you to feel pressured—"

I don't let him finish because I place my finger on his lips. "No," I whisper. "Sleep with me."

He hesitates—understandably—at my words, but I silence his doubts by meeting his lips with my own. We quickly find ourselves upstairs on my bed, Gareth gently yet eagerly pulling my shirt off me between light and playful kisses down my body. His shirt meets mine on the floor, before the rest of our clothes, and once again we find ourselves where we were before.

"Beautiful." His voice is low, husky, his pupils big and dark. Wild, instinctive movements follow as his line of sight moves from my neck down to my thighs.

"Are you sure this time?" he asks, a condom suddenly in his hand.

I panic for a moment, my mind going through all the reasons why I shouldn't. A screaming ghost could appear, or Beasey could come knocking. Heck, I wouldn't put it past Mr. Dodgley to call at this hour. Not to mention Cole could appear again.

But Cole isn't here. And Gareth is.

And everything else can wait, because from the chaos of my

mind to the quiet of this moment, nothing else really matters right now.

"Yes," I reply, pulling him down to me. "I'm sure."

∞ 215 ∞

Nineteen

Sex with Gareth changed everything. They warn the first time can be awkward or uncomfortable, except everything with him felt good. It confirms we are committed as a couple. Boyfriend and girlfriend.

We stayed this way for the following two days; a happy, normal couple, going on walks, eating out, watching movies together, as if everything that happened beforehand wasn't real. Which is probably why, after he kisses me goodbye and leaves with the promise that he'll message me after his classes, as I close my door behind him, when the quiet hits and I'm left looking down at the ruffled bed sheets and condom wrappers telling the story of the past two days that were, that's when I run to the bathroom and throw up in the toilet. And when my stomach feels like it's got nothing left to let out, I look at myself in the mirror. Tears of self-pity stream down my cheeks, all red and puffy, but I don't deserve pity. I deserve nothing good. I feel like a traitor, a cheat.

Because I like Gareth. A lot.

But I still love Cole.

Is this how normal people feel when they move on after losing their loved ones from a break-up or death? *Am* I moving on, considering I still see Cole around?

My phone flashes again. Beasey's trying to call me but it will have to wait, along with the other twelve calls and messages he's left about wanting to see me this morning, because I have class shortly.

But as soon as I step beyond my apartment block I see the all-too familiar motorhome pull up and Beasey stepping out to face me.

"Charlotte, enjoyed your sleep in? Nothing like a mid-morning slumber while innocents are being murdered."

"Hey," I snap, quickly deflating my anger as I mumble, "I was busy."

"Sleep faster next time." He gestures inside. "And check your voicemail. Don't you kids always have one eye on your phones?"

"There's a difference between checking messages and replying to them," I chide as I grudgingly step inside. I glance at Cole before quickly looking away. As if I have something to hide. To which I'm not even sure if I do.

I sigh internally. I'm terrible at acting inconspicuously.

"Well I got fed up with calling so I sent Cole after you, but for some reason he refused." He looks at Cole quizzically. "Not another drama, I hope?"

Cole and I avoid eyes, the truth of how I spent the past weekend not needing confirmation.

"What do you want, Beasey? I have class shortly."

Beasey slides his phone across the table. "Scarlet's body has been found."

I clench my jaw, fighting the anger within me from coming out as it sinks into grief. "As expected."

"Read it."

I sigh, but pick up his phone and comply. "Aspiring gymnast found dead in suspected suicide." I look at Beasey. "Suicide? *Suicide*? It wasn't suicide, she was murdered!"

The anger must be fuming out from me because Cole has to step in. "She was. By a sick, twisted individual. *We* know that. And once we can figure this out then maybe her family can know that, too."

I sit down, defeated.

"Keep reading," Beasey orders. "Scarlet was last seen filling up her car with gas across the city on Tuesday evening. But you and I both know she died on—"

"Tuesday afternoon," I finish, the realization hitting me in a wave of anxiety.

Shit.

He's doing it.

Whoever is doing the spirit transfers is actually doing it.

Which means . . .

"Charlotte," Beasey says in a voice of caution, as if he can read my mind. "It doesn't work."

"Right. Because you know best, obviously. Even when the evidence right here suggests otherwise."

"The killer had the body and it still didn't work. The point here is that the police aren't linking the cases together because there's nothing to suggest otherwise. The killer knows their usual body disposal won't work anymore. So whoever was inside Scarlet's body expected the eventual failure of the body accepting them, and made it pass as a suicide."

"They're obviously working together," Cole says. "The killer and the spirit. But why?"

I know why. Beasey knows too, but he's waiting for me to say it, to admit it out loud.

"Love." I swallow. "He's doing it for love."

Beasey nods solemnly. "Love pushes people to do crazy things."

I don't know if that was intended for me but I don't give him a response. Cole, however, isn't as stubborn.

"Different paths."

"The killer is probably finding a replacement for this Melissa lover of his, and given the age of the victims we can assume that Melissa—and the killer himself—are of similar ages. Now, my invisible contact on the inside says that the authorities have nothing to go on with the other young women. That's a good thing; the less attention they get, the better."

"Try telling that to the victims," I mutter.

Ignoring me, Beasey continues, "We still have to find the

killer before the victim tally increases. Or worse, before the killer slips up and the authorities close in."

"And what do we do once we find him?"

Neither Beasey nor Cole give me an answer straight away. I should have figured it out then and there. Maybe it's my lack of caffeine fix, something my body now seems to need, or maybe it's remnants of my childhood innocence refusing to abandon me.

"Charlotte," Beasey eventually says. "Communicators can be very dangerous. We need to stop the killer before they kill even more people. Innocent people."

"How?"

"In whatever way we can. Including the way *we* can."

I huff. I can't believe what I'm hearing. "Are you telling me I've got to *kill* someone?!"

"Not if I'm there to do it," Beasey replies. "But if I can't . . . if there's ever a time when you're in danger and the situation calls for it . . . just like knowing how to use a gun."

"Using a gun is a little different from exorcism, Beasey." I don't even know how to use a gun.

"It's just another method. The results are the same."

"So, what, we're going to train in how to kill people now? Who's going to be the test subject for that? Cole—in all his martyrdom—can't be the sacrifice for that one, even if he wants to be."

"I will."

My eyes bulge at Beasey. "What?'

"You can exorcise me."

"Are you out of your mind?!"

"You can put me back. My body, my spirit."

I look to Cole for support, to confirm that what Beasey's suggesting isn't—as Gareth would say in that accent of his—*complete and utter bonkers*. Only he doesn't say anything, and I'm left to defend my own opinion.

"You're insane." I stand to leave. "You're utterly insane."

"We'll meet after your class."

"I have a study group meetup and then work after class."

"What time does that finish?"

"Five. Hopefully."

"Fine. We'll meet at five. I have the night shift, anyway."

"I'm with Gareth tonight," I hesitantly add.

"Charlotte," Beasey starts, "while I applaud your dating move to a more carbon-based lifeform, please remember that this is a serial killer we're dealing with here. And we need to stay ahead of the police."

"There's still Melissa to find," Cole mentions.

"The name Melissa isn't really a lead."

"It's something we have that they don't."

My phone vibrates. It's Gareth, but I can't reply to his naughty flirtatious message right now. "I have to go to work," I say instead. I pick up my bag. "You're insane," I remind Beasey, pointing at him before pointing at Cole. "And you're just as bad for not backing me up."

I leave and pace off to class, glad neither of them come after me. Are they really insane? Planning to kill a normal (well, sort of) living person? And clearly something is working on the whole body transfer thing. Not that I'm saying the method is right, but even just a couple of hours to be alive again . . . it wouldn't be enough to tick off a bucket list, but to just be able to eat a favorite food or hold a loved one close one last time . . .

This new compilation of thoughts doesn't subside through class and my study group, which really doesn't help me take in anything I'm supposed to be learning. What if I simply couldn't do it and kill Beasey instead? What would I do with his dead body? How would I explain to the jury that my old high school janitor just happened to run out of air and died in my apartment? I sigh and rub my temples, either the stress or lack of caffeine getting to me.

Not being able to contribute much to the study group, I pick up a takeaway coffee from the campus café before heading to work, although Cole's sudden appearance almost makes me drop the cup.

"You're right."

It's the first time Cole has directly spoken to me since Beasey's revelation that Cole won't be coming back to life and since I committed to Gareth. I have so much I want to say to him, so much I want to shout and cry. But I can't right now, so I instead hold it together and simply reply, "Thanks." I pause before adding, "What for?"

"Exorcising Beasey."

I take a sip of my coffee. It tastes cheap, as always. I can now tell the difference between student coffee and café coffee, my taste buds expecting better. It's ironic that I don't buy all my coffees from work, but Mr. Dodgley doesn't believe in staff discounts and I don't believe in supporting Mr. Dodgley.

"But you should still go through with it."

I scowl at him. "Why?"

"I just want you to be able to protect yourself, to defend yourself."

"Wow, how touching. Anything else you wish to say since you came all this way to see me?"

"Charlotte, this is serious." Cole appears in front of me which makes me stop in my tracks. I respect the dead enough not to walk through them, not intentionally at least. That, and it just makes me feel weird. Cole knows this, and since he's blocking the sidewalk I take a seat on a nearby bench and take out my phone. It's ironic how most of my phone usage comes without my phone actually being used.

"You're not passing on messages from grandmas or mailing inheritance forms out to long-lost relatives anymore," Cole continues. "It's dangerous territory you're stepping into, and I won't always be able to save you. So please," he rakes his hand through his hair, "if not for yourself, then for me."

I fold my arms, my frustration turning weak from his concern for me.

"Okay," I say.

"Thank you."

We look at each other, both unsure of what to do or say.

"How's Timothy?" I eventually ask.

"He's doing alright, considering. He keeps visiting his mom. He's still trying to understand, but I think it helps."

"If you ever want me to visit your parents for you . . ."

"Don't worry. I've passed that trauma. I feel nothing for them anymore. As far as I'm concerned I have no family."

"I'm your family, Cole."

His features soften at this, a reminder of what we are to one another. "Yeah," he says, finding a smile. "You are."

"I miss this," I blurt out quietly when the moment is over. "Us. Like this."

"Charlotte, I'm still here for you. Just not in the way you want it to be."

"Then why are you here?" I bite my lip, instantly regretting my big mouth. "Sorry. I didn't mean it like that."

"You know why. But you will always be in my heart."

"Gareth and I had sex."

I regret the words as soon as I say them, but the guilt is consuming me and I'm selfish, selfishly needing to know how his energy reacts. Does it make him angry? Sad? Jealous?

Cole doesn't react, however, still holding his gaze on me.

"Congratulations," he says laconically.

"It was good."

"I would hope so."

"And . . . physical."

Cole exasperates. "Charlotte, I know what you're doing and it's not going to work. I'm happy for you. Really. Gareth's a good guy. You're living as you should be."

Dammit. Why does he have to be so mature?

"Thanks."

He nods, no further explanation needed, but instead of the feared awkwardness he manages a smile. It's small, but it holds.

And that's enough to realize a new truth, the truth that he really is letting me go.

I can't complain. I really can't anymore. Because now I don't have to carry the guilt of my feelings for Gareth.

So why don't I feel relieved?

My phone vibration suddenly takes our attention.

"You can answer him."

I 'm about to say it's not important, that it can wait. But he's done talking; I know the signs. He looks at me, eyes so telling of thoughts so hidden, and as he retreats into himself he vanishes like he usually does.

I eventually answer and listen to Gareth talk about his shift and how a new nurse pulled out a catheter at the wrong time. His work stories are certainly something, and it keeps me distracted until I arrive at work and say bye with the promise to message later. I feel ready and focused for the shift, thankful I don't have to deal with catheter cleanup, however when I enter it isn't Mr. Dodgley counting sugar sachets on the counter or even Juliet looking gloomy at the corner table that distracts me. It's the newspaper on the complimentary magazine stand, slightly flopped at the corner but still easily readable:

'Natural Causes? No Sign Of Foul Play With Women Found Dead In Forest; Police Still Appeal For Leads'

"Hey, Charlotte." Juliet is suddenly by my side. "Those poor young women," she comments. "Didn't they run out of water or something?"

I shake my head. "They didn't plan for a hike."

"They don't have to," Juliet counters.

"No, they—" I pause, remembering to not let on I know what Rory knows. "The police are still working on it," I adjust my words.

"Well, depressing newspaper headlines aside, how have you been? It's been a while."

I don't even know how to answer Juliet. "Good," I lie. "What brings you here?"

"Two reasons: to check out the place you and Kelly work at. I'm surprised I haven't been here before; this place seems cool."

"Really? Here? The coffee's overpriced and the boss blasts

the aircon up if he thinks you've been loitering for too long."

"Okay, I guess cool is a stretch. But the interior's nice."

I look around at the sterile-looking benches and walls. Aside from the few local artists displaying their work for sale on the wall I'd say it's the least-welcoming café I've ever been in. I guess the city-dwellers would see it as 'chic' or 'minimalist'.

"What's the other reason? Kelly's not in until later."

Juliet shakes her head slightly. "Actually you're the reason. I figured I'd tell you myself so you don't hear it as secondhand back chatter, but Rory just broke up with me."

My eyes bulge. "Oh, really? Why?"

Juliet shrugs slightly. "I'm not too sure to be honest. He became distant recently, said he didn't see it working out. I was just wondering if you knew anything?"

"I don't. Sorry."

I see the disappointment in Juliet's eyes that I can't give her any leads. I look away, suddenly feeling disappointed in myself for not being as social with them as I probably should be. I know I've got a lot going on, but friendship is also important.

"Guys can be like that," I add. "One emotion and then suddenly the opposite. And the assumption is that women are the complicated ones."

"Guys suck."

I notice Mr. Dodgley's disapproval of chatter. "I'd better start work. We'll have a proper catch-up sometime soon. I promise."

Juliet smiles sadly and waves bye.

My work shift is boring, but that's certainly no complaint. It gives me time to think things over in my mind, especially while cleaning. As selfish as it is, Juliet's guy drama provides an escape from the usual thoughts about murders, ghosts and mysteries. I'm close to finishing my shift when Kelly walks in.

"Your *uncle* likes my aunt."

"What?"

Kelly adds a stack of dirty plates to the pile. "I see it. It's my talent, remember? It's going to happen. They spoke for ages after you left. Now, my Italian doesn't go far beyond reading a menu, but it sounded as gushy as their gazes were."

If it's possible to both smirk and cringe at the same time I've done just that. There was definitely something there. But then again, it's Beasey. The master of cunning.

"I . . . don't know."

"You know I'm right about these things. Like with you and Gareth. Speaking of such, I haven't heard much from you lately."

"Sorry," I reply. "Been busy. With my *uncle*."

That's all the excuse she needs to back down, but not before muttering, "None of us heard from Gareth lately, either."

I can't help the blush behind my smile.

Kelly smirks, a big smug smile across her face as she places an order on a tray and walks past. "It's quiet enough so no overtime for you. Go escape while you can. But we're *so* talking about this tomorrow."

I do as she says, relieved to be leaving before the night shift gets going. That is until I see Beasey waiting for me.

"What are you doing here?" I almost seethe, but notice Mr. Dodgley is in earshot. "*Uncle*."

"Here to pick up my niece." Beasey grins. "And making sure she doesn't make other plans."

I force a smile as I let Mr. Dodgley know my shift is over and signal good luck to Kelly. As soon as we leave, just as I knew would happen, Beasey is back to his usual self.

"We've got work to do."

∞∞∞∞∞

I can't say I've killed someone before—at least, that was the case until about fourteen minutes ago, according to the clock on the wall. I also can't say I've ever come across someone as glad to be killed as Beasey. It took a lot of practice, but as he rose out from his body in the static that seems to show a staggered disconnect of body and spirit, he graded my efforts a "comforting

A-grade".

Finally something I've scored an A-grade in.

I look down at Beasey still on the floor. His eyes are closed but he's alive again. For now.

"You wanted me to do this," I say without empathy. "Although I guess it's quite something to be able to kill someone and bring them back to life."

"How about one last time to make it official?" Beasey suggests haphazardly.

I nod before picking up my phone. I leave a message for Gareth saying I can't see him after all, and I hope for both our sakes he doesn't come by anyway because there'll be no way to explain my dead fake uncle on the floor next to me.

Not an average night for an eighteen-year-old, but what's new?

"I do hope you'll provide your undivided attention when killing me instead of playing on your phone," Beasey quips, one eye open.

Maybe having someone trained in first aid here wouldn't be such a bad idea, after all.

It's not that hard to grasp, though. A human exorcism, that is. It's just like a regular ghost exorcism, but then in reverse, and the pull of energy is ten times stronger because there's so much more energy mass. Beasey warned it's harder if they're less willing to die, but we're keeping it simple for now.

Yeah, "simple".

"And remember, once out of a body a spirit only has a minute or so before their body starts fully shutting down, and then returning into their bodies gets less likely very quickly."

"No pressure, of course."

I throw my phone aside, not wanting the distraction of Gareth while I need to focus. I take a deep breath in, blocking out all thoughts and getting into that trance-like state to feel the spirit within Beasey. Just as I do so I notice Cole appears across the room. He's supposed to stay away for his own sake. Now he's the distraction, but he has that effect whenever he's around, no matter how much I pull against it.

"Charlotte."

"Not now, Cole. I'm trying to concentrate on killing Beasey."

"Charlotte," Cole says again with a solemn seriousness that puts me at unease. "It's time. Timothy's ready."

∞∞∞∞

I wish I had more time to prepare. Not that I could do much, but a balloon or two at least would have made all the difference. It's dark and cold out, not that it matters to ghosts, but there are no other people around and the playground would still look creepily haunted even if Timothy and Cole weren't present. I watch them play on the monkey bars with Timothy until Cole comes my way.

"It's time," Cole says.

I was just beginning to take to this little family dynamic we had going, even if there is a parental divorce scenario mixed in. It was nice, nonetheless, to pretend it was real.

"I'll take him to his mother to say goodbye one last time." He notices Timothy is now by his side. "Then it's blast off to the stars!"

Timothy mimics Cole's outstretched arm and then turns to me. "Will you be able to see me in Heaven?"

"No. But I'll know that you're there."

"I'll be flying!"

Don't cry.

"Flying high!" I force a smile, trying to remain composed. "Bye, Timothy. It was nice to meet you."

"Bye-bye, Charlotte."

Timothy gives me a wave and then takes Cole's hand as they start to walk away.

It is a sweet moment, watching Cole being like a big brother again, in the same way he was to me. People like Cole have a special purpose in the world, a good mix of empathy and compassion to help others, something this world is needlessly missing out on.

If that thought wasn't disheartening enough, I then overhear Timothy ask, "When are *you* going up to the stars, Cole?"

Cole replies, "Soon, Kiddo. Not now, but soon."

I pretend not to hear. Maybe I didn't; maybe I imagined it. They are almost out of earshot, anyway. *Almost*. They're just words of reassurance though, right? I mean, "soon" is an ambiguous word. It could mean five minutes, or fifteen. It could mean days, like, "the hurricane will make landfall *soon*", or it could mean decades like the anticipated arrival of artificial intelligence taking over the workforce *soon*. Heck, in the grand scheme of things, we will all depart this world soon enough.

The two ghosts disappear and I stay there a while longer, lost in my thoughts. I eventually walk back to my apartment alone, trying to ignore the lurking ache in the pit of my chest that can no longer be ignored, the feeling that Cole may not be around as long as I hope.

It's late by the time I get back, my mind exhausted with the day. So much so it takes me three long seconds after locking my door behind me to realize I'm not alone in my apartment.

"Shit!" I flinch at Gareth moving on the couch.

"Charlotte," he says while stretching awkwardly. "What time is it?"

"It's late. What are you doing here?"

"I was concerned, honestly. Silly, I know. I bet I look like a right twit. But you seemed off in your messages and bailing again so I thought I'd come and see if you're alright. Only you weren't here. So I thought I'd stay to make sure you got back alright and, well, I guess I fell asleep waiting. Anyway, I'm going to stop muttering like an idiot." He pauses to look at me. "Have you been crying?"

I wipe my face. "No."

"Where have you been? It's late, you shouldn't be out on your own." He stops to study me again. "Are you sure you're okay?"

"I'm fine."

"You don't look fine."

"Sorry. Now's just not a good time."

"It never seems to be a good time, though. What's going on?"

"I'm just . . . doing things."

Gareth raises an eyebrow slightly. "*Doing things*? What's up with everyone lately? Rory broke up with Juliet, did you hear?—and you jump between hot and cold. I'm just concerned. Is it me? Did I do something wrong?"

"What? No."

"Is there someone else?"

"What? No," I repeat, although not as strongly.

"I don't want to sound paranoid but I've seen it before, this constant bailing on me. With Ellie."

"I'm not Ellie."

Or maybe I am. Maybe I'm worse, even.

"I'm not saying you are. But I'm trying to understand. Is this about Cole? Letting go 'n all that? I really think you should see someone about that."

"I can assure you I don't need to see someone about that."

"Therapy isn't bad, Charlotte. In fact, you'd be surprised how many people—successful people at that—rely on a bit of help every now and then."

"I don't need therapy, Gareth!" I snap, clearly a lie by how I feel myself crumbling inside, but I can't let Gareth know that.

"Then why do you keep avoiding me? What are you hiding?"

I don't know how to answer that, which doesn't exactly ease up the situation.

Gareth picks up his jacket and heads to the door. "Fine. Clearly there's not a level of closeness between us I thought we had."

"Gareth."

"I thought you were different, mature for your age. Clearly I was wrong."

I cross my arms. "Hey! I don't have to share everything with you, you know."

"You don't have to hide everything either," he replies as he slips on his sneakers.

I sigh, rubbing my forehead between my eyebrows. Not only am I distancing my friends, I'm now also distancing my boyfriend. I need to give him something to ease his concerns, some truth without the truth. In other words, a white lie.

"I just said goodbye to someone I cared about. I'll be fine, though. I just need a long hot shower."

This at least makes Gareth stop at the door. "Another person you know died?"

I nod. "A child I used to babysit."

Gareth leans back on the door. At least now it's closed. "Blimey."

I think that's enough to calm him down, and yeah, okay, I'll admit I'm appreciating the oncoming sympathy and care I'm starting to feel from him. It's enough for me to slowly make my way to him, hoping we can put the past few minutes behind us, when he suddenly says, "Death is good at throwing punches."

I look at him and frown. "What?"

"I guess you want a quiet weekend indoors, then?"

"What do you mean, death is good at throwing punches?" I ask, ignoring what he said.

"Well, you really never know when it's your time, something we get reminded of a lot at the hospital. But you've just got to—"

"Go for broke," I say at the same time as him. "Because that's how we all come to end."

"Yeah," Gareth replies.

Heaviness falls through me and I need to grip the kitchen counter next to me. That phrase, the one that Scarlet recalled, is no common saying. In fact, I've never heard anyone say it before until now.

I look at Gareth—*really* look him—this sudden stranger in my apartment facing me. Who is he really, and what does he really know? Does he know who I am, what I can do? Is that why he's with me? Because why else would someone like Gareth be with someone like me? Is he even British?

My mind is a twister of thoughts, and I begin to wonder if I'm in danger and how quickly I can reach the knife drawer, but his eyes remain untelling, his posture relaxed, a slight smirk prodding up that dimple of his.

I wonder how many seconds have passed, but it must have only been one or two because Gareth continues, "That's what Rory says."

Twenty

It's just a coincidence.

Surely it's just a coincidence. I think. I *hope*. Because if what Gareth says is in fact true then Rory is just like me, able to communicate with the dead. The thought elates me: a friend who can understand me, the side of me I've had to keep hidden for so long. We could be a team, help one another out.

But that would also mean that Rory is the guy we've been looking for the whole time. Rory can't be the killer. He is always so . . . *normal*. Which makes me angry. Angry that he can have his normal. And angry that I can't.

Did I miss the signs? Was it right in front of me this whole time? I think back to the first time I saw him, at the party. Did he see Brad and Ricky, too? I can't remember. And what about Cole? It doesn't seem like it. He likes Juliet, or at least he did. Why hasn't he killed her yet if he's the killer? And where is this Melissa? I haven't seen her.

Then again, he has access to dead bodies. Or does he? Maybe he didn't access the autopsy files of those young women, maybe he just told me what he already knows. Come to think of it, why would he risk so much to get access to those files in the first place just to help some pal with an assignment? As for ghosts, well, if I can ignore ghosts in public, he can as well.

And then there's that phrase . . .

I could just be overreacting. Nonetheless, I need to know for sure. Which is why I leave Gareth hanging without a proper

∞ 232 ∞

excuse—again—and decide to pester Beasey at *his* job for a change.

Not that it's as easy as that. The hospital is a big place after all, and they don't let just anyone walk around. Thankfully Cole checks in on me and fetches Beasey, and soon we all convene in the staff parking lot.

"It's late," Beasey says. Not upon greeting me, but after I've explained everything.

"Late?" I echo, expecting more for such a discussion.

"You've had a long day."

Again, I look at him expecting more of an answer. He's not wrong and I suddenly feel the tiredness from the day, not to mention the sorrow of Timothy now gone. But how can I sleep knowing what Rory could be?

"Get some sleep. We'll rendezvous tomorrow in the AM."

I huff. "We don't have time. If the killer really is Rory we need to—"

"Do absolutely nothing," Beasey speaks over me.

"But what if he kills another woman tonight?" I argue.

"What if he kills *you* tonight?"

Okay, that got me. Rory wouldn't . . . no, he wouldn't. We're friends, that would be too obvious.

Wouldn't it?

"Nothing good comes out of a rushed plan," he says to my silence. "You've had a long day. The little kid's gone. I'll look into this Rory and Melissa. Get some sleep." Beasey then turns to Cole. "And you stay out of it, too. Unless you want to risk your passing at the hands of Rory."

Cole nods stoically in agreement.

I give in. "Fine." I start to leave but call back, "Any new victim can visit *you* during *your* shift."

Cole appears as soon as I slam my car door shut. "He's—"

"Don't say he's right. I know he's right. Beasey's always right, right?"

"Maybe. Probably. But an innate part of me knows you follow your own compass."

"My own compass?"

"Your moral guidance. That thing that makes you do things you probably shouldn't do, even when others warn you against it. You're good at that."

"I thought I was just stubborn."

"You are," Cole admits with the slightest of quirky smiles. "You care about others. But don't forget to care about yourself."

I huff quietly. I could seriously do with a spa day once this is over, or a weekend somewhere warm with a good book and a smoothie. But the reality is I have study to catch up on, work shifts to do, I have Gareth I owe a good explanation to, and Juliet—

"Juliet." I turn to Cole, my eyes now wide. "Rory suddenly broke up with Juliet when they were so happy together. That's out of character."

"A lot about this guy is starting to be out of character."

"But why would he suddenly break up with her? Or even be with her for that matter if he loves Melissa?"

Cole looks at me poignantly. "You could ask yourself the same question."

I frown, but I falter quickly at my hypocrisy. "What I mean is we've been thinking about Rory but not Juliet. Why did he suddenly break up with her?" I take out my phone and look up the dead women. "Maya Tilly had blonde hair, blue eyes, and a slim build. Monique Sharpe had dark red hair, gray or possibly blue eyes, and a slim-to-medium build. Lucia Turnball, strawberry-blonde hair, blue eyes, and a slim build. Paula Voss, strawberry-blonde, blue eyes, and slim. Scarlet Barnes-Curtis, strawberry-blonde, blue, slim."

"There's a type," Cole speaks my mind.

"Juliet has strawberry-blonde hair. She also has blue eyes and a slim build." I look at Cole. "You don't think . . . ." I swallow, unable to finish that sentence.

"I'll check up on her."

"No." The seriousness in my voice stops him from leaving. "You remember what Beasey said. If he is what we think he is and Juliet is with him, you shouldn't be around that."

"Then what do you suggest?"

"You go and relay this to Beasey. I need to find out where Juliet is and make sure she's safe."

Cole leaves. I call Juliet to invite her over to mine, at least to make sure she's safe if not to be a better friend. I leave a message when she doesn't pick up, hoping a romcom and ice cream therapy at mine is enough for her to return my call.

I'm not convinced, however, so after stopping by her place with no such luck I stop by the café to see Kelly.

"Kelly," I say as I pace up to the counter in front of a customer.

"Oh, hey." Kelly smiles awkwardly. "I'm just taking this customer's order—"

"Have you heard from Juliet? I've tried calling her but I can't get through to her."

"I'm sure Juliet is fine. She's just getting over a heartbreak. I still can't believe Rory just dumped her like that. Guys suck."

The waiting customer coughs impatiently but I ignore him. "Kelly please stay away from Rory."

"What? Why?"

The customer coughs again. "If you don't mind—"

"Hey," I snap back at him. "Go across the street where the coffee is cheaper and better. None of the child labor stuff that's used in the shit we sell here."

With a gape and a huff the customer storms out.

"Charlotte, what the—" Kelly drags me to the office. "It's a good thing Dodgley popped out for a bit. What the hell is going on?"

"I'm not kidding. Promise me you'll steer clear of Rory. And make sure Juliet does, too."

Kelly's eyes narrow. She's certainly not stupid, because she closes the door and folds her arms as she asks quietly yet seriously, "Don't tell me he's another non-existent uncle of yours. Or a cousin this time, perhaps?"

"Something like that," I reply.

Kelly scowls. "My aunt better not be in any danger, mingling with that Beasey guy."

"No," I reply quickly without even comprehending such a thought. The stakes are so high as it is, I couldn't live with myself if anything happened to Maria. "Nothing to worry about there."

"But us? Rory is a friend, albeit a jerk. If I'm about to step in on that—even as a noble bestie—I've got to have reason to."

"Please, Kelly. I don't have time to explain everything right now, but until I know for sure just trust me on this. As a matter of life and death."

"Fuck, Charlotte," Kelly breathes. "What do I do with that sentence?"

Mr. Dodgley then opens the door demanding to know what is going on and why an angry customer complained about the one with the wavy hair. Kelly immediately puts on that well-practiced smile of hers and heads back to the counter before turning to whisper, "My aunt and I are going to Nashville tomorrow for a few days for Thanksgiving. I'll call Juliet after work and convince her to come with no choice on the matter."

She gives me one last suspicious look as she leaves me to get a lecture from Mr. Dodgley. I glance at my watch. It's nearly half-past ten. I should apologize to Mr. Dodgley, go back to my apartment, have a long hot shower, and then go to sleep like Beasey advised. I really should try to explain things better with Gareth.

But a part of me, the part that makes me feel uneasy, tells me Juliet should have returned my call by now.

So I turn and leave—to Mr. Dodgley's indignation—to my car, and when Cole appears and asks where I'm going he doesn't like what he hears.

∞∞∞∞

"You don't have to do this."

I've heard the words many times from Cole's mouth over the

∞ 236 ∞

years, but I didn't listen to him then and I know I won't start now.

"I know." I sigh quietly, not taking my eyes off the house down the road. Cole doesn't approve. Beasey cursingly didn't give his approval either, but at least I can mute those messages. "It's just a stakeout. Just making sure Juliet—or any other redhead—isn't in any immediate danger."

I know the address Kelly texted me is correct because I see his Audi parked on the driveway. The house itself looks lovely, even in the dark with no lights on. Wood timber outlines the exterior with angled roofing pointing out over large windows at the end of the short, sloped driveway. There is a balcony along the side, probably opening up around the back to what I can imagine would be some stunning views of the nearby lake and national park on any nicer occasion than now.

Because we're not here for the views.

I look at my watch. Half-past eleven. "He's got to be asleep by now," I conclude.

Cole repeats what he just said again as I get out of my car. I glance down the road each way. Dead silent except for the distant cry of a coyote.

"You wait here," I warn as I tie my hair back. Stakeouts are never good with hair blocking your peripheral vision, after all. "If Melissa is there and senses you then things could go bad very quickly."

"Charlotte," he says sternly. "Just a peek through the windows. Nothing more. Got it?"

I nod. "Just a peek. In and out. Besides, I'm not his type. Apparently."

I don't think this reassures Cole, but he gives up. He knows there's little else he can do.

Thankfully the moon provides some light, at least enough to guide my way around the house. A peek through the windows shows nothing unordinary. Chairs, tables, various artwork on the wall, one of those old grandfather clocks. A kitchen around the back has appliances any chef would happily take to, and there's a dirty plate left on the counter. I then notice the French door has been left unlocked.

Rory is a friend. And as they say, innocent until proven guilty. In my sudden internal debate of trespassing the house of a friend, I wonder if I should just knock, surprise him, ask to hang out for a bit and do a snoop that way. It's probably just a house. A nice house, but still just a house. Or it could be the place where Scarlet—and the other women, too—were murdered.

For the need to know, I slide the door open carefully and then slip out of my sneakers (because I'm here to scout for a crime scene, not leave a muddy mess) before stepping inside.

Unlike outside, I have to feel my way around inside, the lack of moonlight making it difficult to see as well. I squint at the framed picture on the wall. The Tierney family all carry the stiff faces Rory seems to have, but it's easy to tell they're of the same blood. All somewhat tall, dressed in polo shirts and shorts, even the mother and daughter. Assuming the young adults are all siblings, Rory has two brothers and a sister. He's clearly the youngest, the others at least a few years older than him. I wonder if they're close, but don't hold the thought since a picture can be worth just as many lies as words.

I sigh lightly. What am I doing? This could be an ordinary family photo in an ordinary room, one I am illegally breaking and entering in. I almost turn to leave, until my eyes catch the picture on the adjacent wall. This one is smaller and I have to lean right in to see. There's Rory—that's obvious, even in skiing gear. There's someone else next to him. It's hard to recognize her in all her ski gear, but squinting up close I can just about see what looks like strawberry-blonde hair around her helmet, and I don't like where my conclusion is heading.

"Charlotte?"

I spin in surprise, the voice I know well now so terrifying.

He flicks a light on and the living room lights up. Even with the lights on it's a simple set-up: light pastel-blue wallpaper everywhere, a large television with a games console on the floor in front of it, and as well as the couch there are two matching chairs, a small table with a bottle of whisky on, a large rug over the wooden floor, and a half-empty bookcase which I now know is what I bumped into.

"Rory," I say through a gasp. "I . . ." I try to form up an excuse as to why I'd be here, now, as I am, but my mind melts words to form when I see the bookcase I'm standing against.

Sure, it's a nice bookcase. Antique perhaps, with varnished strong wood, possibly chestnut. The books that were there, however, upon further inspection in the lit-up room, were not the usual college textbooks or study notes one would expect to find. Books on ghosts, books on rituals in ancient civilizations. And on top of the piles and open pages, in the familiar black leather and gold print, is the book titled in large block letters, LIBER MANIUM.

And that's when the confirmation sinks in, the dread I wanted so badly to prove wrong.

The proof that Rory is the killer.

And here I am, standing across from him.

"My research," he starts, following my gaze. "Some things were easier to get than others, but when you throw enough money you can always get what you want eventually." He pauses, but there's little hesitation when he says, "You're like me, aren't you? You can see them, can't you?"

"See what?"

"Ghosts."

As if on cue she appears. I follow Rory's gaze to where she makes herself known, but no introduction is needed.

"Melissa."

Melissa walks around Rory to get a closer look at me. I don't know what she's expecting for a reaction, but no matter how intent her stare is she's not getting one. Not from me. Because I'm too internally flabbergasted right now to know what to do.

She eventually places her arm around Rory's neck, resting her hand on his shoulder. "Finally, we know about her. And it's true."

Cole suddenly appears, and as happy as I am to see him I'm

also full of dread. He smiles ever so slightly my way, most likely in relief I'm okay, only it's then gone to seriousness and staunch.

"How did you know? That I can see ghosts?"

"I'll admit we weren't too sure at first," Rory starts. "Lots of people have a ghost shadowing them, but when I first saw you relaying every number your pal here said at that party I thought surely it couldn't be, surely there isn't someone else here, just like me? I assumed it was just a cheap trick. Even when you looked straight at him I assumed it was just a concussion. Nonetheless, I watched you closely at the hospital, but you managed to totally ignore all the ghosts, including the one next to you right now."

I flash a glance at Cole.

"Yes, that one," Rory comments, watching me. "Gareth also quenched a lot of my curiosity about you when I asked about you that night. He mentioned your failed attempt at impressing him with a trick about relaying the number of fingers he held behind his back. He thought it was funny; "cute" is the word I believe he said. Nonetheless, there was something about you. I searched you up but came up with nothing, not even a Facebook page. I couldn't let Melissa near you, at least not alone, not until I knew what you are capable of. So Melissa watched you from afar. In class. At work. You never looked her way."

I look at Melissa again, now recognizing her from the Korean restaurant, the cinema, and probably other places, too. She was there all along, watching me. *Spying* on me.

"I used Juliet to get closer to you, and I made sure Gareth and I just happened to go to the Korean restaurant too, even though I can't stand the food. When you denied believing in ghosts I let my hunch go, and when Kelly mentioned the backstory of Cole, your beloved friend lost so tragically too soon, him haunting you made perfect sense. Pining a lost love. I get it, I do. It seemed you were totally oblivious to him every time he was there, like at the hospital and firepit when you kissed Gareth right in front of him." He pauses as my eyes falter at the memory. "It was that moment at Halloween, when I so cleverly dressed as a ghost, when Cole here commented that he couldn't see the similarities, and your reaction . . . and when those other two schmucks finally buggered off, when you flinched at the light, that's when I knew."

"Congrats. Next time just ask."

Rory half-smiles at this. "Would you have answered honestly?"

"Yes." Probably. Maybe.

"Just like you have told Gareth, huh? Because he's clearly aware of what you can do? And your secret love for Cole on the side, too? I bet you're totally open about that with him."

I don't answer that because I can't.

"Thought so," he responds to my hesitation. "Don't worry, I said I don't judge. I'm glad, actually. Glad that someone understands why I've done what I have."

I swallow, dreading what he will say. "And what have you done, Rory?"

"It was almost a year ago now, the day it happened," Melissa starts. "We were skiing in Canada. There was a drop off a ledge, one we didn't see until it was too late. Rory landed on a pile of soft snow without a scratch. I landed on the rocks next to him." Melissa takes a moment to remember, a frown now suddenly forming. "Ridiculous, isn't it? How life can end so quickly. One moment, one movement. One decision."

"Melissa died, but she wasn't really gone. But of course no one believed me. Throughout my life they sent me to doctors, to hospitals. Sometimes they left me there," Rory says, looking at the framed family photo. "They said it was all in my head, but I knew it wasn't. I knew it wasn't."

There's something about how he repeats himself, as if he's reassuring himself that he's not as crazy as he may have once thought. I guess it's also how I felt when I accepted I wasn't crazy.

"I always thought I was alone. When my parents couldn't find any more help for me they just threw money at me to go elsewhere, to keep myself busy. But there was Melissa." His voice cracks. "She was the only one who believed me, the only one who loved me for me."

"So you wanted her back," I say, filling in the gaps. I pick up the top piece of paper from the bookshelf, the unmistakable picture of Scarlet Barnes-Curtis next to hand-written notes. I place it back, my hand shaking. "Through any means necessary."

"She was the nicest. I felt really bad for her. I felt bad for all of them," Rory replies.

I look back to the shelf and fear what other contents I may find.

"We can't bring the dead back to life, Rory," I repeat Beasey's words with a tinge of sadness.

"Bringing back the dead is no easy feat," Rory admits.

I want to know what Rory knows about that, but then again I don't.

"I started practicing at the hospital, but the bodies were too far gone by the time they reached the morgue. I needed fresh bodies."

I feel sick at the thought.

"We would scout the hospital, clubs, parties, looking for people Melissa could be. We figured the closer in resemblance to Melissa, the more successful it would be."

"Juliet," I mutter.

"Doesn't she look like Juliet?" Rory asks, obviously hearing me. "I actually thought that Juliet *was* Melissa for a moment when I first saw her. The resemblance is uncanny. So much so that we were going to save her for the final attempt, when I knew I had it right."

Rory isn't wrong; she does look like Juliet. In the same way chest-length strawberry-blonde-haired five-foot-eight slim young women do. But so do millions of other young women in the world. Was Juliet just some pick of the crop? Surely there were some feelings from him? I saw it, Gareth saw it, Kelly in all her talent saw it.

"Rory, surely you like Juliet as much as she adores you?"

Rory glances away, the only sign there's still a bit of humanity left in him.

"It doesn't take much effort with the stupid college girls; they just take one look at his clothes or car and they're lured," Melissa replies on behalf of Rory. "Rory flirts a bit, gets to know them, figure out their life. And when he's busy I follow them, watch them, copy them, so when I become them nobody will wonder otherwise," Melissa says proudly of herself.

"I wasn't talking to you, bitch," I sneer in anger, leveling down Melissa's own energy. "Rory, whatever this is, it has to stop." I say, showing far more staunch than I know I've got. "I can't let you kill anybody else."

"I have to, though. For her."

"It's okay, babe. I'm here. I'll always be here with you. We'll be together."

I cringe at the way she cups his face, the way she stands over him and looks down at his wretched eyes. Rory thinks it's love, but the more I hear the more I am beginning to see otherwise. I don't see love in Melissa's eyes and I don't feel love in her energy, at least not in the way I feel from Cole.

"Melissa loves me. Melissa believes in me." Rory then looks to me for validation, eyes weak and vulnerable. "She's all I have."

I swallow, the empathy hitting all too strong. Being haunted doesn't only mean the stuff of horror movies. It can be a persistent heartache, a vector of the mind, growing and taking over while knowing there's nothing you can do. And I almost feel sorry for him. No, I *do* feel sorry for him, which makes me feel horrible for both how I feel and what I'm about to say.

"Rory, I'm sorry for what you went through growing up. I get it, I really do. But what you're doing is not the answer. You're *sick*, Rory. And Melissa is using you for her own gain."

Melissa clearly doesn't like what I say from the rage emitting from her. "Babe, I know you were excited about her, but I knew this would be a bad idea. I said she wouldn't understand us. No one understands us, Rory. Can't you see that?"

"Rory, can't *you* see that *she* is manipulating you?"

Rory shakes his head. "Stop it, Charlotte."

"Killing others for personal gain is never okay."

"Collateral damage. Try to see the bigger picture here. This is world-changing, Charlotte. This can change society—heck, transform humanity. What are a few lives to that? Besides, isn't that why you're here? We want the same thing."

"We do not want the same thing," I sneer.

"Don't say you wouldn't do the same for Cole," Rory sharply replies back. "Admit it: you, Charlotte Durane, are just like me."

"I am nothing like you!" I snap back. "You're a killer, Rory. A murderer!"

"Enough," Melissa bellows and then turns to Rory. "It doesn't matter what she thinks. She's here. Do it."

"We don't know for sure if it's true, Mel."

"One way to find out."

"Do what?" I demand to know.

"Bring the dead back to life. I can do it now."

Cole, who has been watching on in his usual contemplative silence, suddenly whispers in my ear, "Don't listen to him. One spirit, one body, remember?"

"If you think you're going to kill Juliet then you're deluded! I won't help you with that."

"She doesn't know," Melissa almost giggles to him.

"Know what?" I demand to know.

Rory looks away, as if he's about to deliver some unwanted news. "People like us . . . not only can we communicate with the dead, but we can also *host* the dead."

"What do you mean by that?"

Melissa snickers, an unsettling reaction. "You don't get it, do you?"

I'm not sure what she's getting at, but by the way Cole holds my wrist I think he does.

"I didn't break up with Juliet to take *her* body," Rory answers me. "I broke up with Juliet to take *yours*."

Twenty-one

I blink. Then again. And again. "*My* body?" I ask, dumbfounded. "What do you mean?"

"None of the test subjects lasted for long. Even if they did last longer, the body ultimately rejected Melissa's spirit. But upon more research I figured it out. The key to permanent spirit transfer."

"Which is?"

"You."

"Me?"

"Us. Those who can see the dead are the ones who can host the dead—permanently."

I don't react. I don't know how to. I'm a Communicator. I can communicate with ghosts, and this is what makes me the way I am. But instead I'm designed to be a vessel, some bodily sacrifice? That's a fate worse than death, having someone else *be* me, living *my* life. And no one would ever know the truth of what happened.

This makes me angry. No, more than angry. It makes me furious. And Rory wants to utilize that? Any sympathy I had for him growing up with the struggle of who he is and being on the receiving end of Melissa's influence has suddenly dissipated.

"What the hell, Rory?" I clench my fists, trying to remain strong under the sweat of dread on my neck. "Do you seriously think I'm going to let Melissa take over my body?!"

Melissa smirks, then suddenly she's out of sight.

"I'm not a fan of the waves," I say, looking at my hair. I then smile and do a little sway. "But I guess I can make it work. Nice height, nice shape."

Melissa is suddenly in view again.

"What just happened?" I then ask, confused.

"You were possessed," Rory replies.

"I was what?" I look down at myself. "I don't feel any different."

It then comes to me that this has happened before. It was only once, prom night to be precise, when a very angry ghost happened to be exerting her rage through me, so much so that I felt like she *was* me. It didn't last long, but it was weird enough that I still remember it vividly.

"Something we're vulnerable to. It only lasts a few seconds, though. Hence the more permanent solution." Rory lifts a bottle of whisky from the table stand and pours himself a glass. "Gareth likes whisky. He bought this for me, actually. It's his favorite. Anything from Islay." Rory takes a long sip of whiskey, not taking his eyes off me. "Poor guy. He's not going to like you leaving him for me. If it makes you feel any better we have no intention of continuing our lives here."

"What you're saying is disgusting," I seethe.

"This wasn't the time we planned, but clearly you are more agile than I thought because here you are." Rory takes a couple of steps closer to my couple of steps back before he places his whisky glass back down on the table stand and takes something out of his pocket. "So I am giving you two options: take these pills and it will be quick. Don't take the pills and it won't be. There'll be a struggle, but you'll lose. Maya Tilly found that out the hard way, but luckily for you Melissa can do it on your behalf. Either way you're about to die, and for what it's worth I'm sorry. At least you'll be with Cole."

At that moment Melissa makes for me again, but Cole's already there. That is until Rory holds Cole in place with the same familiar chant I've come to know recently.

I don't know what Rory is capable of, but the same could

be said about me, especially when Cole's wellbeing is involved. Rory knows I can see the dead. But he doesn't know what else I can do. Playing on that, I put Melissa in her own hold.

"Don't think about doing anything you wouldn't want done to Melissa," I warn.

"My, my. She's been doing her own research," Melissa snarls. "Look at this unfortunate little stalemate."

"Nobody is harming Charlotte." Cole's voice almost startles me, now part of the confrontation. His expression is deadpan, his tone final, as if what he says will be the rule.

I smirk a little. My hero, as always.

Cole looks at me. "Charlotte, you know what to do."

I do? It's a fifty-fifty situation at play as far as I see it. I can't exorcise Rory as chances are he'll be too strong. I can't exorcise Melissa as chances are Cole will fall into the mist of the afterlife as well. The only other option would be to leave, but even then Melissa and Rory would catch up to me. And none of those scenarios bode well for Cole, either.

"Cole," I cautiously whisper. If he has a plan up his sleeve I don't know what it is. "Rory will exorcise you."

"I know."

My mouth falls, but no words come.

There is no plan.

"I'm not leaving you," I whisper in protest. "I can't let him take you."

"Exorcise her, Charlotte. He can't do anything to you if he's distracted with me," Cole whispers back.

"If I do that then I won't be able to protect you."

"*I* protect *you*," he says solidly.

"Cole—"

"It's okay," he says. I question the sudden softness in his voice, if I really see a smile on his lips. "As long as you're okay."

"Cole," I say again, almost a beg.

Don't make me do it.

Cole looks me in the eyes. "*Do it.*"

On that note he turns back to Rory, his training paying off as his energy is soon strong enough to break free from Rory's hold, and suddenly Rory takes the two pills down with the last of the whiskey in his glass.

"No!" Rory crouches over, trying to throw up what Cole just made him consume.

I turn and face Rory. I want to punch him and shout at him while he's down, tell him he was a friend, have him comprehend the damage he's caused. But people this far gone from reason usually won't listen.

Beasey's arguments and training are suddenly making a lot of sense. Not all ghosts are sad; some ghosts are just bad. Melissa is bad. Rory won't stop the pursuit to play God at the cost of innocent lives, nor will Melissa stop until she's alive again. Which means they need to be stopped.

Which is why I know what comes next.

I won't call it a plan as much as an experiment. It will either go one way or the other. And I can only try to make sure it's the way I want it to go.

Now that Cole is no longer in Rory, I move Melissa in place of Rory because a two-in-one situation should be easier to control.

I hope.

Naturally, neither of them like the unfolding situation. Melissa is possessing Rory, only I'm holding her in place within Rory, meaning she's not going anywhere and neither is he doing anything like getting those pills out of him (which I'm really hoping will kick in shortly).

Not that they're taking it lightly. It's tiring me out quickly, fighting both Rory and Melissa, and Melissa has a lot of bad words to express my way.

Or is it Rory?

Probably both.

"Charlotte."

"Stand back, Cole," I say through chanting. "I'm going to exorcise them both."

"It's too much for you," he says, probably seeing the beads of sweat I feel forming on my forehead.

"I know what I'm doing."

I have no idea what I'm doing.

"You have no idea what you're doing."

The voice almost makes me lose my hold of Melissa and Rory. Never have I been so happy to hear Beasey.

"About time."

"I'm almost tempted to throw you in with them," he says, striding straight up to me. "What did I say, Charlotte? And what do you go and do?"

"I thought Juliet was in danger."

"Juliet is with her sister, had you remained calm and waited to find out for yourself."

My sigh of relief loosens my hold and I quickly tense back up as I feel my strength waning.

"It's probably relayed on that phone of yours you never seem to answer. At least Cole felt it best to let me know of your impromptu little stakeout attempt."

"Do you mind?" I ask with stress.

"Interesting," Beasey comments at the situation unfolding. "And just where were you heading with this?"

"Beasey!"

Beasey takes over as my arms begin to flop. "I take it your theory on Rory is true, then?"

"Yes."

"And you know what comes now?"

"Yes."

"Do it," Cole encourages. "Put an end to all this."

Beasey nods. "We're not strong enough to do both at the same time. I'll release Melissa."

"Won't she possess me? Or you?"

"Not with the pull of the exorcism we're about to perform." Beasey glances back at Cole. "Your choice, too."

Cole takes a couple of steps back, and then a couple more when I glare at him. On Beasey's command I prepare as he releases his hold of Melissa. Rory flicks his head out of confusion and back to himself, but before he can do what I know he wants done to me, Beasey and I, in unison, exorcise him instead.

Even with Beasey's training and help, exorcising someone alive and struggling to remain alive is a heated effort. And he puts up a fight alright. But then he's there, screaming, static, and the mist comes, slow and growing, assured with the yells of protest from Melissa across the room. I half expect her to run after him, or at least try to pull him out of the mist in vain, something tragically heroic. Only then I realize, as Rory gazes at Melissa, as he struggles to reach out his hand for hers, that Melissa isn't moving towards him, to pass on together in the light, but away from him. And the last thing I see of Rory is the heartbreak in his eyes, his outstretched hand empty of a hold, the last of him to disappear as the pull of the afterlife consumes him in a flash.

My arms flop in tiredness and all heads turn to face Melissa. For a moment none of us know what to say. I guess I shouldn't be surprised, but the depravity of some people—alive or not— always finds a way to surpass my expectation.

Melissa doesn't protest or possess me, however. She doesn't even yell or charge. Instead, as Beasey and I raise our arms for another round, she backs up and is quick to disappear, Cole already engaged to pursue her.

Only my arms weren't raised at her.

"No!" I order Cole with the hold of his energy. "Stay."

I had hoped, of course, in the back of my mind that this would all work out. That Melissa could be held inside Rory. That Rory could be exorcised. Not only for my life—something I have a newfound appreciation for still having—but for Cole's. Because as it is right now, a lifeless body of a Communicator lies in front of us. One that, in theory, can host a spirit.

"Charlotte?" Cole asks, confused.

"No." Beasey catches on first, but it's Cole I'm focused on. He looks at me, eyebrows slightly slanted in lack of understanding. His eyes then move to the lifeless body of Rory across the room and then back to me.

"Charlotte," he cautiously warns, his head starting to shake.

"I can do this," I say, harboring the energy of Cole in my grasp in desperation. "I know I can!"

"No," Beasey says again, this time softer. I can tell he's trying to think of reasons not to go ahead with what I'm about to do, but not even he can give reasons not to, his desire to see it work presiding.

It's a good thing I'm willing to find out.

Cole looks at me again, eyes wide and perturbed. A small sound escapes him as I pull him into the body of Rory. I don't know what to do except continue the holding chant, holding him in place as Rory's body twitches and trembles until it stills again, stiff and unmoving.

Beasey places a hand of caution on my arm as he leans in closer over the body of Rory. There is complete and utter silence with only the seconds ticking by on the grandfather clock and the pulsing of my heartbeat in my ears as I take a step closer, peering down intently for a sign of life.

And that's when he opens his eyes.

Twenty-two

My mother once told me that I have the power to change the world. Of the few memories of her I still retain, this one sticks out the most. Me, power, change the world. I remember feeling like a superhero, and it got me excited. No way was I going to fall asleep after hearing that.

Maybe my mother was wrong. Maybe fatal attribution error is at play, my ego too large for its own good. Because right now, looking at the body of Rory staring up at me with blank stone-gray eyes, I don't feel like a superhero. Right now I feel like a villain, taking my selfish desires too far, and I can't help but wonder if my attempt at playing God will be met with disastrous consequences.

"Cole?"

My voice is a crackle above a whisper, the air from my lungs escaping me. He lies there, stiff and solid, his eyes still and void of any sign of life.

"Beasey." I grip onto his arm in complete trepidation. "Do something. Please do something."

I want answers, I want advice. But even Beasey, usually so knowing, is at a loss on what to say.

"Charlotte." The trepidation in his voice matches my own. "What have you done?"

I look up at Beasey, my concern clear. I don't know what I've done. I thought I was doing the right thing. I thought that if there's a chance—if there's *hope* that Cole could ever have the life he deserves back—this would be it. A Communicator's body. Similar age, similar build. Isn't that enough? Rory said that was enough. But what if Rory was wrong? What if Cole is trapped in some type of coma purgatory?

I start to panic at the possibilities, wondering if it's too late to undo what I've done. Any form of Cole is better than no Cole, after all.

I then feel a hand on mine. It's light, almost feather-touch.

Except it's so much more.

"Cole?" I lean in close to the eyes now looking straight at me. They're still gray—Rory's gray—but it's Cole I feel.

"Charlotte."

It's barely a sound, but it's enough. He then gasps, fighting to breathe, organs so long forgotten with him.

"Cole!" I hold his head to my chest. "Oh my god, oh my god." I repeat the words as I rock him tightly, my lungs now also fighting for air. "It's you. It's actually you."

"Let him breathe." Beasey cautions my grip on him, now too leaning in close. "Welcome back, I guess. How do you feel?"

Cole blinks twice, confused. He looks from Beasey to me once more before looking down at himself, his new body. He slowly lifts an arm, flexing his fingers into a light grip. "I feel . . . heavy. And hungry. Yeah, hungry."

I stifle a laugh. "Typical."

He tries to sit up but slumps back down with a light moan.

"Careful," Beasey warns, hoisting him upright. "Gravity is something you'll have to get used to again."

"Charlotte." Cole breathes weakly over unsettled breaths, barely able to lift his head up to mine. "Why?"

"Because you deserve it, Cole. Regardless of what I want."

Cole looks at my eyes and into my soul. Sure, it'll take some getting used to, but I feel it, the connection of us, regardless of what he now looks like. He shakily lifts his arm and brushes the loose lock of hair hanging down my cheek and curls it behind my ear.

"You have no idea how many times I wanted to be able to do

that," he says, a whispered laugh shared between us.

I cup my hand on his cheek, brushing away the tear in the corner of his eye with my thumb.

"Your skin is soft," he adds before breathing in. "You smell nice, too. Like coconut. And something else. Wow, coconut."

I smile, now brushing away the tears in my own eyes. Cole tries sitting up a bit more, noticing his glass reflection in the glass of the nearby table stand. He rakes his hand through his hair. So many times I wished I could watch him do that. It's different now; he's not doing his telltale sign of being stressed, rather curious and cautious. Still, it's something. It's amazing, in fact.

"This is going to take some getting used to. I liked being blonde."

"We'll pick up some hair dye at the store. Whatever you want."

"I don't want to dampen your little moment, but don't get too felicitous," Beasey interrupts, scouting through Rory's bookshelf. "You're in the body of a serial killer, don't forget."

"But the police don't know it's him," I say. "Do they?"

"If they don't yet then they probably will soon," Beasey replies, his words offering no reassurance. "And when they do—and it will probably be a *when*—you'll need a plan ready."

"What sort of plan?"

"I suggest Alaska. Or better yet, with Mr. Tierney's budget perhaps a yacht in the Caribbean."

I frown. I want to say his suggestions aren't funny, but I then notice how he's wearing latex gloves and touching everything carefully and realize he's serious. Why does he always have to do this, ruin such moments with depressing reality?

"Here we are," he mutters as he picks up that familiar book. He leaves me with that depressing reality as he scouts the rest of the house.

"Hey." Cole looks into my eyes. "Live for the now, remember?"

I kiss him softly on the lips. "For the moments," I quietly reply.

Cole goes in for another kiss, at first just a touch of our lips, soft and sweet. Only he holds me there as he carries on exploring my mouth, my cheek, my ear with his lips.

"I thought you said you were hungry?" I say, giggling.

"I can wait. There's something I crave more than food." He then kisses my neck, his body close to mine, igniting even more sensations between us. I soon hear a sound, a small groan trapped through closed lips, and the kisses deepen.

He suddenly pulls back slightly, an indecision in his eyes. By now he's supposed to say he's sorry and that he won't do it again.

Except he doesn't. Not anymore.

Instead he kisses me again, strong and passionately, clearly enjoying every sensation as much as I am. He pulls me in closer to him, stumbling slightly as he relearns to balance, but I catch him, our teamwork in play as he slides his fingers down the side of my jacket to my jeans.

"That'll have to wait." Beasey bluntly ruins the moment as he walks back into the room. "Your friend Kelly has been making calls of concern about you, including to Maria. Your other boyfriend is on his way."

Beasey brings forth a good point, of course. I suddenly feel guilty for having just kissed Cole. I'll forgive myself given the circumstances, although there's an undeniable feel of betrayal for Gareth I can't ignore.

I glance at Cole who picks up the same thoughts because he subtly shuffles away from me.

Beasey crouches down to us. "Look, you can hide the evidence, and even pretend to live as Rory, but you should start planning. What about Melissa?"

"She scuttled away," I reply. "Pathetic. But when she comes back, we'll be ready."

"And what about the parents?"

"Rory wasn't close with his parents."

"I didn't mean Rory's folks, although that should also be a consideration. I meant the parents of his victims. They deserve closure, too.”

There we are again with that depressing reality.

“Beasey’s right,” Cole concludes. “It’s only fair for them.”

“Hold up.” I shake my head. “There are too many things to consider at once.”

Only, as I say it, I wonder if there really are. I mean, the police aren’t actively looking for a serial killer, rather just trying to find a reason for a few odd deaths. Plenty of unexplained deaths end up being X-filed indefinitely. And it’s probably better that the parents don’t know that their daughters were murdered. I’ll break up with Gareth, something that does scrunch up feelings in my chest, but then again I think we are pretty much there anyway with how our last conversation went. Besides, since he doesn’t believe in ghosts it was probably never meant to be. And, okay, Kelly and Juliet will hate us. And okay, that will suck, especially since I finally feel as though I have a friend base. But this is too complex and consequential to let Kelly in on, and there are other friends to be made out there in the world, I’m sure. And as Beasey implied, Cole has suddenly inherited a small fortune. We’ll leave town, start anew. In Alaska or on a yacht in the Caribbean if need be. It doesn’t matter where as long as we’re together.

“I always thought a Bonnie and Clyde life would be fun,” Cole muses. “I don’t think it realistically has any hold, though.”

“There’s always a cost,” Beasey recapitulates.

“That cost is payable when *we* decide.” I hoist Cole up to his feet. It’s a wobble or two, but he manages to hold his newly acquired weight on two feet. “For now though, Cole has suddenly inherited an Audi and a wallet full of credit cards to the Tierney family accounts. He wants a feed, so we are going to a diner to eat the best waffles his money can buy.” I wrap Cole’s arm around my shoulder as I lead the way. “I’m driving.”

“Just when I thought you couldn’t be any sexier,” Cole smirks as he kisses my cheek.

“Fine. But this isn’t over. We need a plan. A solid plan. And be careful; Melissa is still out there.”

I say okay and promise to bring him back a coffee. It's only once we're in the Audi and start down the road does it really sink in. I look down at Rory's—I mean Cole's—hand on my own. Granted this new appearance of Cole will take some getting used to, especially for him, and it won't happen straight away. But there's time, time and a whole future awaiting us from this moment forth in a new life together.

Cole is finally with me.

It's always such moments that get ruined, though. The ones where there are hopes to be dashed. It's as soon as I turn off Lake Crescent Road and pass the golf course, as the bridge across the lake comes into view, as I rub little circles on Cole's hand resting on my knee. I think we both feel it, the unsettling sudden presence. He turns to me, his eyebrows furrow, but before he can finish asking me what is wrong I chuckle under my breath.

"You didn't think you were going to live happily ever after, did you?" I say, a lopsided smirk forming across my mouth as I push my foot on the accelerator and turn the steering wheel sharply to the left. Across the embankment. Into the water. Where everything goes black.

∞∞∞∞∞

I notice the dark-red smear on the airbag before I feel the pain on my head. It's pretty dark outside, but still light enough to see around me.

"Charlotte!" Cole's tone catches my attention. Sharp and snappy, something I don't associate him with, especially with his new voice. He mutters something inaudible, gripping me tightly.

"Cole?"

His fierce eyes soften briefly, relief flashing across his face. It only lasts a moment, however, as he then says, "Water's coming in."

I blink once or twice, trying to get what he's saying, then I feel a sharp cold sensation on my feet. I turn on the car light and

∞ 257 ∞

see water currenting into the car and realize that I'm in the lake.

"The door won't open!" I panic as I push at the door, my feet swashing in protest to the cold water seeping in through the fabric of my shoes and socks.

Melissa, I then notice leaning across the back seat, giggles. "You really thought I would just let everything go? After what you did to Rory?"

I seethe through my chattering teeth, ready to put my exorcism skills back to the test.

"Forget about her, there's not enough time," Cole says with an unsettling urgency.

I scream as the water seeps in over my legs.

Cole grips my shaking arms. "Charlotte, listen to me." His voice is strong yet low, like a parental warning. "The car is going to fill up with water with us in it. But then the pressure should equalize enough to open the door."

"I can't," I hesitate.

"Yes you can. I'll be here with you," he replies as the water rises up our chests. He flicks one quick glance at Melissa before saying, "Just don't look back, keep swimming up."

"So cold," I chatter through my teeth, unclipping my seatbelt and crouching up on the seat, my hands pushing up on the car roof for balance.

"Don't panic. Just take a big, deep breath in when I say so." He grips my hand. "You can do this, Charlotte. Ready? Breathe, now!"

"Cole!" The word sounds weak and frail as I gasp in the last of the air as the water floods over us.

The water is thick, my eyes fighting the little bits of moss and dirt in the darkness. Cole pulls on my hand, guiding it to the car door handle. I pull on it, but it won't open much. I keep pulling, and then start kicking, the door refusing to move. I punch my arm out through the gap and feel the crunch of my knuckles on a rock. My mouth opens to yelp and my air escapes in a small flurry of bubbles. I barely feel Cole tugging me to the other side of the car. He kicks at the passenger door, each kick widening the gap as it jars against the sludge of the lake floor. I feel Cole push me out before I feel Melissa's unsettling feel through me exhale the last of my air. My chest feels tight. I turn and look for Cole and I think I see him with Melissa, but the mud from the disturbed lake floor makes me blind. My chest starts convulsing, my arms and legs begin to frail.

I start kicking but it feels like there's an anchor inside of me weighing me down. I try to cough but nothing happens. My body spasms in protest and before becoming totally numb I feel a heavy grip on my shoulders pulling me up.

I feel myself lifting higher, the light above beckoning me to it, becoming closer and brighter until I'm through the surface. I open my eyes to the relief of moonlight shining over me and everything I felt before melts away as a euphoric rush vibrates through me.

I then notice Cole in front of me, his amber eyes staring into mine. Sweet, sweet Cole. My savior.

He says my name, a soft gasp that carries in the air. I smile, but then notice his eyes are panicked. I reach out my hand to him, and then Cole is suddenly there, holding me. I turn to see where I need to swim, but instead I find myself looking down at Gareth struggling to the riverbank, pulling something out of the water.

Me.

My lifeless body.

"Oh." It's all I can say.

"No, please God, no." Cole quivers, his fingers pulling through his hair as his eyes flick between the me below him and the me in front of him. "Not this way. Not now." He turns his head and snaps to the sky, "Please!"

"So this is how I die." I watch Gareth start CPR on my body. It feels odd, seeing myself looking peacefully asleep. I probably should care more, especially since Melissa is trying hard to jump into it and take my place, but being here feels so soothing, like a lullaby.

"No. No, don't you say that!" Cole bellows at me.

"It's okay." I place my hand on his, inviting him to feel my peacefulness. I look down at our fingers entwined. It feels nice. "Look, we're the same now."

Cole looks at our hands, then paths up to my eyes. Without hesitation he places his lips on mine. The kiss is passionate and strong, his arms intensely wrapped around me, and I feel every sensation of him—his thoughts and feelings dominated by love for me—flowing through me in warm bliss.

I could happily stay like this, and I realize I can. Cole then slowly breaks the kiss, his forehead on mine, his hands on my face, holding me close, together as one.

Finally together.

"Live." His voice is a whisper in the air, gentle and soft and consoling. He suddenly pulls away, his voice strong. "Live."

I open my mouth to speak but I suddenly feel myself recoil. I glance at Cole, hand reaching for him as I close my eyes to the heavy dizziness I feel.

"Breathe." I hear the word from Cole except he sounds like Gareth.

I open my eyes again and see Cole.

"You can do it, Charlotte. Go back!" Cole says intensely. "Go!"

"But—"

I can't even finish that sentence, because all the bliss I felt before is robbed from me as my mind spins, and then suddenly everything becomes dark and heavy.

"Breathe, Charlotte." The sound is faint behind the ringing in my ears. I open my mouth but nothing happens. I begin to see again but everything is gray and blurry and stings.

"Breathe!"

Suddenly my body jolts. I see color again as liquid vomits out of me. My head twists, the disgusting taste of dirty water coming out of my mouth. My body twitches and my throat gargles all sorts of cries, like a newborn baby demanding the world know it exists.

But Gareth doesn't care. "That's it," he pants as I choke in air.

He wraps himself tightly around me, his racing pulse felt along my stiff cold body, my chest on his as he rocks me close, his heartbeat knocking mine, synchronizing to the beating rhythm of life. "Breathe."

∞ 261 ∞

Twenty-three

Drowning is no fun. It's not like on television where the damsel in distress coughs up a few teaspoons of water and then stands up to carry on flirting with David Hasselhoff. No, it's lying in a hospital bed, fighting for every breath with lungs that feel like iron. It's throwing up bits of blood and gunk and who knows what in a porridge of bile and brown stinking water. It's flashbacks of suffocating in darkness when you try to sleep. And it's looking at your parent's face when they thought that they had lost their child.

That's the most painful part.

Dad doesn't leave my hospital bedside except to use the bathroom or to get a coffee from the vending machine in the hospital foyer. He has quite the used paper cup collection building up on the side table, and it is only when the doctors reassure him that there is no more chance of secondary drowning or complications, and nagging from me that he needs a shave and a shower and sleep in a real bed, that he finally leaves to take a rest in my apartment with the promise to be back first thing in the morning.

Not that getting here is easy, given the press camping at the entrance for the chance of statements or interviews, followed by the resulting extra security presence. Beasey the forever inconspicuous janitor, however, strolls on in without getting a second glance to keep me updated whenever I'm alone.

Like Juliet, I only give a brief statement to the police officers, and I do exactly as Beasey tells me to: that I went over to Rory's lake house to check up on him post-breakup, but found the material relating to the victims from the news along with his psychotic notes of resurrecting the dead. He then tried to kidnap me. Where to? I don't know, probably to where he killed the other girls. But it doesn't matter, because I fought him in his car and his fancy Audi ended up in the lake. I managed to get out. Rory didn't.

From what Beasey tells me, the police did a search of his place and found enough DNA matches and written material showing just how twisted and deranged he was that our statements were more or less a formality to wrap the investigation up.

Once the police officers leave, Kelly gets in to see me first. She explains in one long rushed and expressive sentence that Gareth kept pressing her about what was going on, and because neither me nor Juliet were answering our phones, she concluded that there was something wrong and sort of spilled the beans of my suspicions regarding Rory. For that she says she's "sorry, not sorry" for probably saving my life since Gareth saw the car go into the lake and got to me just in time. She then goes on to hate herself for not picking up on the bad vibes from Rory.

I tell her that she did the right thing since I probably wouldn't be here otherwise, and that she shouldn't be hard on herself because he fooled us all. Once that's settled, she then brings in her now official boyfriend, Carlos. They give me Italian snacks and peach iced tea, which is to help me get through all the class notes she gathered from my professors for me. Kelly does her best to remain upbeat; she and Carlos are in that honeymoon phase where they hold hands and feed each other samples of their food, in this case with mini pizza rolls and some nougat candy. While it would be seriously cheesy if it were anyone else but them, instead it's just funny.

Juliet, on the other hand, is clearly traumatized from finding out that her ex-boyfriend was a serial killer who almost murdered her and her friend. She keeps coming back to profusely apologize to me as if she's done something wrong, which always stirs up a chain reaction in me because then we both start becoming emotional messes apologizing and embracing each other. Maybe it's survivor's guilt. I'll have to ask for a psychoanalysis from Kelly on this sometime to boost her spirits after being so wrong about Rory. Kelly mentioned that she has started reading up on psychopaths and killers, but it's another trigger for emotion so I leave it for now.

Just as I thought the visits were over for the day, Kelly slips back in and once she knows that we're alone she asks me to fill her in on what happened—what *really* happened, that is.

"Wow," she exhales, taken aback by it all. "Credit where credit's due, you certainly do lead an extraordinary life."

I huff. She wasn't wrong there. It almost makes the boring alternative of the pile of lecture notes on the side table to read through seem desirable.

Almost.

"So, now the big questions. Gareth?" she asks.

"He stayed with me in the ambulance. Called my dad. Apparently he involved himself quite a bit with my hospital admission until the other doctors politely yet firmly told him to—as he would say—sod off."

"So romantic." She sighs. "And Cole?"

"I . . . haven't seen him since." I swallow, the truth hard to acknowledge.

Kelly's eyebrows furrow. "You don't suppose, like, since you technically *died* and came back to life, your ability has, like, gone?"

My eyes bulge. "Kelly!"

"Just a thought. Or maybe after he finally got his true love's kiss or whatever, maybe he finally crossed over?"

"Kelly!" I repeat, this time more uneasy.

"Sorry." She shrugs. "He's probably just moping around, doing what ghosts do. Gotta wonder, though."

She is right. I have been wondering, every waking minute, where Cole is. Kelly was wrong about her first theory, however; over the past twenty-four hours I've helped fourteen ghosts cross over, a record for me before Beasey took the rest. But in the ghost hub that is the hospital, none of them are Cole, and Kelly's second theory reverberates through my anxious mind.

Carlos comes back, and it's casual conversation again. We plan a pizza night for when normality has returned in my life, and I promise to make one of the Durane family pies for dessert. When the nurse gives the final polite warning that visitor hours are finishing they grudgingly leave. Kelly peers back through the door, however, and discretely asks me what happened to Melissa.

"Don't worry," I reassure her. "She won't be a problem anymore."

That's what I'm assuming, anyway. I don't want to worry Kelly that Melissa is standing right beside her, at least because it's not her that she's staring down at. Melissa has been popping in here and there, watching me with a malicious grin. I don't know what her game is; maybe she doesn't like possessing damaged goods, or maybe she just likes seeing me suffer. I prefer to think that Cole, my protector, is around and keeping her at bay.

Whatever the reason, I'm not willing to find out. Which is why, after the nurse turns down the lights and the other patients settle down to sleep, I calmly and collectively sneak across to the ICU ward and step into Room Six.

I don't need to see Melissa to know she's there; I already feel her, stalking me from behind. It's an acquired skill picked up since crossing over to the other side, Beasey confirmed. I feel them now more than before. And I can control them better too, without the need for any ancient tongue chant.

Which is handy in moments like this when I would rather skip the talk and get straight to the point.

"This is Simona Martinez," I start, holding Melissa in place with one motion of my arm. "Simona was out horse riding along a country road when she was caught in a hit-and-run, poor girl. Fifteen. So young. Her horse had to be put down, too. The surgeons did all they could. They worked on her for hours. But unfortunately Simona didn't wear her helmet that day and, well, the brain is fragile."

I drag Melissa across the room to the bed, right to the beeping machines and tubes attached to Simona. It seems to make her uncomfortable, perhaps a trigger from her own demise.

"She's brain dead, but that's not stopping her parents. They're hopeful, you see, praying every day, believing in miracles, relying on those cases you read about in women's magazines of patients waking up from their comas years later. They're also rich, and by that I'm talking yacht and overseas vacation home level of wealth. No amount of money will fix their daughter, however. But even against the advice of top neuroscientists, they're not prepared to let her go, and have set up twenty-four hour home-based life support."

I look up as Melissa sputters out sounds in her struggle to fight free from my hold of her. It's a struggle in vain as it doesn't even tire me anymore, but I don't tell her that.

"We both know that there's no spirit in there; I helped Simona to cross over."

"Just what do you think will happen? You can put me in there but I'll just get out."

"A normal body resists. But this is a broken body, a body too damaged to know or do otherwise."

I want to say that the fear forming in her eyes makes me feel valiant, that *I* pull the lop-sided smirk at *her* for a change.

But I don't.

It's beyond jubilation because the result will still be the same: Cole is dead—again—because of her.

So instead I'm deadpan and serious as I continue, "You will be trapped, conscious and alone and uncomfortable for as long as they let Simona live—and they really want her to live. You will wish, every minute of your forlorn existence, that you took the easy way out with Rory. And if, one day years from now, you do manage to open your eyes or breathe on your own, you'll still be in a body so brain-damaged you'll struggle to say words or do even the most basic tasks." I raise her into the air. "And if they do give up and turn off the life support then you will cross over immediately in mercy. Because if not, if I ever see you again," I pull her down to me and say through my gritted teeth, "I'll find another body and make you do it all over again."

"Wait, no, please!" she begs, suddenly desperate and pitiful.

"You want a body so badly? Well then here you go!"

With a final pleading wail from Melissa, I place her into the body that belonged to Simona Martinez and hold her there. I watch as the body twitches and trembles, enough to make the machine blip once, twice, and after a pause it blips twice more before it accepts the spirit of its new host and returns to its stiff and unmoving state, Melissa's screams heard no more.

I lower my arms and lean down to whisper in her ear, "You will suffer for what you did. To Maya Tilly, Monique Sharpe, Lucia Turnball, Paula Voss, Scarlet Barnes-Curtis. To Rory Tierney. And to Cole McCroy."

I stand and turn to leave, only then noticing Cole standing at the doorway. I expect an argument or a lecture on morale to happen, or at least a frown and comment.

But he does none of that.

Instead, with a small nod he vanishes again.

∞∞∞∞∞

I sleep peacefully for a while, but I wake up to Gareth at the door, his shoulder leaning on the doorframe, one arm hanging limp in the pocket of his long white coat, the other behind his back.

"Gareth. How did you get—"

"Doctor privileges," he replies. I don't believe him because it's late at night, but I'm not going to ask further. I'm just glad to see him.

"If you're tired I can come back another time—"

"No," I quickly reply, patting the empty bed space beside my legs.

He takes the hint and timidly sits himself down on the edge of the bed.

"They didn't have much to choose from," he says, holding out a bouquet of small white and purple flowers in his hand. His eyebrows dip slightly, debating his choice. I can't help but smile imagining him standing in the hospital florist analyzing each choice based on factors such as color, quantity, symbolism and longevity.

"They're beautiful," I say as I take them from him and see his face relax. "Thank you."

"They say you can be discharged tomorrow morning." He gets distracted by the medical chart at the end of the bed, picking it up and scanning it in doctor mode.

"They said I could be discharged at the end of today, but then changed their minds for no reason at all." I look at him skeptically.

"They must have a good consultant who ensures the patients are properly looked after for the full recommended recovery time and not kicked out at the earliest convenience to appease discharge rates to maximize bed usage for the bureaucrats upstairs," Gareth replies all too smoothly, his accent on the word "bureaucrats" a sexy tone of his tongue. "You have recovered well, though." He holds my x-ray up to what light there is. "And you have a hearty set of lungs in you."

"Thanks. I'll remember that next time I'm in the shower and want some music."

Gareth immediately looks at me straight in the eyes, his tone now serious. "Shit, Charlotte. What were you thinking? If I hadn't pestered Kelly about you as much as I did, if I hadn't driven out and seen the car go under from across the bridge, if I hadn't gotten to you in time . . ." I open my mouth to reply but he continues, "When I saw you . . . when I felt how stiff, how cold you were . . ." he shakes his head slightly as thoughts he refuses to allow come to life.

"Sorry." It seems to be the only word I can come up with lately to everyone. Being a Communicator is not only a thankless job, but an apologetic one too it seems.

"It wasn't the first impression I wanted to make with your father, either."

"I think it's a good thing. He appreciates you saving my life, and for that he probably won't kill you once he catches on we have, uh, history."

Gareth glances away at this, the stress visible in his creased forehead. "Why didn't you tell me?"

"I haven't really had the chance to explain how my dad is a bit of a traditionalist—"

"Not about your father. About everything." He turns to me, the disbelief still in his eyes as he lowers his voice and says, "Rory *killed* innocent women. He could have killed *you*."

I look down at the hospital bed sheets. "I didn't know for sure. Besides," I then look him in the eyes, "would you have believed me?"

"I . . . don't know," he replies truthfully. "I thought we were close, yet I had no idea who he truly was, what he was capable of, what he did. But thinking back, there were times when he did something or said something that wasn't like him, almost like he was another person entirely."

He probably was, but I leave Gareth to his thoughts.

He soon continues, "You're not a liar, Charlotte, you're right about that. But you hide so much, just like Rory hid so much, and Ellie . . . I don't know who or what to believe anymore."

Ouch.

Putting me in the same pile as his murderous friend and his cheating ex-girlfriend, really? Okay, so me alongside Ellie I could understand. But Rory, *really*?

"So . . . this is goodbye?"

"I need time to process everything, to decide what I want. And so do you."

He's right. It hurts, but the truth usually does. Because Rory was my friend, too. And Cole—whom I love and probably always will, came back to life only to die again to save me.

It's a good thing I don't go to therapy because I doubt there's a therapist qualified enough to deal with my issues. Nonetheless, I admit I need a lot of personal reflection time.

And that includes where I stand with Gareth.

"The hospital's a frenzy. Things are really stringent around here, now they know that one of their own . . . well, things are crazy. Not to mention the reporters trying to sneak in here to meet you. Police officers don't usually stand guard checking our credentials to enter, you know."

"Yay me."

Gareth looks at me pitifully and then stands up, his normal work demeanor back in action. "You should rest. I have to get back to work, anyway. Legally we're allowed breaks, but I'm already getting too many messages from the admin department asking why I don't respond while I'm eating or on the loo."

"God bless American capitalism."

He holds back a smirk. "Sleep well, Charlotte."

"How?" The word comes out as I think it, and it catches him at the door. "The car was twenty feet below. It was dark. It could have been days before my body was found." I internally wince at the thought. "How did you know exactly where I was?"

He stops, then turns his head slightly, eyes fixed on the ground. I can just about see the intensity in his silhouetted face when he opens his mouth to reply, "I didn't. Cole showed me."

He leaves before I can respond, but I'm left utterly confused and speechless.

Twenty-four

I'm officially discharged at ten o'clock, but I wait around for the press at the front of the building to tire themselves out and leave knowing they're not going to get a story out of me. I also know that Gareth is sleeping right now, which sucks because I have some burning questions in my mind that I want clarification from him on. Even though he would be very disappointed if he saw what I am doing right now.

Beasey's disappointment, on the other hand, I care less about.

"Fancy seeing you here," he mutters as he takes out a cigarette from his pocket.

"It's the smoking area." It's also freezing cold and the humming and subsequent smell of the nearby hospital cafeteria vents is terrible, but I guess they want the designated hospital smoking area to be as uninviting and as out of view as possible.

"You don't smoke."

I inhale before replying, "I do now."

"You drowned. I'm no doctor but I don't think that's good for your lungs."

"I'm fine," I reply, suppressing the strong urge to cough out the sickly tobacco I can taste down my throat.

"Smoking is bad for you."

"You smoke," I haphazardly retort back.

"And since when did you aspire to be like me?"

He has me there. He always has the right reply to stump my tongue when he wants to. With one more long exhale of tobacco I snuff the cigarette on the wall and then flick it into the designated trash can.

Beasey passes me the newspaper from his hand, the headline *'What One Does For Love'* streaming across the front page. Taking it, I see the pictures of the five women, the same pictures the press has been using since this all began, and now there's a picture of Rory and Melissa on the front page too, the caption below them referring to the saga as a twisted tale of star-crossed lovers.

At least I'm only featured on the second page.

"The families of the victims have been notified. It won't help their loss, but they'll finally be able to rest a little better knowing why." He turns to me. "*We* of course know more, but they don't need to know those details." He inhales deeply, and I wonder if it's the fresh air or tobacco smoke he's sniffing for because it certainly can't be the hospital cafeteria risotto. "There's a balance in the air now. It's come full circle. Everything turned out for the best."

Almost everything.

"I know it doesn't feel that way now," Beasey reads my mind, "but things will begin to make sense. In time."

"Make sense?" I throw the newspaper onto the ground. "Of all the billions of people in the world, why Rory? I came here for a fresh start, to get away from all of this. So of all the places and people in the world, why *him*? It's almost as if . . ."

"There's some sort of divine intervention." Beasey finds the words I couldn't. "Maybe there is. The Lord works in mysterious ways, after all."

I huff. "I still don't know if I believe that."

"Maybe you should. Why did you choose to study at Hillcrest, of all the other colleges and universities across the country?"

"I don't know," I admit. "Because nobody would know me. It's better than State. And it just felt right."

"Something guided you here. Rory might have felt exactly the same way, too. Maybe you two attracted one another."

I snort. "Murderers aren't my thing, Beasey."

"You wanted to be normal. To feel less alone. And deep down Rory wanted the same thing. Who knows how things could have been had you two found each other earlier . . . or later."

I frown. "Oh, so I was meant to find Rory so I could ki—" I hold my breath and glance around before my voice seeps out in a crackling whisper, "So I could *kill* him?"

"I did most of that part. Besides, you saved lives. People are alive right now who will stay that way because of you."

That I know. I do, and I keep reminding myself of it to make it more okay. Except, I didn't regret it then, and I don't regret it now. Rory was a killer, he needed to be stopped, and so I stopped him (or Beasey mostly did, if his reassurance is true). And as for my revenge on Melissa, well, I certainly haven't lost any sleep over her so far.

But what does that make me?

"And this was all part of some divine plan, huh?"

"You choose your path, Charlotte. And you chose the right one."

"How do you know it was the right one?"

"Because it was worth it, wasn't it? To save lives, to meet your friends, for the precious time you had with Cole."

Cole.

My own twisted tale of star-crossed lovers.

"Remember that, Charlotte." His face and words spoken are strained, distracted only to the inhale of tobacco. He loosens up somewhat to add, "I also hear you've taken care of the other problem."

"Cole has spoken to you then?"

"He has. And I have to say I'm impressed. Proud, even."

"That's a morbid sense of pride you've got there."

"It's a morbid life we live." He exhales deeply, his face lowered and pensive. Then, once his usual frown sets shape on his face, he walks back inside the building.

I pop a mint swiped from the hospital cafeteria in my mouth and then go back inside to find Dad who is waiting for me in the foyer. We avoid any determined journalists still lurking around by sneaking out a back exit to Dad's car parked a few blocks away. Since I don't want to go back to my apartment room and it's Dad's first visit here, we decide to go to the national park. It's nice and quiet, the visitors gone now that the colorful fall leaves are piles of sodden brown on the cold ground. That doesn't concern me, though. While I used to hate this time of year it now seems as equally divine as the other seasons, part of a bigger purpose only to be accepted wholly. Maybe it's a trait of someone who's familiar with the other side, who's been exposed to a new level of life and death. Either way I make the most of it for what it is.

After a short while I head back to see Dad sitting alone, immersed in thoughts that weigh heavy on his features. I sit next to him, tossing aside the strands of grass I braided together.

"You were always such a bright little girl," Dad says, looking down at my creation on the ground. "The number of times your mother and I had to stop you drawing on the walls with a crayon or marker pen . . . you found a use for everything, you did. Your mother and I were sure you'd turn out to be one of those loud subversive arty types with a nose ring and a dreamcatcher tattoo."

We share a chuckle, but I feel Dad's mood change, his face scrunching up.

"But then you went quiet. Not straight away, so we barely noticed. Then I started to hear you talking to yourself. I thought they were just imaginary friends at first, didn't think much of it. But then you started talking about them in detail, things little girls wouldn't normally say, and it bothered you as much as it bothered us. And every time *they* came, you became stressed, anxious. You got in trouble at school, your grades dropped, you came home crying. And I didn't know what to do to make it better. So I tried therapists, I tried pills. This diagnosis, that medication. Nothing worked. I hated it, but I just wanted you to be your normal happy self again." He takes in a stifled breath before saying, "Then Cole came. And he didn't leave."

I look at him in shock.

"What? You think your old man's clueless? I see you in the garden or hear you in your bedroom, talking to someone, *something*. But whoever—whatever—Cole is, it makes you happier. It's there for you in ways I know I can't be. So as much as I disapproved of it at first, as long as you are okay I ignore it. Because I don't want to lose you, Charlotte. I can't ever lose you."

Dad then does something in front of me I've never seen him do before: he cries.

"When I got that call . . . when Gareth told me what had happened to you . . ." he chokes between sobs. "Don't ever scare me like that again."

"You're not going to lose me, Dad," I say, hugging him tightly, my face now covered with tears of my own. It may be against his staunch ways, but it doesn't show because he pulls me in his arms and holds me tight in embrace, his emotions open to the vulnerability he never shows. "You'll never lose me."

∞∞∞∞∞∞

It's a weird feeling to have died and come back to life again. To have stepped on the boundary between this world and the next. I haven't really had the time to myself to process it until now, which is probably why after a long and heartfelt session with Dad, I take a walk alone to begin facing the thoughts and feelings I don't want to confront.

"Hey."

I twist to see Cole standing nearby. His head tilts, a side smile grows. His aura is a tint brighter than usual, his mood pleasant.

"You startled me," I reply. "You haven't startled me like that since . . . since I was twelve years old in the haunted house at the state carnival."

"You needed the VIP experience. Nothing else scared you." Cole smirks at the memory.

I frown, hands on my hips. "Where have you been?"

"Watching you be awesome from the sidelines. I'm impressed, by the way."

I take the compliment but don't show it. "I was worried about you."

"You were worried about me? How sweet."

I fold my arms, unimpressed.

"I'm sorry," he says, serious this time. "Are you okay?"

I look away, instead choosing to focus my sight out over the lake. It's a clear and sunny afternoon which means I can see all the way across the water to the boundary of the golf course, and if I stare hard enough, I can just about make out *that* lake house.

I blink away the wet in my eyes. "I died, Cole."

"I know."

"I was there with you."

"I know."

He comes close and caresses my cheek, the feel of his fingers on my skin now back to the all too familiar feather-touch.

"When Dad heard what had happened . . . when he saw me in the hospital . . ."

Cole hushes me as I start sobbing. "You're okay, now." He kisses my head, his voice soothing and reassuring. "You're going to be okay."

We stand side by side and stare at the lake, the water that took us, thinking thoughts that don't need to be said. Thoughts like what could have been and what should have been. Kelly warned the "what if?" questions would come as I try to process everything. It's pointless though, because for all I am, for all I can do, I feel absolutely powerless to change anything.

"I miss Timothy," I eventually say.

"I do, too. But he's okay. I know he is."

"It's my fault. I messed up. I went into Rory's house without a plan."

"You acted on your instinct."

"Juliet wasn't even there."

"But what if she was? It's a happy ending, Charlotte. Rory and Melissa won't be harming anyone anymore, and you and

Juliet are safe."

"It's not a happy ending, Cole. You died again."

"But I was alive again."

"Not for long."

"Long enough." He steps closer to me, his voice softer now as he says, "And how incredible it was. I got to touch you, hold you, kiss you."

"It's not enough," I try to hold back a sob. "It's not fair."

Cole places his arm around me. "It never is. But it was nice while it lasted."

"We'll find another Rory."

"Charlotte."

"We've done it once; we can do it again."

"Charlotte—"

"If there's a chance—"

"Charlotte—"

"Just give me time—"

"Stop."

"I just need time." I struggle to hold myself together. "I'll think of something."

"Something tells me I'm just not meant to be in this world anymore."

"Don't say that," I protest. "We need to do all those things we promised we would. It wasn't long enough. You shouldn't have . . ." I bite my lip, try to hold the emotion in. "You should have survived. You should have saved yourself."

"That was never my purpose, Charlotte. Protecting you was."

"What about *you*?"

"Do you remember my eighteen again birthday, how you had me make a wish? I never told you what I wished for, did I?"

"No."

"I wished that I could touch that darn loose lock of hair of yours and curl it behind your ear. Just once." He chuckles as I do just that. "Yes, that's the one. *Just once*, that was my wish, my bargaining plea. And I did. It actually came true." He looks at that same lock and strokes it with his hand. It doesn't move, but I don't think he tries. "My wish was granted. I can't expect anything else."

"What are you saying?"

Cole then looks me in the eyes. "Charlotte, please understand. I defied death and it was worth it for those precious minutes I got with you. But now I . . . I have nothing left to carry on for."

"You have me," I say, almost insulted at his words.

"I wish that was true." He covers his eyes with his free hand, failing to hide the pained expression on his face. "My god I wish that was true."

"Why can't it be true?" I press, feeling my face scowl.

I wait for an answer I don't receive. Cole silently stares out ahead. It's a quick change of emotion; what was so well repressed now so quick to reveal itself shows me how sad he really is, and how strong he's been to carry on as he has.

Cole waits a moment longer before replying, "Being dead again . . . it's different. I feel it. The light. Pulling me. And I can't hold on much longer." He turns to me again and swallows, guilty of his admission. "I'm tired, Charlotte."

The words are a punch in the gut. I clutch my chest, the physical manifestation of pain forming, except there's no wound. It's a different kind of pain, one that I sadly know all too well.

Heartbreak.

I'm completely and utterly heartbroken.

It's not cheating, but I feel betrayed. Like the life I lead, my life *with* him and all that I offer, is no longer good enough. Like there's more I should do to earn his keep. Except I tried. And like Beasey—who always has to be right—said, there isn't anything I can do.

Cole is dead.

And life is for the living.

I realize I'm crying again. Not just crying, but a total and utter incomprehensible mess. Because the truth hurts. It really fucking hurts.

Cole has his arms on me, leaning in close and kissing my head. He whispers how sorry he is, over and over again, but it doesn't change anything. Reality has shown itself, like the glaring morning light after waking up from a dream, saying that this is the real world, now deal with it.

"Shh," Cole hushes. "Don't be sad. I got to spend ten crazy years with you. I'm blessed."

"You can spend ten more years with me. Twenty more, even. Just the two of us. Please?"

"One path for you, one path for me. That's how it was always going to be, remember? You've got to play out the rest of yours. Establish a career, get married, have two kids and a puppy in the suburbs."

The thought of being a wife and mother right now makes me sob even more.

"But we'll always have us," he comforts. "Our memories together. That's all we have in the end. That's how we live on."

I pull away from him, trying to find more air to breathe. I don't want him to see me as I say these next words.

"What if I forget you?"

"You won't," he reassures.

I want to believe his words, I really do. But the thing is, the photos of my mother that I have are the only images that keep her alive in me because the memories I have of her have almost all faded away. And I'm only eighteen years old. In another eighteen years I'll be thirty-six years old. Will I remember the details of Cole's brown eyes or dimples of his smile or the sound of his laugh when I'm thirty-six years old, or will they be taken over by all the new memories I'll make? What about eighteen years after that?

"Come here," he says softly, offering his hand. "I want to try something. I need your permission, though."

"Permission?"

Cole nods. "Do you trust me?"

"Of course."

Both of his hands meet my own as he comes in close. So close, in fact, I think he will kiss me. Instead, however, he places his forehead against my own, making a conscious effort to inhale deeply, a smile forming at the corners of his lips. His glow brightens, the close proximity between us making me need to close my eyes, the energy of him so immersed in my own I wonder if he's going to possess me.

"Cole—"

"Shh," he whispers. "Keep your eyes closed."

It starts as waves, throbbing like a tension headache. And then it's as if his invisible wall that's always been shielding him suddenly disappears, along with everything else.

For a moment I'm in my bedroom. I see myself, only it's through Cole's eyes, and I feel as he feels. I'm seven years old, and I'm crying in bed until I look up and scream in fright.

I gasp and pull back, the overwhelming guilt I feel emitting through Cole almost too much to take on.

"Hold on with me," Cole whispers, the palms of his hinds now tightly over my own. "It gets better. I promise."

I close my eyes again as he presses his forehead further on mine, concentrating as he wraps his energy around me, cocooning me into him.

It's faint and distorted at times, but I find myself back into what I realize is his consciousness, transported to glimpses of his memories. I see what he sees, feel what he feels. Moments of us play out: the first time he saw me, the heavy weight of dark energy he carried; the anger he had for his parents and the tears he carried because of them, suffering in secret; the letting go of Danielle and his friends as they moved on without him; the first time he saw me smile, that shimmer of hope he held onto; all the nights he spent sitting outside my bedroom door keeping ghosts away, wanting to protect me; the longing for his final home when he watches the stars; his awe at all the little parts of nature working together; the stab of jealousy he felt as he watched my first kiss and the effort he upheld to not let it show; the reservedness when Venessa kissed him, his lips on hers yet his mind on me; the way he lit up inside when he saw me in my prom dress, thinking how beautiful I was; the wave of light extinguishing his dark when we shared our first kiss.

Then I witness his subtle concern as I branch off and start living, his presence needed less, my independence needed more. He's both happy and sad, watching me study, work, and getting along with my friends and Gareth. I see how he had to leave before Gareth and I kissed at the firepit, how he withdrew after he saw me with Gareth in bed. But there's no dark; he pushes for what's best for me, even at the cost of his own happiness. He knew he had to keep pushing me away from him because otherwise I would forever hold back.

I want to stop there and reassure him, but then I see the moment he opened his eyes, born again, to see me looking down at him. And when he could finally feel me, kiss me, hold me, how he never wanted to let go.

The visions then get stronger, and I feel overwhelmed at how he fought to distract Melissa enough for me to survive, even as that meant as a ghost, and how his only worry when he died again was for me. I feel fully through me how our souls connected when we were together in death, and how relieved he was to watch me wake up in the arms of Gareth so that I could live on.

And then I feel the light, the pure light of whatever is tugging at him. He does his best to ignore it, but it's there, on the sidelines, slowly growing bigger and brighter, emitting love and welcoming compassion like nothing I've ever felt before. He's holding on, but he feels it, the calling for home. For God.

I don't realize I'm crying until he pulls away, the mirage now over.

He was there. Even when I thought he wasn't, he was watching me, feeling for me. He was always there, my guardian angel, his forbearance for his promise to protect me and make sure that I'll be okay.

"Charlotte." His soft brown eyes are on me, gentle and concerned. "Are you okay?"

"What was that?" I manage to ask through the waves of emotion only now starting to settle within me.

"I just shared my memories with you, Charlotte. That's

something nobody else will ever have."

I look him in the eyes. He must think I need more of an explanation because he continues, "I didn't know if that would work or not, but with the whole possession ability thing I—"

I don't let him finish, because I pull him in and kiss him, more passionately than I ever thought possible. If my light could be seen it would be glowing, just like his, because I see—finally see—just how much we are to one another, a connection that can't be understood. Or forgotten.

When I eventually pull away I can't help but sob. "I'm sorry."

"Don't be." Cole cups my face, his fingers splayed across my damp cheeks. "I am so, *so* glad for all the moments I've had with you, Charlotte. Some people don't get something like that that in a long lifetime. We may not be life mates, you and me. But we're *soulmates*."

I can't help but smile. "Forever."

∞∞∞∞

It's a slow hike up around the lake to the viewpoint. I messaged Dad to say I'd only be a couple of hours, but he can wait because I do my best to make it last as long as the day allows. Cole does most of the talking, but it's mostly remarking about the world around us. It doesn't tire him, but that's how he looks. Maybe it's from what he did before, but I know it's because he really is tired, his spirit finally waning the strength to hold back much longer.

When we reach the peak we stay close, hand in hand, no words needing to be said as we watch the last streams of sunlight move behind the hillside to shades of pastel oranges and blues.

"Heaven is here," Cole echoes, taking in the view.

I turn to face Cole. He looks different, but I'm not sure how. He seems a little lighter, his eyes wholesome, his composure serene, as if not a single worry of the world exists. Just him, me, and this magical landscape.

And yet I fear what comes next.

Cole looks at me and smiles. A smile that then melts down to something serious. My fingers fall from his. He has that look where he's about to say something I know I don't want to hear. My head slowly starts to shake.

No. Don't say it. Please don't say it.

"It's time, Charlotte."

I freeze. The world stops, a glitch in the matrix, something I can't compute. Then like a shock of life, pain hits my chest, a reminder that this is real and happening.

I inhale a short, sharp breath. "I'll get my car then, we'll go for a road trip."

"Charlotte—"

"Let's go to the coast. It's been years since I've seen the ocean."

"Charlotte—"

"I'll hire a car, a Cadilac."

"Charlotte—"

"It's too soon. I need more time." My voice breaks, my throat closes. My body begins to feel like jelly and I hold onto the boulder behind me. "There's not enough time!"

Cole looks at me, head tilted, a sad smile. "There's never enough time."

My chest tightens with his words. "I can't carry on without you."

"But you *can*, Charlotte." Cole takes a step closer, his eyes doting on me. "You've come so far from that needy little girl crying in her room ten years ago."

"I still need you," I protest selfishly.

"That's the thing, Charlotte. You don't need me. Not anymore."

I shake my head and look away, trying to focus on the mountainside through my tears. "How can you say that?"

"Because now you have your Dad who finally understands you, and you have Patricia, and Kelly and Juliet and Gareth. And Beasey, of course. But most importantly, Charlotte, you have yourself.”

Cole grins like this is a joke, like the punchline is about to reveal the hidden cameras and I’m supposed to be all surprised and we then all laugh it off and go home. Only the punchline doesn’t come.

“Don’t you see, Charlotte? You have grown into a beautiful, strong, independent young woman. You are not afraid anymore. You are not alone anymore.” He rubs his thumb under my eye. “Don’t cry.”

Am I crying? I can’t even tell if I am breathing.

“You can have a happy life now, and have a real relationship, with a real man.”

“You’re the one.” The reply comes quick, almost instant.

Cole manages to smile, but it’s bittersweet. “I know, and I’m sorry I can’t give you this lifetime. When your time is up, whatever lifetime comes next, I’ll be waiting for you. But you must live a happy life with the time you do have, okay? Promise me that.”

I look at him, fighting myself to say the word, unable to accept this day, this moment I feared and refused for so long, has finally come.

“Okay,” I promise. I have to say it. Not for me, though; this isn’t for my sake. It was always for my sake, everything Cole did. This is for Cole. To let him finally have the peaceful passing he so deserves. To let him finally rest in peace.

I can now see him glowing a pale light and I know what follows.

It is time.

It is really happening.

I want to make it stop, but I can’t. How am I supposed to sum up how much he means to me in these last moments?

“I can’t breathe.” I feel shaky, my breath short. My head starts throbbing and my knees begin to buckle beneath me.

“One breath at a time.” Cole smiles, those beautiful dimples protruding over the corners of his lips. His focus then falters and his mouth opens slightly as his eyes trail around. His eyes glisten, his lips twitch, and a tear falls down his cheek as an enthused huff escapes him. He has the face of silliness and laughter that warms my heart, even now.

"I love you."

Cole looks back at me and with no hesitation he places his hands on my cheeks, his smile full and eyes intense. "And I will forever love you, Charlotte Durane."

Those words. Those eyes.

I get light-headed as he glows even brighter. I feel him slipping away.

This is it.

He's finally letting go.

He moves in close, his face inches from mine. "Close your eyes."

I do as he says, holding his image in my mind. I feel the gentle tingling of his lips on mine, the euphoric rush from my stomach letting me know he is there. A light shimmers through my eyelids—quick and bright and dizzying—then it's gone, the touch of him no more.

"Cole?" My voice cracks through my tight throat.

Nothing.

I refuse to open my eyes. "Cole?" I push the sound out. "Cole!" I try moving but my swirling head sends me to the ground. I keep saying his name, louder and louder, all the while trying to keep his image in my mind.

But there's no reply.

And it's the moment I accept that I'm alone, that he really is gone, that I become a mess. A hysteric, sobbing mess.

My eyes stay shut, my frame of mind gone to my emotions as they convulse from within me. After a while I hear my name. It's faint at first, like an echo from the stars replying to my calls. What if he is still there in some way? What if he is able to come back?

"Charlotte?"

I hear it again.

"Charlotte!"

Panting. Footsteps.

"Oh my god, what happened?"

"Cole."

"You're cold stiff!" Hot breath on my hands. "We've got to warm you up in my car. Your father's worried about you. Charlotte? Open your eyes."

I open my eyes. The sky is now the dark purple hue of late twilight almost black. And where Cole was Gareth now stands, concern emitting through his heavy blue eyes, his warmth felt through my hands making my shivering body crave more.

"No!" I protest my eyes shut again. "I can't forget him, I can't forget his face!"

"Whose face?"

"Cole's," I reply, realizing my teeth are chattering. "He's gone, Gareth." The words stab in my chest. "He's gone."

There is a short silence until Gareth slowly says, "Charlotte. Look at me."

I manage to comply.

"You won't forget Cole." He lifts me up. "Now get in the car."

Twenty-five

He's gone.
I want him here.
Except he's not here. We're so far apart.
When I look for him I am only met with a world I don't want to face.
So I close my eyes again.

Twenty-six

Nobody really knew what to do with me once Gareth got me warmed up in the back of his car. I don't blame them considering I wasn't in a very coherent state. Gareth had to go back to the hospital and Dad wasn't taking any chances with me so he drove me home with him, concluding that I was suffering some sort of onset post-traumatic stress disorder. He tried to get me to talk, to find out what was wrong, but every time I tried to explain I began to weep. And every time I got close to forming full coherent sentences the reminder that Cole wasn't coming back hit again and I began to weep more, so we both gave up trying.

I must have fallen asleep from exhaustion because when I wake up on the couch with Pippi it is late afternoon the next day. Patricia manages to get some warm tea into me, one small sip and motherly gesture at a time. Dad, of course, being frantic with worry takes time away from his diner to keep an eye on me. He's trying, and I appreciate his efforts, but opening up to him will take some practice, too. We'll get there, but for now we default to what we've done so many times like this before: make a pie and watch whatever sports game is on.

I'm pretty sure I have flunked my first semester of college, but I am too numb to care. I certainly don't care about my job at the café, and I doubt Mr. Dodgley cares about me. Kelly calls frequently to check up on me. We have casual conversations, mostly about classes and Juliet and Carlos, but I don't talk about what happened. She doesn't push, either. I promise to tell her in person when I see her next. Until then she reassures me that Gareth is feeding Shark.

I still think about Cole all the time. He pops up in my mind in the small moments I think he's not, like when I look outside and suddenly expect to see him lying on the trampoline watching the clouds float by, or when I want to tell him something—a thought I had or an interesting fact I know he'll appreciate or just a simple hello.

But he doesn't show.

And it hurts. So, so much.

I try to avoid such triggers as best I can, including protesting to Dad to get rid of the trampoline I can never go on again. It's something he's wanted to do for years, and although he is confused at my sudden change of heart, a neighbor down the street is coming to take it for his kids and I know that they'll enjoy it as much as Cole and I did.

But for the times I can't avoid the thoughts, I allow myself to feel the pain as a reminder that he was here, that he existed, and that he is loved and missed dearly.

It is exactly a week later, while Dad and Patricia are finishing dinner and doing the usual distraction by setting up a movie to watch, I step outside for some alone time when Pippi alerts me to an unexpected visitor. She's quick to ignore him though and gets back to sniffing out wildlife.

"You really should stop that before it becomes a habit."

I look at the cigarette in my hand. "It's just the one."

"I take it you're hiding out here in the dark so your father doesn't notice?"

As it turns out, Dad has a good sense of smell so even with gum I can't have any more than one without receiving a lecture, and since I'll be sitting by him for the next three hours to watch *The Hobbit* I should probably stop now.

"What would Cole think?"

Those words are painful, raw.

"It doesn't matter what he thinks anymore, Beasey. He's not here."

"Stop that now."

"Stop what?"

"That loathing self-pity. You know that would disappoint him."

I roll my eyes and snuff the cigarette out against the wall harder than necessary and flick it into the empty terracotta plant pot with the rest. I'll have to get around to discreetly disposing of them at some point, but for now the weeds hide my evidence well enough.

"Things are just a bit hard right now, Beasey."

"It's not meant to be easy. But it's not meant to be suffering, either."

I huff. "Both of you have said that living is suffering."

"Oh, it is. But you decide how much to suffer."

"Sounds like a shit deal to me."

"Only you can control how you feel. All the world was, is, and ever will be are moments fueled by feelings. Some moments are better than others, but all measure up, and sometimes along the way you might just come across defining moments, moments worth remembering, moments worth loving."

I huff again. "That's what makes it worthwhile? Because along the way we may just have some good moments? I'm supposed to hold on to that?"

"Yes," he replies. "The world gave you Cole, remember?"

"Only to take him away!"

"But it gave you Cole."

"But he's gone!"

"*It gave you Cole,*" he says again, sternly emphasizing each word.

I'm then unable to stop the tears suddenly bursting from my eyes and the suppressed weeps from my mouth. He pulls me in, holding me tightly as he whispers the words over again to my ear as prayer to my heart, gratitude in my mind, and eventually—not straight away but soon enough—for the first time since Cole left

I manage to smile, something I didn't think I would be able to do again.

"You got to have Cole," he says once more. "And that's what you hold on to."

"So what now?" I manage to ask as I wipe my wet eyes. "Just carry on? I don't know how to."

"You need support. From people who understand, people who have been through what you are going through."

I wish I still had that cigarette. Since I don't, I start picking at my fingernails instead. "I don't think therapy would work here, Beasey."

"I'm not just talking about your broken heart, Charlotte. You've learned a lot; you're powerful. More so since you were born with your gift and have been in spirit form. Rory is an example of what can happen without such support."

"I have—*had* Cole. And I have you, I guess."

"And where would you be otherwise?"

I gulp at the possibilities.

"Go to Italy."

"To join your cult?"

"To learn about it. All of it. Without judgment."

"Rory had a copy of your Communicator book."

"Yes, he did."

"He was one of you."

"No, he was not."

I frown, expecting a better explanation than that. "Then how did he have a copy? I thought it was members only."

"It is. And that's a good question."

I raise my eyebrow slightly, expecting him to explain further. "What do you mean?" I ask.

"There are things, things you don't yet know about. I'm not going to go over them now, but it's something you should to be aware of. Whether you want to continue down this path or not I'll leave up to you. But just know that it doesn't involve the possibility of Cole returning. His story is over, but the book of Cole remains within you."

"Will joining your Communicator club help me get over Cole?"

"No. If anything it will make you miss him more. But there are still plenty of Coles out there, Charlotte. Not the one you want, but the ones you can still help."

No spirit will ever amount to Cole, but I get it. Our hearts are amazingly able to carry on loving, even after being broken and scarred.

"I'll think about it," I eventually reply. The truth is I have been thinking about it, long and hard. With Cole gone this place feels too empty, too quiet. So maybe a fresh start (or, at least, another one) is the way to go.

Then again, I can't keep running forever. Life on the road may be Beasey's choice but it isn't mine. And since I can't escape it I might as well face it head on.

Defining moments.

Beasey echoes my thoughts. "Death doesn't disappear, Charlotte. It catches up to you."

"I said I'll think about it," I reply, leaving it at that. "What about you? Will *you* go to Italy? Or will you just drift onwards to the next ghost town? Pun intended, by the way."

"I'll do what I usually do: try to clean up the mess of this world, one job at a time."

It hits me then, all that Beasey does. It's mostly thankless and easily forgotten work, and he's barely even noticed or recognized by the world. But he does it anyway, straight from his heart, guided by something greater than himself. I guess he really is doing the Lord's bidding.

"Will you stay nearby, at least?"

Beasey lets out a small chuckle. I guess I opened myself up to all kinds of responses there. He doesn't taunt me about hanging around though, instead replying, "I have a good job at the hospital. Never a dull day there. I like the area, too. Good food, nice people. Maria sends her love, by the way."

Beasey places a small woven basket from behind him onto the steps beside us. Even though there's a red and white tea towel covering it, I can just about smell the fresh bread in the air.

I smirk. Maybe Kelly does have a special talent for reading people, after all. She will be pleased to know. Or maybe not, considering the vibe she gets from him, but I'll just have to reassure her that it's just a good façade, and that he's not that bad once you put up with him long enough.

"You came all this way to deliver her baking? You're into her, aren't you?"

"Charlotte, Maria is a very respectable woman whom I appreciate spending time with. We happen to have a lot in common."

"Sure, sure. You are *totally* into Maria." I stifle a laugh. It feels refreshing, such an action, like for a moment my chest doesn't feel heavy anymore.

Moments worth remembering.

Beasey doesn't say anything, but his smile, the rarity that it is, reveals enough. Sometimes that's all it takes: a look or a nod or a smile. Sometimes gestures don't need words. Cole was like that, wanting to protect me from his thoughts, even his pain. His end.

"He told you, didn't he?" I can only face the ground as I ask, "How else would you know he's gone?"

"Yes. At the hospital. He felt his time was coming, the light too strong to ignore any longer. And the way you took on Melissa confirmed to him that you have it in you to be strong enough without him. It was Cole's final request to me that Gareth be there for you after he crosses over."

"So that's how Gareth knew where I was," I mutter.

"I'm a man of my word, Charlotte. And as a man of my word I shook his hand and made that promise to him." Beasey sighs softly as he pulls out a cigarette of his own and lights it. He inhales, deeper than his usual puff, but I don't judge. "He was a good one, that Cole. It was the least I could do."

"One of a kind," I say, taking in the stars and sky we both spent so many nights gazing up at, talking and laughing and losing track of time and everything else, just the two of us.

Moments worth loving.

"That Gareth guy didn't need telling twice, either. He really cares about you."

"I don't know about that." I haven't heard from Gareth since Dad took me out of his car, but I don't blame him.

"It's a lot to take on. Understandably he's confused, but give him a chance."

"I wouldn't give myself a chance. I'm an emotional wreck, Beasey. I don't know if he even wants to see me again."

"Why don't you ask him yourself?"

I follow Beasey's line of sight to the car pulling up at the end of the driveway. "Is that Gareth? How does he know where I live?"

"I may have given some directions," Beasey mutters before straightening up. "I'll leave you to it."

"There's extra turkey in the fridge if you want to stay. We're having a bit of a late Thanksgiving dinner."

"Maybe next time. I've got places to be, ghosts to see."

"Thank you," I say, from the bottom of my heart. "For being there for me, and every time before that. It means a lot to me."

Beasey nods with a small smile. "You know how to contact me if you want to."

"Hey," I call out as he starts to walk away. "Are you ever going to tell me your first name?"

Beasey cracks a chuckle before calling back, "Try asking me when you're in Italy."

"I didn't say I would go."

He doesn't reply though, just as I knew he wouldn't. With a nod shared with Gareth he leaves while Gareth navigates Pippi the gate guard. She's more excited to meet Gareth, a stranger with a new scent, but once she's had a quick sniff and pat she settles back down.

"Your uncle is like you, isn't he?" Gareth speaks first.

"He's not my biological uncle, but yes, he is."

"Is everyone like you? Am I the weird one here?" He pauses. "Wait, I didn't mean it like that."

"It's fine," I quickly reply. "I've heard worse. And no, Beasey and I are the only weird ones around."

An awkward silence follows. I should try to think of something to say, but since I'm a nervous wreck right now I can only think about wanting another cigarette.

"How are you?" Gareth eventually asks.

I look at him before turning away. How can I answer that? "Been better, been worse," I conclude, wanting to change the topic. "Why did you come all the way out here?" I settle for asking instead.

"I think you know why. There's a lot to talk about."

I swallow, bracing myself for the worst. I don't expect him to still want me, not after all I've put him through. At least I'm already broken inside so we might as well get it over with now.

"Did you make those?" Gareth asks, suddenly taking note of the windchimes hanging down from the gutter over the front porch behind us.

"Yeah. Just something I used to do."

"It seems there's a lot about you I don't know about."

An awkward silence.

"They're cool, though. You have a gift for art."

I can't help but feel good at this, guilty of such an emotion amid the darkness I've been in.

Another silence between us.

"That night," Gareth breaks the silence first, "after Kelly said enough to make me concerned, I drove out to Rory's lake house. I noticed his car coming towards me from the other side of the bridge—even in the dark how can you not recognize a car like that?—before it swerved and went into the water.

"I immediately pulled over and ran up to the embankment, but I couldn't see anything except the faint blur of headlights. And that's when I saw him, floating above the water, looking at me." He shuffles uncomfortably. "It was the scariest thing I've ever seen. You read about ghost sightings on the internet without much believability. I think I watched *Ghostbusters* when I was a kid. But you don't really consider it in daily life. To see a real ghost . . . it wasn't what I thought it would be. His face . . . he looked troubled, in pain, like he was yelling except I couldn't hear anything. Then he looked down at the water and was gone.

"It was only a couple of seconds, and I didn't want to believe it. Then I saw bubbles coming from the water and I just knew that you were down there and in trouble." He sits down on one of the steps leading to the front door, the heaviness of such thoughts weighing him down. "He sure was some guardian angel."

Poor Cole. To conjure up so much energy to be seen by Gareth, even for only a second or two, would have been an effort.

"He was."

Was.

The word makes me wince inside. I feel like a traitor using past tense. I look at Pippi, who's now quietly curled up sleepily by my feet. I keep expecting her to bark once to mark Cole's entry, but she doesn't.

Gareth snickers to himself. "My father always told me those swimming lessons would pay off one day. I guess I should let him know."

"Please pass on my utmost gratitude to your father," I reply in a bad British accent.

Gareth flashes a smile. "Will do."

For a few seconds things feel nice, as if normal again. But I then see Gareth's forehead crease, and he crosses his arms over his lap.

"I'll never be at his level, will I? It will always be Cole in your heart."

I look at the black sky above. The stars seem exceptionally bright tonight. I wonder if Cole is up there now, part of the great cosmos expanse. Is he be watching from above? Maybe I'm being selfish expecting him to still dote on me. He chose to leave, after all. To go where I can't—not for now, anyway.

But Cole was right. This is the land of the living. He died so I could live, and it's time I do just that.

"I love Cole, Gareth. I always will. He was there when I needed someone, when I was lost and alone, and the only person

I could be myself with. He was safe—and, crossing some very odd boundaries of friendship and plains of existence—I gave him my heart for that." I turn to Gareth, his expression stiff yet hurt. I take in a long, strained breath. "But he was a ghost, only in my life because I needed him. You, on the other hand, are part of the life I choose to lead. Not because I need you but because I want you. And Cole only hung around long enough for me to realize that."

This seems to ease Gareth, who relaxes his staunch composure a little.

"And . . . *ghosts*?"

"They're around. They'll always be around. That's not going to change. *I'm* not going to change. I can communicate with ghosts."

Gareth shifts uncomfortably.

I breathe in heavily, asserting myself for what I say next. "Look, I'm not expecting things to go back to the way we were. A lot of crazy shit has happened recently—sorry about that, by the way, but that just comes with the territory. However, I don't belong to the dead. I have my own life to live. So, while I would really like to start over again, if that's too much then I'm sorry that who I am won't work out for you. But, if you were to forgive me and consider taking me back, it would be with me—that is, the whole me. Ghosts 'n all."

I feel my cheeks going hot, my eyes watery as Gareth says nothing.

I start to leave.

"Charlotte."

I turn around, arms crossed tightly to my chest.

"I've had plenty of time to think. About what happened with Rory. About us. And I'm still trying to figure it all out, to have it all make sense in a way I want it to."

I get it. I do. The logical part of the human mind yearns for comfort in the ordinary, things it can sense and analyze, which is why people like me get ridiculed so easily.

Gareth continues, "I just don't get why you didn't say

anything. Why you didn't trust me. Why you had to pull away and go at it alone."

"It's not that I want to do this alone, Gareth. I'm just used to it." Alone with Cole, that is. And now truly alone, in the horribly isolating and demonizing sense of the word. "It's easier this way than trying to explain, to get people to understand."

"But you didn't try. Not with me." Gareth's dark eyebrows lower into a scowl. "Am I not worth that?"

"It's *because* I want you that I didn't tell you, Gareth. So that you wouldn't leave me."

"I wouldn't have left you, Charlotte."

"You said it yourself that you don't believe in ghosts and that you don't know if you would have believed me."

"True. But I wouldn't have left you. Not for being who you are. The secrets, however . . ." He sighs, pinches the bridge of his nose and mutters something through his thick accent about women being complicated.

"You don't need to say it. I'm sorry you came out all the way here to break up with me. Kelly mentioned you're still feeding Shark and I appreciate that. But I'll be back in a couple of days so you can leave my spare key here or with Kelly. You won't need to see me again."

Gareth looks up at me. His gaze narrows but I cut his view as I walk past him to the front door.

"Charlotte." He grips the bottom of my jacket. "That's not what I—" he pauses to stand. "Look, no more secrets from now on. I'll deal with the ghost stuff—somehow. Heck, I think it's an amazing gift you have, and you seem to help a lot of people. But I need you to be honest with me. It's not like I can tell if some hot ghost guy is flirting with you—and it's still cheating even if they're dead, by the way."

I bite the inside of my lip, careful not to reveal more. Since all cards are on the table, part of me thinks I should come out and tell him the rest of what happened, the real story before he found me drowned in the lake, but I quickly decide against it. It's still hard enough for me to get my head around, let alone poor Gareth who has already been through enough. Some things should remain dead.

And for what it's worth, what happened with Cole, well, that is just between me, Cole, and a time now gone.

So I smile, fighting the tears in my eyes as I confirm his words. "No more secrets from now on."

Gareth puts his hands on my waist and smiles appreciatively at me. His warmth is felt both around and within me, an acknowledgement in my heart that I can be with him for all that I am.

We lean in to kiss and almost make it until a couple of taps on the window take our attention. Dad's now watching, a bowl of popcorn in his hands and a stern curious look on his face. I smile back, a signal for both of us that everything's okay.

"Come," I say, gently tugging Gareth's arm. "I think it's time I properly introduce you to my father."

Epilogue

"Now this," Kelly says, sitting up to take a sip of her freshly squeezed juice, "is what living is all about."

I can't agree more. Lying on a beach towel in a string bikini in eighty-two degrees of sun and clear-blue sky is not something I had planned for spring break, but I'm not complaining. And better than the cold pineapple juice beside me and the nice tan I can see coming on are the people I'm with. I lift my sunglasses and watch Gareth, Juliet and Carlos throw a volleyball around on the sand. The beach is packed with young adults having a good time, lounging on the sand or water, with the odd couple taking off in jet skis. Other tourists watch on; some walking by, some joining in, the odd older couple strolling along the sidewalk hand-in-hand. And there's not a single ghost in sight.

My mood suddenly drops and a ball in my throat forms, sharp to swallow. A reminder that Cole is gone.

"Hey," Kelly must have noticed me. "Happy vibes only, remember?"

I force a smile. She's been a big support these past few months, keeping me going when I couldn't even muster the motivation to get out of bed. The rest of the motivation comes from being busy with everything that's changed. I withdrew from university and now attend a police academy with the intention of becoming a detective. The idea solidified within me as a poster on a bus shelter I was standing in after getting caught in a sudden downpour on what was only a slightly cloudy day. I'm sure it was just a coincidence, although I have a feeling I'm going to have a really interesting journey down this path. I figured I should put this gift of mine to a more income-generating and productive use while being able to help all the Coles and Scarlets and Timothys out there find their peace, and since it's what I seem to do anyway I'm getting good grades for once. It also means I can do investigative practices more legally and with more resources and training—which, considering my history, would be a bonus.

And Cole was right; *Detective Durane* does have a good ring to it.

Gareth and I are stronger than ever. I couldn't take the quietness of my loft apartment so Shark and I ended up spending time at Gareth's apartment until it became permanent. He still has moments of unease, usually when I start talking to thin air and he catches on we're not alone, but it's an adjustment he's taking on well.

Dad and Patricia are looking forward to us visiting next weekend, a trip we try to do every few weeks. It seems Patricia's stay at home has also become permanent, but I don't mind, and it makes me glad to see Dad the happiest he's been in years. But I'm still his number one, so if I don't make an appearance every now and then he gets worried and threatens to come up to see me. Considering I'm not too sure how he would take to finding out his little girl now lives with another man (Gareth and I are keeping that on the down-low for the time being), I prefer to visit them instead. I feel bad for dragging Gareth along, especially when he's so busy at the hospital, but he insists it's good to get away from the hustle of the city every now and then. I thought we would eventually be planning a future together in England, but small-town USA seems to be growing on him. Maybe Foxton does have a unique charm I haven't yet realized. Then again, it's probably just the better weather.

Home visits won't have to be an issue for much longer though, because I will be announcing to Dad and Patricia that I have been awarded an exchange scholarship to study in Italy, but it's just for one semester, and I'll be back home before they know it. I'm sure they'll be delighted as well as anxious for me, but I'll tell them not to worry because my best friend will be visiting me for a holiday during semester break, and her aunt and new step-uncle are teaching me basic Italian. Learning languages is not my forté, but at least I'm getting lots of "taste adjustments" with their delectable homemade Italian cuisines during these lessons, so I can't complain.

Gareth will also be visiting his home in England, so I'll be making the trip to meet his family for a week. I'm nervous, but Gareth reassures me that they'll love me, even my Southern accent.

Cole is still on my mind every day, but every day that passes the loss of him hurts just a little bit less. Maybe the grief will never fully go; maybe that's the price of such love. There will always be a part of me that feels empty without him, but day by day, slowly yet surely, instead of letting the loss of him hinder me, I let the existence of him strengthen me. And with that, life becomes easier. Not because time heals though, but simply because life carries on, demanding to be lived in the time each of us has remaining. Nevertheless, Cole understood me, more than anyone ever can. And for that my undying love for him remains, kept alive through the memories of him in my mind and the feelings for him in my heart, places that are secretly and freely mine.

Sometimes—as short and unexpected the moments are—I feel him. And in those moments, I close my eyes and I see him, just the same as when he crossed over. In those moments, wherever he is, whatever he's doing, I know he's watching over me and I know I'll be okay.

Gareth walks up to me, dripping wet from a quick jump in the ocean. Kelly squeaks as he shakes himself over us. Suddenly I'm being hauled across the beach in his arms. I squeal in disapproval as he lets go and a wave breaks over me. I breach through the water, inhaling the beautiful air that fills my lungs, and wipe the saltiness away from my eyes. In that moment of heightened adrenaline I feel more aware: the crackle of pebbles raking against one another on the foreshore by the swell, the salt spray feathered along the fine hairs on my arms and face, the heat of the sun on my skin, the cry of a gull flying overhead as it dives down to the water below. And I see Gareth, looking at me with adoration in his eyes, and a warmth in my heart lets me know that I am loved.

He slips in a cheeky apologetic kiss, but I don't protest. I kiss him back, our bodies supporting one another in the waves, and I know I have everything I need to live a happy life, as promised.

From The Author

When I decided to give myself the time and space to do a freestyle creative writing piece I had no idea it would span multiple books over multiple years. What started as the first sentence of this book, characters came to life over a plot that extended over hundreds of pages. Not that it has been a bad thing; in fact, it has been an absolute joy for me, and likewise I hope it has been an absolute joy for you, the reader, to be a part of this journey as well.

I debated for a long while whether or not this would be the end for Cole and Charlotte. For those reasons, I have left some openings that can be visited in the future, if such a thing is meant to be. While Charlotte's story continues to make itself known in my mind in small, inspiring ways, Cole's story, however, is put to rest.

While this may be sad news for some, if you are not ready to fully say goodbye to Cole, don't fret! *The Way We Are*, based on the life (and afterlife) from Cole's point of view, is on its way!

The Way We Were

It wasn't meant to be like this. There was meant to be more. College, careers, marriage, kids. Many wants, many wishes, yet now there's only one . . . to be alive again.

Coming Winter 2025

About The Author

A perpetual global nomad, Olivia Norton has so far lived in five different countries over three continents. With a background in English teaching and outdoors instructing, you'll either find her exploring the great outdoors or curled up reading a book with a cup of tea (no milk!)
She currently resides in New Zealand.

To stay updated (or to leave a review, which I appreciate), please visit my Goodreads author page on
www.goodreads.com/author/show/42842710.Olivia_Norton, or follow me on Instagram under
www.instagram.com/olivianorton_author